Eldoron

Book one

Volto's Rise

Graham R. Moore

Enjoy the adventure

All communication should be sent to
eldoronthebook@outlook.com

ISBN: 9798857745588

"Introducing Graham R. Moore, a passionate new voice in the world of fantasy literature. He was born in the heart of Lancashire, England. With a heart full of stories and a lifelong love for words, Graham has brought his debut book, 'Eldoron, Volto's Rise,' to life. This captivating novel follows the journey of Eldoron and his family in the never-ending fight between good and evil. Graham's writing is a blend of vivid imagery and heartfelt emotions, inviting readers to embark on a journey of their own. As a first-time author, he is thrilled to share his creative vision and hopes to inspire others to explore the magic of storytelling. When not crafting tales, Graham enjoys listening to music and photography and finding inspiration in everyday moments."

CONTENTS

Eldoron

1 - The Old Tomb

Volto, the scruffy young vagrant had been walking around the cemetery for hours waiting for his friend Eldoron to show up. Eldoron was, as he describes himself, a wizard from a long-forgotten era. He was always late, but never this late. He thought,

"Just one more circuit around the old cemetery and that is it. If he doesn't show up, I am going home, wherever that may be tonight. Maybe under the pier again or in the multi-story car park. At least the car park was dry". The glare of car headlights coming from the road just beyond the cemetery wall was starting to hurt his eyes; it was a miserable, cold, damp evening. As he turned back to enter the old graveyard for the last time, there he was; waiting. Eldoron, the old wizard dressed in grey, as he always seemed to be. His hair seemed longer and more straggly this time, and he looked worried or stressed. No smiles this time either, he was always pleasant, something was wrong he could sense it, but he said nothing, just guided him to the entrance of an old tomb and said,

"Wait there a moment while I remove the sealing spell." This was odd; they had only ever chatted, sometimes for hours. They had never gone near any of the tombs. The tomb looked ancient and ominous. There was a sizzling sensation in the air around him, and Eldoron came back and said,

"You can go in now, but be careful, it's dangerous in there. I'll be nearby if you need help." The sizzling came again and the old wizard said,

"Just shout my name if you get caught." He then faded into the stone wall and was gone.

As he slowly turned around to see what was there, he heard voices coming from within the tomb, whispered voices, in a strange language that seemed very hard and guttural and yet had a soft feminine quality. They sounded like ancient curses or prayers, uttered by unseen lips. His first thought was to flee, but he could not move. He felt paralysed and he had to listen, though he knew not what was being said to him. He somehow knew the voices were talking to him, trying to communicate something important or sinister. He stepped inside the entrance to the tomb, or to be more accurate he was pulled inside, but not physically. It was as if a magnetic force was drawing him in, against his will. He listened to the voices and they drew him in, all he could do was follow. He was powerless to stop himself.

After what seemed hours, the voices suddenly stopped. He came to his senses in a flash and turned around to see where he was. He had moved into the tomb about 20 yards. That was impossible; he thought he had been walking for hours. The air was stale and cold, and he could smell dust and decay. He looked ahead into the dark passage, and he could see a faint glow on the wall in front of him, quite a way off, but there was something there. It looked like a carving or a tapestry, illuminated by some unknown source. He had to have a look, he didn't know why because he was sweating with fear and his knees were trembling like mad.

He took a step forward and found the ground soft beneath his feet, which felt very odd because it was a hard flagstone floor a moment ago. He reached down to the ground and felt the floor; it was grass or soft lichen. He stood up again and started to walk towards the small glow on the wall. Every step seemed to take forever, but the distance he covered was amazing. He reached the glow on the wall in about ten paces, even though it must have been 100 yards away. He stood in front of the glow staring into it. It was a mural of some kind, depicting a scene of horror and beauty. There were figures of humans and animals, twisted and distorted, in agony and ecstasy. Some symbols and signs made no sense to him but seemed to hold some hidden meaning. The colours were vivid and bright, contrasting with the darkness around him. The mural was mesmerizing and terrifying at the same time. He had to look away; it was sucking him in. He felt a strange sensation in his eyes and his mind as if he was being drawn into another world or dimension. He stepped backwards and its power lessened, he stepped back again and it got weaker still, with another step, it was almost gone. The glow before him suddenly split into three appendages, coiling tightly around his helpless body. Immobilized and constricted, he struggled to break free, but the suffocating grip held him in tightly. The urge to scream consumed him, yet no sound escaped his constricted throat. Desperately, he called out in his mind, pleading for Eldoron's assistance, but the silence remained deafening. The coiling arms pressed against his body, searing heat emanating from their touch. Violently, they burst into flames, scorching his flesh as they writhed and fell to the ground in a blazing heap.

His ears throbbed with excruciating pain as if they were about to burst. The screaming suddenly stopped. A blazing orange fireball erupted from the wall, hurtling toward him with astonishing speed, yet moving with an unnerving slowness. The fireball collided with his chest, propelling him across the immense tomb. He crashed onto the floor, rolling helplessly, trying desperately to smother the flames still clinging to his clothes. Struck again by the relentless fireball, he was hurled higher into the air, only to be sent plummeting into a frigid lake below. The shock of the icy water stole his breath, and he found himself sinking deeper, dragged down by an unseen force.

He felt himself plunging deeper and deeper into the lake. He had to stop and get to the surface for some air, but he was going deeper and deeper as if he was being dragged down. Amidst the watery depths, a figure emerged, grasping his hair and forcefully pulling him back up. He reached up, feeling the touch of a woman with long, sharp nails. Agonizing pain gripped his chest, his desperate need for air intensifying. He drew in a massive gulp of breath, only to have his lungs fill with freezing water. Darkness enveloped him, and he slipped into unconsciousness.

When he regained consciousness, his chest throbbed relentlessly, his throat seared with agony, and his head pulsed with a bleeding wound. Opening his eyes, the blinding light assaulted his senses. He found himself in a vast cavern, a makeshift bed supporting his body with a soft pillow beneath his head. Adjusting to the light, he observed tapestries of various shapes and sizes adorning the walls, while stone furniture filled the chamber. The walls emitted a radiant glow, extending from the floor to the vaulted ceiling.

At one end of the cavern, an enormous stone throne commanded attention, flanked by two small chairs, all presently unoccupied. Struggling to sit up, he was overcome by the pain in his chest. Footsteps approached from behind, and he attempted to turn his head, only to be seized by a woman who forcefully pressed her hand over his mouth, driving his head back into the pillow.

"Make a sound, and your life ends here and now,"

she warned in a hushed tone. He lay there in silence, save for the thunderous pounding of his heart within his chest. Slowly, she removed her hand from his mouth and spoke,

"Remain silent, or He will tear you apart."

"Who is He?" he whispered.

"He is Zeraphos, the master of the underworld."

"The underworld?" he repeated, perplexed. The woman's eyes widened, a sudden roar echoing from somewhere near the throne.

"Now you've done it! He has awakened!" She exclaimed before swiftly fleeing from the cavern.

Approaching footsteps resonated, but he couldn't bring himself to look. The sense of impending doom intensified as He drew nearer, emanating an overwhelming aura of dread. A massive, hairy foot, adorned with razor-sharp claws, descended near his head, rendering him paralyzed with fear. Standing tall over him, Zeraphos's booming voice reverberated through the chamber.

"So, you are the fabled one, the one destined to face me, Zeraphos. Many have tried and failed before you, and so shall you."

"Who are you?" he managed to utter.

"You already know who I am; I bear many names in your world." The Devil? he pondered. Zeraphos laughed, mocking his thoughts, and replied,

"The Devil? A name that has faded from memory. Yes, I can perceive your thoughts. Now, rise and prepare for battle. I have waited many years for you."

"Battle?" he stammered. "I am not prepared for battle; I have never fought before."

"Do battle!" I said, "I cannot do battle, I have never done battle."

Zeraphos raised a leg and stamped down just missing his head. He rolled over and jumped out of the way, but he grabbed Volto's arm and threw him across the room. He heard his leg break as he landed awkwardly on the stone floor. Zeraphos was coming again, but Volto could not move this time. Panic-stricken he shouted,

"Eldoron! Eldoron, help me!" Zeraphos froze in his tracks, fixing him with a glare.

"Eldoron? Do you believe that a feeble wizard can enter this domain? Only those who are invited can cross the threshold." With a malevolent intent, the chamber's walls turned an ominous shade of orange, then exploded. Eldoron materialized amidst the chaos, radiating an intense orange glow that gradually subsided. Zeraphos turned to face Eldoron and let out a derisive laugh.

"Well, well, it seems you have grown stronger. But you were not invited to partake in this game. Leave, or choose death."

"I will not leave, and I cannot die as long as you live. I was invited here by young Volto," Eldoron proclaimed. Zeraphos raised his hand, hurling a ball of green fire in their direction. Eldoron swiftly caught the projectile, effortlessly diverting its destructive path into the nearby lake.

"Ah, a nice touch, wizard. I see you have been studying. Was it the book you stole from me the last time you trespassed in my realm?"

"The time for battle has not yet come. Volto is not yet fully prepared, and not all prophecies have been fulfilled. He must live!" Eldoron asserted.

"Wizard, you disappoint me. You send this man to me prematurely. Take him and depart. But be warned, you cannot return to his world; you must remain here in my realm until he is ready. Leave, wizard, and take your Volto with you."

Zeraphos seated himself upon the throne, slowly fading away. Eldoron approached Volto, placing a hand on his broken leg.

"It is fractured. We must mend it."

In a blaze of orange light, they floated toward the wall through which they had entered, eventually passing through it and emerging in a rocky meadow.

Eldoron

2 - Voltos' Injuries

They came to rest under a large tree, an old oak. Tired, battered, and burned, Volto just lay there gazing up at the tree and the sky. The sky was so blue and cold looking, like a frozen lake. The tree was so big and full, its leaves rustling in the wind. He could almost feel its weight pressing down on him as if it wanted to crush him. Eldoron sat there with his head in his hands, muttering something under his breath. Volto could hear the pain and despair in his voice.

"What are we going to do now?" Volto asked.

"Examine you for a start young man, you nearly got yourself killed back there, and we don't want that, do we." The old wizard stood up and went over to him.

"Where does it hurt the most?" He said.

"It doesn't hurt" Volto replied, "I am numb from head to toe, I cannot feel anything."

"Well that doesn't mean that you are not hurt, things can be a little different here, just keep still while I check you over." He placed his hands on the top of his head and started muttering to himself again.

"What are you saying?" Volto asked.

"Be quiet for a while, just until I finish this, you won't want me to make any mistakes will you?" Slowly he worked his way down his chest and then onto his legs. Each time he moved his hands, he could feel a cold tingling sensation. Eldoron sat upright when he had finished and said.

"This is too much for me to deal with, we need Valadora here."

"Who or what is Valadora?" Volto asked.

"Valadora is my wife young man, and we need her here before you bleed to death. Your left leg is broken as I said before. Only it is worse than I first thought, the bone has torn the muscles in your thigh and you are bleeding quite badly inside, it needs attention right now. I must get in touch with her immediately."

With that, he stood up and turned round; with his arms raised to the sky, he whispered something and a brilliant orange light appeared at his side, then vanished leaving a tall slender woman in its place. She looked stunning, dressed in a dark green long dress, with very long dark hair shot through with silver-grey streaks, she was holding a hairbrush in one hand and pointing threateningly with the other at the old wizard. She said in an icy cold voice.

"I told you the last time you did that I would reduce you to a gutter rat, this better be very important old man."

He looked at her, then at me and said,

"Look who I have brought for you, my dear." She took one look at me and took a step back saying as she did.

"By the fires of hell, what is he doing here, it is not his time yet, and look at the state of him, he looks like he's been through a war."

"Err… well! He has, sort of. He needs attention pretty quickly. That's why I called you," the old wizard explained.

"Let me examine him," she said.

"I have done that already, he has a badly broken leg, severe bruising to the left shoulder, and burns to his legs, stomach, arms and face." She came over to me and placed her hands on my head, the same way that Eldoron did, with the same cold tingling sensation.

She worked her way down my body in the same way too. In a more relaxed manner, she said to Eldoron,

"Summon the children now, I need assistance." Eldoron once again raised his arms to the sky and started to mutter. A bright orange light shone on both sides of him, on his left side a young lady of perhaps twenty years old appeared. The light on his right flashed a few times and vanished. Eldoron spun round, his face full of anger, and then shouted. "How dare he refuse my summons!"? He raised his arms higher and shouted at the top of his voice. The words, Volto could not understand, but the power in them was like a thunderbolt at close range.

This time, there was no orange glow or flash, just a young man lying naked and dripping wet on the grass, his head full of soapsuds.

"How dare you refuse my summons boy" Eldoron screamed.

"But father I was in the bathtub," shouted the young man, trying to hide his naked body. At that, Valadora stood up and said very firmly,

"Enough you two! That is enough." She turned to the naked young man, pointed at him, and said something in a strange tongue and the young man was suddenly dressed in a black robe with a red cord around his waist.

"If we have quite finished, I need a shelter for this man, and I need it now," said the tall slender woman.

"Doron go and find something to make a shelter, and you Dora, see if you can get some food, we are all going to need something to eat by the time we have finished here", said the old wizard.

Valadora came back and sat beside Volto again and said,

"You have got to go inside yourself and mend that broken bone before you bleed to death."

"Go inside myself? What do you mean?" he asked.

"Oh dear," she said looking rather upset. "Do you mean to say that you don't know how to do that yet?"

"I have never been inside myself before; I didn't know you could do that."

"I will have to do it for you then, I'll show you how as I do it, so try to remember everything that I do, it is very important, do you understand?"

"Well yes, I guess so."

"Don't guess, do you understand or not?"

"Yes, I understand," Volto said.

"Good then let's make a start. Close your eyes and imagine that you are inside your head; you can see everything that is wrong with yourself. You must go to the place that has the worst injury first; in your case, it is your left leg. You have to go down the inside of your spine, out of the last vertebra and through the pelvic cavity to the top of your leg. You can feel the break from here, can you feel it?"

"Yes, yes I can, but there is no pain."

"Good, that means you should be able to manipulate the bone back into place yourself, now let's go a little further down and see the damage properly. Don't worry about the blood; that will sort itself out when we have finished. There you see that jagged bone right there? It needs to be put back onto the end of this bit that we are on. We will have to go very carefully down to the end of this bone and reach over to pull that one back into place, but we must not trap any blood vessels or nerves. Now carefully push your mind towards that piece over there and pull it over here. Easy does it, mind that vessel; move it away with your mind, it will move, just will it out of the way. Now pull the bone and hold it tightly in place while I seal it up. That's excellent, just a little

11

longer, there we're done; we just need to stop that bleeding over there now. You should be able to do that on your own, just straighten out that artery, and seal it up, that's it done. Let's get back to your head and out before you go unconscious, or else we will be stuck in here for hours. We have to go back, and it has to be exactly the same way that we came, or else we might get lost, so follow me closely and quickly. How do you feel? Volto, how do you feel? Don't you pass out on me now, let's get moving, come on Volto quickly you can do it, just a little further now, there we are, and out we go. Now you can let go, sleep for a while, I'll be here with you when you wake."

Valadora sat back against the tree and said to her husband,

"When we are done here, I think we need a little talk, you have possibly ruined everything we have worked for, for the past nine hundred years, you do realise that don't you?"

"Oh, will you just shut up for a while, you really do get on my nerves with your bloody self-righteousness; do you think you could have handled it any better? Just get on with patching him up, and let me think for a while."

She slowly turned her attention back to Volto,

"I'll have to splint that leg and put some lavender on those burns and some comfrey on his shoulder," She said to herself. When Doron came back with some wood for the shelter she asked him to get a piece long enough to make a splint for his leg, Doron asked,

"How do I measure it? I can't take his leg with me." The glare from his mother was enough; he said, "Only joking" and went on his way rather quickly, chuckling to himself as he went.

On his way back out of the woods, he saw his sister Dora stalking a large hare in the field. He shouted her over and suggested that they helped each other, and then they could have some fun, she thought that was a good idea and said they should finish the shelter first. It didn't take long to gather the rest of the wood; they even found a piece that was perfect for the splint for Volto's leg.

They took the wood back to Eldoron and started to erect the shelter for Volto, the old wizard said to them.

"That took you long enough, now move over and I'll show you how to make a shelter in next to no time." A big blue flash and there it was, a bit rackety but it was a shelter. Valadora looked up and saw the thing between the two trees, and started laughing and said,

"You call that a shelter? I could have made a sturdier one out of water."

"Give me strength! You never give up, do you? Why did I ever marry you?" Grumbled the old wizard.

"Because you loved me then just like you love me now, you old sod. Now do us all a favour and re-do it, so that we all get a good rest tonight. We don't want to wake up dead in the morning, do we? Dora, did you find any food? I thought not; never mind, I need some help with his dressings before he wakes up, pass me the bottle of lavender, will you? We need to take his clothes off so that we can see where he is burnt and bruised."

When they had sorted out Volto's injuries, and Eldoron and Doron had finally finished the shelter; Doron and Dora went to find some food. They returned a couple of hours later with two hares and several different roots and vegetables, which Valadora made into a strong-smelling broth.

When it was ready Dora went to wake Volto. He woke up with a start and tried to sit up, but the burns on his stomach would not let him, the skin had started to dry out and every time he moved it felt like his stomach was being ripped open.

"Hey steady on lad!" said the old wizard. "You

should be a bit more careful with those injuries you have, they'll be sore for a while yet. Valadora is good, but not that good, it takes time as well as sorcery to heal bones and burns."

"All right Eldoron," Valadora said as she came over to Volto. "Here you must eat as much of this as you can, it will speed up your body's healing process. Try not to sit up for too long either, just long enough to eat this, and then you should lie down again. Here I will feed you, tell me when you've had enough. We don't want you to throw it all up again now do we?"

Volto ate as much of the broth as he could, and then led down again.

"How long have I slept for?" asked Volto.

"Not long enough yet, you'll have to sleep until morning, and then you should be ready for the journey to our home," Answered the tall slender woman. She passed her hand in front of his face and he fell asleep once more.

"I think we all should get some rest now, it looks like we are going to have a hard day tomorrow." Said Dora; nobody argued against that, Doron put some more wood on the fire and went into the shelter to make some room for everyone. It didn't take long before they were all asleep.

Eldoron

3 - Dark Moods

Volto woke up just before sunrise, his face felt like a gigantic scab and his stomach like a piece of meat on a butcher's block. The sounds of his groaning woke Valadora. She rolled over to face him and quietly asked him if he was all right.

"Oh yes, I feel just great. How do I look to you?" He sarcastically remarked.

"No need to be like that. I have had enough of that with these three. I was only concerned about your health," Valadora replied.

"Sorry, my face and stomach are in excruciating pain, and I can't move my leg."

"Well, before you attempt to get up and worsen your scabs, let me apply some more lavender oil on those burns. It will help if you let it soak in. As for your leg, only time will heal it, but you can take a look yourself if you feel up to it."

"I think that I might pass on that for now, if you don't mind."

"Okay but don't leave it too long or else you will forget how to do it, and I don't want to waste time showing you again. Now stop talking while I put this on your face."

The others woke up while Valadora was putting the oil on his burns.

"I'm starving, does anybody want some food? We can finish off the broth from last night," said Doron. Eldoron suggested that they all have a good breakfast before they set off for home because it will be a hard journey if they have to carry Volto.

"That's sorted then; I'll get the fire going again and warm it up," answered Doron.

Breakfast was a solemn affair; everyone was lost in thought, contemplating how they would manage if they had to carry Volto over a long distance. The silence was broken by a sudden shriek from Dora. All heads turned to see what was wrong.

"Look at that mountain over there! It's on fire!" exclaimed Dora. Eldoron was the first to leave the shelter, followed closely by Doron and Valadora. Volto strained to see what was happening but couldn't get a good view from inside the shelter.

"What is it?" he shouted.

"It's just a volcano," Valadora replied

"What do you mean 'just a volcano'? Are they common around here?"

"No, we haven't seen one in about six hundred years, but don't worry about it now. I'll explain its significance later," she assured him.

Oh great! Volto thought. A volcano erupts and it's treated as no big deal. What kind of place is this?

Eldoron returned to the shelter with a wide, childlike grin on his face. Valadora looked at him as if he were crazy

"Well, come on, everyone! We need to pack up and leave right away," the old man declared.

Volto tried to stand up but fell halfway, landing on the ground. He rolled over and massaged his leg. Dora came over and helped him up.

"You're going to have to get used to standing with that splint you know." She said to him.

"I will. I just lost my balance, that's all. Anyway, how far is it to your house?" He grumbled.

"I haven't a clue. I don't even know where we are. I've never been here before. But I'm sure my parents know. Now, try to walk a bit while we pack up."

"How did we end up with so much stuff when we 'arrived' with nothing?" Doron asked his mother.

"Don't start asking silly questions, Doron. You know perfectly well where it all came from and where it's going back to."

"Well, can't it go back the way it came? It would be much faster and easier to travel, especially if we have to assist Volto."

"Hey! The young man has a valid point there, sweetheart," Eldoron said, grinning broadly.

"It's not a good point, and don't call me sweetheart. We have a long way to go before nightfall, so let's pack up and get moving," she retorted.

"Wow is she always in such a good mood first thing in the morning?" Volto asked Doron. "I'm saying nothing, but if you want to see tomorrow... Well, just don't annoy her."

For a while, nobody spoke or acted out of turn. Once everything was packed and the shelter dismantled, Valadora stood gazing up at the sky.

"Alright, let's go this way!" she suddenly announced, picking up the pace. There was a frantic rush to gather everything and catch up before she got too far ahead. Volto had a stick to assist him with walking, making his burden lighter compared to the others.

The sky was overcast with heavy clouds approaching from the south. Dora broke the silence, questioning Eldoron on how her mother knew which direction to go when the sun wasn't visible.

"Easy," he replied. "She just looked through the clouds to find the sun. It's simple really. I thought you already knew how to do that." Eldoron chuckled and suggested, "Let's play a little game. Let's see who can locate the sun. Doron, can you spot it?" He stood still and looked up at the sky.

"Yep, there it is," he said, pointing to a small lighter patch in the clouds.

"Well, Dora, where do you think it is?" Eldoron inquired.

"I believe it's over there," she responded, pointing in the opposite direction to Doron.

"Volto, what about you?" Volto paused and looked up.

"Well, I think it's over there," he said, gesturing vaguely towards the west.

"You need to be certain," Eldoron remarked. "Doron was right. Now listen, both of you, I'll explain how to locate it."

"Well, tell them as we walk," Valadora interjected. Eldoron glanced at her but remained silent before continuing.

"You need to focus on one part of the cloud. For example, that darker patch over there. Concentrate on it, imagining it slowly becoming transparent, like a pool of water clearing in the sky. With practice, you should be able to see right through it." Dora expressed her intent to keep practising, while Volto commented,

"I think it's a bit silly and probably impossible for me. I'm not like the rest of you." Valadora spun around and shouted at him,

Valadora spun around and shouted at him, "You will practice, and you will learn. Otherwise, you will fall into the hands of Zeraphos, and he will triumph, leading us all to our demise. You will practice everything we teach you. Do you understand, Volto?" Stunned by her sudden outburst, he glared at her, recalling Doron's earlier warning:

"If you want to see tomorrow, don't annoy her." They continued walking in silence, with Volto glaring at Valadora's back, consumed by fear, anger, and hatred. Despite the pain in his leg, his rage fueled his determination.

After about an hour, his anger escalating rather than subsiding, he looked up at the clouds and attempted to focus. He saw straight through them, fixating on the sun directly. The sun appeared to be staring back at him, reflecting his emotions and intensifying his anger. He felt himself on the verge of exploding into an unprecedented rage. The sun taunted him, provoking him. His head spun, his chest burned, and he stood motionless, locked in a gaze with the sun.

Dora noticed that something was wrong and shouted at her mother. She turned around to see Volto standing there. The air around his body shimmered, and his hands started to smoke. She and Eldoron simultaneously made rapid gestures with their hands, while Valadora shouted to Volto, but he did not hear her.

Eldoron mentally shouted his name. That did it... he snapped; he exploded into a rage, a rage so strong it knew no right or wrong. He screamed, raised his hands, and sent balls of fire flying toward the sun. The others dropped to the floor as Volto turned around and started throwing fire in every direction.

"We've got to stop him," shouted Eldoron to Valadora.

"Oh, and how do you propose doing that? With that much power, he will rip us apart." Dora rolled over to a nearby burning branch, stood up, and ran towards Volto, completely ignoring Valadora's shouts to stop. She swung the branch at Volto, aiming for his lower back. However, the branch exploded into splinters before making contact, and Volto turned to face her, his face contorted in a painful grimace. Then, with a sign of recognition, he raised both hands above his head, white lightning flashing between them. Slowly, he drew his hands together and, with a thunderous shout, threw one massive thunderbolt towards a small hillock on his right. The explosion completely blew the side off. He fell to the floor, and the grass all around him burst into flames. He was completely engulfed, but he wasn't burning himself. He just lay there, staring up at the sky.

Eldoron and his son slowly edged their way towards Volto, extinguishing the burning grass as they went. When they got near him, he turned his head towards Eldoron and quietly whispered something. The old wizard couldn't hear him and went a little closer. Suddenly, Volto sat up, sent another fireball flying into the sky, and shouted,

"Keep back! Or I might kill you all! I'm dangerous, I'm lethal, I'm angry, I'm frightened, I'm... Oh, please, help me. What is happening to me?"

Eldoron stood up, went to him, and took him in his arms, holding him tightly. The others stood up and approached them. Valadora took Volto from Eldoron, held him in her arms, and said,

"Oh, my son... I'm so sorry. I should learn to control my temper with you." She let him go, stood up, and said, "Let's get out of here right now. Okay, you old wizard... you win. Take us home." The old man stood up and waved his arms. Suddenly, they found themselves on the grass in front of a cave entrance. The grass was lush, green, and slightly damp. Dora stood up and started to brush the dampness off her clothes. Doron said,

"Maybe you should ask Volto to dry your clothes for you."

"Any more comments like that, and you'll turn out like your father," replied Dora.

"Doron, help me get Volto into the cave, will you?" shouted Valadora. Doron went over to Volto, picked him up, and carried him into the cave. He placed him in the spare room, the one that Valadora calls the junk room. He laid him down on a large pallet. Volto was still and pale, and his breathing was very shallow. Doron momentarily thought he was going to die, but Volto started to stir and moan about his leg. Valadora said, "That's a good sign," but the others were not convinced.

"Get some rest; I think we have a lot to discuss tomorrow," she said to him. "Right, everybody out, and let him rest for a while." With that, they all went back outside in silence.

"Well, do you still doubt that he has real power?" said Eldoron. Obviously, nobody disagreed with him.

Eldoron

4 - Along Comes Jorgon

Eldoron and the others had spent the entire night engaged in deep debate, striving to formulate a plan for Voltos' education. Exhaustion had settled in, but they knew they had to devise a strategy before allowing themselves any rest. Time was undoubtedly not on their side on this particular occasion.

Just as Eldoron was becoming frustrated with the lack of progress, a familiar song drifted through the air, bringing a sigh of relief to the weary gathering. It was Jorgon the Small, as he was affectionately known, singing the same tune he always sang during his travels. Jorgon approached along the edge of Valadora's field, waving to them as he walked. He seemed taller than usual. Dora got up and ran to meet him, and he lifted her in his arms, hugging her tightly. Jorgon had always held a special fondness for Dora. He carried her on his shoulder back to the makeshift table where they were working on Volto's learning program.

"I think it's time for a little refreshment," Eldoron suggested.

"Not the kind of refreshment you're thinking of," replied Valadora. "We have too much work and too little time."

"Oh! Have I chosen a bad time for a visit? I have such a strange tale to share with you. How unfortunate!

Well, I suppose I'll have to come back another time," Jorgon joked.

"Oh, I give up!" exclaimed Valadora. "Doron, could you fetch a barrel for the two of them and bring two tankards as well?" Doron stood up and headed towards the cave entrance, then turned to his mother and asked,

"Should I bring six tankards, Mother?" She looked over at him and noticed Volto standing at the cave entrance, looking horrified at Jorgon.

"Volto? Is this lad 'The Volto'?" Jorgon stood up and looked down at Volto, "He is rather small for a…"

"Jorgon!" Valadora shouted, interrupting him mid-sentence. Volto strained his neck, gazing up at Jorgon; he had never seen anyone so tall. Sensing the tension, Dora said,

"Jorgon, come and sit with me." Her words broke the tension on Valadora's face, and she let out a sigh of relief before asking Volto how he was feeling.

"Um… I think I'm okay, but who or what is that?" Volto inquired.

"Sorry, young man," Eldoron intervened, "this is Jorgon the Small. He is a dear friend of ours and hopefully will become a good friend of yours too." Volto couldn't help but burst into laughter, leaving the others staring at him. His laughter was so contagious that Jorgon began laughing as well, his deep and resonant laughter prompting the others to join in, whether laughing with them or at them. When they finally settled down, Jorgon stood up, approached Volto, and placed a massive hand on his shoulder.

"I think you and I will be great friends. I haven't laughed like that in far too long." Jorgon sat on the floor in front of Volto, extending his hand in friendship. Volto gladly took it, although his hand felt small like a baby's hand being held by its father. He still had to look up to see Jorgon's face, but he resisted the urge to giggle.

"Maybe this place isn't so bad after all. Since I arrived here, all I've experienced is pain, and I don't think I'm meant to be here yet."

Doron returned with the barrel of ale, and they all gathered around the table with a tankard in front of them, except for Jorgon, who sat on the floor and still towered over them.

Valadora turned to Volto and said,

"How does your leg feel today?"

"It's much better today, I think. I had a dream where I visualized it healing, and now it feels a lot better. Can I really do that in a dream?" Valadora looked at Eldoron, seeking answers. He simply shrugged his shoulders and replied,

"We don't know the full extent of your powers, Volto. That's something we need to discover soon, although it may not always be pleasant. We've been up all night trying to devise a learning plan for you, but we haven't come up with a good enough one yet." Volto looked at him and inquired,

"When is the battle supposed to take place then?"

"We don't know that either. Some prophecies need to be fulfilled, and the volcano was the first," Eldoron answered.

"Um... if I may interrupt, Big El, I believe the volcano was the second. That's why I came to tell you!" There was a stunned silence.

"What are you trying to say, Jorgon? What don't we know? Don't just sit there grinning like a fool, tell us... tell us everything, I mean everything."

The big man was grinning from ear to ear, and said,

"Well, I was on my way home the last time I was here, and I unexpectedly ran into an old friend... or rather, she ran into me. It's been a very long time since we last saw or heard from her. It must be nearly a hundred years. Maybe you've seen her without my knowledge. Anyway, I was camped out in a field on the edge of Sormoving Wood. I was fast asleep under my small blanket, as I was exhausted from a long journey through the woods... It was only a small camp by my standards because I was very tired after a very long journey through the woods..."

Valadora grinned at Eldoron's expression and suggested that Jorgon gets to the important parts.

"Well, he did say everything," Jorgon replied mischievously. "Rosella tripped over me while I was asleep in the forest. You know... Rosella, the seer."

"Hmm," Eldoron pondered. "She's been silent for quite a few years. What did that blind old bat have to say after all this time?"

"Once you get to know her, she's actually a nice person. She used to be a good friend of mine until your bad temper nearly killed her," Valadora remarked.

"That blind old lady, as you so kindly refer to her, informed me that there is another person of my kind in this Old World of ours. I was told to find her in the Gehenna Coves. That was almost three years ago, as you know. So, I went straight from Sormoving Wood down south to Gehenna, and let me tell you, it's a God-forsaken place."

"Why did you not come back and tell us Jorgon? That is a very dangerous place you know... There have been thousands of murders and sacrifices there, those Gehenneons have a very strange religion, and like to sacrifice strangers in the name of their Gods," said Valadora.

"I'm aware of that, M'lady, but it was faster for me to go alone and find her."

"And what did you discover down there, considering you haven't brought her with you?" Doron sarcastically chimed in.

"Hey! Who said I haven't brought her with me, young

man?" Jorgon replied, beaming with a smile and a chuckle.

"Well? Have you? Have you, Jorgon? What's her name? What's she like? Where is she?" Dora asked eagerly.

"As a matter of fact, she'll be here very soon. She needed to stop by the village for something. You know how women are…"

"Thank you, Jorgon, and we women know how men are too, don't we, Dora?" Valadora retorted, teasingly grinning.

"Yes, we do, Mother," Dora chuckled.

Eldoron stood up to fetch another drink from the barrel and noticed that Volto was once again staring at Jorgon.

"What's the matter, young man? You look like you've seen a ghost," Eldoron remarked. "I'm confused by all of this; I don't understand any of it. And to make matters worse, someone has started talking to me," Volto replied quietly.

"What do you mean, talking to you? Are you hearing voices in your head now, boy?" Eldoron whispered as he sat next to him.

"Somebody is trying to communicate with me, but I can't hear them properly. They're too far away, too faint," Volto explained.

"Quiet down, everyone. I think we might have something important here. Valadora, come over here and try to enter Volto's mind. Let's see who is talking to him," Eldoron said urgently.

"Eldoron! You know I can't do that. It's not possible anymore; Zeraphos put a stop to it the last time we saw him, remember?" Valadora protested.

"Damn! This could be very important. Volto, try your best to listen to it," Eldoron suggested. Volto looked perplexed and disturbed as he responded,

"It's not like that. I can't try harder; it's just there. It's not really like listening at all. But I recognize the voice; it's a woman's voice." Eldoron leaned back, rubbing his beard, lost in thought.

"Hey, big El!" Jorgon interjected. "Don't worry too much. Just wait until Jarreen gets here. She has the gift."

"What? She's a listener? How is that possible?" Valadora exclaimed.

"Rosella told me she has the gift, and she was right. So be careful with your thoughts when she's around. She's a formidable warrior, and I wouldn't want to be on the wrong side of her. She won't be long now; I can sense her presence growing stronger," Jorgon explained

"Mother, she's over there! I can see her!" Doron shouted excitedly, "She looks even bigger than you, Jorgon."

"Aye, lad, she is," Jorgon replied, standing up and waving to her. Jarreen waved back and started running toward them. Jorgon walked down the road to meet her, and when they came face to face, they embraced tightly, their strength evident. It was a beautiful sight, albeit peculiar, such size and power combined with tenderness.

Finally releasing each other, they approached the small table where the rest of the group was seated.

"My friends, and Eldoron, of course," Jorgon said playfully. "Allow me to introduce my wife, Jarreen. Jarreen, meet Valadora, Eldoron, and their children, Dora and Doron. And this is..."

"Don't tell me. This is the One, the Chosen One, Volto. My Lord, I am honoured to meet you. I am humbled in your presence, Lord Volto," Jarreen bowed respectfully...

"What do you mean, Lord? The Chosen One? I'm just Volto," he responded, taken aback.

"Oh no, M'lord. You are not just Volto; you are the

Chosen One. I can sense your power and strength. You are the one this world has awaited for thousands of years," Jarreen insisted.

This statement nearly overwhelmed Volto. Eldoron intervened, explaining to Jarreen that Volto had arrived a bit too early and didn't fully comprehend his role in all of this.

"Well, perhaps now is the right time to explain everything to him," Jarreen suggested.

"Not just yet, Jarreen. We need your abilities for something else first, if you don't mind, of course," Eldoron replied

"And we also need to eat. Did you manage to get anything from the town, my dear?" Jorgon asked Jarreen.

"Yes, of course. I wasn't just wandering around. I brought enough food and wine to last us a few days and more... Shall we start preparing the meal first, and then you can tell me what you need from me?" Jarreen suggested.

Jarreen, Valadora, and Dora took the supplies and headed inside the kitchen, where they began preparing a small meal consisting of various cheeses, meat, and bread.

"What happened to your leg Volto?" Jorgon asked when they had all finished eating.

"He had a little encounter with Zeraphos on his first day here," Eldoron answered.

"Is that the issue you need me to address? I've heard that Valadora is more qualified than I am for that sort of thing," Jarreen remarked.

"I've done all I can for his injuries. It's up to Volto and time now. I believe he will recover quickly. And as for your mind, Volto, it's functioning well, isn't it?" Valadora assured.

"You think my mind is fine? After what happened

yesterday on our way here, and me 'going inside myself' before that? Not to mention the encounter with Zeraphos, as you put it. And that woman in the cave... It's her! It's her voice. Now I know who's been talking in my head," Volto exclaimed.

"Hold on, young man... Hold your horses! You haven't mentioned this woman before. Who is she?" Eldoron interjected.

"I don't know who she was. She pulled me out of the lake in the cave, I believe, and she might have saved my life. She held me down and covered my mouth so I couldn't speak. She warned me not to wake Zeraphos, but I did, and then she ran away. She was beautiful, with the most perfect face I've ever seen," Volto recounted.

"Volto, don't let your emotions cloud your judgment. I have a suspicion about who we might be dealing with here, and she's not a pleasant character, Volto," Valadora cautioned. "Please enlighten us, Valadora. Share the secret with all of us," Eldoron urged, sounding quite impatient.

Jarreen sat down on the floor next to Volto and informed him that she was going to enter his mind and teach him how to properly listen to the voice. She began humming a soft tune, and he felt a tingling sensation on top of his head. Suddenly, Jarreen rolled backwards, letting out a loud shout that nearly deafened everyone.

"Wow! What kind of power lies within? Who is this lady we're dealing with? You should have warned me about her strength, Volto... She just threw me out, and that has never happened before. You'll have to talk to her and let her know that I'm going to reenter," Jarreen exclaimed.

"How do I do that? Can I communicate with her?" Volto asked.

"Of course, you can... Just think that you're speaking to her, and she should be able to hear you, with a bit of practice," Jarreen explained.

Volto pondered this for a moment and then burst into laughter.

"This can't be real... It's like something out of a storybook, not real life. What the hell am I doing here?" he exclaimed.

"Okay, Volto," Eldoron interjected. "Here's the story so far..."

"No, wait, Eldoron!" Jarreen interrupted.

"I need to address this woman first. I have to find out who she is. I can't be thrown out like that without knowing why or by whom," Jarreen declared.

Volto jolted as if he had just been pricked by a needle and said,

"My name is Selika, and I am here to help. Valadora, if you want your listening powers back, I can restore them... Eldoron, I can resolve your little issue as well. And you, Jarreen, you're new here, and you're quite powerful, which I admire, but be cautious. There is much for you to learn. If we try, I believe we can all get along splendidly. I will join you in person soon, but for now, I must attend to some matters. Before I go, a word of caution... Stick together, no matter what, for troubled times lie ahead. He knows the time is near."

"Well, is that who you thought it was, Valadora?" asked Jarreen.

"Selika? No, I have never heard of her before, and what a strange name. Has anyone else heard of her?"

"Well, we will have to just wait till she comes back then, or just pops round the corner unannounced," said Eldoron.

"This is serious, Eldoron. We don't know who she is or what she wants. She kicked Jarreen out of Voltos' head and seems to know a lot about us," said Valadora.

"What did he, I mean she, mean about your problem, Father?" asked Dora. Eldoron chuckled and hung his head in embarrassment.

"It's just a personal issue that some men experience later in life, Dora. It's something I don't wish to discuss right now."

"You realize she probably knows everything there is to know about all of us, Eldoron? This little problem of yours... If you even consider it a problem, which I certainly don't, is known only to you and me," said Valadora.

"Hey big El, you never told me about this 'little problem' you have. You can get help you know. It is probably just psychological, why don't you have a quiet word with Jarreen, she is very good in that department," Jorgon said mockingly.

"Will you all just let it drop? It is embarrassing enough, without everybody going on about it."

"I've not said anything about it Father." Doron chipped in wryly. "But you might have said something to me... A problem shared is a problem halved, as you used to say to us," They all started laughing, and Volto said,

"Whoever this Selika is, she has a wicked sense of humour. I think I am starting to like her, I can't wait to meet her in the flesh."

"What have you put in this ale Valadora?" Asked Jorgon.

"I thought it might be helpful if we all relaxed a bit; so I just added a few herbs to the barrel, nothing much really, but I might have slightly misjudged the strength of the new crop... Oops!"

"I'll have a refill then, anyone for a top-up?" Said Eldoron, standing up to reach the barrel. "I think we might as well forget any serious conversation today... This stuff is much too good to be serious over, and I feel a great need to finish the barrel."

"Eldoron, I hope you are not leading my husband

astray, you know what he's like when he has had a drink or two…" Jarreen said jokingly.

"Oh he knows full well what he is like; they have been doing this for centuries… and always with the same outcome, a couple of bad hangovers in the morning. The rest of us would be better off leaving them to it and finding something else to occupy our minds…"

"Mother, is it not true that I am an apprentice to my father?" Asked Doron.

"Yes my son, why do you ask, when you know that already."

"I think I will stay here a while, I might learn something," He answered with a sly smile on his face.

"You get more like your father every day young man… You will be ill in the morning, and then you will want me to make a potion for you. Well I won't, you will have to suffer and learn the hard way."

"It's alright Mother, I will make one for him, after all, I am your apprentice, and I need the practice," Dora said.

"I don't believe this, you're encouraging him. I think I have totally lost control over you two. Be it on your heads then. Volto, I take it that you are staying too?"

"Yes I would like to, but I don't think that I can take much more of this ale. I am not used to it, though it is very nice, and it does help the pain… Well, maybe I will have a couple more and see how it goes."

"Hey Volto, don't have too many, you never know when your friend will be back, or how it will affect her," Jarreen said.

"You're joking, aren't you? It can't affect her can it?" He said a little worriedly.

"You never know, do you? Right, we will leave you all to it for a while, I think Valadora and I have a lot to discuss."

Eldoron

5 - Selika

Jarroth was conducting his daily inspection of the battlements being constructed around the city of Gehenna when a young woman abruptly pushed past him, nearly causing him to stumble.

"Seize that woman!" he shouted to one of his army captains.

The woman had stooped down to retrieve an apple core discarded by one of his captains. Cadderman, the captain of the Eastern Regiment, grabbed her arm and forcefully brought her before Jarroth, the Clan Chief.

"What is your name, peasant? And why are you trespassing near the battlements when you know this area is off-limits to your kind?" Jarroth inquired.

"Sir, I..." the woman began.

"Lord Jarroth to you, peasant," Cadderman interjected with contempt.

"Lord Jarroth, I have been working with the construction gangs on the battlements and haven't eaten for three days. I require sustenance to continue my work, my Lord. I implore you to show mercy," she pleaded.

"My dear young peasant, indeed I shall show mercy. I cannot have my workers starving to death, can I?" Jarroth replied. "Soldier, escort this peasant to the castle and confine her in the dungeons. We can sacrifice her in the morning, then she won't die of starvation... How's that for mercy, my dear peasant? I have just solved your hunger problems for you."

Cadderman seized her by the hair, forcefully pressing her face against Jarroth's feet.

"Now, kiss his boots and express your gratitude for his mercy," Cadderman ordered. Reluctantly, she complied, muttering something unintelligible into Jarroth's feet. Cadderman then yanked her up by her hair and handed her over to the waiting soldier, who caught her and bound her wrists together behind her back.

Fear and hatred emanated from her gaze as she looked at Jarroth. Cadderman moved toward her, raising his hand to strike her, but Jarroth halted him with a wave of his hand.

"Do not harm her," he commanded. "There is something peculiar about this little peasant. I will see her when I return to the castle. Soldier, take her away and ensure she is not left alone until my arrival. Also, see to it that she is provided with food and a bath. She cannot be sacrificed looking and smelling like that."

"What is your name, soldier?" she inquired as they marched up the cobbled stone road leading to the castle.

"Keep quiet and keep walking, lady. Don't attempt any foolishness," he barked.

"You're different from the other soldiers, aren't you? You don't approve of what's happening here," she observed. In response, the soldier grabbed her hair and hissed in her ear.

"Nobody likes what's going on here. One misstep, and they'll publicly sacrifice you. So just stay quiet and speak only when spoken to." They continued their journey in silence.

Once in the castle, he took her down to the bathing rooms and shouted for one of the servants to help bathe her. He took off the binds around her wrists and started to rip her clothes off. She objected very strongly, but the soldier just carried on oblivious to her shouts and screams. He then tied a rope around her neck and pushed her into the hot pool.

"Now wash, and be quick about it," he ordered. The servant woman joined in, helping to scrub her.

When she had finished, she climbed out of the pool and dried herself; put on the gown that the servant had brought and started to comb her hair in front of the wall-sized mirror. She said to the soldier,

"Why do you not look at me Petterman? That is your name, isn't it? Do you not like the look of me? Am I not beautiful to your eyes?"

"I cannot look at you, for you are not mine to behold. And how do you know my name? Did the servant tell you?" the soldier replied.

"No, it was not the serving woman. I know quite a bit about you, Petterman. I know that you are married and about to become a father, and that your father passed away a few months ago," she answered.

"How do you know these things when I don't even know your name?" Petterman asked, puzzled.

"You will learn my name soon enough, soldier. But for now, you may call me M'lady," she responded.

"I will call you a peasant or a whore. I don't address prisoners as 'M'lady'," Petterman retorted, gripping his temples as a pain shot through his head.

"If you are ready, M'lady, we can go and get something to eat," he said, his temples throbbing.

"That's better Petterman, a little more civilised I think, don't you?" She said with a look of satisfaction.

"You're a witch!" He hissed at her.

"Oh, come now, Petterman. You don't really believe that, do you? Such thoughts can be quite painful." The pain shot through his head again, bringing him down to his knees.

"Very soon, Petterman, you will need my assistance.

So be kind to me, or you will regret it. Besides, I require your help too. As I mentioned earlier, you are different from the others. You seek a way out of this predicament Jarroth has thrust upon you. Every day, you risk your life for this man you despise..." she continued.

"Stop! Stop the pain woman, err... M'lady. You are right, I loathe Jarroth, but what can any man do against the power he has? He holds a piece of the 'Sacred throne', and why should I need your help?"

"Does he hold a piece of the 'Sacred throne'? How do you know it is from 'The Throne'? There are lots of fake pieces around. You could pick up any stone and say it is from the throne... and with the right mental attitude, you can make others believe you, and once they believe it, they will start to fear you, and so you have great power over them."

"He does possess a piece... It is common knowledge. He wields the power of Zeraphos," Petterman insisted.

"Have you personally seen this fragment from the 'Sacred Throne'? Or witnessed its effects?" she inquired.

"Yes... well no, he keeps it in a pouch around his neck, and no mortal man may cast his eye upon it, for fear of being turned to stone..."

"And how then, did Jarroth acquire it? Did he just find it on the road?"

"No, he has travelled extensively... He spent his early years as a trader, dealing mainly with stones, metals, and furs. Have you not seen his sword? He never goes anywhere without it. It is crafted from a foreign metal, harder than any found in this land, and adorned with a large red crystal in its pommel," Petterman divulged.

"I have heard of the sword, but it does not concern me, it is the fragment of the Throne that I would like to know about. What can you tell me about it Petterman?"

After she finished brushing her hair, Petterman took out the ropes to bind her wrists again.

"I don't need those, Petterman. I am right where I intended to be. I have no desire to escape."

"Very well, but only because I have been ordered to remain by your side. Try any tricks, and not only will you wear these ropes, but your feet will also be bound. Now, let's find some food," Petterman warned.

As they walked silently through the corridors of the castle, she became aware of the noise and the hustle and bustle of the servants going about their business.

"Petterman, would you be willing to show me around the castle after we've finished eating?"

"What's the point? You'll be dead by morning... Besides, this place is enormous. It would take hours, and I've been ordered to lock you up in the dungeons once you've had your meal and bathed."

"As a last request then; before Jarroth comes back? I will be good I promise. A quick tour around for my last dying request Petterman, how about it?" She asked with a little mental push. "And he won't be back for some time..."

"Okay! Just a quick look round, where is it you want to see?"

"Everywhere, of course... but just a quick overview," she replied, grinning mischievously.

He took her to the main hall, where they found a large wooden table overflowing with various foods. They each grabbed a substantial pewter platter and loaded it with cheese, meat, potatoes, fruit, and a large cob of bread.

"Is there a special occasion happening here tonight?" she inquired as they made their way to a table tucked in the corner of the hall. "And don't look at me like that... I haven't eaten in three days, I'm absolutely famished."

"I bet you can't finish all of that!"

"Then you've got yourself a bet. If I manage to eat it all, you'll give me an extensive tour of the castle. What

37

say you?"

"Hahaha, alright then. And I'll also promise not to insult you by calling you a whore or peasant for the rest of your life if you succeed."

"That is a very tall order for you because you don't know for sure how long that will be, do you?"

"Quite a simple task really, you have about twelve hours left to live. Don't forget that you are to be sacrificed at dawn."

"We'll see... It's a bet," she declared, diving into her food. To Petterman's amazement, she finished her plate with ease and even went back for seconds.

"Well, you never know when you're going to eat again do you?"

"You most probably won't do."

She ignored his comment and said,

"And you don't really know when you will eat next, so it might be wise for you to get some more."

"I will be fine; supper will be waiting for me when I get home. Then in the morning, after my breakfast, I will be back here to take you to the sacred hall, and then I will have the usual sacrificial meal. That's three meals that I know about. Now when you are ready, we will make a start on your tour."

She stuffed another couple of mouthfuls down her throat, then stood up and said.

"Okay, I think I have had enough now."

"Right let's get going before he comes back and finds me giving you a tour of this hell hole of a castle."

"Ah! See... You admit it now; you hate this place don't you."

"I never really denied it, did I...? Now let's start at the top of the East Wing and make our way down, down to the dungeons."

They made their way to the East Wing and ascended the stairs to the highest floor.

"These are the servant quarters; all the rooms are the same here, small and functional."

They walked along the long, bare, narrow corridor to the far end. Where there was a large common room for the off-duty servants. This room was decorated with all sorts of tapestries and paintings, mostly of battle scenes; some of them looked very old and faded. Petterman told her the story behind them as they passed each one. They passed through a door at the far end of the room that led to a small narrow stairwell with two young boys playing a game of tag. As soon as they saw the two adults coming down the stairs, they stopped playing and stood to attention against the wall. Petterman said to them,

"At ease young soldiers." They relaxed a bit and stood staring at the woman. She said to them in a soft but firm voice.

"And you will not remember seeing us, will you…"

"No M'lady," They both said in unison and promptly went on playing their game as if they had never been interrupted.

"Before you die, you must teach me how to do that. It might come in handy for me one day."

"You already possess the ability; everyone does. However, it is rarely utilized, causing people to forget how. Your brain is an underutilized tool, and you'll be astonished at what you can achieve with proper training."

"And I suppose you're going to offer me that training in exchange for helping you escape," she interjected.

"Petterman, I shouldn't tell you this, but you'll need this forgotten knowledge tonight. Earlier, I mentioned you'd require my help, and tonight is the night. However, I can't say more at the moment, so please don't ask for further details."

They had descended to the middle floor of the East Wing.

"This floor is for the servant's overseers and their families. This room, just as on the upper level is their common room, but during the day it is used as a nursery for the children, as you can see with all the toys all over the place. They are allowed to have only two children. The women look after them until they are eight years old; then the children are trained in household duties. When they are fourteen, they are enlisted into the army training camps to the north of the city. The ones that fail in the camps are either set to work as labourers in the fields or return here to take up servant duties. The rest are then enlisted as soldiers, and spend the rest of their days in the legionnaire's villages."

Along the corridor, she noticed that all the rooms were family-sized and nicely decorated, but this was not the part of the castle that she was interested in, so tried to hurry him along a bit.

They reached the stairs at the end of that corridor and went down. The lower floor was the food preparation and cooking area for the whole castle. Two burley guards stood barring their way into the kitchens. Petterman explained that Jarroth had only one fear, and that was the fear of being poisoned. As they approached, she said to him,

"Well, this is your chance to see if you can use your powers… But don't worry I will assist if you mess up." As they got closer to the doors, the two guards suddenly turned and blocked their way. The guard on the right said.

"Sorry sir, but you are not permitted to pass through these doors. Please turn around and go back from where you came."

"We can and will pass through these doors, and you will not remember," Petterman replied. The two guards immediately lowered their pikes and advanced toward them. Petterman went to draw his sword but was too slow and the guards pinned him against the wall with their pikes against his throat.

"Sir, you have been asked to turn around and walk back from where you came. You have not done that, so we are now forced tò arrest you and take you to the dungeons until our lord returns, where you will have to answer to him personally. But, because we know you, Sir, we will ask you one more time to walk away." Petterman was shaking with anger at the thought of these two soldiers of a lesser rank than himself, putting his life at risk. He silently shouted at them,

"Drop dead you simple morons!" Suddenly, the two soldiers turned and faced each other and drove their pikes into each other's hearts, in seconds they were both dead. Petterman stared in total amazement and disbelief. The woman standing next to him started laughing and said. "Nice work, but did you have to kill them? You could have just ordered them aside and forgotten that they ever saw us like you first said to them. It is not right to kill you know, I think you have a lot to learn about the ethics of using your natural powers. We will overlook this one but never do it again without first considering what may happen to you afterwards. For now, until I have the time to instruct you more, just remember that whatever you do to nature may be returned to you three-fold. I had to act very fast then, to turn your work around so that they killed each other instead of you killing them."

"What would have happened to me, if you had not made them kill each other?"

"Well, only time would tell that my friend, you see, Mother doesn't like you messing around with the balance that she has created. Come on let's see these kitchens that are, or should I say were, so closely guarded."

They entered the kitchens, and it was obvious from

41

the start that there was nothing of interest to her here. She kept pushing him forwards till they got to the far end and out of the door.

"Well that was a waste of time, and such a waste of two lives just to see nothing, could we not have gone through another door and bypassed the kitchens?" She asked him.

"No, there is no other way out from this end of the castle, now shall we start towards the West Wing and see if that holds more interest to you? It is the residential quarters for the dignitary and the Lord's meeting rooms."

"I'm not that bothered about seeing that part of the castle, if it's fine by you, I would rather go and see the collection of tapestries that are hidden away from public view."

"Ah! That's where your interests lie, is it? Now, why would a person want to get into the castle, by any means possible; just to look at a collection of tapestries that are as old as the hills?"

"They are not just old tapestries Petterman. They tell the history of this world from before we existed on it, and no we aren't the first to inhabit this world."

"Oh, now you are going crazy, who was here before us, besides our ancestors?"

"Show me the tapestries and we will see... This is one of the reasons that I came here. I'll tell you more about it another day..."

"There you go again, have you forgotten your appointment with the sacrificial knife in the morning?"

"I've told you once Petterman, I will not die tomorrow, there are some things that need to be taken care of before I go to my grave, and it will take a long time to sort them out. But we have not got much time here so we'd better get going." Just then a loud trumpet started its' fanfare announcing Jarroths' return.

Petterman quickly ushered her towards the dungeons. "Come on move yourself... the tour is over, Jarroth has returned and if he finds me giving you a tour of this place, we will both be in the quagmire, without our entrails..."

"Where would our entrails be?" She said jokingly.

"Thrown to the wild women in the Coves. Now stop joking around and start moving." He said irritably.

"You're frightened of him aren't you Petterman, he will not harm us, take my word for it. And those wild women are my friends. He wants to talk to me because he knows that I am not like the other women around here and he senses that I have a power beyond his comprehension, and he does not like that one bit, he is worried that I mean him harm."

"And do you?"

"Well not at the moment, but I cannot guarantee that for the future.

He possesses numerous artefacts that don't belong here, and eventually, they must be returned to their rightful places."

"And you're planning to steal them. I suspected you had ulterior motives; you're nothing more than a common thief, aren't you?"

"No, not I, Petterman. That task will be entrusted to others. Besides, I cannot steal what already belongs to me. You will understand soon enough."

They walked the remaining distance to the dungeons in silence. Once inside, they sat down on the damp floor. Petterman pulled his legs up under his chin and wrapped his arms around them, and then he spoke.

"You mentioned that I fear Jarroth, and it's true. But you, you worry me more than he ever could. You know more about me than my own wife, and you know things about my wife that you shouldn't. How do you possess this knowledge? Who are you exactly? I had a comfortable life here until today. Then you came along, telling me what I already knew but never admitted: that I despise it here. And now, you've awakened a strange power within me that I never knew existed, nearly causing me to kill two of my comrades. Explain to me, what the hell is happening here? Why am I involved? And how can a simple soldier like me assist someone like you?"

"I cannot answer all of your questions right now. I will do so later. For now, you must go to your wife immediately. She has started the birthing process, and something is wrong. Go and help her, Petterman. The child must not die. If you need me, call for me later."

"What are you ranting on about now? How can I go, when I am ordered to stay with you until he gets here, and how can I shout for you when I don't know your name and you are imprisoned here?"

"Jarroth is on his way down here now; he will let you go, just tell him why. I will make sure he lets you go. You must find a way to call me from within yourself when I hear you… I will come. That is all I can say right now."

"Jarroth is on his way down here. He will allow you to go; just explain the situation to him. I will ensure he lets you go. You must find a way to call me from within yourself, and when I hear you, I will come. That's all I can say at the moment."

Suddenly, a door farther down the corridor slammed open, and the sound of marching feet filled the air. Petterman stood at attention near the door. Two of Jarroth's guards entered the dungeon, surveying the surroundings. Then Jarroth himself entered the small room and addressed Petterman.

"Well done, soldier. You are dismissed."

"My Lord Jarroth, my wife is…"

"Yes, I'm aware of the situation, soldier. Go to her if

you feel the need. If she gives birth to a boy, I want to see him as soon as possible. That's an order, soldier. You two, escort this soldier to his home and then report back to me.

"Now, peculiar one, tell me everything about yourself," said Jarroth.

"I think you know most of what you need to know Jarroth don't you?"

"My Lord Jarroth is the title I prefer, not just Jarroth. Even my own wife would never address me as simply Jarroth."

"You have no wife, Jarroth. Your entire life is built upon lies, and you're well aware of it. Your only power lies in the fear people have of you, which compels them to obey."

"How dare you! I show you mercy after catching you stealing food, and this is how you insult me?"

"Jarroth, I wish to see the tapestries. That's the reason for my presence here. It's why I stole the discarded apple core, so you would grant me entry into the castle, sparing me the trouble of breaking in and sneaking past your soldiers."

"And why do you desire to see the tapestries? What interest do you have in those old, moth-ridden rags?"

"I thought you knew more about me than to ask that question. You do have a reputation for being knowledgeable about the events in this realm but never mind. I am a historian, of sorts, and the tapestries hold significant importance for my research. Particularly the ones concerning the 'Nogho-Tilabive' and 'Na-Vot.' Though I would truly appreciate the opportunity to see them all."

Jarroth took a seat on the bench in the cramped cell, feeling the weight of his current predicament. She knew that his authority stemmed solely from the fragment of stone in the pouch hanging around his neck, leaving him powerless in reality. If she truly was a historian, shouldn't she be more intrigued by this stone than the worn-out tapestries below, despite their undeniable value?

"Are the tapestries all that interest you?" he inquired, hoping to extract more information from her.

"Primarily, yes. But as I mentioned earlier, I am a historian, and I would be fascinated to see all your artefacts. That includes a glimpse of the Throne fragment, your notorious sword collection, and the two rings of power, one gold and the other white gold," she responded.

"The rings, my precious rings, they have quite intriguing tales behind them. The gold one was rumoured to be the 'One Ring,' a ring meant to rule over all others. It bears peculiar inscriptions that reveal themselves when heated in a fire. However, I have never deciphered their meaning. There's also a claim that wearing it grants invisibility, but that has never occurred to me. So, I assume it holds no power in this realm. The white one is just as peculiar. Its size and weight appear to fluctuate, and when one grows irritated while wearing it, it emits a warm glow of shimmering white light. Though its true purpose eludes me," he explained.

Why go about it this way? Why did you not just ask to see them?"

"I have sent numerous requests, but they have gone unanswered. So, I took matters into my own hands and ventured down here to try my luck. It has been three days since I arrived, and every time I inquire, I am dismissed. That's why I devised this little scheme, and it seems to have worked splendidly, wouldn't you agree? At last, I have your attention," she remarked.

"Yes, you have certainly caught my attention, but in doing so, you have also secured yourself a date with the executioner's blade tomorrow morning. Was it truly worth it?" he retorted."

"We shall see. It is not yet morning, and you have not decided whether or not to show me the artefacts," she replied.

"I see no reason to withhold them if that is all you desire. I only hope you won't be disappointed. Death is a hefty price to pay for anything, but then again, sacrifice is deemed honourable, isn't it? It will be an honour to sacrifice you, young woman," he stated.

"To whom or what do you intend to sacrifice me? I hope it is something worthwhile and not just another act of murder. From what I've heard, you dispose of anyone who challenges your authority. If you were truly as strong and powerful as you claim, you wouldn't need to resort to murder. You would assert your dominance and govern your people properly, treating them with decency. In return, they would respect and willingly obey you, fostering a contented military and civilian workforce," she argued.

"You don't speak like a common peasant, and now that you're cleaned and dressed, you certainly don't look like one either. However, how I treat my people is none of your concern. They follow orders, and the tasks are accomplished. End of story," he retorted.

"Without a contented populace, they may eventually turn against you and sacrifice you in the name of 'Big old Z'," she warned.

"Watch your tongue, woman! He can hear you through this stone. If he unleashes his wrath upon you, you will deeply regret it! he warned.

"Oh! I am well acquainted with his wrath; I have been studying him for years. That's partly why I'm eager to see the tapestries. They are the oldest existing records and, as far as we know, the only authentic ones.

"So, it seems you're a Zeraphite priestess researching His origins. Why didn't you mention it earlier? I would be delighted to show you the artwork, or as I like to call it, the collection. Come to think of it, I haven't been down there myself for quite some time. It'll be refreshing to take another look at everything. I've been preoccupied with other duties for far too long. Let's go now before it gets too cold; the temperature drops significantly down there at night."

"Ready when you are, boss. I've waited a long time to see these tapestries. I hope you're well-versed in curating, as I might have a few questions about some of them."

"You can ask as many questions as you like, but I don't possess extensive knowledge about them. I merely collect them because of their rarity, and some were quite a challenge to acquire. I had to search far and wide, both on land and at sea, and as you'll see, some of them aren't in the best condition."

They left the dungeons and descended into the strong room, where all the treasures were kept. At the beginning and end of each corridor stood two soldiers. Every time they spotted Jarroth and his prisoner, they snapped to attention, blocking their way. And each time, Jarroth commanded,

"Make way for your 'Lord Jarroth'," and the soldiers stepped aside, holding their pikes upright.

As they passed each pair of guards, the prisoner silently whispered,

"Your shift has ended; go home to your families and forget that you saw us." She chuckled at the thought of a trickle of soldiers leaving the vaults halfway through their shifts, leaving Jarroth and herself alone.

They arrived at a large pair of wooden doors adorned with black runic writing across the middle.

"What do you know about this entrance?" she inquired, trying to gauge Jarroth's knowledge.

"Nothing; it has always been here. It's the sole

entrance to this network of caves, known as the Gehenna Coves. There are other coves along the coastline where the 'mad women' live, but these are unique, as you'll discover once we enter."

"What about the writing? Do you know what it means?" she probed, seeking to uncover the extent of his knowledge.

"It is said to be in the language of the ancient gods, from a time before we inhabited this land. The wood is incredibly hard and cannot be scratched or marked in any way. That's why I had the castle built around them, to preserve them. The wood has almost turned to stone; that's how old they are."

"If they are unmarkable, then why build a castle around them? They should be on display for the public to learn about this land's ancient history. Instead, you've made them one of your personal possessions, and I believe that's wrong, Jarroth.

However, setting that aside, little is known about the writing. It is said to translate as: 'The safest, the strongest, the best, the last. She who enters shall be our last.' And I am 'She,' Jarroth; now you know who I am…"

Jarroth stared at her in disbelief. "You cannot be. She is nothing but a myth, a myth from ancient times. You are no god! You are flesh and blood just like everyone else... I could draw my sword and sever your head from your shoulders."

"Jarroth, keep an eye on the doors," she commanded in a loud, authoritative voice. She then raised her arms high and, with a thunderous voice, said,

"En Sephi Farragho, Annall Na-Graffico!"

Instantly, Jarroth summoned the guards and unsheathed his red-pommeled sword. The red crystal emitted a glow as if it were ablaze from within.

"There are no guards, Jarroth. I sent each one of them

home as we passed them in the corridors," she declared.

He spun around to face her, but before he could utter a word, he noticed the red crystal glowing in his hand. Thinking it would burn him, he dropped the sword to the floor and took a step backwards, his face drained of colour and his voice trembling with fear as he asked,

"What is happening? What have you done? You're going to get us killed..."

She just smiled at him and said softly.

"She simply smiled at him and spoke softly,

"I have come to seek my destiny and claim my rightful name. From this day forth, I shall be known as Selika, daughter of Zeraphos and Selenika. I am the embodiment of your greatest dreams or your worst nightmares. Watch the doors and remain silent, Jarroth."

Reluctantly, he turned away from her and gazed at the massive old doors. Once again, she whispered,

"En Sephi Farragho, Annall Na-Graffico."

This time, the writing on the doors began to glow, first red, then white. More letters appeared around the top of the door as if someone or something was inscribing them. The air crackled with electricity, and a faint hissing filled his ears.

"Open the doors, Jarroth," she commanded.

He placed his hands on the doors and pushed, but nothing happened. He pushed again, still to no avail.

"They always open easily, but not now; I think you have locked them," he surmised.

Once again, she chanted the words,

"En Sephi Farragho, Annall Na-Graffico." In an instant, forks of electricity shot across the doors, throwing Jarroth to the ground.

Then, the doors began to open on their own. The sound of whispering voices emanated from within the caves, sending a cold shiver down Jarroth's spine. Thousands of voices whispered in unison,

"Welcome, sister, and welcome home."

Jarroth slowly sat up and peered into the cave. Bright balls of green light floated and bounced all around, some of them venturing into the corridor and hovering above them before darting back into the cave with incredible speed. Jarroth gazed at Selika and gasped. She was suspended in the air, arms outstretched, tears streaming down her face. She looked at him and pleaded,

"Pull me in, Jarroth."

"Never! We will be killed if we go in there," he protested.

"You will not be harmed, Jarroth. You are safe. Your stone will protect you. You must pull me in now before it's too late," she urged.

Reluctantly, Jarroth rose from the floor and reached for her hand. As soon as their hands touched, a bolt of electricity surged through him, but instead of throwing him down, it bound their hands together. He pulled her toward the doors, surprised at how effortlessly she floated along. A ball of green light brushed against his head, and although he tried to swat it away, his hand passed straight through. Another settled on his arm, sending a chilling tingle through his body. They reached the doors, and the whispering ceased and all the green orbs hovered at eye level, he pulled her into the expansive cavern, and the doors slammed shut behind them with a mighty bang.

A voice from the far wall spoke,

"Welcome, Selika. You are the last. You have much to do and must not fail. We cannot help or interfere. Your role is to lead and guide, for the final task, does not belong to you. A child born in this city tonight must live; she is the next leader of Gehenna if you succeed. We have a limited amount of knowledge to impart before you depart. That is all we can do. You know your mission. Do not fail, for if you do, this land and all its inhabitants will perish alongside our parallel world.

Jarroth, you are no longer the leader of this kingdom. You have a task that you brought upon yourself. All artefacts not native to this land must be cast into the fires of Quenilith when she erupts. The piece of stone that you carry must also be thrown into Quenilith. Take it out now and place it on the floor. He followed the voice's instructions, placing the stone on the floor. Two green balls of light moved toward the stone, settling on either side. They lifted the stone off the floor and started hammering on either side of it. Suddenly, the balls turned red and exploded into sparks, causing the stone to fall back to the ground. The voice from the wall said,

"I have diminished its power, it will no longer cause harm. Take it and cast it into the fires of Quenilth with all the other artefacts. The tapestries will remain here and be restored by others. Go now, Jarroth, and prepare for your tasks."

A green ball of light touched his hand, releasing his hold on Selika. Jarroth picked up the stone and put it back into its pouch around his neck. He turned around and walked toward the doors, which opened as he approached them. Once outside the cave, the doors closed again with a loud bang.

"Selika, when we have given you the gift, you must walk straight out of the doors and begin your task. You are being summoned from the city. We can say or do no more. May you have strength, luck, and success"

An orange ball suddenly appeared and struck Selika squarely in the face, knocking her back a few paces. She fell to the floor with the ball stuck to her face, screaming in agony as it began to sink into her eyes. Just as suddenly as it started, the pain in her eyes ceased. She rolled over, sat up, and rubbed her eyes in an attempt to clear her vision, but horror struck her as she realized she could see nothing. There were noises and flashing lights inside her head, but she was blinded by that terrible orange glow. Slowly, she stood up, unsure of her direction, and began to walk, hoping it was the right way. Unfortunately, she walked straight into the wall, hurting her knees and head.

"Jarroth!" she shouted. The doors opened immediately, and Jarroth rushed in.

"Over here, M'lady. I was waiting outside the doors for you. Dear God! What happened to your face? It's a terrible mess"

"Jarroth, I cannot see anything, get me out of here."

"To where M'lady?"

"Anywhere… Just get going."

"To my quarters, then, M'lady. And let's clean up your face a little."

Jarroth guided Selika through the now deserted corridors to his quarters. The castle was silent; never before had he experienced such an eerie quietness, which made him quite nervous.

"There's something not quite right here, M'lady. I've never known this old place to be so silent."

"Shh…" She said quietly. "They are just learning of your abdication and Cadderman temporarily taking over."

"Who's informing them?"

"I am, now let me concentrate; it's not easy telling over a million people at once, that you're going on walkabouts."

Jarroth led the rest of the way in silence.

They reached Jarroth's quarters just as Cadderman knocked at the door.

"My Lord Jarroth," Cadderman said, bowing low. "This news comes as a shock to us all. What has brought this about so suddenly? And why have I been chosen, sir? Moreover, why is this prisoner out of her cell, sir?"

"First and foremost, Cadderman, this lady is a

prisoner no longer; she is the most esteemed guest this establishment has ever hosted. Her every wish shall be granted. Do you comprehend, Cadderman? This is my final and most crucial command as your leader and lord. Is that clear?"

"Yes sir! Crystal clear sir and it has been a pleasure serving under you sir…"

"Don't lie to me Cadderman; you hated me just like everybody did. I reigned through fear, fear of being sacrificed. That must stop. Let all the prisoners waiting for sacrifice go; send them back to their homes."

"It will be seen to straight away sir, along with quite a few other things too sir."

"Don't call me Sir now Cadderman, you are in charge here now, not me. I will be coming and going for a while yet, I am relocating everything in the vaults to a safer place, everything except the tapestries, which will be renovated and kept here. Now, I believe we should seek assistance for our guest, don't you agree?"

"I don't need assistance," she said. "I need to get to Petterman's house without delay."

Cadderman summoned one of his soldiers and provided him with instructions. Within minutes, he was on his way, leading the now blind woman to Petterman's house.

Eldoron

6 - The Birth of a Child

Selika and the soldier arrived at Petterman's house to the sound of screaming coming from the upstairs bedroom. They went straight into the room from where all the noise was coming. The room was crowded with women, shouting, panicking, and trying to give instructions. Petterman saw them standing in the doorway and shouted over the entire din.

"M'lady, please help. I shouted to you but you did not come, and now I think it might be too late. Elita, my wife, she is struggling, she can't…"

"I know Petterman, I know. Soldier, will you get rid of these interfering women, leave me with just one helper and Petterman."

The soldier physically removed all but one of the hysterical women after guiding Selika to the bed. She still could not see but knew instinctively that things were not going well.

"What happened up at the castle M'lady? We have heard some startling news, is it true?"

"Yes it is true, I will tell you all about it later when this little problem is all sorted out. Soldier, do you have other orders for today?"

"I have other duties, but they will wait if need be M'lady."

"Good, I will have a few jobs for you, if you don't

mind. What is your name? I can't just call you soldier all day."

"My name is Norak, M'lady, and I will do all you ask."

Another wave of pain shot through Elita and she started screaming again. Selika turned to her and said.

"Things are not going well here Elita; I need to help you before you get too weak. I need to send myself inside you and try to turn the baby around; it is too big to turn from the outside. It is trying to come out feet first."

"Do it, just do it please," cried Elita.

"I need you to relax so that my mind can penetrate yours…" Petterman interrupted her to tell her that there was blood coming out of her birth canal.

"Damn, this is not good! Norak, hot water and plenty of it, towels and blankets too, as quickly as possible please."

"Yes, M'lady right away." He said and then marched out of the room.

Selika sat on the bed and put both hands on Elitas' swollen abdomen and said to the others in the room. "Silence now please, while I do this. One mistake could prove fatal for both the mother and the child. Elita, I am going to try and turn the baby around, it cannot be done from the outside because it is much too big, and her feet are stuck in the birth canal. It will be very painful but it is the only way."

"Do it, please do it before the pains come again, I can't take much more… please."

"Okay, Elita, try and relax and I will try and make things right." Selika closed her eyes and started chanting to herself. Her mind entered Elita's and she started to relax a little. The voice in Elitas' mind told her that the baby was very special and had to be born safely at all costs. Without waiting for a response Selika set off down inside the woman's body, heading straight for her womb.

She entered the womb and was appalled by what she witnessed, so much so that she instinctively recoiled, accidentally tearing through the engorged lining of the woman's womb. With great caution, she slowly positioned herself beside the baby, who seemed to be looking at her. Moving around to the baby's back, she reached around and gently pulled up its knees, bringing its feet out of the birth canal. Elita experienced excruciating pain as she did this, and Selika felt a sudden release of pressure as the mother's waters broke, pouring out and leaving no room to manoeuvre the baby. Selika attempted to turn the baby around, but it became clear that the woman was unable to carry such a large child.

In her desperation, Selika suddenly shouted,

"Dearest Mother Goddess, in whom we live, be present now within this woman, descend and bless your hidden child."

Screams and shouts reverberated through the streets below as an earthquake shook the town, causing all the houses in the vicinity to tremble. A piercing screech emanated from the sky, descending like a diving eagle, transforming into a deep and powerful sound that stunned the entire city.

Far away, in the Burning Mountains, Quenilith, the dormant volcano, erupted, sending smoke, fire, and molten rock high into the sky. Despite being fully aware of the chaotic situation outside, Selika remained steadfast.

Suddenly, the wall of Elita's womb split wide open, flooding the small chamber with blood. Thinking and acting quickly, Selika pressed the unborn child into a ball and, utilizing the blood as a lubricant, turned her upside down, forcing her head into the birth canal. The contractions resumed, and Selika shouted,

"Push now, Elita! Push hard. Elita, bear down and push." Unfortunately, there was no reaction; Elita had already gone into shock due to the loss of blood and the traumatic events unfolding.

Temporarily withdrawing from Elita's mind, Selika addressed Petterman and the other woman.

"When the baby's head emerges, assist in delivering the rest of it swiftly but carefully." She then returned her focus to the baby, pushing it down the narrow canal in sync with Elita's contractions. Gradually, the baby's head progressed through the canal, with each push from Selika moving it closer to the open mouth of the birth canal and into the new and unknown world. A powerful contraction struck, and Selika pushed as hard as she could. The baby's head emerged from its mother's body, entering the realm in which it would play a significant role

Petterman and the other woman shrieked in horror at the sight of the baby's head, even though it was covered in blood. They could discern that something was amiss—its skin was green with black blotches and completely devoid of hair. Tentatively, Petterman took hold of his child's head and attempted to guide it out in rhythm with the contractions. The woman had fainted and collapsed onto the floor.

"Pass those towels, soldier!" Petterman shouted. Norak, the soldier, promptly responded, throwing the towels near Petterman's feet, then recoiling in horror at the sight of the baby's oddly coloured skin. "Norak, if you cannot bear witness to this, then attend to the woman on the floor," Norak dutifully responded, grateful for the distraction.

During the next contraction, instead of the traumatized Elita, Selika pushed while Petterman pulled. The shoulders emerged, displaying the same peculiar colouration as the head.

"What in God's name have I brought into this world?" Petterman thought. In the subsequent contraction, the baby's torso was delivered, leaving only the legs, which came out relatively easily.

Petterman wept openly, cradling the blood-soaked baby in one hand while tugging the still-attached umbilical cord with the other. Selika emerged from Elita and quickly tended to the cord. Norak had revived the collapsed woman, who was now sobbing and muttering something.

"What are you saying, woman?" shouted Norak.

"I'm sorry, M'lady. It was too much for me to bear. I lost my baby just last week. He went to sleep and never woke up again." She took the baby from Petterman and started checking her, making sure she was breathing. There were no problems there as she started to cry.

Petterman turned his attention to his wife, who was still bleeding profusely from between her legs. Norak had brought two large bowls of water, one for the baby and one for Elita. The woman was washing the baby, and Selika and Petterman were trying to stem the flow of blood from Elita's body.

"What has gone wrong, M'lady?" Petterman asked softly.

"Nothing went wrong. Mother Nature has taken over now. There is nothing we can do now but comfort her until she has passed over. I am so sorry Petterman; I got here as soon as I could. I was blinded at the castle, temporarily I hope, and that hindered my journey here. Maybe if I had arrived sooner things might have been different."

The sound of the baby crying suddenly stopped, and they both turned around. What they saw surprised them both. The baby was suckling on the woman's breast, and tears were pouring down her face.

"I am so sorry," The woman said, looking very embarrassed and pulling the baby off her breast. "It just happened and it felt so right. Sorry Sir, sorry M'lady."

She started to hand the baby back to Petterman but he stopped her and said,

"I am so sorry," the woman said, looking embarrassed and pulling the baby off her breast. "It just happened, and it felt so right. Sorry, Sir, sorry, M'lady." She started to hand the baby back to Petterman, but he stopped her and said,

"Please, no. Carry on, she needs feeding. Elita cannot do it now; she is dying. Please, please feed her." He broke down sobbing on the floor. Selika stumbled over to Petterman, still blinded by the earlier events, and put her arms around him. She whispered something into his ear, causing him to sit up slightly. She whispered again, and he started to stand up, glancing from his child to Elita, then to Selika and back again.

"I must tend to my wife," he said in a very strained voice. He went to the bed where Elita lay, blood still oozing from between her legs. He knelt on the floor next to the bed and, with a damp cloth wiped her forehead. She still looked beautiful to him; she always will.

"Elita, my love, I don't know what to do with our baby. Don't die, please don't die. I am a soldier, not a mother." Elita slowly opened her eyes and turned her head to look at him. She whispered,

"My Soldier, don't worry. I think she is in good hands now. She has stopped crying, and I can see her feeding. It's strange; I can see her, I can see everybody in here, yet I am looking only at you. I am sorry I did not tell you about her. I thought it was just a dream I had months ago. She is very special; I don't know why, but I was told she will do great things." With tears rolling down his face, he tried to ask how she knew, but she interrupted him.

"My love, you must go with the blind woman. She needs you. Leave our baby with Vadoma, the lady who is feeding her. She knows how to care for her, and I trust her to bring her up in the right way. I know I am dying. Please, my love, promise me you will let Vadoma raise her." He took her hand in his and took a deep breath,

"My darling Elita, I do not know this woman. How can I entrust the life of our child to her?" He felt a strange sensation in his head, and his ears started to feel very warm. He looked over to where Selika was; she was looking straight at him through her sightless eyes, and her intense glare frightened him.,

"I do not have any choice do I?"

Elita gripped his hand so hard it hurt, his attention was back to his wife, and she whispered,

"My love, strange powers are at play here that we know nothing about. It is my destiny to die now, but you do have a choice. Please, my love, go with the blind woman and be her eyes. It is why we are here. I can see it all so clearly now, the good and the evil…" She suddenly curled up in pain,

"Oh, God! Please take the pain away I cannot bare anymore. My Love, hold me a while; I think I need to close my eyes now. Go with the blind woman my Soldier, my time here is done."

Petterman felt her fall into death; her lifeless body relaxed, and the flow of blood slowed then stopped, he pulled her towards himself and held her in his arms,

"Sleep well My Love, 'till we meet again in the next life."

Selika stood up and came over to Petterman, sensing where he was by the sound of him quietly sobbing. She put her hand on his shoulder and started to say something, but he interrupted her with a sudden burst,

"Why? What has gone wrong? She isn't meant to die, she's my wife. She should be looking after our daughter, why woman; why?" Selika knelt next to him,

"Petterman, I am so sorry, there is more going on here than you can ever know, but I can tell you a little of it if you can give me the pleasure of your company for a while longer. I need you to take me somewhere up north, I cannot go alone, I need you to guide me; be my eyes until I can see again. Will you do that for me Petterman? I think Elita would have wanted it too." Once again he felt like he had no choice in the matter and simply nodded his head in agreement,

"I need a few days to arrange Elita's funeral and sort things out with our child, and talk to Cadderman and Jarroth at the garrison," He said quietly.

"Of course Petterman, but you won't need to talk to Jarroth, Cadderman is in charge now." Petterman looked at her with a puzzled expression,

"I'll explain later, now you get things sorted here, I have to go back up to the garrison. I will talk to Cadderman for you while I am there. We have to leave for the north in a few days from now, so you must get things moving as soon as possible. I need Norak to take me back to the garrison; I will see you in a couple of days. Good luck with the funeral, I will try to be there."

Eldoron

7 - The Na-Vot

Valadora led Jarreen into the cave, and what she saw surpassed her expectations. The main living area stretched fifty or sixty paces in length and at least thirty paces wide, with several doors leading to other rooms. Valadora guided her through one of the doors near the cave entrance, which turned out to be the kitchen. Long racks held pots and pans of all sizes, and a massive stove stood against the wall. This kitchen could easily cater to an army.

From there, Valadora took Jarreen to a large cupboard on the far wall. Opening the door revealed another surprise—shelves that acted like a hidden door, leading to a secret room. They quickly entered and closed the doors behind them. The room, although smaller compared to the kitchen, still felt spacious. It was carved straight from the rock as if shaped meticulously with a hammer and chisel. The room lacked any decorations or ornaments, appearing entirely bare except for old wooden benches with thrown-on cushions. Arranged in a circle around a small fire pit, the benches offered comfort. Despite the absence of windows, the room emitted enough light to see. The walls emitted a faint glow, casting peculiar shadows in the darker corners. It was an eerie space, to say the least.

"Welcome to my sanctuary. Nobody knows about

this room, and I prefer to keep it that way," Valadora said. Jarreen walked over to the circle of benches and found them surprisingly comfortable.

"What do you do in here?" She asked,

"I do all sorts of things here. From planning meals to keeping an eye on the 'past ones.' I can see them clearly in this room. Only Eldoron knows, but he doesn't know how or when I observe them. Lately, they've become more active, which puzzles me. That's one reason I brought you here. I'll show you how to use the fire later, and then you can see for yourself."

"Valadora, please excuse my ignorance but who are you referring to? Do you mean the Ziton's? The old ones that failed to rid Zeraphos of his powers?"

"Yes if that is what you call them, we just refer to them as the past ones."

"But I thought they had all perished one by one, as Zeraphos killed them."

"Oh no, we now know that he cannot kill their spirits, only their bodies. Their spirits endure, strangely enough, all in the same place. It's as if they live together or have been confined there for some reason. However, that's not the only reason I brought you here. I've devised a way to train Volto and wanted to hear your opinion before discussing it with the others." Jarreen's face turned ashen as she contemplated Valadora's intentions.

"Send him to the Zitons?" she thought to herself. "Over my dead body!" Valadora interrupted her thoughts,

"Let's have a drink of our own, just like they are doing outside, only we can drink it in the warmth of this sanctuary. What's the matter? You look like you've seen a ghost."

"Valadora, you don't mean to send Volto to the Zitons do you?"

"What? Send him to the past ones? No, never, he is

much more powerful than all of them put together. I don't think that they could help." Jarreen's whole body relaxed as she let out a big sigh of relief.

"Here, let's have a drink, did you think that I would do something so foolish and potentially dangerous? No Jarreen, I was thinking of training him from within; entering his mind and teaching him that way. It would be much quicker than creating countless lessons for him and allowing him to make mistakes, only to repeat them until he gets them right. That would take years. Instead, we can expedite his training through mental guidance." Jarreen lowered her gaze to the faintly glowing embers in the fire pit and took a sip of her drink. Valadora noticed the embers brighten slightly, but Jarreen remained fixated on them.

"What do you see?" asked Valadora, aware that she was toying with fire by the way it moved. The embers' glow began to swirl in a circle, growing brighter at the centre. A small flame danced just above the circle's midpoint. Gradually, the flame ascended from the fire, hovering at head height. It appeared to have a fading blue tail trailing an inch or two below it. The flame started to spin, starting slowly and then accelerating. Its blue tail vanished into its core, and its colour began to shift from yellow to red. Valadora grew concerned, for she had never witnessed such a phenomenon before.

"What are you doing, Jarreen? I've never seen anything like this," Valadora exclaimed. The spinning flame changed colour again, shifting from red back to a vibrant blue. Little sparks fell from it, crackling as they landed back into the fire. Jarreen sat back, looking puzzled by the flame.

"I'm not doing anything, Valadora. I'm not controlling the flame. I thought you were displaying your talents," Jarreen responded. The flame started to solidify, forming a small, vivid blue orb floating in the air. Another orb rose from the flames and hovered beside it, followed by a bright red orb that settled between them.

Both women appeared worried, and Valadora cautiously inquired.

"Who are you?" The blue orbs ceased spinning and gently tapped the red one. With each tap, the red orb grew slightly larger until it reached the size of a fist. The three orbs then stood motionless for what felt like an eternity. This time, Jarreen asked the question.

"Who or what are you?" she asked. The red orb began to shimmer, and in a loud booming voice, it declared,

"We are the Na-Vot, the soul keepers. We desperately seek your help. We can no longer maintain the balance between life and death." Valadora attempted to speak but was instantly silenced by the pulsating blue orbs, which, in a deafening voice, said,

"Do not interrupt the Na-Vot." Both Valadora and Jarreen were stunned into silence. Jarreen, speaking with a shaky voice, apologized,

"We apologize, Na-Vot. Please continue; we are listening." The two blue orbs moved toward the women and hovered menacingly just above their heads. Though unsure of the orbs' capabilities, they instinctively knew they could be very dangerous. The red orb resumed speaking, albeit quieter this time.

"We can no longer hold the balance of life and death. Zeraphos has stolen millions upon millions of souls from us and is using them to create an army, unlike anything we have ever seen. This army is not composed of humans; instead, Zeraphos allocates three souls to each creature. This disruption has upset the balance, resulting in more souls alive than dead. We must retrieve the souls to restore equilibrium; otherwise, life as we know it will cease. If we fail to restore balance, we will perish, and all of humanity, not only in this world but life in all other worlds will also perish. Furthermore, Zeraphos has taken millions of animal souls, and we remain uncertain of his purpose. The animals, too, will face extinction if we do not restore balance. This world will perish soon if we cannot rectify the situation."

Jarreen and Valadora just sat there pale-faced, staring into the fire. Jarreen and Valadora sat pale-faced, gazing into the fire. Valadora broke the silence with a nervous cough and asked,

"What can we do to assist you? We know nothing of your kind or your predicament. We are mere commoners compared to you. We are unaware of this army or the stolen souls you speak of." The red orb started to pulsate and said,

"The red orb pulsated and replied,

"You possess the stranger, the young one known as 'The Child.' He must reclaim all the souls and return them to us as soon as possible. The survival of all our worlds depends on it. We understand that he lacks knowledge, but we have been observing him since he arrived in this world. It will be perilous for us to share some of our knowledge with him, as he is only a mortal and may not possess the strength required to wield the powers he will need to succeed, but we have no alternative but to try."

Jarreen sat up straight and reached for her drink. The blue orb nearest to her descended and hovered right in front of her eyes. Instinctively, she tried to wave it away, but the orb reacted by shooting out a thin, bright light towards her forehead. Suddenly, the fire burst into life, and hundreds of blue orbs flew out, encircling Jarreen and trapping her in an eerie blue cage. She looked terrified. The red orb addressed the others and they backed off. Turning to Jarreen, it said,

"We apologize for our nervousness around you. Your

touch could cause great harm to us. They were only protecting me. Please move slowly, and everything will be fine. I am the last of my kind, their elder and mother figure." Jarreen looked very angry and replied,

"Jarreen appeared angry and retorted,

"If you pull a stunt like that again, our fragile alliance is over. I am a warrior who believes in self-preservation. Next time, I will defend myself, regardless of the consequences." She relaxed slightly and slowly picked up her drink, gulping it down. "I need another one of those, Valadora. Now." Valadora began to rise, but the red orb intervened, saying,

"Please, allow us." A few blue orbs came forward, took the cup from Jarreen, and dropped it into the fire. The cup shimmered, rose from the embers, and floated back to her. She held out her hand, expecting to get burnt, but the cup was cold and filled with a strange-coloured, thick liquid.

"What is this?" She asked.

"That is the only beverage we consume in our world. It has sustained us for millions of years. It will not harm you; in fact, it will likely benefit you. Valadora, please drink," the red orb explained."

"I will not touch it until you have explained exactly what it is made from; you may be here to poison us for all we know." The slight glow from the walls started to get a little brighter and turned a nice warm shade of orange, the fire started to flicker and small flames reappeared, it smelled like fresh peat had just been put on it. The red orb spoke again,

"Valadora, Jarreen, we have not started off on the right foot, have we? We mean you no harm. We are not a violent race, though we will defend ourselves when necessary, just like you. We are incredibly delicate in your world, and even a slight touch from you could kill us. We have no physical substance; we are pure spirits.

All souls reside within us, yet we are neither a place nor a being. We simply exist. This drink is our elixir of life, if that's what you would call it. Unfortunately, it is tasteless, but if it had a flavour, it would be the most exquisite drink you can imagine. It is incredibly nourishing and fulfilling, capable of making those who consume it quite euphoric. Similar to the concoctions you create for your husband. So, please drink with us. I promise you won't be disappointed," assured the red orb.

Reluctantly, both Jarreen and Valadora accepted the drink and took a sip. As the orb had described, it was tasteless, cold, yet warming as it went down. It was the kind of beverage that would be most welcome on a cold winter's night, yet refreshingly cool like pure spring water on a hot summer's day. The small drink helped to calm their moods. Valadora then asked the red orb about reclaiming souls and why it posed a danger to him. Was it a life-threatening danger? The orb seemed to settle down, and its pulsating slowed.

They leaned back and looked at each other, worry etched on Valadora's face and lingering anger on Jarreen's.

"You mentioned that he would need powers for this task you're asking of him. What kind of powers are necessary? How will he employ them? And how will he know when to use them? When to stop using them? Is it going to be dangerous to him when he is using them?" Jarreen put her massive hand on Valadora's arm and said,

"Slow down. You're talking too fast, and nobody can understand you. I have an idea. Instead of trying to explain everything ourselves, why don't we let this Na-Vot thing," she pointed at the red orb, "do the work for us? They can implant our knowledge into Volto while giving him their own. What do you think? Could that work?" The red orb confirmed that it was indeed possible. However, the powers they would give Volto would be time-limited, so he would have to act quickly. The knowledge, on the other hand, would stay with him forever.

"Bring the young one in and let's start this." The orb said, rather insistently.

"Yes, the sooner we start the better" agreed Valadora.

Jarreen interjected,

Hold on a moment. We haven't figured out all the details yet. We don't know which parts of our knowledge we should teach him. And more importantly, we haven't even asked Volto if he's willing to go through with this. After all, it's his mind we'll be tampering with, isn't it? We should wait until morning when we have clear heads and can discuss it with Volto."

Valadora stood up and walked around the fire, feeling its warmth without disturbing the orbs. She said,

"You are right, Jarreen. We need to think this through, but it's an incredible opportunity to prepare Volto for his destiny. It could save years of training. We can't pass this up." She turned towards the red orb and asked, "Is it safe? What you're proposing, is it safe?" The orb paused, changing colours slightly, contemplating the question. Finally, it stopped and turned bright red again.

"Ladies, we cannot guarantee that Volto will not be permanently harmed, but it's highly unlikely. He's incredibly strong, as you can see. We can't fully comprehend the extent of his power, which worries us. If he were to join the wrong side after gaining all this power and knowledge, he could destroy the very fabric of time and space. That's a grave concern. However, the alternative is equally dire. If we don't retrieve the souls, life as we know it will cease"

Jarreen was pulling at her cheeks and lips in a very anxious manner, and mauling her face.

"There is something not right here and I cannot put my finger on it. Something is bothering me, some gut instinct. Have you ever heard of these Na-Vot things before or had any dealings with them? I haven't. Can we trust them? They might be evil things trying to get Volto on their side or worst; they might be doing this because they know he is going to be very powerful and instrumental in winning the battle against Zeraphos. Or they might be some sort of clever spies."

The orb was turning slowly and bobbing up and down slightly, quite strange but also very compelling to watch, almost hypnotic. It said.

"You are very suspicious of us and rightly so Jarreen; you don't know a thing about us and we have been here since the beginning of time. After this world was created, we were the first beings to inhabit it, and we did for millions of years. Then we ran into trouble, the trouble of our own making. A bit like the humans are doing now. I have seen the making and breaking of many races and species, even the demise of my own race. I am the only one left of my race, and we were classed as immortals, these others you see here with me are not the same as me. They have been created from different races and creatures to help, serve and protect me, whatever the cost. The Creator, The One, whatever you wish to call it, we have always called it Nogho-Tilabive, simply 'The Creator' in our tongue. It knows there are troubled times ahead. It knows we are approaching a precipice but cannot interfere. If Zeraphos, as you call him re-awakens fully and gains control over the humans, then this world is over for good. All the humans will kill each other and poison the animals. It will be just a dead rock floating in space. Zeraphos must be stopped at all costs. Jarreen, we are not here to do you or Volto or anyone any harm. We are here for the same reason; to stop Zeraphos from killing us all. We just have a very pressing matter to deal with, something that will give everybody time to prepare for the upcoming events."

Valadora sat down once again, burying her face in her hands. She spoke softly,

"We need to speak with Eldoron and Volto. We can't proceed without them. We require their input and Voltos' perspective on this. It's his mind we're dealing with, not ours to tamper with. However, we must ensure this room remains a secret. We need to move the orbs out of here, either to the kitchen or outside." The orb interjected, stating that it could go wherever there was fire. If they gathered around a fire outside, it would follow them there.

"There isn't a fire at the moment, but it won't take long to start one. Let's go and figure this out, Jarreen."

At that, they both got up and went out of the secret room back into the kitchen, where Valadora picked up some wood from the stove and lit it on a small fire in the hearth. Feeling like fools, they took the burning log outside to where the others were seated and announced that they were going to light a fire for them, to keep them warm. It was a warm summer's evening and in no way did they need a fire, Eldoron and Jorgon looked at them in disbelief,

"Ladies please; it is plenty warm enough without lighting that. We were considering removing a layer of clothes, not lighting a fire! Doron, will you get us all a refill while your mother and I discuss the necessity of a fire in the middle of summer."

"Doron, the drinking has been suspended for the time being. We need your attention, your full attention now!" Jarreen shocked everybody with the tone of her voice; the jovial atmosphere disappeared in a flash. She was serious and they all knew it.

"Certain events have just happened while Valadora

and I were talking in the kitchen, and you are all going to see what has transpired. We just need to light this little fire to show you, not to keep you all warm. We have had a visit from a race known as the Na-Vot. They want to talk to us all; they have a special need that needs to be taken care of."

Eldoron almost jumped out of his chair,

"The Na-Vot have not been heard of for thousands of years, what is going on? They were thought of as just myths to most folk, only a few from the higher order knows their true purpose, and as far as I am aware no living person has ever clapped eyes on them. There must be something serious going on here. Where are they?" Valadora looked up from lighting the fire and said to Eldoron,

"Don't get too excited old man; we are a bit spooked by all this, as you will be very soon. You really need to keep a level head and bring your old training to the forefront. Things are going to happen tonight that may change the course of our lives if not history itself."

"I'm confused with all this. I just want to go back to a normal life," Volto said to Dora. "You're not on your own there Volto, things are a bit mad here at the moment, it is usually so quiet and calm, apart from Mum and Dad arguing over things that are way beyond me, or the odd visit from somebody like Jorgon."

"Why is it, when you want to start a little fire the wood is always wet through?" Jarreen said quietly. Doron jumped up and said excitedly,

"I will light it for you, just watch this!" As he raised his arms to the sky; both Jarreen and Valadora shouted at the top of their voices,

"No stop!" That made them all stop and look and scared the life out of Jorgon, who was already on his feet and spinning around to see what all the fuss was about. Valadora glared at Doron and said,

"Step away from the fire and slowly put your arms down, then sit back down and do not move. You got that?"

"Whoa! Chill, I was only trying to help; I didn't intend to incinerate us all."

"Sorry Doron, as I said we are a little bit spooked at the moment. You will understand very shortly, but for now please just sit and be quiet. I need this fire to be small."

The mood now was icy cold and very strained, Volto and Dora stayed well back out of the firing line. Jorgon and Eldoron were looking at each other but said nothing, their expressions were enough.

"Please, stop standing there with your mouths agape, the two of you. Will you kindly arrange some seating around here, but ensure it's not too close to the fire? Everyone should have a good view of the flames." Neither Eldoron nor Jorgon argued or made any sarcastic remarks. They simply obeyed in silence, understanding that it was for the best.

Once Jorgon and Eldoron had organized the seating, Jarreen and Valadora beckoned everyone to come and sit around the fire. Jarreen decided to narrate the events that had taken place in the sanctuary, but she cleverly altered the setting to the kitchen with the small hearth, keeping the location of the sanctuary a secret. She described in great giantish detail how the embers started swirling and a small flame rose up, and out of the fire to head height. The two blue orbs and then the red one, the orbs talking to the two of them and the drink that they were given. As Jarreen told the tale, the embers started swirling just like she described. Eldoron thought it was a trick and a good one too, and started giggling to himself. Valadora gave him a look that killed the thought stone dead. A blue orb arose from the embers again but this time a lot bigger. It hovered over the fire. Jarreen sat down, looked at the fire and raised her hands and cocked an eyebrow in a gesture of 'What more can I say? Just watch and see.' The second orb joined the first, and then the red one slowly, gracefully rose from the embers and nudged its way in between them. They were a lot bigger than when they appeared to Valadora and Jarreen. Once again the blue ones started tapping the red one and then dropped a few feet below it. The audience was transfixed; they had never seen a show like this before, and not even the best side shows that the travellers give had anything on this.

The Na-Vot spoke to Valadora again,

"Thank you Valadora, please; before we start telling our needs, will you explain to all around the fire that we must not be touched or even approached? We will be moving around out here more than in your kitchen in the cave. We also need to give you all a little drink, the same as we gave you two inside. Do you agree to this?"

Eldoron and Jorgon were looking at each other, then at the two women.

"What is going on Jarreen? We do not understand any of this, do we Eldy?"

Jarreen stood up and said calmly and quietly,

"Please, let the orbs speak for a few minutes. We must hear this directly from them. We were conversing with them in the kitchen before coming out here. They offered us a drink, which they claim to be their elixir. I'm still alive so it appears that it is safe."

Doron fidgeted nervously in his seat next to Jarreen and whispered,

"I already have a drink that suits me. I don't need another one yet." To his surprise, and everyone else's, Jarreen suddenly struck him forcefully on the back of his head and spoke in a strange voice, "Do not drink any more of that. They will provide you with a drink, and you will drink it!"

Startled, Doron's leg kicked out involuntarily,

accidentally knocking a small branch near his foot into the fire. Instantly, hundreds of bright blue orbs erupted from the flames, flying toward him without making contact but coming dangerously close. The orbs closest to him had needle-like spears aimed in his direction. Volto, seated beside him, swiftly moved toward Dora and Valadora, his ears ringing loudly, and the front of his head began to burn. Jorgon rose to his feet, his face twisted into an angry, battle-ready expression, his massive hand reaching for his sword. Eldoron grabbed his arm, stopping him without knowing why. Valadora rolled back off her seat and stamped on the ground with one foot, causing a slight tremor, and an eerie black light descended upon the circle of so-called friends. Eldoron stood up, his voice unusually menacing as he said,

"Back off! Back off into the fire from whence you came! Na-Vot-Na, approach slowly and explain yourself. Valadora, release the shielding, and the rest of you, sit down."

The darkness disappeared and everyone sat down again but the orbs remained suspended, pinning Doron to the bench. Jarreen reached for her sword and addressed the large red orb, now concealed within the fire.

"Release him or I will slay you all."

The red orb emerged from the flames once more, growing in size as it ascended. When it reached head height, it stopped, now twice its previous size. It pulsated with a strange hue of purple. Wet strands of purple plasma suddenly shot out toward Jarreen's sword, halting any further movement. The orb spoke calmly.

"Stay your sword, warrior. This aggression is unnecessary. In the cave, I informed you that we mean no harm. On this day, no one will be harmed if we can all show a little tolerance. The Na-Vot cannot be touched, and you do not wish to be touched, so let us respect that. Let us sit in peace, and rid ourselves of mistrust and doubt. We are here on a vital mission that cannot fail, but we need your assistance."

As the orb spoke, the blue orbs covering Doron receded back into the fire, vanishing before their eyes. The strands holding Jarreen's sword fell to the floor and disappeared. However, calm had not fully returned to the circle. Jarreen trembled with anger, while Eldoron and Valadora hurried over to their son Doron, who remained seated in the same position as when he was pinned down, pale and trembling. Upon inspection, Valadora determined that he was physically unharmed, only shaken up. Jorgon sat beside Jarreen, offering comfort. Both were safe. Eldoron turned to Volto.

"Are you alright, young man?"

"My head feels like it's burning from within," replied Volto. Valadora interrupted the conversation, saying,

"We will address that matter shortly." She shot an evil glance at the Na-Vot.

Dora was the only one not affected by the incident, though she was shocked at the strength in her father's voice, she had always seen him as a very gentle quietly spoken man. How wrong was she?

Once everyone was seated, the atmosphere gradually became more agreeable. The large red orb spoke again.

"Please, place your tankards near the fire. I will have them refilled for you. I assure you, it will not harm you, as Jarreen has already confirmed. Drink, please, for clear thoughts, are necessary to understand the gravity of our message. Our elixir will remove the effects of any other drink you've had this day."

"What a waste," said Volto, "I had just started to feel better, then all this happened, never a dull moment in this household eh?" Jorgon started to giggle.

"It's not been like this for countless years Volto; something is afoot here; mark my word. We have just got used to living a mundane life and look what happens."

The blue orbs started to pass the tankards filled with their elixir. The red orb addressed Jorgon.

"Jorgon, this marks the end of the mundane. From this day forth, you may face death around every corner. The people you encounter in towns and villages may not always be as they appear. Higher forces are at play, unbeknownst to you. But fear not, by the end of this night, you will have a better understanding of why we have called this gathering.

Please do not drink until we all have one. Eldoron was the last to receive a drink and turned to the red orb.

"What about you? Will you not drink with us to prove it is untainted and not poisoned?" "Yes, I will drink with you if that is your wish, and if it helps dispel your mistrust. However, I cannot consume it as you humans do. Normally, we savour the moment, considering the elixir a special offering that has sustained me since the beginning of time." The orb shimmered slightly, and around fifty or sixty blue orbs rose from the fire. They gathered beneath the red orb, tapping against each other and slowly merging to form a small, shallow bowl. More blue orbs emerged from the flames and guided the bowl, without physical contact, back into the fire. All present witnessed the bowl filling with the same gooey liquid they had in their tankards. The bowl rose again and floated just beneath the red orb. Both the red orb and the bowl moved away from the fire, settling a couple of arm's lengths away from the group.

Slowly, the orb descended into the elixir, causing a small amount to spill onto the grass. To everyone's astonishment, tiny flowering plants sprouted where the elixir had landed, and colourful flowers began spreading in every direction. Within seconds, the vibrant blossoms had almost reached the cave entrance, leaving everyone dumbfounded. The scent was incredible, strong yet delightful and butterflies and bees soon made their appearance. Valadora observed the happy, smiling faces of her companions, all gazing at the ground, seemingly letting the flowers grow beneath their feet. Meanwhile, the orb continued to soak in the elixir, while the flower's expansion gradually slowed and the butterflies fluttered less fervently, though the bees remained industriously collecting pollen. The trance was broken when Doron succumbed to a fit of sneezing, a victim of his springtime pollen fever. Valadora rose and offered to find some "butterbur" for his sneezing, but the orb intervened, addressing Doron directly.

"Doron, just drink some elixir. It will cure your ailment once and for all; I promise you that. Nature can remedy nearly any affliction or ailment".

Dora playfully chimed in,

"Hey Father, it might just fix your little problem too." Eldoron glanced down at the floor, his face betraying obvious embarrassment.

"Okay, so I'm going to be the target of your jokes and comments today. Bring it on... I can handle it. Just remember, you'll all pay for it later; trust me."

Valadora shifted uncomfortably, interjecting,

"Old age cannot be reversed, nor can the clocks be turned back. Let's leave it be, shall we? The old man is embarrassed enough, and we have more pressing matters to discuss. Na-Vot, please enlighten us about the purpose of your visit"

The Na-Vot addressed them, conveying grave news.

"Zeraphos was planning something immense. He managed to steal millions of souls from the realms of the departed and has begun forging an army of peculiar creatures, each possessing three souls: human souls and an assortment of animal and insect souls. This is highly perilous, as any major disruption in the balance of souls could spell the end of not only this world but all other worlds, including the one you came from, Volto."

Volto, who had been somewhat detached, as this was not his homeland and didn't directly concern him, suddenly paid attention. Though he didn't have any genuine family connections with these people, he had grown rather fond of them. Valadora referred to him as "my son," but he was aware of the distinction. However, Na-Vot's statement seized his focus. His homeland faced annihilation, and while he didn't have many friends or family there, being an orphan who had lived independently for several years, there are billions of innocent people who don't deserve to perish. It was then suggested that the orbs enter his mind to impart some knowledge or abilities. Volto placed his tankard down on the fresh grass and began to listen intently.

"What we are saying Volto, is that we intend to enter your mind and impart some information and special abilities that you will need to retrieve the souls from these creatures, you won't know how to retrieve them until the time comes, which is not far off. The abilities will not last for long so you will have to act quickly to release all the souls back into our care.

This will not destroy Zeraphos, but it will setback him somewhat. Our mission is not to destroy him. Strange events are currently unfolding in Gehennah that may hinder your progress. Unfortunately, we cannot provide further details at this time. Volto, please come and lie down on your back near the fire so we can begin."

"Wait! Just a minute! Are you planning to enter my mind and alter me? What do you intend to change? I've seen people with altered brains before, and it's not a pleasant sight. They suffer greatly and end up living in asylums for years if they ever recover at all. No, I cannot allow you to do this. It's already difficult enough with her presence in my mind, and I don't think there's any room for more. I'm overwhelmed with information, and my head feels like it's about to burst right now. How will it feel with all of you in there too? There's no space for all of you! And none of you has even had the courtesy to ask me. You simply assume that I will just lie down and accept it! Well, no. I won't spend the rest of my life in an asylum. I won't allow it, not now, not ever. You can delve into someone else's mind and manipulate their thoughts. Give them the special powers if you want, but I don't want them. I don't want to become a murderer, killing millions of creatures just so you can reclaim their souls"

"Volto, calm down. There's a strange glow surrounding you. Remember what happened in the field when you lost your temper. You don't want to harm anyone here, especially the Na-Vot," Eldoron said, approaching him to help calm him down.

Everyone, except Doron, Dora, and the Na-Vot, slowly moved closer to Volto in an attempt to help him regain his composure. A peculiar purple aura now enveloped Volto, and it seemed like he was on the verge of losing his temper at any moment.

The blue orbs gathered strength around the large red one, shielding it from any potential threats that Volto might pose. The orbs rose higher from the fire, out of reach of the group. Eldoron now sat beside Volto with Valadora on the other side, the two giants flanking him. Doron and Dora remained on the opposite side of the fire, staying out of the way. Volto spoke in a calm voice,

"Step away from me, or I will move you all" Jorgon chuckled and said in a lighthearted tone,

"Come on, lad, you can't move me. I weigh more than ten times your weight, and you'd be pushing me uphill." Volto stared at him with fiery eyes, slowly raised one hand, and calmly said, "Move." Suddenly, Jorgon slid along the bench and onto the grass. Volto then turned his gaze toward Jarreen, who appeared ready to pounce on him, and once again uttered, "Move." She tried to resist, but she slid along the bench and onto the grass, just like Jorgon. Eldoron and Valadora took it upon themselves to move before he had a chance to look at them. Volto's aura turned bright red, matching the colour of the towering Na-Vot, now as high as the top of a large tree, surrounded by thousands of smaller blue orbs.

Volto knew that he had to find some form of release, even in his mental state as it was now, he remembered destroying the side of the hill and he did not want a re-occurrence of that. He kept looking around for something to stop the mounting pressure inside him, his eyes wild with fire. Nobody knew how to handle him because nobody knew what he was capable of.

Suddenly, some of the blue orbs descended in two distinct lines: one heading towards Jorgon and Eldoron, and the other towards Jarreen and Valadora. Jarreen began to draw her sword, but the big red orb, which had lowered itself slightly, boomed in a deafening voice,

"Giant, stay your sword! Nobody will be harmed on this day." She returned the sword to its scabbard again. The two lines of blue orbs, seemingly forming a barrier, positioned themselves between Volto and the people on either side of him. The large red orb, still encircled by countless blue orbs, moved over the top of Volto. He hadn't looked up and did not know they had moved at all.

The new grass and flowers, along with the bees and butterflies, had all but disappeared, bringing back the earthy autumnal smell that was present before the day's events. The pressure continued to build as the orbs formed a seemingly impenetrable barrier between Volto and his friends. The red orb rose higher, intensifying the mounting pressure. Volto was aware that he was losing control but felt helpless; he knew he had to release the tension. The pressure reached its breaking point, causing his head to feel like it was undergoing a slow explosion, and his vision took on an eerie reddish hue. He wanted to stand up and run, but he found himself almost paralyzed and weighed down. The sensation of fire being drawn into him added to the mounting pressure.

Suddenly, the fire transformed into a loud whisper that he could hear but couldn't comprehend. The volume of the whisper increased, growing even louder. The words enveloped his entire body, coating it in a strange purple glow.

Eldoron and Jorgon were looking at each other with great concern; they knew that they had to do something to stay his anger, but what could they do against an unknown power? Valadora and Jarreen were also looking at each other in the same manner. For some reason, though nobody knew why, they all started to move slowly forward towards Volto, forming a circle around him. Dora and Doron joined them without being asked, they didn't know why either.

The blue orbs that had acted as a barrier changed course, encircling them all. The distant red orb remained out of reach but faintly visible. Fear reflected in their eyes as they looked at one another, their minds filled with confusion and a lack of understanding regarding the imminent events. They closed in on Volto gradually, as if attempting to suffocate or suppress his power.

Volto now recognized the words he heard. She had returned at the exact moment when he was on the brink of exploding, that was all he needed, he thought. She was singing, singing in a voice that was so beautiful it made him falter. The others could hear her too, in their minds. They could not make out the words, they were in a strange tongue, and Eldoron thought that he knew the song but dismissed it. Time seemed to stand still while she was singing. Volto stood up and raised his arms above his head as though he was about to direct his anger and all his power at something far out of reach, the singing suddenly stopped and they all heard a loud screech in their minds, Volto collapsed to the ground, covered in a purple glow, as if attempting to bury himself in the earth. After a moment, he sat up and gazed at his friends, his face contorted with terror. He began speaking, but instead of his voice, it was Selika's voice that emanated from his mouth.

She addressed all of them through Volto, almost ordering them to refrain from approaching him. The blue orbs, now spinning rapidly and emitting the same noise as Selika's singing, encircled them. Selika explained that she had to quell Volto's anger before he harmed everyone. She instructed everyone, except Volto, to remain silent and motionless. To Volto, she spoke in the same enchanting singing voice as before.

"Volto, you must trust me and follow my instructions. Channel all your anger through yourself and into me. I will remain unharmed, extinguishing your fire here. Nobody will be harmed if you comply. Just direct all that fire at me. If you refuse, everything will be lost. I know you have the Na-Vot nearby, and they must be protected."

Volto felt immense confusion. He had never been so furious before and couldn't understand why. Last time, he had released his anger towards a hillside and it had dissipated, but this time he couldn't let go. The magnitude of the anger felt too immense as if it could shatter the entire world. Selika repeated her plea.

"Volto, throw the fire at me. I can handle it, and it won't harm me." As she spoke, his purple aura began swirling and spinning, accompanied by a deep droning sound. The blue orbs moved in one direction, while his aura moved in the opposite. The entire group could sense the overwhelming power in the air but were powerless to act. Suddenly, Volto rose to his feet, his aura doubling in size and spinning faster. He stretched his arms upward, splaying his fingers wide, before collapsing into a small ball and screaming at the top of his lungs. His aura expanded further before abruptly retracting into his body. The screaming suddenly stopped and the blue orbs flew at lightning speed past the circle of friends and collided with Volto, totally smothering him. There was a huge thunderclap overhead and the ground shook like an earthquake knocking everyone to the floor. The red orb was still way out of reach up in the air far above them all but was now swaying side to side as if it was dangling on a string.

Everything fell silent for a moment, and then Valadora slowly approached Volto. The blue orbs still covered him, swirling slowly like a seething mass of blue slime. Eldoron also moved closer as the red orb lowered itself to just above head height. It announced that his anger had somehow disappeared, and the swirling slime transformed itself into thousands of blue spheres, moving away from him, perhaps to allow Valadora to examine him for any injuries. Jarreen stood up and went to Jorgon's side, and together they approached Volto. Jarreen said to Valadora.

"I think I need to enter his mind and see what has transpired in there. Let's just hope there is no damage."

"You can't do that! You've already been thrown out once by that woman. For all you know, she's still in there, waiting for you to try," Valadora replied.

Volto lay on his back with his arms covering his face, trembling as if in a fever. He started to move his arms and tried to sit up. Valadora placed her hand on his forehead, steadying him and checking for signs of fever.

The shaking subsided somewhat, and he felt cool to the touch. Valadora thought that such power should have permanently damaged his mind.

"How do you feel Volto?" She asked.

"About what?" he said. "And why is everyone standing around as if they're about to go into battle with me? What happened? I just remember being annoyed with all of you discussing altering my brain without my permission. Oh no! I remember something now; the red mist came again, didn't it? What did I blow up this time? I hate to say this right now, but I feel good. I feel... refreshed. Light. Like something has been lifted away from me. Did those orb things do something to me?" Valadora said she wasn't sure but didn't think so.

Volto said,

"I think that woman in my head stopped me from causing too much damage. I'm starting to remember now. She told me to throw the anger and the fire at her. I think I remember seeing her in a large lake surrounded by flames, but she wasn't burning. The water was boiling, but she seemed unharmed. I hope I didn't hurt her in any way. Or even worse, kill her."

"I somehow don't think you harmed her. She wouldn't have asked you to throw the fire at her if it endangered her life. But I would have liked to witness what happened wherever she is. Did you say she was in a large lake? Can you describe it? Were there mountains or snow or anything that could give us a clue about its location?" asked Valadora. He replied, "I didn't see any mountains or snow, just a large clearing with a big lake in a forest. A very big forest."

"Sormoving Wood, it must be," said Eldoron and Jorgon simultaneously.

"That's not the friendliest of places. Why would anyone want to be in that dark, forsaken place?" Jarreen wondered

"It looked nice and peaceful from the glimpse I got," said Volto.

"We'll tell you about that place another day. Trust me, you don't want to go there anytime soon," Eldoron assured him.

Valadora asked Volto how he was feeling again. He said he felt fine, just a slight headache. Valadora was relieved.

"I think we should return to the business with the orbs before it gets too late. Shall we gather around the fire again and get this over with?" No one argued, and they all returned to their original places around the fire.

The red orb descended from the sky, and most of the blue orbs returned to the fire, leaving only a small guard for the big red orb. The red orb addressed them all, urging them to relax and finish the elixir they had been given. It would help ease any anxiety they might have. Once they finished, it would explain again the importance and urgency of the situation.

After a few minutes of quiet conversation, the big red orb began to explain once more that all the souls needed to be returned to the holding rooms. It provided details on what would happen if the balance wasn't restored and emphasized that it wasn't just this world that would be affected. It promised Volto that the procedure to impart the required knowledge and abilities would be painless, and wouldn't last forever. Volto would need to start making plans as soon as possible after this day.

"What? Today? Do you mean you're going to do it today? I'm not ready. I have no idea what I'm supposed to do. I can't just go out tomorrow and kill millions of animals, creatures, insects... I'm not ready to battle anyone or anything, let alone millions of three-headed monsters or whatever you want to call them. I've never been a fighter!"

The big red orb approached Volto and said,

"Young man, listen to me and trust my words. You won't be going into battle as you imagine it. This won't be a physical battle. It will be a battle of the heart and mind, so to speak. These abilities or powers, as you call them, aren't physical powers. You won't be able to pick up a sword or a bow and become a master. They are internal powers that will give you the ability to perceive and understand things and to react before they happen. Your body will serve as a vessel, temporarily holding the souls until they can be returned to us. So you must not die or lose consciousness during this time. If you do, your body will become the permanent resting place for all the souls you've collected, and I don't think you'd want that, would you?"

"Okay, so this thing you're going to do to me won't hurt or harm me, and it won't last forever. But how long is 'not' forever? Will I be aware if it's there? How long will it take? And how can I make plans if I don't know what or where it is, or how to access it?"

"Volto," said the big red orb, "Don't worry. You'll know when the time comes. I can't tell you how it will work because only you will know that. Even the lady in your head won't know. You won't end up living with the Zitons"

"The Zitons, who are they? Asked Volto.

"They're the ones who previously tried to rid Zeraphos of his powers and failed. But that's not your concern at the moment. We can talk about them another day if you want to know. We usually refer to them as 'the past ones'," explained Eldoron.

Eldoron

8 - I Can Fly

The large, red orb floated over to join them, staying just out of reach to prevent any damage. It began speaking in a soft, feminine voice, a stark contrast to the hard, guttural tone it had earlier. Volto thought it was attempting to show a caring side, perhaps to calm him down before the procedure. However, it sounded so insincere that it only heightened his suspicions. After all, this orb was an ancient being, possibly billions of years old, having witnessed the birth and extinction of countless species. Why would it care about him? Besides its own survival being at risk if he failed to return the lost or stolen souls, was its display of concern just an act of self-preservation? Or did it genuinely possess a sense of compassion? Does it actually have a heart, (so to speak)?

"Please, Volto," it implored, "just lie on your back, close your eyes, and relax. You won't feel a thing. This will be over in a few seconds. I'm going to administer a small amount of the elixir into your body. You may experience a pleasant, warm sensation."

One of the small, blue orbs rose from the fire and approached the large red orb. It rotated slowly, emitting tendrils of steam. As the droplets fell to the ground, the grass began to grow again, mirroring what had occurred earlier. The blue orb floated just beside Volto as if awaiting the cessation of the drips or instructions from the large red orb. Another blue orb emerged from the fire and hovered on the other side of Volto, also dripping and waiting. The crackling and sparking of the fire grabbed everyone's attention. Blue orbs continued to emerge from the fire, forming what could only be described as a funnel, wide at the top and tapering towards the base. The base, still enveloped in flames, gradually turned green and appeared to bulge, as if something lay within. The bulge then ascended the funnel, heading toward the wide opening at the top—a radiant fluorescent green orb. Upon reaching the summit, it halted, slowly rotating and emitting green sparks. More blue orbs emerged from the fire, creating a path or bridge that led to Volto and the large red orb. The green orb commenced its slow journey along the path, accompanied by a smaller blue orb on each side, as if preventing it from straying. Upon reaching its destination, the green orb stopped, while the large red orb awaited its arrival. The two blue orbs gently glided over Volto's face, the dripping having ceased, and the large red orb began uttering words in an unfamiliar language. The ethereal and melodious quality of the voice was almost pleasant to hear. Volto felt his eyes growing heavy, attempting to resist but failing.

He felt a small droplet hit both eyelids simultaneously, startling him and causing him to instinctively turn his head. The large red orb reassured him, "

"Remain perfectly still while the elixir seeps in. It won't hurt or harm you. Soon, you'll feel a warm sensation in your eyes. Volto shuddered as the thick, viscous liquid permeated beneath his eyelids and into his eyes. The warm glow he experienced confirmed the truth of the large red orb's words; it was surprisingly pleasant He felt himself drifting as though he was going to sleep, but he knew that he was still wide awake. It felt strange, he could hear big red muttering away in that strange-sounding language and thought that he could still hear the others chattering away as though he was not there. Maybe they were talking about him? He thought.

Suddenly, a sharp, piercing pain shot through both his eyes, as if a slender needle had been thrust into the centre of his pupils. The pain travelled downward, coursing through his eyes and converging at the centre of his head. Volto shouted, or at least he believed he did,

"You said this would be painless!" But there was no response from anyone. The pain transformed into an intense burning sensation, rapidly engulfing the inside of his head and then descending down his neck. It felt as though his throat had been seared from within. He screamed in agony, or so he thought, but there was still no response from the others. He felt his head and neck swelling, as the burning sensation spread to his shoulders, down his arms, and into his hands. He could almost sense fire erupting from his fingertips. This was only supposed to take a few seconds, he thought. The fire continued its relentless journey, engulfing his chest, stomach, heart, and lungs. He felt nauseous as if he would vomit fire instead of the contents of his stomach, though he managed to keep it down. The burning sensation intensified as it reached his groin and hips, reminiscent of a long-past infection. It travelled down his legs like a slow-motion bullet, causing unbearable agony. Was this the end for him? Just another failed attempt in the never-ending battle against Zeraphos? He tried to call out for Eldoron, as he had been instructed, but to no avail. Although he felt like he was writhing in agony, he was lying motionless on the grass. The burning spread further into his feet, and he imagined it spewing out of his toenails and onto the grass. His entire body felt as if he had consumed molten lava from the volcano the other day.

Suddenly, the inside of his body turned icy cold, as if he had been turned inside out and thrown into a frozen lake. His heart stopped and turned to ice, his brain froze instantly, and his limbs became solid and lifeless.

"I think I'm dead," he whispered to himself. "They have killed me, but I can still think. I can't move, but I can see everything around me, like an out-of-body experience. The burning has stopped, and now I'm freezing. I can see Eldoron and the others, all gathered around me by the fire. None of them are moving, and the fire is perfectly still, like a frozen moment, like a photograph. I think I can fly, yes, I can."

The pain from the burns had vanished, and the freezing sensation was subsiding. He marvelled at his newfound ability to see everything.

"This is incredible! The orb lied to me; it said it would be painless. Just wait until we meet again, and I'll show it what painless truly means."

"I'm flying! Where should I go? Up, yes, up. Let's ascend." Higher and higher he soared, surpassing the mountains and floating above the fluffy white clouds. Still ascending, the air grew thin and colder.

"I don't think I'm breathing, but I can feel the cold in my lungs. I can see the sun, but I can't feel its warmth." He looked down again through the breaks in the clouds. "I can barely see the group, still gathered around me. To my right, I can see the coastline. Let's take a closer look. I used to love visiting the coast in a past life." He banked to the right and glided toward the coast, with a sense of wind in his hair...

"Oh! I can't feel the wind. I'm flying at great speed, but there's no wind. That must mean I'm dead!"

He continued his journey towards the coast for a brief period; he spotted movement in the water; people swimming.

"Can they see me?" he wondered, descending for a closer look, he realised that they were bodies; human bodies floating in the water, thousands of them; all dead, drowned. Overwhelmed by this dreadful sight, he nearly lost control of his flight. However, he swiftly regained composure, as if he had been flying for years, and began ascending once more. Still shaken, he flew back to his starting point. The group was still there, just as they had been before. Something was definitely amiss. Perhaps the procedure had gone wrong, or the elixir had poisoned him, explaining the excruciating burning sensation.

This time, he veered left and flew for what felt like hours, observing a vast forest below. "Could this be Sormoving Wood? The forest that Eldoron mentioned earlier?" He noticed smoke rising from its centre. "No, the forest can't be on fire," he thought, flying closer. It became apparent that the fire originated from the middle of a large lake. He recognized it as the same lake he had seen in his vision during moments of anger. This couldn't be the fire he and Selika had started; it should have been extinguished hours ago. Drawing nearer, he noticed more bodies, thousands more bodies floating in the water. Overwhelmed by shock once again, he turned around and flew back to the group.

Once overhead the group, he began to descend slowly. They remained motionless, gathered around him, while the big red orb continued to hover just above him. As he approached, he could once again hear the strange, enchanting voice of the red orb, but nobody moved. Even the flames in the fire remained still, resembling a frozen scene. When he was directly above the gathering, he realized that he could pass through them while they remained motionless. He flew past Dora and gently stroked her hair, but she showed no reaction.

"Am I truly dead? Am I now a ghost?" He suddenly realized that when he touched Dora's hair, some strands got caught on his wrist and were pulled out. As he tried to clear them away with his other hand, he noticed scales instead of skin. He was thoroughly shocked—burnt, frozen, and now transforming into a dragon, lizard, or some other grotesque, scaly creature. Carefully, he floated back toward his motionless body, along with the others and the motionless fire, resembling a photograph. There was no sound, no movement—nothing. Lowering himself to the ground, he glided past the group without making contact. He couldn't feel the floor; it was as if he were floating just above it.

He then felt a familiar pulling sensation, the same as when he had first entered the tomb. Was it Eldoron pulling him back to his body? Was it the Nah-Vot giving him his life back; seeing as they had killed him in the first place? The pulling got a lot stronger; slowly he glided all the way to the side of his body.

It was a very frightening thing to be standing right next to your own body, looking at it, still and lifeless. He said to himself,

"I look quite healthy considering that I was all burnt and broken a few days earlier, all the burns have healed up nicely and my leg looks... well not broken anymore." The pull had stopped pulling while he was looking at himself. He looked up at big red, which was still floating motionlessly above the group, he could sense it watching and studying him.

"Can you see me? Or hear me? Am I dead?"

"You are not dead, Volto. You have stopped time. That shouldn't be possible; it's a very dangerous thing to do. Only the ancient elders of my race could accomplish it, and only for a brief moment. They are all gone now. You have halted time for far too long, but it appears you have survived. You need to re-enter your body so we can discuss what has happened and what may happen," replied the big red orb."

The pulling sensation suddenly intensified, drawing him back into his own body. For a moment, he feared that the burning and freezing sensations would return, but they vanished in an instant.

As soon as he opened his eyes everything started moving again. Valadora and Eldoron were just looking at him as if waiting for something to happen. He said to them,

"What's wrong? Don't look at me that way I didn't do it; they were already dead!"

"What are you talking about young lad? Nobody has died, who are you meaning?" Eldoron replied.

Big Red said to them all,

"I think we all need to go back to the fire and discuss what has just happened,"

Jarreen said,

"Nothing has happened yet, we are still waiting for you to do whatever it is that you are going to do to him."

"It is all done, the knowledge is imparted. Volto why don't you tell us all what has happened and how you now feel."

Volto started to tell them all how the procedure was not painless at all. He told them how the burning pain started in his eyes, and how it seemed to travel all through his body. He described in great detail how he flew to the coast and the forest and saw all the bodies floating in the water, and the lake still on fire. They were horrified and wanted an explanation from the Nah-Vot as to how all this could have happened in no time at all.

Big Red said,

"I have only given him the gift. The gift was dissolved in the elixir, which was absorbed into his being. The rest was Volto's doing. Nothing whatsoever to do with the Nah-Vot. It appears that Volto has stopped time itself for a few hours. We are not entirely sure how, but this hasn't happened since my elders were alive, possibly millions of years ago. Only a select few were powerful and trusted enough to control time, and it required three of them due to its fragility and danger.

Volto has achieved it all by himself and for a much longer duration than the elders were permitted. If not properly controlled, it could bring about the end of the world. Time is the apex of the universe, and any disturbance could result in its collapse, causing the known universe to implode. Even Zeraphos would not survive such an event. We still don't know how or why this has happened. Perhaps it's a simple premonition of what will occur if the souls are not recovered and returned to us. Moreover, we sensed an animal presence within him, possibly a small dragon or gryphon— something with scales and the ability to produce fire without being harmed by it. We also saw wings, but they could belong to another creature carrying him, or he himself might have the ability to shape-shift. Perhaps this is the reason why the gift was as painful as he described." Big Red explained. Volto said,

"It was me that was flying; I was not being carried by anything else."

Doron was listening intently;

"Show me how you fly; I want to be able to fly as well. It must be amazing, Father; can I fly? Please; will the round ball-like things teach me to fly? That would be very useful when we are hunting for rabbits and stuff."

"Doron!" Eldoron shouted, "Show some respect, these round balls are the Nah-Vot; they are older than the world itself, and they deserve more respect than anything you have or ever will see in your life."

"Young man, we did not show Volto how to fly; he has done that himself. We were not even aware that he might be able to do that. So, unfortunately; we cannot show or teach you how to fly." The red orb said.

Volto continued, "It didn't just feel like flying. It was more like I had died, and I was observing myself from above. Only when I reached a certain height could I look around and start moving. As soon as I began moving, wings seemed to manifest. It was as if I had possessed them all my life; I instinctively knew how to use them. It was a wonderful feeling of freedom until I saw all those bodies floating in the water; thousands, maybe hundreds of thousands. It frightened me and made me falter in my flight. They appeared so real; do you think they were actually there or just my imagination? And then there was the fire in the lake; not even the water could extinguish that. What have I become? I don't think I like it very much. I used to have a peaceful existence before all this. No worries because nobody bothered me in my normal life. I lived on the streets of a big city and slept wherever and whenever I chose. My normal life is coming back to me now; I remember things from my world; cars, planes, trains, cities, towns, and villages where I lived. People, beautiful and horrible, cruel and kind. Drunkards, druggies, and homeless people. I was one of the homeless, and I had to beg for food. It was a hard life, unlike here. Here it is beautiful, and there is plenty of food. Everyone is friendly and kind to me. You all wear nice clothes and look and smell clean and tidy, unlike what I'm used to. I'm more accustomed to being ignored or pushed away. Sometimes, I would get beaten up by thugs who thought they were the bosses, the kings of their group. Occasionally, there would be a kind person who cared, but that was rare. The majority were not nice at all. Right now, I could go on and on, describing how nasty and evil my world sometimes is, but I don't think you want to hear that at the moment, and to be honest, I don't feel like talking about my world right now either.

I want to know more about what has happened to me and what I'm supposed to do next with all these souls. How do I find them? How much time do I have? How do I retrieve them? Where do I place them, and how do I put them where they belong? Can I touch them? Can I see them? Will they want to come to me? The questions are endless..." Volto expressed his concerns.

"Volto," Big Red interrupted, "When the time is right, you will have all the answers you need. That is all I can tell you for now. The gift I have given you hasn't been activated yet. The time for that has not yet come to pass, but soon you will feel it. You will know what to do, and there's no need to fear it. However, you must learn to control it, as it could potentially start controlling you, which could be dangerous. The lady who communicates with you in your mind will leave you alone, at least for the time being. I have placed a block to prevent anything or anyone from entering your mind and observing what has happened or may happen soon. All of you should rest now and gather as much strength as you can. The next few weeks may prove to be very challenging for all of you. We, the Nah-Vot, will soon return to our normal existence and may never see any of you again. However, one never knows. I recall saying the same thing to someone here a few thousand years ago, although he may not remember."

Eldoron

9 - A Funeral Fit For A Queen

Petterman was acutely aware of the need to make arrangements for Elita's funeral, but he found himself in a state of mind that hindered his ability to do so. Overwhelmed with grief, he felt the urge to drown his sorrows and be alone for a while. He had already requested assistance in preparing Elita's body for burial.

The first person to arrive was Norak, who was taken aback by Petterman's distressed state. Norak knew Petterman was upset, but he hadn't expected him to be in such a condition. Petterman had consumed copious amounts of ale and mead, rendering him almost unconscious. Realizing it would take hours for Petterman to regain any semblance of usefulness, Norak sought the help of several of Elita's friends. Norak dragged Petterman into the living room and just dumped him on the floor to sleep off his inebriation.

The ladies who came to assist were remarkable and clearly experienced in preparing bodies for burial, given their familiarity with the number of sacrifices ordered by Jarroth. Within an hour or so, they had completed their task while Petterman still snored in the living room. With everything set for the burial in the morning, the ladies bid their farewells and returned to their homes. Norak decided to stay with Petterman, recognizing that he was in no condition to be left alone. He knew Petterman would need some strong encouragement to be ready for the morning. Norak fashioned a makeshift bed on one of the chairs and quickly fell asleep.

The sounds of Petterman rummaging around in the kitchen roused Norak from his slumber. To his surprise, Petterman was wide awake, cooking eggs for breakfast. Norak approached the kitchen, and Petterman greeted him with a broad smile.

"Would you like some eggs and toast before we begin preparing Elita?" Petterman asked, oblivious to the fact that all the preparations had already been completed.

"Err... Yes, thank you. Are you feeling alright, Petterman? I mean, Sir, you were very drunk last night. Don't you have an unbearable hangover?" Norak inquired.

"I can't remember last night. I needed to grieve in my own way. After we lay Elita to rest, I'll be leaving this place, and I probably won't return for a long time. You don't have to call me 'Sir' anymore. I'm no longer in the service. I've been tasked with escorting the blind woman somewhere, although I know not where. I believe things are about to change dramatically around here and for the better. Cadderman is now in charge at the garrison, and I've always respected him. He was always fair to everyone. Hopefully, all the sacrifices will cease."

After they finished breakfast, Petterman suggested going upstairs to begin preparing Elita. However, Norak interrupted him, urging him to sit and relax for a while.

"All the preparations have been taken care of while you were... well, out cold, err... grieving, that is."

"In that case, let's get this dreadful time over with. Then I can go visit my daughter and see if Vadoma needs anything," Petterman replied.

"Petterman, please sit down. There's nothing for you to do. Everything has been arranged. The blind woman informed me, although I haven't seen her personally. We just need to stay here and wait for the carriage to arrive for her, which should be anytime now."

Not long after, they heard the sound of a carriage

come clattering down the rough track leading to Petterman's house. It was an open, flat-backed horse-drawn carriage, exquisitely painted and adorned with flowers. Four jet-black horses with large black plumes on their heads pulled the carriage. Two men, dressed entirely in black with black hats bearing matching large black plumes, occupied the front seat.

"Norak, my friend, who is responsible for all of this? I can't afford such extravagance; it's far beyond my means. I couldn't possibly pay for a funeral as grand as this, even though she's worth ten times the cost."

"As I mentioned, Petterman, everything has been taken care of and paid for, or so I believe. You must have good connections and friends."

The carriage came to a stop right outside the front entrance, and the two men stepped down from their seats and approached the house. Petterman had never seen them before. The man on the right introduced himself.

"Sir, I am Franklin, and this is Vermolt. We have been summoned here for your wife, Sir. We won't be going to the usual burial ground. We have been instructed to take her to the garrison where she will be laid to rest. Would you please accompany us there?"

Petterman was taken aback and speechless, but Norak stepped in and agreed to go with them.

Overwhelmed with tears and distress, Petterman was helped onto the rear seat of the carriage and told to wait there. Norak, Franklin, and Vermolt went inside and upstairs to where Elita lay. She was wrapped in customary muslin sheets, tied with torn strips of muslin from the sheets, and a small bouquet of fresh flowers adorned her chest.

Franklin examined the body and turned to Norak, speaking quietly.

"This is not fitting for a funeral of this stature. This will not do. Vermolt, please fetch the appropriate gown and dressings for her from underneath the front seat of the carriage. Hurry now; we don't have much time."

When Vermolt reached the carriage, Petterman inquired if something was wrong. Vermolt reassured him,

"No, everything will be fine in a few minutes. Please stay seated and wait." He went back upstairs, and they changed Elita into attire befitting a queen's burial. Vermolt went back down to fetch a piece of strong canvas and two poles; he slid the poles through the hemmed sides of the canvas and laid it on the floor. Franklin and Vermolt took the head end, while Norak took the foot end. Carefully, they lifted Elita off the bed and onto the stretcher. Carrying her down the stairs posed no challenge as she was small and light.

Outside, a crowd had gathered, dressed in their finest attire. Petterman, not looking back, was unaware that his beloved was adorned in the most luxurious silks money could buy. Elita was gently placed onto the carriage and covered with more exquisite silks.

As the carriage embarked on its final journey to the garrison, children began tossing flowers onto it. The gathering behind the carriage grew larger and larger, but Petterman still did not turn around to witness the multitude bidding their final farewells.

Upon entering the garrison, Petterman was struck by the scene before him. The entire courtyard teemed with soldiers, all dressed in their finest regalia. The sight overwhelmed him, tears streamed down his face and his vision was blurred, he found himself unable to speak. Trembling from head to toe, he remained frozen and could not move.

A deep, resonant drum began to toll, and the carriage started forward again. As they passed by the soldiers, they stepped aside and bowed low. They proceeded past thousands of people, all respectfully bowing as they made their way toward the large arched wooden doors leading to the burial grounds at the far side of the garrison.

Petterman turned to Norak and whispered,

"This is where commanders, heads of state, and a few heroes are laid to rest; not where ordinary folks like us find their final resting place. Why is this happening?" He could see, straight in front and at the far end, a new crypt had been built, still under wraps. After circling the garrison three times turning from east to west, as was customary, they headed straight for it. The carriage stopped just to the side of the new crypt, and Franklin and Vermolt disembarked from their seats, gesturing for Norak to assist.

"Please remain here until we are ready to proceed inside," Franklin said to Petterman, who was still in a daze and couldn't muster a response. The three of them walked around to the rear of the carriage and lifted Elita out. They waited a moment until the crowd had gathered around and some crowd it now was.

They brought her forward and put her on a trolley with large wheels, Petterman's astonishment grew as he saw her covered in a delicate silk sheet. Two soldiers began removing the sheets that concealed the crypt where she would be laid. Selika stood at the entrance, emanating an aura of strength despite her obvious blindness. She too was adorned in exquisite silks, and the morning sunlight only enhanced her stunning appearance.

With slow, deliberate movements, Selika raised her arms and murmured unintelligible words. Suddenly, her voice resonated clearly in everyone's minds. Advancing toward Elita's lifeless form, she removed the silk covering, prompting Petterman to shed tears once again. He had not anticipated witnessing his beloved dressed so elegantly.

Selika then proceeded to uncover Elita's feet and anointed them with fragrant oil. The entire gathering spoke in unison:

"Earth my body,
Water my blood,
Air my breath,
Fire my spirit."

As Petterman prepared to descend from the carriage, tears streamed down his face. This was no ordinary funeral; it was a queen's farewell. In his mind, he heard Selika's gentle voice whispering,

"You will understand in time. Trust that everything will work out and your unnamed daughter will be well cared for."

Selika turned towards the crypt doors and began a slow, purposeful walk towards them. Petterman positioned himself at the front of the trolley carrying Elita's body, gripping one handle, while Norak grasped the other. Franklin and Vermolt took up positions at the rear, and together they carefully pulled the trolley into the spacious, well-illuminated crypt. Torch-lit sconces adorned the walls, casting a warm glow within. Opposite the entrance, a designated spot awaited Elita's remains. With utmost care, the four of them laid her body on the stone slab that would serve as her final resting place

As they emerged from the crypt, the crowd continued their solemn chant:

"Earth my body.
Water my blood.
Air my breath.
Fire my spirit."

The children encircled the crypt, scattering petals around it. After completing three revolutions, they gathered in a circle, joining hands, swaying gently, and singing their own mournful dirge.

Selika silently addressed the assembled,

"This soul shall now rest in peace, at least for a while. Thank you all for attending. Find solace and return to your lives as Elita would have wished. As you know, changes lie ahead, and for now, you shall be safe. Farewell and be at peace."

As the crowd gradually dispersed, Petterman approached Selika, seeking clarity about what would follow. Clearly, this was no ordinary funeral for a soldier's wife. Ignoring his question, Selika asked with concern,

"Are you alright? We must embark on our journey as soon as possible. Can we leave from here at first light tomorrow?"

"Why the hell not; I have nothing keeping me here anymore. While I was on my way here, I pondered suggesting to Vadoma that she move into my house with the baby. I won't be needing it for a while, and her current residence is in disrepair."

"That's a wonderful idea. You should ask Norak to arrange it for you. Do you have any belongings you need from the house? Norak can retrieve them. I don't think you should return there; you might be tempted to start drinking again, and I'd have to intervene and sober you up for tomorrow. It promises to be a long and challenging day, and we both need as much rest as possible."

Eldoron

10 - The Sacrificial Altar

Petterman rose well before sunrise, as was his habit. Sleep never came easily to him, especially in an unfamiliar bed. Curious about the weather, he approached the window to determine whether they should pack summer or winter clothing. Additionally, he pondered the duration of their journey. Realizing the only way to find answers was to awaken Selika, he rapped on her door. To his surprise, she promptly opened it, seemingly poised for their departure.

"I have been awake for quite some time. I believe it's time we gather a few essentials for our journey. Travelling light is advisable. I have already requested a light breakfast and some provisions for our trip. As for the horses, I've made what I believe to be suitable choices, but you might possess more knowledge about them," Selika replied.

"Where are we heading, M'lady? I'm unsure of what attire to pack and how long we'll be away," Petterman inquired.

"Pack something warm, as you can always shed layers if it becomes too hot. As for the duration, it's uncertain. It depends on how long my blindness persists. This morning, I noticed a glimmer of light from the wall sconces, an improvement from yesterday. Perhaps this condition will last only a few days, eh…?" Selika speculated.

Petterman guided Selika to the refectory, where their breakfast awaited them. A plump woman in a stained white dress arrived with a bag of food for their journey. Petterman thanked her, and she said,

"I've included your favourite cheese, along with some meat and fruit, sir. M'lady, I apologize for not knowing your preferences".

"I think that whatever you have packed will be perfect; thank you", Selika said.

Petterman finished his breakfast and quickly went back to his room and gathered a few belongings and clothes. He was back down in the refectory before Selika had finished her breakfast.

As soon as she had finished, they made their way to the stables so that Petterman could inspect the horses that she had picked. They were both large heavy-set black horses, definitely not built for speed. Petterman thought that she had chosen them for a long steady trip. How far were they going? He wondered.

"I want to go to the sacrificial altar first, I have a couple of things that I need to do there, and then to the burial site for the sacrificed, shall we mount up and make a start?" Selika said.

Petterman guided Selika to one of the chosen horses and helped her up onto its' back.

"Petterman guided Selika to one of the chosen horses and assisted her in mounting it.

"To reach the altar, we need to take the west road. May I inquire about your intentions there, M'lady? It is heavily guarded, nobody gets in there without good reason," Petterman said.

"Worry not, soldier. We'll be fine. We will gain entry without trouble. At this moment, your only task is to ensure a smooth journey. I am aware that the road is rough, and I do not wish to fall from this horse. It's a long way down when you cannot see the ground," Selika assured him.

Slowly and steadily they made their way, it wasn't far, maybe 10 minutes away. The gates were already open;

"That is very strange; these gates are always locked and guarded unless there is an imminent sacrifice," Petterman said.

"It is okay, I have sent them back to the garrison on other duties, we will not be disturbed for a while, and I think it may be wise if we leave the horses here at the gate while I do what needs to be done. Please close the gates behind us." Petterman closed the gates and helped Selika from her mount, they made their way from the gates to the altar easily as it was a well-trodden path.

The altar itself was a remarkable sight, captivating in its grandeur. It stood as a colossal rock, intricately carved on all sides with a plethora of depictions: humans, animals, trees, and symbols of various sizes and shapes. Its top surface was smooth and polished. Surrounding the altar's perimeter was a small channel that led to a spout at the head, designed to collect and drain the sacrificial blood into a finely crafted stone vessel. Although unable to see what lay within, Selika possessed an uncanny sense of the exact location she needed to reach.

"Petterman, it would be wise for you to stand away from the altar," Selika suggested. "I don't want you to get hurt. I intend to open it, as there is something inside that I require".

"But M'lady, how can there be anything inside? Legend has it that this altar was hewn from a mountainside near Quenilith and transported here hundreds of years ago," Petterman replied."

"My dear Petterman, this altar stone was never hewn from a mountainside. It was stolen from my homeland nearly two thousand years ago. Just as it was then, it remains a sacrificial altar, although not for human sacrifices. Our ancestors were not so barbaric. This altar was used for sacrificing animals to the gods they believed in at that time. The sacrifices served to invoke protection spells and mark the rites of passage for young men and women venturing into the old forest—now known as Sormoving Wood. That is precisely where I intend to go after we visit the Gehenna Coves."

"M'lady! We cannot enter that forest. Many soldiers who fled the garrison, for various reasons, have attempted to pass through it and were never seen again. It is said that the trees move unexpectedly, suffocate you, and drag you underground, devouring you. If we enter, we will undoubtedly perish before reaching the other side. I do not wish to be consumed alive by those ancient trees or any other creature lurking within."

"Petterman, that is precisely why I need to open the altar. There is something within that can aid us in traversing the forest. If its potency remains intact after all these years, we need not fear while journeying through the woods."

"That is a significant if. How long has it been since it was last used? According to local folklore, the altar has been in this position for centuries, and nobody knew it could be opened or that a door lies within. I am unaware of any locks or keyholes," Petterman questioned."

"Petterman, please just trust me, I think that I know what I am doing, but just in case things don't go to plan, go and stand further away, you are my guide and I do not want to injure you, there may be some bright lights bouncing around. We don't want the blind leading the blind, do we... My guess is, that it should open with relative ease, but I am aware that it has not been accessed for over two thousand years and something inside might be very volatile. Now be quiet please, I need to concentrate for a few minutes, but before you move away will you help me to get on the top of the altar."

Petterman gave her a hand up onto the altar and then moved away. Selika knelt on her knees with her hands resting on the ridge where a head is supposed to go, even though she could not see anything, she closed her eyes and started to sing quietly to herself. Petterman was watching intently, he could not hear the words and so took a few steps closer, he could feel a strange sensation in the air all around him and the hairs on his neck stood on end. The fallen leaves on the ground around the altar started to move and blow away, there was dust blowing away in all directions from the altar in the windless air, and a swirling sound like a strong wind, but all was calm. It was very eerie, her words slowly became louder, and gravel and small stones started to roll away from the altar. The bottom of the altar started to glow a faint green colour, her song became a little louder and the glow got a little brighter. On the top, Selika, now lying face down on the altar's top, her arms outstretched, appeared to be in agonizing pain her singing was getting louder and the glow was getting brighter. Suddenly a flash of green light came from the ground at the base of the alter and Selika was thrown off and onto the rough ground at the foot of the alter. Petterman ran over to her, but she was okay, just a little angry. She expressed that this process might take longer than anticipated, as the stone felt lifeless, having remained dormant for thousands of years.

Petterman said, "What do you mean it feels lifeless? It is stone, it is not alive."

"Oh, you are so wrong, Petterman. I thought you knew more than that. Look at your name for a start. Petterman or Petraman means 'Stoneman' in some older languages. You have a lot to learn about the old world. Things have been forgotten and lost that should not have been. The whole world is alive to some extent. You think the stone is dead, but it is not. It just takes a long time to do or say anything. In my former life, I was known as Selika Stone Melder. I could hear and speak to the mountains, and I could mould the rock into different shapes just with my mind and hands. There were only a few of us who could do this. Sadly, the others are no longer with us, and I am the only one left. I just cannot remember how to do it. It has been a long time since it was needed, and that lore has almost faded away. But I must remember. Soon, I think I will be needing it again. There are people up north who might be able to help me with this, and that is where we will be going after we've been to the Coves. But back to the issue at hand, I still need to open this altar, and it is not cooperating. I can feel and access the power within, but it will not open. I think I have neglected to do something. Maybe I should read the writing, but that can't happen with this blindness, can it? There is one way, but you will have to agree for me to do it. I will enter your mind and use your eyes, and then I might be able to read the writing."

"No way, I have seen what you can do to people's minds, what will it do to mine? What are the dangers?" He said.

"No dangers at all, I promise you, you will not even know that I am looking through your eyes, you will only know that I am inside you when I move your eyes to where I want to see, and that may make you feel a little unbalanced. Do you agree to me doing this?"

"Well; with what happened to Elita, no I do not want you to do this, but do I have any choice in the matter? If I say no, what will happen then, you will not be able to open the altar and we cannot go through Sormoving Wood. Do we need to go into that forsaken place?"

"We do need to go through it. Yes, I need to go in there. Something is going to happen. I do not know what yet, but I can feel it, and I know that I need to be near the lake. We could go around it, but that will cause unacceptable delays to things that have not yet happened. I wish that I could explain more, but you must trust me. Things are starting to happen that have not occurred for a thousand or more years. Quenilith was one of them. Please trust me, Petterman. Let me use your eyes this once."

Reluctantly; Petterman agreed, Selika asked him to go to the altar and stand at the back of it, turn his head toward the altar, and then slowly walk around it, heading to the foot end first, keeping his head turned to it all the time. He started to walk in the direction that she said and nearly lost his balance,

"Carefully does it, Petterman. I don't want you to fall over. It will hurt me as well as you." He felt his eyes moving, looking at the markings. He could see them, but they meant nothing to him. He instinctively tried to look at something else but could not. She said to him,

"Relax and let me do the looking. Just slowly walk around it until I see something. It might take a few circuits before I see what I am looking for, so just keep walking slowly."

On the third circuit she saw it; a small symbol on the head end of the altar, it was a neatly carved image of a dragon, with fire coming out of its mouth,

"That's it she shouted, how did I miss that. Now, I must try again, help me back onto the top of the altar, then go back to where you were, and thank you for the loan of your impeccable sight".

Petterman once again assisted Selika onto the altar, then returned to his previous position. He could still hear the faint singing and observe the silent rustling of leaves and stones. The bottom of the altar emitted a faint greenish glow once more. Selika lay on top of the altar, clutching the head block. This, however, the atmosphere felt different. The air crackled and fizzed around him, drawing him closer to the altar. It wasn't as if he was walking but rather floating, while his feet remained firmly planted on the ground. Selika's sightless eyes glanced at him with a troubled expression. He couldn't resist the slow forward movement; he was being pulled into the proceedings, whether he desired it or not. A hint of concern crept into his mind because Selika had instructed him to stay out of harm's way. The singing grew louder, clearer this time. The greenish glow expanded, spreading onto the ground surrounding the altar and reaching towards the rugged path and the trees. As soon as the glow encompassed him, a sharp pain shot through his head, causing his legs to buckle. He should have fallen to the ground, but instead, he hovered just above it. The singing intensified. Petterman worried that if it grew any louder, it would reach the garrison. Or was it all occurring solely within his mind?

Suddenly, the sound of stone grinding and a hissing noise started coming from the altar, which was now all covered in the eerie green light, Selika again knelt up, this time at the foot end, her arms stretched out to the front. Her fingers were pointing at the head block, it looked like green lightning was emanating from her fingers to the block. The block started to turn like it was unscrewing, it then fell to one side with a thud. Thick green mist started to rise from where the block had been, it rose to her fingers and seemed to sink into them, turning her arms a vivid green. She turned to face Petterman and told him to come closer. He didn't have any choice as he was being pulled closer to the altar all the while, he couldn't have walked if he tried. As he reached Selika, she turned her head to face him and said.

"Now, Petterman, you must climb on top with me to receive the protection of the ancient ones. Climb now."

He pondered to himself,

"How can I climb when I can't even walk?" But within seconds, he was lifted from the ground to the apex of the altar. He soared through the air, feeling completely out of control. He preferred having his feet planted firmly on the ground, but he was powerless to resist. Once atop the altar, facing Selika, the green lightning began to touch his hands. It felt like pins and needles, radiating up his arms, leaving a warm sensation that ascended to his shoulders and then into his chest.

Visions flooded his mind—fire and water, countless lifeless bodies adrift in the water. He was horrified and recoiled from the lightning, but it followed the movements of his hands as if he were tethered to the stone altar. His head throbbed, akin to a severe hangover from a night of excessive drinking with his fellow soldiers.

Abruptly, everything turned black, then white, then green. They were both catapulted from the altar, crashing onto the rough ground. Groaning, they realized they had sustained only minor injuries—some bruises and a small graze on Petterman's forehead. Selika stood up and burst into laughter.

"Wow!" she exclaimed. "That was intense. I've never experienced anything like it before. I was always told it would be a calming experience, and I never imagined it would involve you as well. Now, you too are under the protection of the ancient ones. It's a tremendous privilege. How do you feel, Petterman? Are you alright?"

"Yes, I am fine, but what were the visions about? You know the fire and water and all those dead bodies?"

"I did not see those, I did not have any visions, perhaps you are more sensitive than I thought to all the unworldly happenings, you might be a valuable guide after all. There is one more thing that I have to do before we leave here, I have to change this altar back into what appears to be ordinary stone so that it cannot be used unwittingly. Can you sense the heat emanating from it? That Petterman is earth power; pure and tangible. Just give me a moment; it won't take long. The altar now recognizes us, and we should be able to invoke its power again from anywhere, should the need arise

Just give me a moment, it won't take long, it knows who we are now, and we should be able to call on its power again, from anywhere if it is needed". She stood back a little and quietly muttered a few incomprehensible words, the glowing disappeared and all seemed normal again.

Eldoron

11 - The Burial Grounds

"Come on, let's return to the horses. I'm sure they're already missing us. What do you think, Petterman? Should we give them names? They do seem quite friendly. What colour are they?"

"They are black, M'lady. Pure black. Both of them. It will be quite difficult to tell them apart."

"As I mentioned before, I had a previous life and two very close friends. Unfortunately, they perished in the great battle. Perhaps we should name the horses after them to honour their memory. They were sisters and remarkable warriors. Their names were Decronim and Secronim. What do you think, Petterman? Are those suitable names?"

"I think they are wonderful names. If your late friends ever come back and see them, they will surely be pleased, M'lady. But which horse should be Decronim, and which one should be Secronim?"

"That, young man, I will leave to your discretion, now please help me onto one of them".

"I think this one shall be Secronim, just because you are now on it, and it has the same first letter as you have in your name. So, do you wish to go to the burial site first or the Coves M'lady?"

"To the burial ground first please Petterman, what I

have to do there will only take a few minutes. Then onto the Coves after that."

The burial ground was just around the corner in the next field. Selika expected to see many graves with headstones and flowers, but she was greatly disappointed and disturbed when Petterman described the scene to her. It resembled more of a mass grave, a mound in the middle of the field. The deceased had not been buried but rather cremated to save space. All the ashes were thrown together in a heap at the centre of the field. Petterman noticed Selika's troubled expression and tried to explain that Jarroth had ordered the exhumation and cremation several years ago due to space constraints. He estimated that over one hundred thousand sacrifices had taken place in the twenty years he had been in charge, with the crematorium operating twenty-four hours a day.

"How could this man have gotten away with such atrocities? These people; these ashes, were once someone's loved ones. They should have had the choice of burial or cremation. And if they chose cremation, the right to decide whether to take the ashes home. Isn't that a basic human right?"

"You are correct, M'lady. But anyone who dared to challenge Jarroth was also sacrificed. He held absolute power and did as he pleased. His people lived in fear, and he thrived on it. He was not a kind man, M'lady."

"Hmm... this changes things a bit. Nevertheless, it won't take me long to do what needs to be done. Please guide me to the edge of the ash mound, Petterman. Then help me dismount from Secronim and stand at the edge of the field."

Petterman complied with her request. Once he reached the edge of the field, he shouted to Selika, informing her that he had done as she wished.

Acknowledging his message with a raised hand, Selika dropped to her knees and lifted both arms toward the sky. She began reciting a rhythmic chant, the words unintelligible to Petterman. It seemed to be a language he had never heard before. She repeated the chant over and over again. Eventually, she lowered her arms and motioned for Petterman to join her.

"Would you accompany me on a complete walk around the perimeter of the mound, please? We need to encircle it entirely," she requested. Without hesitation, he complied with her request.

As they made their way around the mound, stopping at each cardinal point, she paused and uttered three times,

"Spirits, rise and be free, your torment is over".

Once they completed the full circle, she gestured for them to return to their horses and exit the field. After closing the small gate, Petterman assisted Selika in mounting her horse again. However, an unsettling rumbling noise emerged from the field, accompanied by an inexplicable sensation. Selika warned Petterman not to observe the unfolding event, as all the souls of the deceased were being released. Nevertheless, his innate curiosity got the better of him, compelling him to turn and witness the unusual spectacle. He watched in astonishment as numerous small, see-through spheres resembling bubbles rose from the earth and slowly floated off into the distance.

The ground started to shake like a small earthquake, and the horses stumbled slightly. Petterman was watching the mound, regardless of what she had told him, he was transfixed by it all. Underneath the mass of blue orbs rising from the mound, a green glow, similar to the one under the altar started to shine, it got brighter and brighter. Selika told him,

"Look forward and run, do not look back." Shocked by the severity of her voice, he faced forward and kicked his mount into a full gallop, still holding on to

Secronim's reigns. As they turned right, toward the coast and onto the path to the Coves, the mound exploded in a bright green flash, the thunderous noise was deafening.

"What in gods name was that?" He asked.

"The field is back to how it should be," is all she said.

"Is that it? Is that all you are going to say, it nearly frightened the horses to death, and me too, I'll wager that there is a massive hole in the ground, and that is not back to how it should be, as you call it."

"Petterman, do you want to go back and have a look and see if there is any damage? I assure you, if you do go and look, you will not see anything unusual, you will only see an ordinary green field that is ready for grazing, no mound, nothing, it has all gone, gone back to how it should be. If we have to come back this way after the Coves, you might even see some cattle or sheep on it."

Eldoron

12 - The Coves

The journey to the Coves proceeded without any noteworthy incidents, except for Petterman's incessant chatter. He seemed eager to comprehend the new life he had found himself in, asking questions about everything he had witnessed. It was a stark contrast to his previous existence in the garrison, where every aspect of his day was regimented and preplanned. In comparison, this new experience was refreshingly different. Although it had only been a couple of days since Elita's funeral, it felt like a lifetime ago. Strangely, this temporal shift prevented Petterman from wallowing in sorrow, as it deterred him from dwelling on thoughts of Elita and becoming emotional once more.

Selika, the enigmatic woman accompanying him, possessed both remarkable beauty and an aura of intimidation. One had to be cautious not to harbour negative thoughts about her, as she seemed capable of perceiving them somehow. Petterman couldn't contain his curiosity any longer and inquired about the green light emanating from the stone and the green lightning that had touched them. Her reply was slow and thoughtful,

Selika responded slowly, her words measured and thoughtful.

"Explaining it fully might be challenging, but I'll

simplify it for you at this stage. The light surrounding the altar was pure nature. It anticipated our arrival and understood our purpose. It also recognized our need for assistance, so it faltered slightly, prompting me to use your eyes. I believe it wanted to test my authenticity by concealing the dragon key, an ancient symbol of my family from millennia ago.

The green lightning wasn't actually lightning; if you had observed it closely, you would have noticed that it consisted of countless tiny green orbs. These orbs represent another form of pure nature, specifically associated with information and learning. Additionally, hidden within some of the green orbs were blue orbs, which serve as protection during our passage through Sormoving Wood. With luck, they will accompany us until we reach the other side of the forest and venture towards the Triohex Mountains."

Selika paused for a moment before revealing her plans,

"In those mountains, I hope to encounter two extraordinary individuals; an older man and a woman. They believe themselves to be several thousand years old, but I know better. I will enlighten them about their true age, as they possess a wealth of knowledge and experiences that you will find incredibly intriguing."

As they made a sharp turn onto a rugged track leading to the coast, a breathtaking sight unfolded before them. Vibrant green fields stretched on both sides, with a deep valley nestled in their midst. The sea shimmered in the centre of the valley, while a couple of small ships lay at anchor near the horizon.

"I never tire of this view," Petterman remarked.

Selika responded, emphasizing the importance of preserving such sights.

"Indeed, these are the treasures we must protect. Scenes like this brighten our hearts, offering a distant beacon of light on a gloomy day, and instilling a sense of joy. Unlike the Coves visible across the fields, let's reach our destination as swiftly as possible."

Secronim and Decronim, their horses, plodded side by side down the rough track, abruptly coming to a simultaneous halt. Despite Petterman's attempts to urge them forward, they adamantly refused to budge.

"What is wrong with them Petterman?

"I'm not certain, M'lady. They must sense something unsettling. We might have to continue on foot from here; the Coves aren't far. I've traversed this path countless times. But I must warn you, it's not a pleasant place. They used to make us march here to instil fear; a truly eerie place filled with witches and all sorts of unsavoury individuals".

Selika challenged his perspective.

"Have you ever stopped and conversed with these so-called witches? More often than not, they are kind-hearted individuals with different beliefs than you. Many possess extensive knowledge of remedies and treatments that would be invaluable in case of serious injuries. They have been confined within these Coves for countless years, too frightened to venture beyond these fields due to persecution and sacrifice. I intend to liberate them all, to grant them the freedom to pursue new knowledge and rekindle hope. They have been oppressed for far too long. I consider them my sisters; beings who deserve the opportunity to wander freely and reconnect with the ancient wisdom of the land and nature."

Petterman had never ventured into the heart of the town. In his perception, the entire place seemed like a chaotic cluster of dilapidated houses and tents, scattered in various shapes and sizes on the sloping hill leading down to the Coves. As they passed each house, the occupants emerged, their eyes fixed on them with a mixture of curiosity and disdain, hurling curses their way. Eventually, they reached a rather spacious town square, devoid of any signs of life. Crossing it without pause, they continued on the path that led to the Coves.

"We are nearly there M'lady, you can smell the Coves from here, it smells awful."

"Have you ever wondered why it reeks so horribly down there, Petterman?" Selika questioned.

"No, I haven't, M'lady. I presumed it was due to the uncleanliness of the people here. They simply do not maintain proper hygiene," Petterman replied.

"No, Petterman. The stench has nothing to do with the inhabitants. It is a consequence of all the sacrifices made over the years. The remains of countless victims, thanks to your revered ex-leader, have seeped into the soil, poisoning it. The entire ground needs to be cleaned and restarted from scratch. It has become a breeding ground for all sorts of germs. And as for the Coves, they too need to be emptied and sterilized. Although I've never been here before, I know the Coves used to be a beautiful place to live. Many people I've known resided here and were genuinely content. This decay has occurred only since your esteemed leaders transformed it this way, by preventing the inhabitants from accessing the barracks for provisions. They feared their intelligence and independence and therefore discouraged them from pursuing a military life.

I am going to have a meeting with them all shortly in the town square. During that time, I want you to go to the Coves and sprinkle a handful of a special powder that I have in my bag into every single Cove. Make sure you don't miss any; otherwise, it won't be effective. You may bring one person along to assist you, but I'll need the others with me in the town square."

"It will be an arduous task to cover each and every one of them. Do you have any idea how many Coves there are?" Petterman inquired.

"We're about to find out, aren't we? You're a fit young man, and you can accomplish it quickly. As for the ones that are out of your reach, that's what your helper is for. Just lift them onto your shoulders and instruct them to throw the powder into the doorways," Lady Selika explained.

As they approached the first Cove, Petterman realized that the job of sprinkling powder was not as time-consuming as he had initially thought. The doors were fairly close together and only two levels high. A swift count revealed approximately thirty Coves.

"He meticulously described the scene to Selika, providing her with intricate details. She nodded with satisfaction and said,

"Perfect. Now, would you kindly take me back to the town square? I need to gather the townsfolk, and then you can choose one of them to accompany you. Don't forget this powder." She reached into her bag and withdrew a sizable bag of white powder.

Petterman was astonished and inquired,

"How and when did you manage to fit that in your bag? It seems larger and heavier than the bag you're carrying. Perhaps I should leave it here on this stone and retrieve it on my way back."

"As you wish Petterman, as long as you trust these so-called unfavourable townsfolks not to steal it, and use it for some other unknown, unsavoury purpose."

"M'lady, I apologize if my previous description offended you. It was not my intention. However, it has been ingrained in us that the townsfolk are unwelcoming, as evidenced by their exclusion from the barracks."

"Petterman, we need to change our attitudes towards these common folk. They are the foundation of civilized society. They are not witches, as you label them. They are ordinary people trying to survive, much like you.

The only difference is their belief system. They place their faith in Mother Nature, while you do not. Who can say who is right or wrong? Who has committed more evil deeds? Is it them or is it you and your followers? Have they killed tens of thousands in the name of a god? I think not. I am willing to assist them in any way I can, and so should you. Perhaps it's time for you to reevaluate your beliefs and consider how much good you can do instead of resorting to violence against those who disagree."

"M'lady, I did not participate in the killings or support Jarroth's barbaric practices. I found them appalling and inhumane."

"Alright Petterman, let's leave it there, for now, maybe it will be a good conversation to have on our journey north."

Upon returning to the town square, Selika requested Petterman to arrange a seating area.

"Will they assist us? If you could see their faces, you would hesitate to ask for help. They are giving us some very dirty looks M'Lady."

"Petterman, leave me here and approach the nearest person. I assure you they will offer their assistance. They are not monsters, despite their appearances."

Following her instructions, Petterman approached the closest person, an elderly woman dressed in tattered clothing. She appeared famished and emaciated, her former elegance diminished over time due to years of oppression and fear. Petterman inexplicably felt a profound sense of guilt, as if partially responsible for her condition. In a tremulous voice, he asked if someone could help set up seating for a meeting on the square. She raised her head to meet his gaze, her eyes were wide open but she had no pupils, they were just milky white and bloodshot. She was obviously blind, but she seemed to be looking, boring deep into his soul. Her face was so long and thin, her skin, wrinkled and almost transparent. Her hair was a tangled mess of grey and white strands hanging halfway down her back.

"What is your name soldier?"

"Petterman madam, my name is Petterman, but I am no longer a soldier, I have been relieved of my duties up in the garrison by this lady in the square, she needs to speak to you all about some up-and-coming changes."

"We know who she is, Petterman. But who are you, now that you are no longer a soldier? We will gladly assist the lady, but we are uncertain about helping you. We have seen you here before, haven't we, Petterman? Marching around, capturing us, and taking us up there to be slaughtered like animals. And for what? To please your god? Do you believe any god would desire to kill in their name? No, my child, you have been led astray for far too long. You have forgotten the ways of old, haven't you, Petterman? You have forgotten what should never be forgotten. You and your kind are not welcome here. Help for the meeting is on its way. Now go and do what needs to be done, then leave this place and never return. Do you understand, Petterman?"

The old woman's words deeply disturbed Petterman. He had never realized the extent of this underground community. He had assumed there were only a few shacks and makeshift tents, but it seemed there were hundreds of people going about their daily lives.

Unbelievably, as he made his way back to Selika's location, the square had transformed into a gathering space with an array of seats and benches of various shapes and sizes. They were arranged in a semi-circle, with Selika seated proudly at the front, facing the audience.

"Thank you, Petterman," Selika acknowledged. "I hope the old lady wasn't too harsh on you. You can't blame her for her lack of trust or dislike towards you.

She has likely endured a lifetime of fear from Jarroth and the rest of the barracks. But let it go, for you probably won't encounter her again after today. I have found a helper for you—a perfect fit for the job. She's relatively small, which will allow her to access the narrower spaces. The last doorway on the ground floor is crucial. Ensure you don't place any powder there, as there might still be people in the passage up to the barracks."

"A secret passage, M'lady?" Petterman inquired. "How has it remained undiscovered? How long has it been there? And where does it lead?"

"Petterman, it is no longer your concern," Selika reassured him. "Consider how these wonderful people managed to survive here. Now, go and place the powder in the Coves, and return to me once you're finished."

He set off on the track back down to the Coves and a short woman jumped up from her seat and started to follow him, she was a darkish-skinned woman about 20 years old, but looking much younger, her hair was very dark brown and long and flowing in the breeze.

"Sir, she said to Petterman, my name is Sol, I am to help you with the powder bombs in our homes."

"Bombs? I don't think they're bombs," Petterman replied, perplexed. "Just some powder that needs to be thrown into the doorways. It should be a straightforward task for us." He noticed that the bag she brought back was no longer filled with loose powder, as he had seen earlier. Instead, it contained small leather pouches, securely tied with string.

Pondering the events that had transpired in town, Petterman and Sol exchanged few words as they made their way to the Coves. He couldn't help but contemplate whether the old woman he encountered in the square had recognized him, despite never having laid eyes on her before. Had she perhaps traversed the secret passage to the barracks to pilfer food? Was she spying on their activities? Did her awareness explain how they were constantly aware of their capture attempts?

Upon reaching the first of many closed doorways on the ground floor, it became apparent that the strong sea breeze facing them had prompted residents to shut their doors. Sol inquired,

"May I throw the bags into the houses? You can open the doors, and I'll take care of tossing them inside, please, sir."

Petterman readily agreed, and as he pushed the door open, Sol flung the bag deep into the room. With a resounding bang, he half-expected a flash or a minor explosion, but nothing occurred. They continued to the next doorway, repeating the process until they reached the final one. Sol looked at Petterman and raised a concern.

"Do we have to do this one too? This one is special."

"No," Petterman responded. "We've been instructed not to open this one for some reason. However, now you need to climb onto my shoulders to reach the second floor."

Sol positioned herself atop Petterman's shoulders, and he handed her a pouch. She opened the door, tossed the pouch inside, and closed the door once more. They repeated this procedure until they returned to their starting point. Sol hopped down from Petterman's shoulders and took the bag from him, noting,

"There's one left. We must have missed one."

"We haven't missed a single door. We've opened all of them except for the last door. There must be a spare door in case one gets broken or something. We'll ask her about it when we return to the square," Petterman explained.

"I'll run up and ask her. You can wait here. It'll only take me a minute. I'm a very fast runner. You sit down, and I'll be back soon, Sol volunteered.

She was gone before he had time to answer her. Petterman found a large rock by the side of the track and sat down, facing the sea. He took a moment to appreciate the view when he felt a peculiar sensation in his head. He couldn't help but wonder what Selika was saying to the townspeople, recalling a similar feeling he had when he showed her around the garrison.

Soon enough, Sol returned and confirmed that there should be one pouch left. However, she also mentioned that Petterman should wait there for her because she would be coming down with the townspeople. They sat in silence for a while until they heard voices approaching. It wasn't just ordinary voices; it was a chorus of voices singing in unison, creating a melancholic melody, almost dirge-like, that resonated through the air.

"That sounds so sad," Petterman remarked.

"It's our moving song. We all have to learn it. It's about the entire town having to relocate for some reason. We must be going somewhere, all of us. The song tells us that everyone has to move out, but we'll return soon, Sol explained."

The townspeople, led by Selika and an old hag, came walking slowly down the track in two orderly lines. Two young boys guided them, and they all sang the same haunting song as they approached. When Selika reached Petterman, the procession halted, and the boys led Selika and the old hag towards him. The singing continued, everybody except Selika and the old hag was still singing.

"I've learned some things about you, soldier. I might have misjudged you, but I don't regret what I said. I still hope I never see you again. Your kind has taken the lives of too many of my people for me to ever forgive you. I did hope you'd rot in hell, but from what I've heard, you might have a purpose in this world before you meet your end. So tread carefully. You haven't yet discovered your true calling in life. Don't die before your time."

The two boys rejoined the line at the front, leading them past the doorways, singing the same song as they went.

"You did leave the last Cove empty, didn't you?"

"Yes, M'lady I did exactly as you asked."

As the last of the congregation passed them, Sol and the old woman joined them. The two boys at the front of the line were just entering the last doorway, all the others were following them inside.

"Where are they going? Why are they leaving?" Petterman asked, perplexed.

"They have to depart temporarily. This place needs to be cleansed and purified. The secret passage lies within that last doorway if you know where to look. Nobody resides there; it's solely used for storage. They'll be in the barracks soon, and then I can clean up the mess your kind has made. They may choose to return in about a week or so; it's their decision. They are now free to go and do as they please, and I genuinely wish them all the best. But for now, let's return to our horses. I'm sure they're missing us."

"But what about the cleaning, my lady? How will it be done? Or perhaps I shouldn't ask." Petterman inquired, sensing the complexity of the situation.

They slowly made their way back up the track towards the now deserted town square. The atmosphere was even eerier than before as if the town had been abandoned by spirits. Eventually, they located their mounts, grazing peacefully in a lush field, seemingly carefree. As soon as the horses spotted Petterman and Sol, they let out a loud whinny and trotted over to greet them.

"Petterman, I need you to lead them to a location near

the burial grounds and wait there for approximately ten minutes. After that, come back here for me. Hopefully, we will be done by then, and we can begin our journey north to Sormoving Wood. While you're there, you may hear some noises and commotion from the Coves, but don't let it concern you. Everything should be resolved by the time you return."

After Petterman had safely relocated the horses, Selika began humming and chanting. Petterman could feel the vibrations of her voice resonating in his head. The chant seemed to be in an ancient language, but he couldn't make out the words. Nevertheless, the tone and intensity sounded quite aggressive.

Selika stood on a large, flat stone, facing the sea and the coves. Her chanting grew louder and stronger. Suddenly, the air around her shimmered, and small white orbs emerged from the stone beneath her. They spiralled in a wide circle, starting from her feet and rising to her head before ascending high into the air. As they soared higher, their size doubled and then doubled again. Eventually, they crashed into the ground, twenty or thirty feet away, vanishing as quickly as they appeared.

The ground trembled as the orbs struck the soil, and the tremors travelled toward the coves, resembling an extended earthquake. The last orb rose from the ground, spiralling towards Selika's head, growing in size as it ascended. However, unlike the others, this orb remained afloat in the air, slowly increasing in size and rotating. It emitted a bright, sun-like glow with long, radiant white tendrils dangling from its lower edges. The orb drifted towards the Coves while Selika's chanting slowed and ceased. She sat down, crossed her legs on the stone, and rested her elbows on her knees. Her gaze fixated on the descending orb, seemingly observing its movement as it approached the seafront.

The orb lingered in front of the Coves' doors for a

few minutes before pulsing with increasing brightness. Its tendrils extended, growing longer until they nearly touched the sandy beach. Suddenly, the orb expanded tremendously, and its tendrils shot towards the doors— one tendril for each door, except the last one on the ground floor. They hung there as if gripping the handles, preventing anyone from exiting.

Petterman sensed that the allotted time had passed and left the horses once again, making his way back to Selika. As he approached her, he noticed her troubled expression. Before he could speak, she interrupted and instructed him to take her back to the Coves. Petterman complied, guiding Selika along a track that had turned into freshly ploughed dry soil, devoid of any grass. It proved challenging to keep his balance, let alone support Selika. Eventually, they arrived intact, and as they rounded the final bend, the colossal orb came into view.

Petterman exclaimed, "What in the gods' name is that?"

"Worry not, at least for now," Selika replied. "Something has interrupted the process, and I must determine what and why. Please provide me with a detailed description of what you see, Petterman. I need to understand the situation we are facing."

Petterman meticulously described the scene to Selika, but as he neared the end of his account, the last door began to open.

"M'lady, the last door is opening. I believe someone is emerging. It's Sol, and she's accompanied by that old hag. They are walking toward the sea, M'lady. Oh no, it seems they're trying to evade those long appendages extending from the massive orb in the sky. Yes, M'lady, they are now approaching us. This old hag despises me. Would you like me to remove myself while you speak with her?"

"No, no, Petterman, I want you right here. She

doesn't hate you personally, but rather what you represented as a soldier, and rightfully so."

Sol guided the elderly woman, Rechina, to where Selika and Petterman were standing.

"Well, merry meet and merry greet. It's been a long time since we last met. By what name do you travel this time?" Rechina greeted Selika.

"The same to you, Rechina. Merry meet and merry greet. This time I travel under my rightful name, Selika. It seems you were not blinded the last time we saw each other. What has happened?"

"Selika, I have wronged this man you brought along. I didn't know you were also blinded like me. I have heard a few good things about him and his late wife, Elita, but I seriously misjudged him. I believe his name should now be Goodman Petterman. Goodman Petterman, please forgive me. I was wrong to judge too quickly. This blindness came about by doing exactly what you're trying to do. It won't work this way. I now know what needs to be done. Pass me the spare pouch, and I will finish this once and for all."

"What do you mean you got blinded by this? It shouldn't be that dangerous. I've cleansed the altar and the burial grounds, but something is still preventing it."

"It's the last door that's blocking us, Selika. That's why there's one tendril still hanging. Sol told me she could see it. It needs to be attached to the last door, but then there will be no escape for us. Only one of us can stay and complete the task. I am old and done with this life. I am ready for the change, whatever that may be. I would like to come back as Rechina again, but I don't know if that's possible this time."

"Grandmother, no! You can't do it. I will have nobody if you do it. Please, I don't want to be on my own."

"You won't be alone, Sol. You'll see. You have a

long journey ahead of you. I can see it in my mind's eye. I think you might be about to embark on the adventure of a lifetime. Now, all of you, go through the last door and leave me to finish this."

"We can't go that way. We need to retrieve our horses and go north through the forest. We've already taken precautions for that. And what's all this about the young lady coming with us? This hasn't been discussed. We're embarking on a very dangerous road through the forest."

"Selika, my old friend, Sol is going to be delivered to Rosella. She'll become Rosella's new apprentice. The forest won't harm her; she's very familiar with it and has been there a few times. She probably knows the way better than either of you. Besides, she has no place here now, and I don't think I'll be coming back from this task. She'll need someone to look after her for a few more years."

"Who is Rosella, Grandma?" Sol asked.

"She's an old woman much like me. She's also blind but can see in different ways, just as I can. I think you'll like her; she's very clever, just like you. We just need to get you to her house. She knows you'll be coming."

"Okay, but only to Rosella's house if we can find it. Are you sure you know what you're doing with the pouch?"

"Yes, now go, all of you. I'll give you fifteen minutes to get as far away as you can, and then I'll activate the process again. Good luck with whatever you're doing. I hope to see you all in my next life. Sol, will you take me back to the last door again, please? Then run back down here so you can go with Selika."

Sol followed the instructions and gave Rechina a big, long hug goodbye, then ran back to Selika and Petterman. Rechina sat down on the stone floor and waited.

Petterman and Sol guided Selika back up the path

once more, leading her to the horses.

"Can you ride one of these horses, Sol?" Petterman asked.

"Wow, they are huge! I think I could ride one if I could get on it. Who do they belong to? Are they twins, Sir?"

"Do you think you could sit in front of Selika and steer the horse for her? It would be much faster if you could do that instead of me leading her everywhere. This one's name is Secronim; you will ride him. The other one is Decronim; I'll ride him. I'll help you both onto the horses."

When all three of them were comfortably seated on their mounts, Petterman let out a loud shout to get them moving. He took the lead, occasionally glancing back to check on Sol. To his surprise, she appeared completely at ease on her mount, riding as if she had done it all her life. Impressed by her natural ability, he shouted for them to pick up the pace, creating some distance between themselves and the Coves.

Selika, sensing the urgency of the situation, shouted to Petterman that they needed to find solid rock as soon as possible and wait for the cleansing process to commence.

"There's a rock to our right, M'lady. We should head towards it. Hold on tight," Petterman suggested, his voice filled with determination.

"Dismount and hold the horses tightly. This might frighten them. There will be a lot of noise and a blinding flash of light," Selika commanded. They dismounted, holding onto the horses tightly, their hearts racing in anticipation. They stood there, waiting for what felt like an eternity, unsure of what was about to happen.

Meanwhile, Rechina remained seated outside the last door, contemplating the passing of time.

"Surely, it has been fifteen minutes now. Maybe not.

I'll give them a little longer," she thought to herself. Slowly, she stood up, still clutching the last pouch in her hand. Turning to face the giant orb, she raised her hand in a gesture for it to see. The final tendril began to move towards her, its power palpable even before it reached her. With a swift motion, the tendril snatched the pouch from her hand and forcefully pushed her into the last Cove. The door slammed shut with a resounding bang.

The soft sand, soil, and rubble trembled all the way up the track to the fields leading to the burial ground. The sea grew eerily still. The tendrils emanating from the orb swelled into massive serpent-like arms, pulsating with energy, extending from the orb to the doors. Suddenly, the doors flung open, and the serpent-like arms ruptured at the ends, releasing millions of white orbs into each Cove entrance. Even the last Cove, with the old hag inside, became inundated with the orbs, flowing out onto the sand. As these orbs touched the sand, they sank into it, disappearing from sight.

In an instant, the orb exploded in a cataclysmic flash, akin to a thousand thunderbolts unleashed at once, the shockwave reverberating for miles. Every single smaller orb detonated, obliterating the Coves and launching the doors far into the sea. The sand, soil, and rubble were sent soaring into the air, forming a colossal funnel-shaped vortex that twirled and twisted like a monstrous tornado. The swirling vortex traversed the beach and the sea until it abruptly ceased, resulting in a tremendous splash as everything plummeted into the water. The ensuing wave, reminiscent of a tsunami, crashed onto the beach with such ferocity that it uprooted all the trees in its path. Subsequently, it pummeled the open Coves with such force that they were instantaneously filled, ejecting their contents—including the old woman's lifeless body—and scattering furniture and personal belongings into the now retreating water. Debris washed ashore in a larger wave, cascading over the tops of the Coves and flooding the fields above, inundating the soil and bare rocks with a thick, slimy layer of mud. Remarkably, the sand settled and remained on the beach, while the mud continued its ascent, coating everything in its path. The lifeless body of the old hag floated out to sea with the receding tide.

Then, the rain commenced, surpassing any downpour ever witnessed in this region. Enormous raindrops pelted the muddy soil, giving it the appearance of boiling mud, as if nature itself was engaged in a vigorous cleansing. The Coves, too, faced the deluge, with torrents of rainwater streaming into each one, purifying them and washing away the remnants of salt.

Shortly after, the lightning arrived—a barrage of colossal bolts crashing into the ground, scorching the sand and soil and sterilizing the landscape. The entire area emitted steam from the heat generated by the lightning bolts. The impact of these bolts resulted in the creation of small, coral-like statues that dotted the beach, marking the spots where the lightning had struck.

The orb, still positioned where it had been from the start, remained undisturbed by the torrential rain and thunderbolts. Suddenly, it started pulsating rapidly, and without warning, it unleashed large fireballs into the Coves. Each fireball found its mark, exploding upon impact with the back wall of each room, engulfing them in flames and sterilizing everything within, including the last doorway.

In the barracks where the occupants had sought refuge, panic ensued. Nobody could comprehend what was happening. Some individuals ran about in a state of hysteria, while others stood in disbelief, watching alongside the soldiers. Sheltered from the rain and lightning, they had a clear view of the Coves and the orb. They witnessed the fireballs striking the final Cove,

Volto's Rise

causing flames to erupt from the secret passage exit
within the barracks. People screamed and scrambled
away from the passage, yet the flames posed no harm to
anyone or anything. Instead, they billowed out and
ascended into the sky, gradually fading away until they
vanished.

Selika, Petterman, and Sol had halted their journey
atop the hill to observe the unfolding events.
Unfortunately, their vantage point didn't provide a clear
view. Selika attempted to narrate the scene, but her
limited recollection of the distant past made it
challenging. Sol bombarded her with questions, but
before she could answer, the thunder and lightning
drowned out their conversation. Frustrated, they resigned
themselves to continuing their trek. After some time,
Selika declared,

"We need to stop and find a stone for me to stand on
for a few minutes. The cleansing is complete, and the
orb must return to its rightful place." They found a
suitable spot shortly after; a rocky area. Selika
instructed,

"Sol, you stay here. This won't take long. I can sense
the orb approaching us now. Petterman, please help me
down onto the rock, then you can jump back on
Decronim."

Silently, the large white orb emerged from behind
them, hovering approximately ten feet above the ground.
Petterman and Sol felt the energy emanating from it—a
tingling sensation enveloping them. They both gazed
upward at the massive, brilliantly radiant orb, yet oddly,
their shadows failed to materialize on the ground.

Selika began chanting, and the orb gradually
diminished in size and luminosity. It continued to shrink
until it resembled the size of a human head. Then, in a
reverse motion, it descended and swirled around Selika,
echoing its previous movements. Eventually, it landed

on the stone ground beneath her, sinking into it as though submerging into a bowl of water, devoid of any splashing.

"Well, Petterman, I believe that concludes this particular chapter of the city," Selika remarked. "It's a pity about Rechina. She was a remarkable woman; a true salt-of-the-earth. And remember, Petterman, although she may be deceased for now, it doesn't mean you'll never see her again, does it? Strange things have a way of happening here, don't they, Petterman? Or should I say Goodman Petterman? Now, could you help me back onto Secronim, please? We must make plans to depart for Sormoving Wood at daybreak. While we can, let's go to the barracks and gather more supplies."

Eldoron

13 – Sormoving Wood

After enjoying a meal at the barracks, Sol expressed a desire to take a walk around the premises. Selika and Petterman didn't object, as they wanted to strategize on how to reach Sormoving Wood quickly without any interference from locals or other inhabitants of the Coves.

However, their plan took an unexpected turn. As soon as Sol exited the refectory, a flood of people approached them, bombarding them with a barrage of questions. They asked about when they could return to their homes, what to do now that Jarroth was gone, who was in charge if there would be more sacrifices if the passage to the Coves was still accessible, and if they were now free to wander as they pleased.

Petterman took charge, standing up and forcefully tapping his tankard on the sturdy wooden table to capture everyone's attention.

"Please, everyone! We cannot answer all of your questions at once, and some we simply don't have the answers to. You'll have to seek those answers on your own. What we can tell you is that several significant events have occurred in the past few days that will likely affect each and every one of you to some extent. I hope this esteemed lady," he said, gesturing toward Selika, "can provide more insight than I can. So please, settle down, return to your seats, and Selika will address you shortly."

A few minutes later, Selika rose to her feet and began to explain the recent occurrences. She described the strange noises and flashing lights and informed the crowd that the altar, burial grounds, and Coves would be off-limits for at least the next week. Only after that period could the residents of the Coves decide whether they wanted to return or move on freely to find a new home. Selika encouraged them to explore and rediscover the forgotten knowledge of the land, emphasizing its importance in the coming years. However, she couldn't provide further details at that time.

Selika instructed everyone living in the barracks to continue with their normal duties until instructed otherwise by their superiors. Petterman, Sol, and herself would be travelling north the following day for urgent matters and needed some privacy for planning. She requested that if anyone had suitable clothing for the cold northern climate, especially for Sol, it would be greatly appreciated since Sol was in tattered rags.

Suddenly a man burst through the doors and into the refectory carrying a lifeless child in his arms, blood dripping from his head, face and neck, the man too had severe lacerations down his face and one arm. Amid the screams and shouts, Selika could just about understand what was happening, she gripped Petterman's arm and shouted at him,

"Tell me that is not Sol, Petterman, who is it?

"I know not, M'lady," Petterman replied. "Their faces are covered in blood, but both of them are badly injured. The child appears to be fatally wounded, M'lady."

In a commanding voice, Selika stood up and shouted,

"Clear the room! Only the healers may stay, if there are any. Clear the room now!"

No one dared to argue with Selika's authoritative tone. The old lady in the room shouted to the healers,

"Bring me rags, blankets, and hot water immediately!" The two healers hurried off in different directions; one went to the kitchens behind the bar for hot water, while the other ran out of the door, presumably to fetch rags and blankets.

The old lady rushed to the injured man with the agility of a young person, effortlessly moving tables and chairs out of her way. As Petterman observed her closely, he realized she wasn't as old as he initially thought. She was a strong and robust woman, perhaps in her fifties, with the appearance of a warrior from a bygone era. Her face bore scars, resembling battle wounds, and she tied her long grey hair tightly in a ponytail. Her hands were large and powerful, like shovels. Surprisingly, underneath her dusty and worn overcoat, she wore fine silks and gold jewellery around her neck. Her skin had a pale yellow hue, and her eyes were narrow slits of vibrant electric blue.

She took the lifeless child from the man's arms and gently placed it on a nearby table. Tragically, they had arrived too late to save the child. Its throat had been brutally torn open. She returned to the injured man, who was now drifting in and out of consciousness. "What happened? Who attacked you?" she asked, but the man was too disoriented to make coherent sense. He babbled deliriously about an intruder bursting into his house and attacking them both.

Selika gestured for Petterman to accompany her and approached the unfamiliar woman. As she got closer, a familiar scent reached her nose, triggering a memory.

"We have met before, though it may have been a long time ago. What caused these injuries? I am currently blinded, but I hope it's temporary."

The old warrior responded with a rough tone,

"Well, look what the gutter rats have thrown out. What brings you here in these changing times?"

142

"Times and fates change, but you don't sound any older than the last time we met. However, I don't seem to remember your name, which is unusual for me," Selika replied.

"I never told you my name because you were so focused on killing me. There was no need for you to know. But now that I'm back, I sense that something is about to happen that could change the world. Surely, you must agree that we need to set aside our differences and find out what it is," the old warrior explained.

Selika inquired further,

"What happened to these two? Are his injuries life-threatening? Will he survive? Can you describe the nature of the injuries?"

"He will survive. It appears they were attacked by a bear or something similar. Unfortunately, the child didn't make it. This man's face is badly scarred, with a missing eye. His arm should recover with minimal damage, but he suffered a severe blow to his head, which explains his incoherence. We may learn more once he regains consciousness," the old warrior elaborated."

"Good to know. He doesn't require immediate bone mending, so I don't need to intervene. I can't linger here for long, though, as I need to prepare for the journey north. We will likely meet again, sooner or later. By the way, my name is Selika, and this is Petterman. The young lady accompanying us is Sol, who will become the new apprentice seer once we reach Rosella's house," Selika introduced.

"Merry meet, Selika. So, you do plan on travelling through the forest? It's not a pleasant place, and I've lost many friends there. I, too, need to journey north, to the Triohex Mountains, to reunite with my kin. They might have awakened from their deathly slumber, as I have. But I'm uncertain, as I haven't felt their presence yet. Something significant is unfolding, Selika, and I don't know what it is. We used to protect the elder ones, and I thought they had all perished. There's definitely something afoot. It might be wise if we all travel together; for safety in numbers. My name is Tomoe," the old warrior, Tomoe, proposed.

"Merry meet, Tomoe. You might be right about the safety in numbers, but I intended to travel lightly and swiftly. The more people we have, the slower our progress will be. However, we can accommodate you, but no more. Four of us will already attract attention in the forest, which is precisely what I wanted to avoid. Petterman, could you please find Sol and ask her to return here? There are tasks she needs to complete before we rest tonight. Tomoe, I believe our meeting has concluded. Can you trust the healers to tend to this man? We will want to speak with him tomorrow, if he's able, to gather information on what we should be wary of. I don't think it was a bear that attacked them; my instincts tell me it was something else, but I can't quite put my finger on it. Somehow, it doesn't feel natural," Selika expressed her thoughts.

Petterman returned with Sol, and together they began their preparations for the journey ahead. Sol headed to the kitchens to gather provisions, while Petterman made his way to the chambers to gather clothing and blankets. Meanwhile, Selika remained in her armchair in the dark corner of the refectory, unable to contribute much to the preparations.

Once everything was ready, Selika invited everyone, including Tomoe, to sit down. She asked Sol to summon one of the kitchen maids to join them. When the maid arrived, Selika requested a light meal for everyone before they retired to rest. Petterman said,

"M'lady, it is not long since we have eaten, surely you do not need more at this time."

"Petterman, we seem to have had this conversation

before, you do not know when you are going to eat again, so take advantage of this kind of hospitality and fill your stomach, who knows, breakfast might not happen before we travel."

After they had all eaten again, they went to their quarters, the night was uneventful and they all had a reasonably good sleep.

The following morning, Tomoe was the first to awaken, never one to sleep after sunrise. Petterman followed shortly after and found Tomoe outside the sleeping quarters, engaging in a series of peculiar exercises on the grass. She wore an ensemble of red and gold silks; a loose-fitting jacket and trousers; with her hair elegantly tied up in a bun atop her head. Today, she had chosen not to wear any jewellery. Petterman observed her movements, which resembled a slow, sensual dance, occasionally punctuated by swift strikes from her fists or feet. He marvelled at this unfamiliar form of combat, wondering where she had acquired such skills. He resolved to inquire about it later, but his thoughts were interrupted by Sol's arrival.

"Petterman, she's calling for you. I think she needs assistance with her preparations," Sol exclaimed breathlessly. "She mentioned that we're running late" Petterman made his way back to the sleeping quarters and told himself to remember to ask Tomoe about the strange exercises.

"Petterman made his way back to the sleeping quarters, reminding himself to ask Tomoe about her unique exercises.

"Good morning, m'lady! I see you're already dressed and prepared. Would you like to have breakfast in the refectory before we depart?"

"No, Petterman. We're running behind schedule. I had intended to leave before sunrise, but it's too late now. Are the others awake and ready? We should set off as soon as possible. Please go and prepare the horses, Petterman. Let's hope they had a good rest because it will be a long day."

"Secronim and Decronim should be ready by now, m'lady. I informed the stable hands last night that we would need them at daybreak. They should be waiting for us. I will bring them to the entrance and return here for you," Petterman replied.

"If you happen to come across Sol, ask her to guide me to the entrance. I'll meet you there. Also, inform Tomoe that we are departing and ask her to collect the food from the kitchen maid. It should be ready for us by now."

As Petterman stepped outside, he spotted the two stable boys leading the horses up the path toward the entrance. The horses appeared to have grown overnight, towering over the young stable boys. It was as if they had nearly doubled in size.

"What on earth did you feed them for breakfast? They look like they've grown exponentially," Petterman exclaimed in astonishment.

"We gave them the same as usual, Sir; some haylage, carrots, and apples, Sir," one of the stable boys replied. "But they've grown, sir. They could barely fit through the stable door. They're quite friendly, though. The blacksmith fitted them with new shoes early this morning, Sir. They should be ready for the long journey ahead."

"Thank you, both of you. You have done an exceptional job looking after them. Now, off you go back to work and stop calling me Sir. I am just a regular citizen now."

"Thank you, Sir."

With that, he joined the rest of the group at the entrance, where gasps of astonishment filled the air upon seeing the horses' sheer size.

"What's with all the gasping?" Selika asked.

"I wish you could see this, M'lady, it is a picture to behold," Petterman replied. "Our mounts have nearly doubled in size overnight. Could this be your doing?"

"Certainly not," Selika retorted. "This has nothing to do with me, Petterman. But if they have doubled in size, how are we going to mount them?"

As soon as she said that, both Secronim and Decronim lowered themselves to the ground, just enough for them to easily climb on and sit comfortably. Tomoe positioned herself behind Petterman, while Sol sat in front of Selika, holding the reins as before. The horses carefully stood up, shaking their heads and whinnying, as if engaged in a conversation.

"Lead us out," Selika instructed Petterman. "Take us on the most direct route to the forest"

Leaving the barracks, they took the westerly road towards the main crossroads. Sol provided a detailed description of everything they passed, and when she mentioned the head of a woman displayed on a post, Selika abruptly called out.

"Stop! Remove that and bury it. It is an insult to humanity" Secronim immediately crouched down without instruction, and Petterman began to descend. However, Tomoe intervened.

"I will handle this. I'll be faster than you." Petterman didn't argue and handed her a small shovel from the saddlebag. Tomoe swiftly dug a hole, removed the head from the post, covered it in a rag, and placed it carefully in the hole. She stood over the grave and said a few words in her native language before filling it in. Secronim patiently awaited her return, and she deftly climbed back onto the horse as it stood up again. They resumed their journey, while Sol continued her running commentary to Selika.

Petterman, eager to learn more about Tomoe,

persistently questioned her. However, she remained guarded and elusive about her past. All she revealed was that she hailed from a village beyond the Triohex Mountains. In a previous life, she was part of the 'Protectorate,' a small race of people who occasionally took an oath to the Elders. Upon completing the ceremony, they became nearly immortal, requiring neither food nor sleep, perpetually on duty and ever-vigilant. They seldom engaged in conversation with others, communicating mentally only when necessary. Initially, the Protectorate had no weapons, relying solely on hand-to-hand combat. It was only later that they adopted handcrafted swords and small daggers.

Petterman persisted in his curiosity, intrigued by an army without weapons. Gradually, Tomoe began to open up, sharing tales of the skirmishes they faced. She explained that at any given time, there were only five women in the Protectorate, as men were forbidden from taking the oath and had their duties at home, such as crafting swords and daggers. Each weapon was meticulously designed for its wielder and could take an extended period to create. Similarly, they fashioned specialized shoes for their horses, like the ones currently worn. These shoes were durable and would last for years, protecting the hooves from injury. Once attached, they could only be removed by one of the blacksmiths from their clan.

Petterman asked her about last night's supper, noting that she ate more than anyone else.

"I ate all that food because, as Selika has already told you, you never know when you'll get the chance to eat again. I have to return to my land, and I feel it's to fulfil an oath once more. Events are unfolding that none of us can hope to understand; the volcano, the death of a mother, the birth of a special child – they all carry meaning in their occurrence. And I don't believe these events will be the last; more strange happenings are to come, mark my words, Petterman."

"Do you have one of the swords or daggers with you? I would love to see it. I consider myself quite a skilled swordsman, having practised almost every day during my time in the garrison," asked Petterman.

"No, Petterman, I no longer possess them. I have no idea what happened to them when I perished in that last battle; that must have been a thousand years ago."

"I saw them disappear when you died, both the dagger and the sword, along with your belt. They started glowing with a strange blue light, and then they simply faded away," Selika said from behind them.

"Wow! Blind as a bat, but you still have the ears of a gutter rat," whispered Tomoe.

"I can still hear you. Will you ever forgive me for killing you? I doubt it, but we could at least make this little journey as pleasant as possible. I think we may need each other before all of this is over, and I believe we'll be on the same side this time. Have you tried to contact the others from the Protectorate? Or have any of them contacted you? Or was that ability taken away from you, like it was for almost everyone else when Zeraphos was defeated?" Selika said.

"I think that ability may have been taken away. I can't sense any of the others, but that doesn't necessarily mean they haven't returned. They might be on their way back to our homeland, just like I am. I don't even know why I was reborn in the same body as last time and at the same age as when I died.

There's no guarantee that anyone will be brought back and put into their old roles. That's why I need to get back to Hemmingstone, the village just beyond the Triohex Mountains, where we, the 'Protectorate,' come from. It's a small village nestled on the slopes of the mountain, beautiful to look at, with two waterfalls on either side falling from the mountain's top, forming a lake at the bottom. The water was always freezing. It may have changed by now, but I hope it's still somewhat like the place I left behind. I left a very long time ago when I entered the service of the Protectorate, it might be a bustling city now, I suppose I will find out soon enough. I would like it to be just as it was when I left, I know that is impossible but I can hope."

"It sounds like a beautiful place," Petterman said. "I can't even begin to fathom the idea that you were killed in battle. I've never heard of anyone coming back from the dead. My lovely Elita, my wife and the mother of my daughter, died in childbirth not long ago, as you know. Will she ever come back to me? I'd love to think so, but surely that's impossible. Reincarnation seems to be reserved for special people like you and Selika, not for us ordinary folk. When we die, we're gone forever."

"So, are you saying you don't believe in reincarnation, Petterman?" asked Selika. "What if I told you that you probably have been and probably will be, reincarnated again at some point, and I can prove it?"

"I'll believe it when I see it, M'lady. As you know, I've witnessed a lot of death while in Jarroth's service, in wars and sacrifices. Never once have I seen anyone return from the dead. But I'd love for you to prove me wrong."

"Petterman, Selika killed me in a fierce battle some time ago, involving many thousands of people. I haven't figured out exactly when it happened or which side won, as I've only been reincarnated for a few days. It was as if I woke up at the edge of a field as if I had been having an afternoon nap. I remember the pain of my injuries and dying as if it were yesterday, yet now I show no signs of any harm. Is this not a form of reincarnation?"

"I cannot answer that definitively, as I did not witness your reincarnation. I imagined it as being reborn as a baby, not as a fully grown woman. There's a possibility that you may be a con artist with ulterior motives, but I hope my suspicion is misplaced because I wouldn't want to be on the wrong side of you, especially if you and four others can take on a full army."

"We didn't engage a full army, Petterman. That wasn't our mission. We were tasked with protecting certain important individuals at all costs. As for the lady I was protecting, she was what your kind would call a witch, but she was a very special one. Her name was Valadora; a young, beautiful woman and the wife of a talented sorcerer. However, they are likely long dead now. I cannot fathom why I have been brought back like this. When others in our kin fell in battle, they were replaced, but maybe there are none left now, and perhaps my race has died out. That's why I need to get back home as soon as possible."

The day passed uneventfully as they continued west towards the crossroads. It seemed further than I remembered, or perhaps we were simply travelling slower than during my service. All the while, the edge of the forest appeared to be getting smaller and more distant, though that should have been impossible since we were heading straight toward it.

By late evening, they reached the crossroads—a well-covered area with trees and some heavy ground cover. There was a small clearing that had been used as a campsite before. A fire pit made of stones and plenty of fallen wood was there. Selika suggested,

"It's probably a good idea to stop here, have a bite to eat, and camp for the night."

Petterman mentioned, "There's an inn just down the road from here that usually has good food and fine ale, M'lady. If you prefer some home comforts, I know the owners well, and I've been there many times."

"No, Petterman. We'll stay here, out of anyone's way,

out of sight, out of mind, especially after what happened to that child and the man. We never got the chance to talk to him about what transpired, which might have been useful knowledge, but never mind."

The two mounts lowered themselves to the ground to let their passengers dismount and stretch their legs after being seated for too long. Sol guided Selika to a makeshift stool, but she preferred walking around for a few minutes to get the blood flowing again. Tomoe and Petterman started preparing the food, lighting a small fire to boil some water. Tomoe mentioned she had some herbs in her bag that could aid them in a restful sleep later if they desired.

Sol walked around with Selika, describing everything she saw. Selika was remarkably observant, a trait that would prove invaluable in her apprenticeship with the seer. However, Rosella was not known for her patience, especially with young apprentices who didn't listen and learn.

They all settled around the fire to eat a small plate of sliced meat, cheese, and bread. Tomoe had prepared a special brew that smelled foul but tasted surprisingly good, with an earthy, minty flavour. Petterman inquired,

"Where did you learn about these herbs, and are they readily available? I didn't expect you to be a herbalist, considering your background as a warrior."

"I watched and learned a great deal from Valadora. She seemed to know instinctively which plants were beneficial and which were not. She could easily identify ones good for burns or bruises or those with intoxicating or restorative properties. Some she boiled, others she crushed and mixed with different oils. It's a shame she's not here now, you could learn so much from her. Sol, you too could be a herbalist and a seer, combining these skills would make you in high demand, ensuring you'd never be short of work."

Shortly after the sun had set, Petterman announced that he was going to tend to the horses and then retire to his blankets for some sleep. Sol asked if she could join him. They both headed in the direction they had come, but to their surprise, the horses were nowhere to be seen; they had broken free from their reins and vanished.

"Where have they gone?" asked Sol. "They were still here when I was running around not long ago." They ventured further into the field, and suddenly Petterman called out, "Decronim!" Now, they could see both horses lying down in the grass in front of them. They had been invisible in the twilight. Satisfied with the sight, they returned to the camp to inform the others that the two mounts were safe for the night. Sol took great pleasure in describing how they had turned invisible, but the group initially laughed, thinking it was her imagination. However, their laughter ceased when Petterman confirmed the truth and even asked Tomoe to see for herself.

"Petterman, do you realize these are no ordinary horses?" Tomoe questioned. "They are the royalty of all horses, a breed that was more common in the past, but now very rare. They are the purest thoroughbred horses to have ever existed. They possess incredible abilities - they can change size and shape to suit different situations, and they're as fast as the wind or as strong as an ox. They used to carry us when I served in the Protectorate. These horses demand respect and won't let just anyone ride them. They had already assessed us long before we first mounted them; if they didn't like any of us, they would have refused. We are incredibly lucky and privileged to have been accepted by them. If they wander off, they'll know when to return; it's a mysterious sense beyond our understanding. This is another sign that something momentous is going to happen"

"M'lady, did you know all this when you chose them

in the stables?" Petterman inquired

"Yes, of course, I knew," Selika responded. "They had been following me for months, staying hidden but still present. Sometimes, I felt them in front of me, and other times, I sensed them behind. When I asked for your approval, I was thrilled when you said they were fine animals. As for the blacksmith finding the special shoes, I have no idea how he knew about them, but I did hear the stable boys mention a new blacksmith in town. Perhaps someone informed him that his unique services were required, prompting him to make the journey south."

"So, if it was one of my kin who journeyed south, at least some of my people still live! This is exciting; I haven't seen any of my kin in such a long time. We must push on tomorrow and make our way through Sormoving Wood as quickly as possible if it allows us to pass," Tomoe said with enthusiasm. They all settled down for a restful, uninterrupted night's sleep, just as Tomoe had foretold.

The next morning greeted them with a bright, sunny day, though a little chilly. The sky was clear and vivid. Selika once again sat near the fire while the others went about their tasks. Tomoe and Petterman prepared the food, while Sol packed up their belongings.

After a light breakfast, they all mounted their horses. The majestic animals communicated with each other through whinnies, and they set off on the north road without needing guidance from Petterman; it seemed they knew instinctively which way to go.

As they rode, Sol described everything she saw to Selika, painting a vivid picture of the sparse landscape, occasional woody outcrops, and the distant forest. Selika listened attentively, envisioning the scenery as Sol narrated the details, including the movement of the clouds and the wildlife they encountered.

Meanwhile, Petterman and Tomoe engaged in conversation about their pasts. Petterman shared stories of his life in Jarroth's service, where he wielded power through fear and sacrifice. He also revealed the fragment of the sacred throne that he carried in a pouch around his neck. He also told her about Selika and her visit to the garrison, how she had tricked Jarroth into showing her the tapestries, and how she had helped during the birth of his daughter and arranged the funeral of Elita. Tomoe, in turn, shared stories of some ancient battles, how she had kept Valadora safe from harm, and how she and the others from the Protectorate had hidden their companions from Zeraphos's soldiers, who outnumbered them by a hundred to one. At that time, Zeraphos was an overwhelmingly powerful force, having suppressed all types of magic and left everyone vulnerable to his troops. She also briefly mentioned Selika's role in her downfall and how powerful and evil she was back then. Tomoe admitted that she still didn't entirely trust Selika because of their past, wondering why Selika had changed allegiances and was no longer the Zerapite princess she once was.

As the day passed uneventfully, they made camp for the night by an outcrop of rock halfway up a small hill. It appeared that nobody had been there for years, and a small stream running down the hill provided them with a water source to refill their flasks in the morning.

Selika gathered them all around the small fire that Petterman had lit, after a bite to eat she said to them,

"Be on guard this night, the way Sol had described the scenery, I know that we should be close to the edge of the forest." Sol tried to explain that the forest was still miles away, but Selika dismissed it, and said,

"The forest could be all around us by the time we get up in the morning. This forest is like water; it moves, and nobody knows how or when, but you can go to sleep on the outskirts and wake up in the middle, not many people come out from here alive, it is not a friendly place. Be on your guard. Many years ago, I used to travel through it quite often, and for some reason, it let me. When I knew Rosella, when we were both younger, I could go and visit her whenever I liked and just walk out of the forest, but Rosella could not leave, whenever she tried, her way out was blocked. Once we tried to get out together but the forest stopped us both. It can be a very frightening place, but it is also very enchanting and can make you feel like you do not want to leave, it is then that it is most dangerous, if you go to sleep in there, more than likely you will not waken up, the trees will drag you under the ground and devour you. A lot of the trees are carnivorous and just love a tasty little snack. It is also said that you can hear the trees talking to each other, maybe it's just the breeze; maybe it isn't, who knows. These are the oldest trees in the world, it is the largest forest in the world, and it has a large lake in the centre that is nearly always freezing, even in the hottest summer.

If we are still on the outskirts when we rise tomorrow, it will be a short ride into it, and who knows how long it will take to get to the other side, only the forest knows that; it may be a day or it may be a week, Rosella lives near the far shore of the lake, we will be heading there first, to drop Sol off. Then we will be going north again, heading towards the Triohex Mountains. Petterman, will you and Tomoe sort the horses, please? I would like a private little chat with Sol." Petterman and Tomoe wandered off to get the horses settled for the night.

Sol slid over to where Selika was sitting and cuddled up to her, Selika wrapped her blanket around Sol to keep the chill evening air out, then pulled her in close.

"Sol, do you know anything of this woman Rosella?

Or this forest?" asked Selika.

"No M'lady, I know nothing about the lady except that she is a seer, and sometimes not very nice to know. I have heard lots about the forest, Grandma says that I have been to it many times, but I don't think I have. I thought that the stories were just old wives' tales, they are not are they, M'lady, it is true isn't it?"

"Yes Sol, unfortunately, most of it is true. You are going to have to think very hard tonight as to whether or not you really do want to go to Rosella's house. You know that her house is in Sormoving Wood and that she can never leave it. This may be the same for you, once you go in there, you may never come out again, I may be wrong, but you have to realise what you are getting yourself into. If you have any doubts about being her apprentice you had better speak up tonight, or it may be too late, once we go in, there may be no turning back. She is quite a lovely woman, and I believe you'll get along just fine with her. However, try not to annoy her too much as she has a short temper. She's very old and has a treasure trove of interesting stories, most of which carry a moral, so be sure to listen carefully. As for the forest, she can tell you more about it than I can; she's lived in it for over a thousand years and helps nurture and protect it, preventing any harm to herself. Now, take some time to think about it, and let me know in the morning if you still wish to visit her house."

"M'Lady, I know what I want to do. I've talked to my grandmother many times about it, and I've decided to become her apprentice. You see, I have this ability to perceive things that others don't, I sometimes see events before they happen. It used to frighten me, but my grandma said it is a gift, and I should embrace it and strengthen it. I didn't consider that I might be stuck in the forest forever, though, and that does worry me. I don't want to end up being eaten."

"Don't fret about that. I'm sure Rosella has already informed the trees that you're coming and not to harm you. So, you're set on this path then. Well, get some rest now; tomorrow might be a long day."

Petterman and Tomoe came back from sorting out the horses, they were already nearly invisible when they located them. The three of them sat around the little fire chatting for a short while, then slowly one by one wrapped themselves up in their blankets and fell asleep.

They were all woken up in the early hours, just before dawn by the thunder and lightning, Petterman got a large cover from his bag and stretched it out over them all, propping it up with some branches that he found earlier for the fire, Sol jumped up, shouting that she loved the thunder and lightning, Tomoe called her back and said to get under the cover. She quietened down and came back toward them, then suddenly stopped,

"Petterman!" She shouted, "There is something in the bushes watching us." Petterman was on his way out from under the cover when Tomoe flipped over him and landed right at the side of Sol.

"Over there look, you can see its eyes, it has blue eyes." Even before Petterman had exited the cover, Tomoe had moved away from Sol and was making her way around to the back of the bush. Petterman approached from the front, and Sol took cover with Selika under the rain cover. She was out of breath but managed to tell Selika what was happening. Petterman charged at the front of the bush at the same time as Tomoe hit the rear. They captured a creature, a very odd-looking creature. It was on all fours but had hands and feet, and it was about the same size as a fully grown goat but could stand up and walk. It had a head like a man but was smaller and grunted rather than spoke. It was very strong for its size, its body was covered in thick fur. They managed to subdue it and brought it back to Selika.

"Maybe this is what attacked the man and his child the other day," Petterman said. Selika just sat there for a while and then said,

"No this is not the same creature, I have just entered its mind and it is just a wild beast. There is no intelligent thought process in there, I think it just wants food, and it thought that we might be its next meal. But this is no natural creature, it has been made in some way. Something is certainly not normal about it."

Is it a spy of some sort or a scout?" suggested Petterman.

"No, I don't think it has the brain power to accomplish such a task. Maybe we should just set it free and see what it does, and where it goes. If it goes toward the forest, it will probably get caught and devoured by the trees."

"Let us set it free then, it has not done us any harm," Tomoe said.

Petterman slowly released the rear of the animal while Tomoe was holding on to its head and arms. It was not struggling to get away, rather, it seemed to be trying to hide. It was shaking and when she let go, it scuttered away under the bush again. Another flash of lightning and they all could see both Secronim and Decronim towering over the bush, they both reared up and stamped down with full force right on top of the creature, so fast that it didn't even have time to squeal.

"Well, that takes care of that little problem. I assume they didn't like the small creature, or maybe they sensed it wasn't natural. We should pack up and start early. It looks like a big storm is heading our way, and it'll hit us hard once the rain comes. It's so dark I can't see the forest, and it might take a while to get under the cover of the trees," Tomoe said.

Another flash of lightning revealed the forest not far away, maybe a twenty-minute trek if they were lucky.

Everyone, except Selika, began packing their belongings. After finishing, Selika stood up and called for Secronim and Decronim. They appeared almost instantly as if they had been invisibly waiting for the command to show up. She started to stroke them on the side of their faces and whispered something into their ears. Their tails thrashed around like they were trying to swat a thousand flies. When she finished whispering, they both lowered themselves to the ground, ready to be loaded with belongings and passengers.

With everything secured and everyone on top, the two horses stood up again, and Petterman led them back toward the north road. It was still very dark, but the horses didn't falter; they knew the way. They were moving much faster than the previous day. The lightning flashes were getting closer and more frequent, but the rain was holding off for the time being. With each flash, Petterman could get a glimpse of their progress and the distance to the edge of Sormoving Wood. At this rate, he thought, they'd be under the cover of the trees well before the rain arrived. Then he felt the first cold droplet splash on his face. He urged Decronim into a gallop, and Secronim instantly followed.

The dawn was just becoming visible to their left, though somewhat delayed due to the thick clouds. Petterman could now clearly see the edge of the forest, and it was getting closer rapidly. In just a few more minutes, they would be there.

Suddenly, huge trees started to emerge from the ground on both sides of the road, the forest was coming toward them at the same time as they were going toward the forest. Tree after tree appeared from nowhere, and the dawn sky on their left had disappeared again, it was once again pitch black, but the horses were steady and knew where to dodge the rocks and stones on the rough roadway. The sprouting trees started to encroach on the road, making it more difficult for the horses to navigate at speed, they had to slow down or risk serious injury, trees were popping up right in front of them, making Decronim and Secronim swerve this way and that to avoid them. Selika called them to a halt and said,

"We cannot go on like this, it is madness, we are undercover now, let us slow down." More lightning flashes overhead but still no rain. "Our mounts are too big to go charging through any forest like this."

The trees seemed to be getting closer and closer, the sky above was completely blocked out, and the way ahead was blocked, as was any retreat. The way to the sides was getting tighter and tighter. They were surrounded and more trees were popping up all around them. The horses were getting nervous and started to stamp their hooves on the ground.

Sol jumped down and gave the reins from Secronim to Tomoe. She went over to the nearest tree and flung her arms around it. The lower branches moved swiftly and pinned her to the trunk, it somehow grew and took her with it, it then turned and handed her to the next tree. Then the next and so on till they had gone in a full circle. The tree next to the first one placed her on the ground, and all the trees drew back a little way. They all bent their trunks like they were giving her a bow, and they then started to sway like they were in a strong breeze. Sol returned the bow, and then the trees started to make a very low rumbling noise that echoed right back into the distance. She slowly backed up, back to Secronim, who had now lowered himself enough to let her climb back on. As the rumbling echoes faded and the noise of the thunder passed, Selika shouted,

"What the hell is going on? Where did you go?"

"I went to talk to the trees and asked if they would allow us to pass through. Surprisingly, they responded to me. They lifted me up and passed me from one tree to another, each one granting permission for all of us to pass through the forest, including the horses. Curiously, they referred to the horses as 'The Jumentals.' What does that word mean?"

Tomoe replied, "In my ancestral stories, there were mentions of a race of horse-like creatures that only the ancient Gods and demigods could ride. It was considered a mere myth, with tales of some of these creatures having wings and the ability to fly. Perhaps these trees, being so ancient, might have some insight into whether these creatures were real or not."

Everyone was left speechless as they watched Sol confidently mount Secronim with a broad smile on her face. Selika, with tears in her eyes, embraced her gently and whispered,

"My child, the trees have accepted you as an apprentice, an honour that hasn't happened in over a thousand years. You must be truly special, or it might signify that Rosella's time is coming to an end. Either way, this is a significant moment, and you are about to discover your true potential."

As they turned to move forward, they noticed that the trees had silently moved again, this time forming a road so straight that they could not see the end of it, it just faded into the distance. Petterman urged them on, but they did not move, Decronim came forward and stood next to Secronim, Secronim turned to the left and Decronim turned to the right, then, they both simultaneously reared up, then lowered themselves again, then lowered their front legs and bowed to the trees. They both turned their heads to each other, touched snouts for a second or two, then whinnied and started to trot down the long road with their heads held up high; the road that will eventually lead them to the Great Lake.

Eldoron

14 - A Meeting With Rosella

The road ahead appeared long and arduous, but the chatter among them made it somewhat easier. They hadn't even noticed their mounts had reverted to normal-sized horses, nor that the thunder and the echoes of the trees had ceased, leaving behind an eerie quiet. Selika was the first to realize this, and she shouted to Petterman to stop. Only then did the others notice the unusual stillness and the size of their horses.

"Something doesn't feel right, I can sense it somehow," Selika said.

"Everything seems fine to me, except for the size of our mounts," Petterman replied.

"Well, of course, it would feel that way to you, Petterman. You don't perceive things as we do," Selika retorted.

"What do you feel, then, or rather, what don't you feel?" Petterman inquired.

"I can't feel it, Petterman. I should sense the earth's power, its elemental force, especially in this ancient place. It should be stronger here than anywhere else."

Sol, who was sitting in front of Selika dozing, suddenly woke up and said,

"They are speaking to me again; the trees have closed off the magic. They say it's too loud, and we cannot use it. They will guide us to the Great Lake; we just need to follow the road and not stray for any reason. The magic will be restored if necessary. They mention that winter is approaching, and it's their season of rest. They ask us to be quiet"

It was hard for all of them not to burst out laughing at the situation.

"The trees are telling us to be quiet. What's next?" muttered Tomoe. "Will the ground suddenly heat up and keep us warm through the night? Or will the birds bring us breakfast in the morning? I've never felt comfortable near this old place. It feels like it's watching and listening to everything we do or say. Come on, let's move on. The sooner we're through this forest, the better for all of us. I'm sorry, Sol, but I find it creepy."

"I've been in here many times before, but today feels different. It's as if the forest disapproves of something or someone," Selika said to the group.

Petterman cleared his throat and said,

"It might be because of me, M'lady. The forest might remember me from a few years ago when we were on a search for two deserters from the garrison. We had to camp near the edge of the forest on a very cold night. We heard a strange wind-like noise coming from the forest that sent shivers down our spines, so we left. It just didn't feel right, and we didn't take any wood or anything, honestly. We didn't even find the two deserters."

Tomoe chuckled, "Don't get all paranoid on us now, Petterman. I don't think the trees care about you searching for someone."

Sol interjected,

"He's not being paranoid. The trees are telling me what happened. The two deserters came into the forest and started chopping large branches with axes and swords to hide. The trees didn't like that, so they consumed them. They don't trust you, Petterman. They believe you were one of them and fear you might chop more branches. They want you to throw down your sword. They say you can't proceed or leave the forest."

"I can't just throw away my sword. I have a feeling I might need it at some point. Maybe I can give it to you or M'lady to carry while we're in the forest. Can you ask them?" Petterman asked.

"I don't need to ask them; they can hear you. They can hear everything in the forest, all the way to its northern edge. They say you can give the sword to Selika for safekeeping, but you're forbidden from touching it until you can prove your trustworthiness or leave the forest," Sol relayed.

Sol urged Secronim forward to take the sword from him; she then passed it back to Selika, who held on to it until Sol dismounted and packed it in Selika's belongings.

Throughout the rest of the day, they moved on with no more interruptions or delays. They just rode along the long, boring, straight road leading directly to the Great Lake. By early evening, the lake was visible in the distance. However, with darkness approaching, Selika suggested making a small camp on the road. They all dismounted and walked around for a few minutes to stretch their legs.

Selika stood holding the reins of both horses, their heads together, speaking to them and telling them not to stray from the path. She eventually let go of the reins, and the horses walked a little way down the path before lying down. Surprisingly, they did not fade into the background this night; perhaps their magic had been stopped too.

Tomoe and Sol retrieved the last of the food from their packs, and they all sat down to have a cold meal. Knowing they couldn't light a fire, they accepted that they were in for a cold and miserable sleep. After finishing their meal, they sat and chatted about the day's events for a while. As darkness enveloped the night, they gathered their blankets and huddled together to share their collective warmth, eventually falling asleep.

As the new dawn broke, Sol was the first to wake up. She sat up and started giggling, prodding Selika in the ribs, saying,

"That was very clever. When did you do that? I thought the magic was gone." Selika groaned but sat up and asked,

"What are you talking about? What have I done now?" Then she noticed it: they were all covered in a thick blanket of moss and leaves. Petterman and Tomoe woke up at the sound of their giggling, both amazed by the mysterious occurrence.

"How on earth did this happen? I never heard or felt a thing," said Tomoe. Suddenly, a voice from behind startled all four of them. Tomoe went into defensive mode and Petterman reached for his missing sword, only to realize it wasn't there. The voice calmly explained, "It was I, I did it. I sensed that you all would be cold during the night, so I thought I would cover you all up." The voice was Rosella's, she was sitting on the floor right behind them, with her legs crossed, holding a clay mug to her chest with a steaming hot drink in it. They could smell the drink now, it smelled earthy and minty at the same time. She looked at them through her eyeless face,

"I thought that I would come and meet you, these old trees told me that you had entered the forest, and said that you had a special person with you, normally they would not bother me, but they thought it was important. Selika, merry meet, how good it is to see you again, I thought that you had perished many years ago. There have been so many strange things happening recently, I had a visit from a very old friend of ours not long ago, I thought that he was dead too, but no, still alive and kicking and with a new wife now too, the giant, Jorgon, do you remember him? But to more immediate thing first, who do we have here? Soldier, I remember you,

you did right in turning back that night, or you would not have been here now. The trees never forget, they may get things wrong or mixed up now and then, but never, ever, do they forget.

Now this strange lady, I feel that I should know you, but I keep thinking of another, one from the ancient Protectorate, you are not her, are you?"

"Yes I am, but, I was killed in the Great Battle, and for some reason, I have been brought back, but I am not now in the Protectorate," Answered Tomoe.

"And last, but most definitely not least; you, my young lady, you have been sent to me by your grandmother, as my new apprentice, and I hear that you can already converse with the trees, that is excellent, very promising. No other apprentice has ever been able to do that, not even with training. That is why I got rid of them all, pesky little things. I hope that you will do much better than they did."

Sol blushed a little and said, "I didn't know I could talk to them until we came in here. I could always hear the noise they made at home, but I couldn't hear the words. In here, I can hear all of them talking at once."

"Don't worry about that; you will soon learn to distinguish one voice from another, and their personalities too. Yes, they are all different, as you will see. They all have good moods and bad moods, just like us. The old oaks are the worst; they are plain miserable most of the time. But if you have any questions, they are the ones to go to; they are very intelligent."

Petterman eyed the old woman and asked,

"How did you get all the way from your house near the lake to here so quickly? And where and how did you make that brew?"

"My dear soldier, you know nothing about these trees, and you would not comprehend it if I took the time to explain. But for now, just think of it as all the trees being connected and talking to each other in a way that would blow your mind. A tree from here may talk to a tree on the far northern border of the forest, even further if one of the saplings has gone for a wander. They are incredible beings, but in your ignorance, you just cut them down and burn them. If I had the time or inclination, I would teach you a thing or two so that you would respect these ancient, majestic beauties. Maybe Sol, if she makes it through the apprenticeship, can show you a thing or two."

"Yes!" said Sol with a big smile on her face. "You could be my apprentice, Petterman. That would be fun; you would have to do everything I say. I might enjoy that."

Petterman laughed at her and said,

"Be careful, young lady. You are nowhere near that stage yet."

Selika asked Rosella, "How long will it take us to get to the other side of the Lake from here? I am pushing to get as far up north as possible today."

"Selika, my dear, you know that is a very difficult question to answer. It all depends on what mood the trees are in. They may make the road very long and winding, or on the other hand, they may give you a straight road leading directly to the Lake. And how fast you can travel is another factor. But looking at your Jumentals, it shouldn't take too long. The trees have always had an alliance with them and always let them come and go as they wish. I ride one too; that is how I got here so soon. He is over there with yours, no doubt gossiping about something or other. I have use of a cave not far from here when I am down this way. Do you want to come over for a little breakfast? I don't have much in there because it is normally only me that comes here."

Selika accepted the invitation and suggested to the

others that they start to pack up. They called for the horses and mounted up in no time. The journey to the cave was thankfully quite short. Rosella knew where everything was in the little cave, and being blind was no handicap for her. She asked Sol to get some jars down from a shelf on the far wall; they were full of seeds and berries. Rosella lifted a few trays down from another shelf; they were full of leaves and mushrooms, both dried and fresh.

Petterman thought, "Well, that little bit isn't going to fill us for long." But how wrong was he? Little did he know, but the mushrooms were of a certain extremely rare variety (Amandatonin), locally known as 'mushysnacks'. Just a small handful can keep the largest of men full for a full day, and they are very nutritious. They only grow in Sormoving Wood, and if the stalks are thrown onto the soil, then they will sprout more, thus making it possible to travel for a long time without going hungry and doing no damage to this precious environment.

Between them, Rosella and Sol set out a small breakfast for them all. The brew that Rosella was drinking earlier was made from mushysnack mushrooms. She had made enough for them all to have a couple of mugs each; that would keep them fed and warm for the rest of the day. Rosella told them all how to find them and how to distinguish them from other more poisonous varieties. These safe ones have three raised lumps on the stem; if there are no lumps, do not pick them unless you want to poison someone.

When breakfast was finished and the lesson completed, Rosella informed them that she would now take Sol under her wing and that Sol must leave her old life behind to embrace a new one with a new name. Sol said,

"I want to be called Eve, it was my mother's name

before she was sacrificed, and I've always liked that name."

"Then so be it, Eve. We'll have a proper naming ceremony later, and I'll introduce you to the forest properly. I have a positive feeling about you, young lady, though I can't explain why. Now, let's get these people back on the road; they have a long journey ahead of them."

Eve was the first to step outside, followed by Petterman, who was guiding Selika, and then Tomoe, who was with Rosella. The horses were already there, three black stallions silhouetted against the early morning light. They seemed to know they would be leaving soon and had made their way back to the cave entrance.

Eve went to Secronim and embraced his neck, whispering something in his ear. Then she stood away, and Secronim knelt on one knee, lowering his head. Eve moved forward again and kissed him right between his eyes. Petterman watched with tears in his eyes; he had known the girl for only a few weeks but had grown very fond of her. It felt like she was his daughter and a good friend, despite her young age. This might be the last time he would see her, so he walked over, gave her a big hug, and said,

"I will miss you. I'll miss your silly sense of humour. Take care of yourself and the old woman.

"We will see each other again. I have to teach you the ways of the forest once I've learned them. I don't think it will take me long. I'll ask the trees to keep an eye out for you, and then I'll come and get you."

Eve then hugged Tomoe tightly, saying,

"Look after Petterman; he's my friend, and I have to teach him what I'll learn from Rosella. Keep him safe."

Next, she embraced Selika, saying,

"When you get your eyes back, will you come and

see me? I'll show you all over the forest and tell you what I've learned from Rosella. You can also share all the adventures you've had."

"I'll be coming back through here quite soon, I think. As soon as I've sorted out the business in the north, I'll need to return to Gehenna, and this is the fastest route if the trees allow it. Now, you have a new name and a new life. Staying with Rosella won't be easy; she can be very stubborn sometimes. But remember, she's been in this forest for thousands of years, and what she doesn't know about it is not worth knowing. Listen to her, observe everything she does, and who knows, you might even become the keeper of the forest one day. Be attentive, be her eyes, be her ears, and her legs when needed. I wish you all the luck and best wishes in the world. I can feel her waiting, go to her and enjoy your new life."

Eve walked over to Rosella, who was still standing by the cave entrance, looking taller and more confident than before. "Well, this is it, young lady. This is where you start to work and learn. Are you fit enough to run alongside my horse, or do you need a lift?"

"Err…could I have a lift, please?"

"Come on, I'm only teasing you; you'll have to get used to my sense of humour, just as I'll get used to yours. I think you'll make a very old woman feel young again. Now, let's climb aboard and make our way home."

Tomoe climbed onto Secronim's back, stating,

"I think I'd better lead you now, Selika, now that your young friend has departed. Petterman helped Selika up and then climbed onto Decronim. They headed north.

Eve and Rosella sat there on the horse's back, waving goodbye to them. Their path north looked nice and straight. Hopefully, they would reach Selika's desired destination in no time.

Eldoron

15 - Fire and Water

Petterman gazed ahead and noticed that the road stretched as straight as an arrow, leading exactly where they intended to go.

"M'lady, if we push the horses, we might reach the Great Lake before sundown. The trees have given us a clear path right to our destination. Can't we use some magic to make them go faster?" He suggested.

"No, Petterman. You heard what Sol, uh... Eve said. The forest has silenced all magic because it needs rest. We'll have to arrive at the lake in due time, day or night," replied Tomoe firmly.

They embarked on their journey along the narrow, straight road. The weather was slightly cool, but pleasant, with birds chirping in the trees and an eagle soaring overhead. Petterman spotted a hare in the distance and expressed his desire to hunt it for a meal, envisioning a hearty feast with potatoes, herbs, and mushrooms.

"Petterman, you can't be serious! You just had a substantial breakfast, and those 'mushysnacks' Rosella gave us should be enough. If you keep eating like this, you'll end up with a belly like a beer barrel!" Tomoe scolded him.

"Just thinking ahead. As both you and Selika said, we never know when we'll get our next meal, and who knows how long we'll be in this forest. The mist is already creeping in, and things change rapidly here,"

Petterman reasoned.

As they continued, the mist thickened, though it seemed to move away from them at the same pace they travelled. After a few hours, Selika called for a break.

"I am thirsty and need a drink, and my legs need to move a bit, let us give the horses a rest while we have a drink of the brew that Rosella gave us. It is not looking by the way you are describing it, as though we are going to make the Great Lake today, so tomorrow will have to do. I have a couple of flasks in my bag if you wouldn't mind getting them Tomoe."

They sat at the side of the road, sharing the remains of Rosella's brew, Petterman picked up a mushroom that was growing next to a tree trunk, he examined it and found that it had the three lumps on the stem, he passed it over to Tomoe just to make sure that he was correct in thinking it was a mushysnack, she confirmed it and popped it in her mouth, holding it by the stalk.

"Hey, I found that it is mine, finders keepers and all that." She snapped off the stalk and threw it at him, hitting him on his forehead, he caught it before it hit the floor and tossed it over his shoulder. Seeing where it landed he saw several other mushrooms, all the same with the three spots, he picked one for himself and one for Selika. Then he thought to himself.

"What if I give one to the horses? Would it sustain them as it does with us?" He picked two small ones and took them over to their mounts and offered them one each, they ate them and gave him their approval with a big nod and a whinny. Tomoe was telling Selika what was going on and they both burst out laughing.

"Come on guys, let's get moving again, we have a long way to go yet," Petterman said. The horses were already by them, waiting to be mounted again, they seemed to be in a rush to get moving, maybe the mushysnacks were making them impatient.

As they resumed their journey, the mist moved closer, and an eerie silence settled in as the birds stopped singing. Petterman and the others could feel a chilling wind on their faces, and a sense of anticipation hung in the air.

"Something feels awry here, Selika. I sense a strange presence among us, something I cannot identify," Tomoe said.

"I feel it too. Something is definitely wrong," Selika replied.

Without warning, Secronim and Decronim picked up their pace, transitioning from a trot to a full gallop. The ground trembled beneath their feet, causing the horses to stumble slightly and slow down. The mist ahead was approaching, obscuring their vision, and a sudden rising mist just in front of them brought them to a halt. Visibility was limited, and an eerie silence enveloped them. Soon, they heard what seemed like thunder, but there was no lightning; just the earth shaking with each thunderous rumble.

Decronim and Secronim lowered themselves to the ground and motioned for their riders to dismount, they did as the horses wanted. The horses stood up again and started to nod their heads, and the thunder stopped, the ground felt like it was rumbling like it was talking to something, and the horses whinnied loudly. All of a sudden Rosella and Eve were there, Rosella shouted at them,

"Get back on your mounts, you are needed at the Lake. The trees are moving away from the Great Lake, can you not feel it? The ground is shuddering and the thunder is them shouting to each other. Something has also happened far up north, way over the mountains, Eve has said that she can sense it but not see it, it is too far away. We need the magic back, we need it right now. I am going to ask the trees to give it back for a while at

174

least."

Rosella got down from her mount and went to a large birch tree nearby, she flung her arms around it and started to talk to it in a strange language, the tree started to shudder and some of its branches lifted and started to stretch out to the next tree, that tree did the same, and the next one. A strange bluish light made its way down the birch's branches and when it reached the trunk it started to glow very brightly, then shot down the trunk into the ground, the blue light then, as fast as lightning, spread out in a large circle in every direction, as if in deep conversation with nature itself.

"We will know very shortly if they will allow the magic again, they are discussing it right now, sometimes it can take days for them to reach a decision but I think today it will be very soon."

There was a sound so low that it made the ground shake, and then the blue light that spread outwards came back just as fast and shot up the trunk, along the branches, into the leaves, and then changed colour to bright orange. The light then shot out from the leaves and formed millions of tiny orange balls, these little orbs then spread out all over the canopy and slowly sank to the floor, giving the whole area a golden-orange glow.

"It's done! The magic is back, though I can't say for how long. We must hurry to the Great Lake, Rosella announced.

Their mounts were waiting, led down on the ground, they all mounted quickly and the horses stood up. The mist that was so dense a few minutes ago was now clearing, the breeze had picked up again and they could see far enough down the road to make haste. As they picked up speed, they could feel their mounts growing in size again and felt themselves rising higher off the ground and travelling faster and faster. After a couple of hours of travelling at such speed, Selika called a halt,

"Let the horses rest a little, we are going to kill them at this rate." They stopped and dismounted, Rosella and Eve were right behind them, they too dismounted. Selika started to say something but Eve cut her off, saying,

"The trees are running! They're scared of something, but they don't know what it is. They're asking for your help, Selika. You possess all your magic now; please aid them," Eve urgently implored."

Selika kneeled to the ground, retrieved a root from a nearby tree, and held it close to her head.

"I need to see what's happening up there. Lend me your eyes; lend me your ears," she requested.

The tree root started to pulse in the same bluish light as before, tiny specks of blue light pulsating along the root back to the tree. Then, just as before, it travelled up the trunk, along the branches, and up into the leaves. Waves of blue light passed amongst the upper parts of the trees and back again. The root that Selika was holding started to wrap itself around her head, and the blue light lit up her face. She was quietly muttering something, but it was not loud enough to hear. Then, she blurted out,

"The Na-Vot are here. This could be a good thing or it could be disastrous." Then she said to Eve, "Tell them not to worry about the Na-Vot. They are pure nature, pure spirit, and they will not harm anything."

"It is not them they are concerned about. The new power is not them. They have met the Na-Vot before, albeit many thousands of years ago, but they do remember them. The new power is in human form, a stranger to this land."

"Volto, it must be him. His powers must be coming through properly now. Tell them not to worry; I will deal with this. All these hours without my perception, I could have known hours ago and averted all this. He is good and on our side, though he is not aware as yet. I will have to go to him and find out what is happening."

"You can't just go to him; it must be a few days' ride from here," Petterman said.

"I don't mean go to him physically. Now that I have my magic back, I should be able to project myself to him, look through his eyes, and hear through his ears."

"Can you read his thoughts too? I would not like that. I think one's thoughts are private unless you wish them to be known."

"I agree with you, absolutely Petterman. I do not try to listen to others' thoughts. It just brings bad feelings out. But sometimes, in the past, it has been quite advantageous. When I was younger, many years ago, when I had the looks and the body, I used to find it quite embarrassing to hear what some people thought as I walked past them. With practice, I have learned not to hear them. So do not worry yourself; I have not, and will not, pry into your thoughts or anybody's without their permission."

"We need to get going again if we are to reach the Great Lake before dark," Tomoe said.

They all got back on their mounts and set off again, this time Rosella and Eve kept up with them. Three huge black Jumentals, now at full size again, ran like the wind through the forest.

The road thankfully stayed straight for the rest of the journey, though it did take longer than they expected. They ran through the evening and into the night, and they had to stop when it got too dark to see. Reluctantly, they all dismounted and made a small camp for the night. Rosella took Eve with her and showed her how to look for the mushysnacks without being able to see them. It didn't take long for Eve to pick it up. She told Rosella that she just closed her eyes and pretended she was blind, then opened her sense of smell.

"If you can find them in the dark, then so will I," she

said.

"Who said it was dark? In my world, it is bright all the time. I cannot see darkness. Just because I do not have eyes does not mean that I cannot see. After thousands of years of coping with no eyes, I have learned a different way of seeing. I can, as you have probably heard, sometimes see into the future, but it is not always very accurate. I can see things happening, but I don't know when they will happen. It would be very valuable to you if you could somehow learn that, but I doubt that will ever happen. I have been the only seer to be born in ten thousand years, and not one person has ever learned how it is done, so I don't hold much hope for you in learning it."

They found enough mushysnacks for all of them, including their mounts, who had once again faded into the background. They all ate their snacks in silence, had a drink from a small stream nearby, and then got their heads down for a good night's rest. The mist had started to form again and covered the whole area in an eerie white cloud.

As dawn broke, the mist still enveloped everything, limiting visibility to just a few arm's lengths. They all rose, preparing for another challenging day of travel. The group's mood was noticeably sombre, and the conversation was sparse, to say the least.

Eve took it upon herself to uplift the spirits. Just before they set off into the mist, she called out to them, chastising their gloomy demeanour,

"Well, you're all quite miserable this morning. What's wrong with you? We're alive, well-rested, and well-provisioned with these beautiful Jumentals, embarking on the adventure of a lifetime. We should be happy and full of joy!"

Petterman was the first to respond, complimenting Eve,

"You're an absolute joy to behold, Eve. Your positive outlook on life is unparalleled. No matter what comes your way, you face it with a smile, and that smile is so infectious. You've even got me smiling now."

Tomoe chimed in, agreeing with Petterman,

"I couldn't agree more. Eve is a delight to have around."

Selika simply remarked,

"Rosella, you're going to cherish Eve's company more than you know. She exudes joy just by being herself, and that smile of hers is truly radiant."

"I can see that, (so to speak), and hear it in her voice, and what's more, the trees like her and give their approval, she certainly is special."

"Stop it, all of you, I know you are just kidding and embarrassing me, but it has done the trick and got you all smiling again. Oh! did you feel that wind?"

A cold breeze started to blow from the north, and in minutes, it had begun to clear all the mist. To their amazement, they could see the Great Lake, maybe half an hour's ride away.

"The forest favours us this day, let us take advantage of this and get to the lake before the forest changes its mind," Tomoe said to them all.

The three Jumentals set off together, riding three abreast, with the forest having kindly widened the road for them. Eve asked Rosella if she could ride with Petterman for this last part of the journey, noting that she doesn't need to steer all the time.

"No worries, Eve. You go ahead and enjoy this time with him. It might be your last chance," Rosella replied, passing the reins to her."

She passed the reins over to Rosella and stood up on the horse's massive back, then took a big leap over to Petterman's mount, she landed easily at the back of him, sliding a leg on either side, then flung her arms around his waist and gave him a big hug.

Observing this, Tomoe remarked,

"I sense something between those two. Don't you think, Selika?"

"You're right. I hadn't noticed it before, but they do seem to make a good pair," Selika agreed.

"They look good together, despite the age difference," Tomoe added with a knowing smile.

They soon arrived at the lake and noticed a large area of disturbed ground near the shore. Eve pointed out,

"This is where the trees must have run from."

"I need to be on my own for a short while, I need to contact the stranger before the trees stop the magic again," Selika said.

Petterman suggested that he and Eve go for a walk in the forest, to see if he can somehow restore the tree's trust in him, and to see if they can find some mushysnacks.

Tomoe and Rosella exchanged glances, understanding the unspoken connection between Petterman and Eve.

"Before you go, you two," Rosella pointed towards Petterman and Eve, "will you set out my blanket for me to sit on? I think I may have to perform a little ceremony for this task."

They went to Secronim and retrieved the blanket and some other items from her bags then laid them down on a flat piece of ground. After showing Rosella where everything was, they quietly departed.

Rosella turned to Tomoe and said, "I know of another little cave not far from here. Would you like a refreshing drink while we wait for Selika to do her thing?"

"Absolutely, that would be great," Tomoe replied. So they rode off on Rosella's mount, leaving only Secronim and Decronim behind while Selika prepared for her magic

Selika sat in the middle of her blanket, it was just a plain black cloth, but when she started to draw shapes just above it, different symbols and runes started to appear on it, she was singing and chanting quietly, and smoke, sweet-scented smoke started to rise from the corners of the blanket. There seemed to be a strange haze forming a dome shape around the area where she was sitting. The haze started to turn a pale blue colour. She started to sing in the most beautiful angelic voice, even Secronim and Decronim turned to look at her, Eve and Petterman could hear her voice floating in the air and just said,

"Wow! Who is that?" It was breathtaking, they both turned around to see if they could still see where Selika was, they could just see her, they could see a blue dome covering her, like a big protective bubble. It was like an aura slowly turning with her voice. Petterman remarked,

"Anyone on the receiving end of that must be utterly spellbound. How could anyone resist such a summons without even understanding the words?"

Eve explained, "The language she uses is ancient and believed to have been forgotten for thousands of years. It's a language of the ancient gods, known as the Elohs. Rosella was right; the old oaks truly have wisdom."

Selika continued singing and communicating with someone far away while swaying in different directions. The blue aura around her started to rotate in the opposite direction, and astonishingly, the blanket she was sitting on lifted off the ground.

Petterman and Eve were now led side by side on the ground, watching from afar, and out of harm's way. Eve put her arm around his back, as though to keep him safe. They just lay there transfixed, and silent. The song sounded beautiful and the sight of her rising into the air and floating toward the lake on the blanket was spellbinding. Selika was floating further and further out into the lake, she was floating just above the water. When she was what looked to be about halfway across the lake she stopped, they could only just see her now, the blue dome seemed to be distorting her but they could see that she stood up and raised her arms.

In their minds, Selika spoke to both Eve and Petterman in a commanding tone,

"Close your eyes and cover your faces. Do not watch for a few minutes. This could get very bright."

They did as she said without hesitation. Suddenly out of nowhere, a huge purple flash appeared right across the sky and then descended in a massive funnel directly at her, her song stopped and she screamed so loud that it hurt their ears. The blue dome was protecting her, it diverted all of the purple light around the dome and into the lake, and as soon as it touched the water it burst into huge purple and blue flames. The flames were so big and fierce that surely she would be burnt to death, but no, she was still standing inside the dome with her arms raised. The fire kept on coming from the sky and bouncing off the top of the dome, it was covering the whole lake and coming toward the shore. Petterman uncovered his face and opened his eyes very slightly, he was shocked to the core by what he saw and nudged Eve to tell her to get ready to run for her life. She too opened her eyes and looked through her fingers.

"The trees, Petterman the trees will burn, she must stop this, all the forest will be lost." She screamed at him.

Selika spoke again in their minds,

"Worry not, my child. The trees will remain unharmed; those in danger have moved away. The fire will not harm them."

As the fire approached the shore, Petterman and Eve retreated further into the forest. At the lake's edge, the water began to rise, forming a barrier that deflected the flames back into the lake. The lake resembled a blazing cauldron, emanating incredible heat. But, as Selika had assured, it didn't harm anything.

Rosella and Tomoe rushed up the narrow path to join Eve and Petterman.

"What the hell happened here?" demanded Tomoe. Eve described the scene to Rosella, who could only imagine the intensity, feeling the heat herself. Rosella added,

"Some of the trees are communicating with me. They don't seem too concerned because the flames won't harm them. Selika is controlling the fire, and the trees believe it's the manifestation of the new power."

Selika was still under the protective dome, she could feel the power of the flames subsiding, the flames had stopped falling from the sky, but were still burning all over the lake, the water looked like it was boiling but no dead fish were floating in the water. She decided that it would be safe to make her way back to the shore, the singing started again and she started to float through the flames to the shore. When she floated onto the shore, she seemed to just step out from under the dome and turned back to look at the lake, she had a sudden vision of thousands of dead bodies floating on top of the water. It only lasted for a second or two, then disappeared. The singing stopped and she started to walk towards them with a puzzled look on her face. When she reached them, she asked them if they had seen the bodies floating on the water, but none of them had seen them. The fire was still burning but had started to recede toward the middle of the lake.

"The fire should burn itself out soon," Selika explained. "I tried to keep it contained within the lake's boundaries. The Nah-Vot will probably approach the one responsible for this once his anger subsides. I'm exhausted after that ordeal; it takes a lot out of you.

Some of those mushrooms Rosella mentioned would be very helpful right now."

Rosella came forward and said that she has a few in the pocket of her coat, but it is in the little cave down the narrow path. And right on time, the three horses came strolling up the path, as if they knew that their services were required.

They all mounted up and Rosella and Tomoe led the way to the cave. It was only a small cave, certainly not big enough to fit them all in comfortably, but there were plenty of rocks and branches that had been made into benches to sit on outside. The conversation inevitably came around to the singing that they all heard.

"Where did you learn to sing like that?" Eve asked Selika,

"Sing like what? I have not been singing, that was all in your imagination, all I did was block what you heard from me."

"What? Said Tomoe, "All of us heard the same song, surely it was you singing, a block is a block, so I was told many years ago by Valadora, that was not just a block, that was something else. I would love to be able to sing like that."

"Rosella, what is the best route around the lake from here, would it be better to go past your house or the opposite way, I was just thinking that we could accompany you a little further, that is if you don't mind." Asked Selika.

"It is about the same distance either way if the trees are feeling kind, but it would be very nice of you to accompany us, I have spent enough time in this forest on my own. A bit of company is always appreciated, plus you can stay and rest for the remainder of the day to recuperate from that thing you did out there on the lake, you can then set off nice and fresh in the morning and if all goes well, you should be where you need to be by the end of the day."

They all agreed to that little plan, especially Eve, who was eager to spend a little more time with Petterman, they had grown quite close these last few days.

Once again, Rosella and Eve prepared a little snack for the group. This time, it included mushysnacks, some greens, what appeared to be rabbit meat and a mug of a musty-smelling brew. As they brought the food out to the others, they discovered Selika fast asleep on a bench. Carefully, they placed the trays in front of Tomoe and Petterman without waking Selika. Eve then went to the horses and retrieved Selika's blanket from the bags on Secronim, surprisingly warm, probably due to its proximity to the fire. She draped it over Selika to keep her comfortable. Selika remained asleep for the rest of the day and throughout the night.

During this downtime, Rosella and Tomoe decided to rest but spent most of the time chatting. Meanwhile, Eve and Petterman thought it would be nice to explore the forest. They returned to the lake to check if the fire had gone out when they were stopped by a large tree. To their amazement, the tree spoke to Eve, instructing her to wait because others were returning, those who had moved away from the fire. The tree deemed it safe for them to come back now.

Eve relayed what the tree had said. Petterman suggested they sit on the branch and observe. Neither of them had seen trees move before, and what they witnessed would leave a lasting impression. Trees of various sizes were coming from all directions, some so massive that their movements created a deep thunderous sound, while others glided slowly and silently. The scene was captivating, with trees interacting with each other, exchanging gestures as if communicating or shaking hands. Their graceful movements, tender touches, and overall display of emotion overwhelmed Petterman, who had tears in his eyes. He had always considered trees as lifeless objects, but this experience changed his perspective.

"What is wrong Petterman? Why the tears?"

"Nothing is wrong, I just did not expect any emotion from the trees, I have always thought of them as some kind of inanimate objects, and to see this is just so overwhelming. It is beautiful, you have been granted what must be the greatest honour in the world, to be an apprentice to the woman who is caring for these trees. I feel so humbled in this forest, I will never see a tree in the same light again."

"See I knew it… you are not the big hard soldier all the time, you do have a nice softer caring side, but you just don't show it often enough. Your soldiering days are over now, can we see more of this side of you, I love you like this Petterman".

"I don't think my soldiering days are over yet, I have been brought on this journey for other reasons than just guiding a blinded woman, I think there is more soldiering to come yet. That is why I do not want to relinquish my sword, and what about Tomoe? If her story is true, then why has she been brought back from the dead, and have you ever heard of anybody else coming back alive? It is totally unheard of in my world, and believe me, I have seen a lot of death, something greater than we know is happening, something monumental. You might just be in the right place now, away from all the troubles that are about to land on our doorsteps, you stay in here and stay safe."

"You will come and find me again when all this is over, won't you? I know you have to leave and go with Selika and Tomoe when she wakes up. Just come to the forest, the trees will tell me where you are."

As the trees returned to their positions, Rosella and Tomoe finished chatting, and the group began preparing for the next day's ride. Selika remained asleep, still not having eaten. The others gathered their belongings, ready to mount their horses in the morning. Rosella and Tomoe had already prepared another small meal and snacks for the following day. They sat chatting and eating in a small circle away from Selika so that they did not wake her. Rosella was telling them of her dreams from the other night,

"It was an unusual dream for me because it was in colour. Normally, all my dreams and visions are in black and white, but this one was so vivid. It was a short dream by my standards. I saw you, Tomoe, standing by a river at the bottom of a large valley, engaged in a heated debate with four others of your kind. Selika and Petterman were also present but stood at the side, away from the rest of you. I believe the others were from the Protectorate, but it was strange to see all of you talking or shouting as it's not common for those in the service. Petterman and Selika were also debating, but theirs was not as intense. Selika kept urging Petterman to listen to the stones, saying she knew he could hear them, which is why she wanted him alongside her."

Tomoe was overcome with emotion, realizing she was not alone in being brought back.

"These individuals you saw must be my sisters in arms - Hangaku, Masako, Nakano, and Yaeko. Together, we were the most fearsome group within the Protectorate that has ever existed. I've often wondered what happened to them since my return. Perhaps they are still alive or, like me, brought back from the dead. Selika was in that last battle, and she might know more."

"Tomoe, Selika also fell in that battle, but she was brought back immediately. However, something changed in her during that resurrection. Her real name was stripped from her. Only a few of the elder ones know this, but she shifted allegiances and started fighting against her father. A few years after the great battle, she disappeared and hasn't been seen or heard from for many centuries. Only recently has she reappeared, and she seems stronger than ever, she has also regained her name." Rosella said.

"And what does it mean for me to listen to stones? Can you listen to them too? I can hear them as they roll and clatter down a hillside. Does this mean we'll have a battle on the side of a mountain?"

"No, Petterman, I don't believe that's the meaning. I think you've been chosen by someone or something to have a very special role. You might be able to communicate with the rocks and the mountains. As far as I know, there have only ever been two individuals with this ability. One perished thousands of years ago - she could persuade massive boulders to move just by talking to them, and she could tell the history of a mountain by lying down on its rock and listening. The other was Selika in a previous life. I have no idea why this ability might be bestowed upon you."

Tomoe turned to look at Eve, as she had been so quiet for a good while, she was fast asleep with her head on Pettermans lap, and Petterman was stroking her hair as if it was a normal thing to do. She said quietly,

"I think it must be time for all of us to be like that, we only need to throw our bags on the horses in the morning and we are ready to go, that is of course if Selika ever wakens up. I think if we all stay close together we will be able to survive the cold tonight." With that, they all lay down, wrapped up in their blankets on the cold hard earth and slowly drifted off to sleep.

Eldoron

16 - Rosella's Departure

Shortly before sunrise, Selika awoke and surveyed the sleepy campsite. She smiled, stretching her aching muscles; yesterday's proceedings had taken a toll on her body, and she knew it would take a few days to fully recover. Secronim and Decronim appeared in the camp, nudging the sleeping bodies. Everyone looked puzzled as to why the horses were waking them up, and even Selika seemed confused. The three Jumentals seemed eager to get moving, urging everyone to rise.

After exchanging greetings and some sarcastic remarks aimed at Selika, they decided to forgo breakfast and start their journey. Preparing their belongings on the horses didn't take long. As they set off, a mist began to rise from the forest floor, causing the horses to become jittery, swinging their heads from side to side. The mist grew thicker until Rosella looked at Eve and expressed her concern:

"Eve my child, I cannot hear the trees, they have gone silent, can you hear anything,"

"They are very quiet, but I can just about hear them. They are saying that they have changed the road we need to take, and it's for our benefit."

All three horses suddenly lay down at the same time, sensing the ground shaking like a small earthquake. A breeze blew from the direction of the lake, and the mist started to fade. The road ahead was now completely different, transformed into a wide, straight path that was incredibly smooth. Both Eve and Rosella said in unison:

"They are telling us to go, go now and not leave the path. They say we will reach my house within the hour if we go now."

The horses stood up without any instruction and started to canter down the road, growing to their full size once again. They picked up the pace and began to speed along, covering the distance quickly. Rosella's mount pulled ahead, and Secronim and Decronim followed close behind. The group was near their destination, and Rosella could sense it:

"We are near, I can sense where we are. You should see a cave entrance up ahead. It is only small, but you should spot it easily enough"

"I think this beast knows where to go, I am not leading him, he is just going where he wants, I can see a cave entrance in the distance, as you say it is only small, we seem to be heading straight for it."

The cave entrance was not far, and they arrived within a few minutes. As they approached, they slowed down to a canter and then a nice, slow walk. The Jumentals seemed unusually skittish as they walked the last few paces to the cave entrance, shaking their heads, stamping their feet, and whinnying loudly. Petterman and Tomoe dismounted, exchanging a knowing look.

"Something doesn't feel right here," Tomoe whispered to Petterman. Eve struggled to control Secronim, while Rosella and Selika held onto each other's reins.

Petterman called out to Rosella, "Your entrance door is wide open. Did you leave it like this?" Without waiting for an answer, both Tomoe and Petterman headed for the cave entrance. Suddenly, there was a loud creaking, cracking sound from behind them. A tall, slender tree bent over and, with one of its long, thin branches, snatched Petterman's sword from Selika's baggage. It then raised the sword high and threw it at Petterman, instinctively, Tomoe swung around and nimbly caught the sword in mid-flight, she swiftly handed it over to Petterman who then swung it deftly around for a second or two, just to get the feeling of it again, they glanced at each other again, nodded to each other, knowing exactly what was to happen next.

Without speaking a word, Petterman vaulted for the door and, sword held ready, entered the doorway, there came out of the cave, a loud blood-curdling scream. Petterman was ejected from the cave and crashed into Tomoe, knocking her to the ground, his blood-soaked sword was flung out of his hand and skidded across the floor.

A huge bear-like creature came crashing out from the cave, blood spurting everywhere from its severed arm, it thrashed out at Tomoe, who was just rising from her grounding. Another creature came out holding the severed arm, it raised it over its head and flung it as hard as it could at Tomoe. The armless creature flailing its other arm accidentally deflected the airborne one away from Tomoe and sent it in Selika and Rosellas' direction. Both being blind, they did not see it coming and so could not avoid it.

The arms' claws hit Rosella in her neck, ripping a gaping hole in it. Eve screamed so loud that the trees on either side of them jumped, the one that had taken Pettermans sword swung into action and seemed to slap some of the other trees with its branches, the other trees then sprang into action and joined the first. As the armless creature tried to bolt for its life, the trees blocked its way, then grabbed hold of it and tore it apart, flinging the pieces into the forest. The second creature tried to make a run for it, but like the first, it was caught with ease, ripped apart and thrown into the forest, to be devoured later.

Rosella had fallen from her mount, blood oozing from the wound. Selika demanded to be told what had happened, while Eve shouted,

"No! Please, this cannot happen. She cannot die like this, not now. We have to save her, Selika! Her throat has been torn out by that creature. What can we do?"

Selika jumped down from her mount and landed a bit awkwardly, she stumbled backwards a bit and fell on the ground next to Rosella, she could hear her gargling in her own blood. She fumbled around trying to figure out what the damage to Rosella was, Eve took hold of one of her hands and guided it to the ripped throat of Rosella.

"This does not bode well, I feel that this might be too much for me to deal with, I am so sorry Eve my child, but these injuries are too severe, I cannot possibly stop this bleeding." Eve, now soaking wet with tears pleaded with her, but to no avail, she was dying, tens of thousands of years of caring for the forest, and one unfortunate incident and this is the end.

"It cannot end like this, there is nobody to care for the forest." She cried, "Selika, I know what we can do, just try and curb the bleeding for a minute, I am going to get help." She then stood up and ran to the tall slender tree and started to climb up it, she was talking and shouting all the while she was climbing. A loud thumping started to sound and other trees started to move closer to Rosella, a particularly large willow tree barged its way through, it lowered its gentle branches and carefully took hold of Rosella's neck, it then opened the wound and poured some of its sap into the wound, this almost immediately stemmed the blood flow. The tree spoke to Eve in a very sorrowful voice,

"This is much too serious, we cannot save her, she will become one of us soon. That thing with the stolen souls has done too much damage, they must be stopped before it is too late. Speak to the big old oak over there, she will tell you how to help, I think the ancient ones need to be woken, the Nah-Vot; if they still exist, they are the only ones that can help now."

Selika understood what needed to be done before Eve went to the old oak, she said to Eve,

"Eve my child, we will need to light a small fire if we are to call upon the Nah-Vot, they can only travel in this world through the fire, ask the oak if we can light a small fire, and ask it for some twigs and small branches, we will light it in the cave if necessary."

"The oak said it would be better if you light the fire in the cave, Rosella should already have some fallen branches in there, they let her have the ones that they shed or get blown off, she is also saying that she can talk to the Nah-Vot directly if you want her to."

"Yes; yes, ask her to do that will you please, that will save me a lot of time, I would have to set up and perform a special ritual to attempt to speak to them."

"She is doing it now, she will tell me later what they have said."

"Quick, Eve, we need them now, not later. Can you persuade her to try it immediately? Rosella might not survive much longer."

"Light the fire. She's telling us to do it now and take Rosella into the cave, near the fire."

Everyone sprang into action. Eve guided Selika to the small hearth in the cave and found some small twigs and branches as kindling, setting them up as her grandmother had taught her. With the small flint, she ignited the fire. Petterman and Tomoe carefully carried Rosella in and gently placed her in front of the hearth.

"What now?" asked Tomoe, "Do we just wait and see, or will something happen?"

"We have to wait until the fire is hot enough. Be patient. The Nah-Vot are here; they're waiting for it to reach the right temperature," said the oak through Eve.

Shortly afterwards, the flames and embers started to swirl and change brightness. A small flame rose from the fire and turned blue, spinning slowly into what looked like a solid blue orb with sparks dropping back into the fire, creating loud crackling sounds. Another flame rose, identical to the first. Both flames emerged from the fire and circled the small cave a few times before returning to the fire. Tomoe was mesmerized by the event, recalling the tales she had heard in her youth, though she had believed them to be mere myths. Petterman stood guard at the cave entrance, his sword at the ready

The two blue orbs separated slightly, and a larger red orb rose from the fire to hover between them. The blue orbs moved toward the red one and tapped it twice before coming out into the room. The red orb followed and hovered above Rosella, with red sparks falling on her skin without causing any harm. Selika, unable to see them, knew exactly what and who they were. She bowed her head low and addressed them:

"Merry meet, ancient and wise ones. It has been a long time since we last met, and many things have changed, including allegiances. But as you know, we don't have time for chitchat. Our friend and ally, Rosella, has been fatally injured and needs urgent help, beyond even my healing capabilities. We know of no others who can assist her. You know her well; Rosella, the seer and forest keeper. If we lose her, the forest will perish, and the world will begin to fade and die. Will you help her?"

The red orb lowered itself just above Rosella's neck and dripped a few red drops onto her wound. The drops soaked in, and the ripped skin started to heal, but then the healing stopped. A few more drops were released, but this time, nothing happened.

The orb rose and spoke to Selika,

"This is beyond anyone's power to heal. She has been taken by stolen souls, Selika, the work of your Father.

The only thing that can be done is to retrieve her soul and let her go."

"But I have seen you bring people back, and as you can see one of those is here with us now, she was injured just as badly as Rosella."

"The people of the protectorate were killed by natural causes, Rosella was not."

Eve had been sat there, stunned into silence by the events going on in front of her, but when the orb said that Rosella was dead she objected, saying,

"She is not dead, she still breathes and bleeds, whoever and whatever you are, you are wrong, this woman still lives, therefore still has a soul, at the moment at least."

The red orb moved over to Eve and hovered just in front of her face rather menacingly, the two blue orbs had joined it, and a steady flow of more blue orbs started to emerge from the fire, they too came over to where Eve was sitting and surrounded her.

"And who might you be young lady?" The red orb asked.

I am Eve, formerly called Sol, and my grandmother was called Rechina, I never knew my mother and father because they were both sacrificed, as was my grandfather. My grandmother told me stories about you. I didn't think you were real. Rosella accepted me as her apprentice; she said that I had real potential. Please, will you help her?"

"So it was you who spoke to the old oak! No wonder I didn't recognize you. You certainly do have potential; you are a very gifted young lady. I think I have an idea. We cannot let the forest die, as Selika says. That would be disastrous. What if we made you the new forest keeper? It would work, wouldn't it?"

"But... but I know nothing about her work. I have only just arrived, and we only met the day before yesterday. She has thousands of years' worth of knowledge, and I have none! The forest will fall, and we will all die."

"This is where I can help. I cannot help Rosella, but I can help you. I can give you all of her knowledge, but it comes at a cost. You will never be able to leave the forest again. You will never have children, and you will live as she has, a hermit, for the rest of your life. That might, like Rosella, be many thousands of years. Do you agree to that?"

"I have to agree to it, or else the forest will perish. I have no choice, do I?"

"You always have a choice, Eve," said the Nah-Vot. "You do not have to agree. If you choose not to take on this commitment, then yes, the forest will eventually die. But that may take many, many years, longer than you would normally live for. You could live a normal life, have children, and be happy. The choice is yours and only yours."

"I cannot let the forest die. I have no choice in my mind. I have to carry on the work that Rosella has started. Maybe I can improve on what she has done because I am not blind. I will see when something needs to be attended to, and the trees are already my friends. I cannot desert them; I will not let them just perish and wither then die. I have hope for this forest. I intend to expand it further north and west. I intend to make it the most beautiful forest in the world. I will try to find ways to travel to other forests and help them too; I know it can be done. I accept the position of 'Keeper of the Forest.'"

"So be it then. We have a new keeper of all the forests in the world, and long may she live," said Petterman, sounding a little upset. Eve looked at him, obviously full of emotion.

"I am so sorry, Petterman; we were just getting started. We might have had a lovely life together, but this is so important for all of us. We can still be friends and hopefully more. If I don't do this, then what hope do we have?" Eve said with a tear in her eyes.

Selika interrupted the sadness, "We have to move on this before it's too late to save her knowledge, Eve. Just do exactly as the Nah-Vot says."

The big red orb asked her to lie down next to Rosella, then started to slowly rotate in a clockwise direction.

"Petterman, will you please go to the big old oak and ask her to attend this procedure? The oaks are the knowledge of the world, and it would not be right to exclude them from this. They may even want to have some input. What happens here today must never be spoken of outside of these walls. We, the Nah-Vot, are not in the habit of showing our skills to mortal beings. If word reaches us of chatter about this, then we will be forced to intervene. Is that clear to everyone?"

Petterman went outside to ask the old oak, but to his surprise, she was standing right outside the door to the cave. She lowered a branch and touched Petterman's face.

"We are here, soldier. We are listening, we are hearing, we are agreeing, we are hopeful. We believe your future union with the Sylvan will be good for all. Go back in and tell the Nah-Vot that we are here, we are ready, and we will take Rosella as one of us."

Petterman did as he was asked and went back into the cave. Eve was lying next to Rosella on the floor, and Selika and Tomoe were standing by Rosella's head. The red orb was hovering over them all, and most of the blue orbs that were surrounding Eve had returned to the fire. The red one lowered itself in front of Selika and said to both Selika and Tomoe.

"Please, go and stand over there. I need some space so as not to come into contact with you. If you touch me, I could be fatally injured, and I am the last of my kind.

Life in this world would be out of balance if I perish. I am sure your father would want that, but we do not."

After both Selika and Tomoe had moved away, the red orb lowered itself to Rosella's level, almost on the floor. Eve lay beside her, Eve's eyes were wide with fear or trepidation, visibly shaking.

"Try to remain still, young one. This will be painless, and you should not feel a thing, except a momentary discomfort in your eyes," the red orb assured her. "It will be over in a second or two."

A small green orb started to appear in the fire, it rose a little, then started to spin with green tendrils hanging from it, the orb spun but the tendrils were still in the fire and not moving, slowly it moved out of the fire and over to where the red orb was, they both then started to tap each other in a rhythmic sort of dance, the tendrils still in the fire, a bit like it was tethered to the flames, two blue orbs rose from the embers carrying a small bowl and moved over to the other two, there they stayed. A large bright white orb emerged from the fire, it moved slowly and purposefully toward Rosella, just skirting over Eve's face. As it reached Rosella, the tendrils that were still in the fire swelled up into thick rope-like strands and went quite rigid, the red orb said,

"When this white orb touches Rosella, she will pass from this world into the Arbor world, more specifically the Quercus world, as she has been so knowledgable and helpful to the older oaks, the oaks will take care of her while she is a sapling, then she will be released into the forest to roam at will, may she roam for many ages to come. I do not take readily to humans, but this one, I have known for a few thousand years, and never once have we had a crossed word, I hope for her sake that she has a smooth crossing. May your bark be strong and your leaves be broad, may your sap be plentiful and your roots be deep. Farewell blind seer, your time in this cruel world is done. I take your soul and hand it to the forest."

As the white orb reached Rosella, the tendrils released from the fire and stretched over to the doorway. Petterman opened the door, and a large, thick branch from the oak tree pushed its way into the room. The tendril and the oak's branch touched, and then the white orb moved to Rosella's forehead, sending a very thin spike into her. Her body stiffened for a few seconds, then fell flat and silent. A small swelling moved along the narrow spike to the orb and then into the oak branch, which slowly broke free from the tendril and returned outside.

Eve remained in the same position, not daring to move. The red orb moved toward her, with the green one by its side. The big white orb rose to the ceiling of the cave and then made its way back into the fire, disappearing. The green orb hovered just above Rosella's now pale face, while the two blue orbs carried the bowl over and placed it on her forehead. The green orb pierced a spike into both of Rosella's temples, and a green mist flowed out of her eyes and into the bowl. When it was full, the red orb sucked it up and spoke some incomprehensible words. Then, through a thin tendril, it aimed the mist at Eve's eyes.

"Keep your eyes wide open until it's all in. It will only take a second or two," the red orb instructed. However, at the first touch of the mist, Eve blinked, causing some of it to roll down her face. The green orb quickly moved over, sucking it up with its thin tendril.

"Keep your eyes open, don't blink," the red orb repeated. Eve moved her hands to her face, holding her eyelids open to prevent blinking. When all the green mist was in her eyes, the blue and green orbs returned to the fire and disappeared, leaving only the big red orb.

The red orb addressed Eve, "When you stand, you will feel very light-headed. Be cautious for the next few days and rest to allow all the knowledge to sink in. You may see and hear things—this is normal, and you needn't pay them any mind. These are just some of Rosella's memories that we couldn't remove. I must leave you all now; I have important matters to attend to in the north. But before I go, young man, what is your name? And what is your part in all of this? I sense an ancient talent within you, a talent not used for thousands of years. Can you hear the stone? Can you communicate with it? You need to develop this ability; it could be vital in winning the battle of all battles."

With that, the big red orb floated back into the fire and vanished, just like the other orbs had done.

After a few moments, Petterman broke the silence and said,

"I will find something to dig a grave for Rosella so that we may lay her to rest."

"No need to do that soldier," said Eve. "Just take her outside, the trees will take care of that, she belongs with them now."

Petterman and Tomoe carefully lifted the lifeless body from the floor and carried it outside. The large oak tree stood near the doorway, and as they approached, it extended two thick branches, waiting to receive the body. Once they placed Rosella's body on the branches, something extraordinary happened. Small twigs sprouted from both branches and the thick trunk, enfolding Rosella's body until it was completely cocooned. The big oak then bowed its trunk and slowly moved away, carrying Rosella's body with it, back to where it came from.

Eldoron

17 - The Journey North

After a few minutes of respectful silence, Tomoe approached Eve and inquired about her well-being. Eve responded that she was feeling okay but a bit fatigued, and her head felt fuzzy. As she sat up, true to what the red orb had said, she felt light-headed.

"Woah... that's weird, and look at my arm, there are marks on it, they weren't there earlier, it looks like somebody has drawn pictures of trees on it, this other arm too, ah well, it must be all this new knowledge coursing around my body, I suppose it will be gone in a few days."

Selika, who remained at the far side of the cave, suggested they should prepare to head north again. However, Petterman insisted they stay a while longer until Eve felt better and could walk steadily. Eve assured them she'd be fine with some food, water, and the brew Rosella made. Tomoe agreed with Petterman, so Selika reluctantly agreed to stay for one more day.

Petterman examined the strange markings on Eve's arms, expressing his curiosity,

"I have never seen anything like it before. I've seen countless tattoos on people's bodies, but nothing as intricate as this. Maybe the orb has somehow poisoned you, or perhaps you're turning into a tree? Are you growing bark on your legs yet? Look, they're on your chest too, faint but visible. They seem like flowers winding their way up a delicate trellis."

Tomoe laughed and told Petterman to stop kidding Eve, saying,

"Everything will be fine in a few days. Trust what the Nah-Vot said; they cannot lie."

Selika then suggested having a bite to eat, feeling hungry and asked Eve to guide her to the food. Tomoe offered to help and led Selika to the shelves where they found dried meat wrapped in broad leaves and various types of mushrooms, but none looked like the mushysnacks Rosella had shown them. They also found the pungent brew in a couple of large earthenware jugs. The search for plates and mugs led Tomoe outside, where she found some large flat stones and earthenware mugs. They would have to share the mugs.

After finishing their snack, Selika stood up and raised her mug, proposing a toast,

"A drink to an old friend, may she be happy till the end of all days." They all stood up, with Petterman supporting Eve, Selika passing her mug to Tomoe, and Petterman giving his to Eve. Together they saluted,

"Till the end of all days!"

The rest of the day passed somberly, each lost in their thoughts about the loss of the ancient seer and forestall and how it would impact their lives.

Eve wondered how she would continue the work she had done for thousands of years, still feeling overwhelmed by the knowledge gained from the orb. But, as the orb had mentioned, she understood it might take a few days for everything to settle in.

Petterman pondered the words the orb had said to him just before departing,

"Can I talk to the stone? I've always heard the rumbles underfoot, I thought everybody could. I'll have a talk with Selika about this on the way north. Also, how did I hear the tree? It spoke to me, and I heard it," he thought, somewhat selfishly. "Why should I have to leave here? I've only just started this lovely friendship with Eve, and now it's being ripped away. I don't know what the future holds for me; I'm just a guide for a blind woman."

Tomoe was contemplating her hometown and how it might have changed since she was last there. She wondered about her protectorate sisters—were they on their way there or brought back already? And what about the Nah-Vot? What role would they play in all of this? Surely, they couldn't get involved if the red one is the last. What happens when that one is destroyed? Will the world end?

Selika, on the other hand, was trying to communicate with Volto, but the Nah-Vot had put a stop to that after the fire in the lake. She felt an urge to see what was happening in the north.

The day seemed to drag on and on for Selika, and by mid-afternoon, she was itching to get back on the road, she kept glancing over at Eve, and thought, "There's nothing wrong with her; she just doesn't want to be left alone. I can't blame her for that, Rosella was very lonely sometimes, though she never admitted it. She also doesn't want Petterman to leave; can't blame her for that either. But as things are at the moment, she will just have to deal with it, in her own way, he might come back this way, once things are all sorted in the north, or, he may never come back this way if what the Nah-Vot said was true; that he is a listener of rocks, how can he develop that talent? Ask the rocks, or maybe ask the old oak, she might be able to advise him."

Eve lay on a bed made of straw and leaves, with Petterman at her side. She suggested he go for a walk and explore if any trees would talk to him again. She expressed happiness that he could hear them, making him special to her. Selika added that he should also inquire about the Nah-Vot's statement regarding the stones—did the orb mean specific stones or any stone, big or small? Petterman should bring his sword for safety but keep it hidden so as not to worry the trees.

Petterman asked Tomoe if she would like to walk with him, but she declined the offer, saying that she and Selika still had things to settle regarding their past encounters.

"So be it then", said Petterman, "I'll go back out into the wilds, with who knows what nasty little creatures that may be hiding in the forest, watching me, waiting to jump out and steal my soul, but don't worry your little heads, if I am not back in an hour then chances are that I will be a soulless quivering wreck on the floor not far away from here." They all started laughing at him and Tomoe picked up a cushion and threw it at him, "Oh get out you drama queen, go and find the oak. Shout loudly if you need help."

Petterman stepped out of the door just as Decronim came trotting up the path, surprised to see him, Petterman gave the horse an enquiring look. Decronim came right up to him and nuzzled into his chest, pushing him back slightly. The horse then lowered itself so that he could mount up easily, once he was up on top, Decronim turned and walked off down the path, with no guidance from Petterman.

"Where are you taking me?" Petterman asked, but the horse just shook its head and quietly whinnied, "Ok, just take me to wherever you want me to go." Within minutes Decronim had found the old oak tree and stopped at the side of it, Petterman knew it was the right one because of the very distinctive trunk, it was quite slim and very knobbly and twisted. The tree lowered a slender branch and touched Decronim on the forehead, then she slid the branch over the horse's head and down its neck, it then started to wrap around Pettermans waist, it lifted him from the horse and settled him in the gap between some of its branches, holding him steady so that he did not fall.

A quiet voice came from the tree, though he could not distinguish where it came from, he could not see a head nor a mouth from which the voice emanated, maybe it was all in his head, or maybe the tree was communicating telepathically. The tree quietly said,

"We know what you now seek soldier, the Nah-Vot has informed us that you are akin to the sylvan girl, but your thing is stone, you must go over the mountains with the warrior, to her village, beyond that village is a cave, a very well hidden cave, the warrior knows this cave, there is a small door leading to a secret chamber at the far end, what you seek is in there, a chalice sits on an alter, you must drink from the chalice. When you're done, you must return to the mountain you crossed and then locate the stranger, the one not from this land, the same one Selika is searching for. You might even encounter him on your way to the mountain. Be cautious, as he's the one who started the fire in the lake. He's extremely dangerous, but he's essential for the future of this world. Also, keep in mind that the door will likely be guarded by some spell or magic."

Petterman sat there for a few minutes in silence, contemplating his options.

"I could stay here and assist Eve with her work, or I could venture to the other side of the mountains, find a secret cave, seek a hidden door within it, and find a way to bypass the spell or magic. Then, I must locate a sacred chalice on an ancient altar and drink some mystical fluid from it, likely stored for thousands of years. After that, I have to find a very dangerous man, someone who shouldn't even exist in this world. But then what? Do I merely sit down and have conversations with the mountain? Or do I fulfil my obligations to Selika and give up this crazy endeavour, returning to the garrison and resuming my more predictable, ordered life, as it was before?"

A rustling noise on the ground brought him back to his senses. He looked to his right, through the trees, and noticed movement in the bracken, two more of the creatures that had visited earlier were approaching. They were closing in on him rapidly. He drew his sword from its scabbard slowly and silently, reassuring the tree in his mind,

"Don't worry, I won't harm any wood." The old oak released its grip on his waist, allowing him to act as he pleased. As soon as the first creature passed beneath him, Petterman leapt out of the tree and landed on top of the second creature, driving his sword down into its skull, killing it instantly. Regaining his balance, he swung his sword at the first creature, narrowly missing it as it dodged out of the way and crashed into the trunk of the tree. The old oak shuddered slightly but then swung one of its branches, catching the creature around the waist, lifting it up, and slamming it forcefully against the ground. Petterman seized the opportunity and thrust his sword through its chest with such force that it went straight through the creature and into the ground, causing the tree to wince a little as it hit one of its roots. Petterman wiped his sword clean and sheathed it. Then, he gently lifted the creature from the tree branch that had held it and apologized,

"Sorry if I hurt your root. I didn't mean to be so forceful; I didn't realize they were so soft and squashy. I should get back to the others. Thank you for your help, and I believe we'll meet again in the not-too-distant future."

As he turned around to call for Decronim, the horse came into view from behind an outcrop of bracken, trotting toward him. Petterman, still filled with adrenaline from the fight, jumped up on top of the horse. Decronim reared up, kicking both his front legs in the air and emitting a loud, deep roar. Petterman had never heard a horse make such a noise before, and it surprised him enough that he nearly lost his balance. But then he laughed out loud and shouted,

"Decision made then... Let's find that cave!"

Tomoe was running down the road to meet Petterman, they had all heard the roar of the horse, and she was out of the cave in a flash, Decronim slowed down to a trot as they drew close,

"What the hell has happened and what was that noise?" She shouted. Petterman responded with bloodlust in his eyes,

"Prepare yourselves; we ride north at first light. This place is swarming with evil creatures. I just encountered two more, and they have been dispatched."

"Well, thank you for calling for help. I could have used a break from the boredom. Did you find what you were looking for?" She asked.

"Yes, I found what I was looking for, or perhaps it found me. We'll never know for sure. The two beasts disrupted my contemplations, and their actions made up my mind for me. Let's get back to the cave, and I'll tell you what happened. I think you'll find it intriguing."

When they returned to the cave, Petterman discovered Selika sitting on the bed with Eve, who was now wide awake. They seemed to have been deeply engrossed in conversation before the unfortunate disturbance, and Eve appeared to have been crying.

"We'll leave at first light tomorrow; we have a long way to go... Eve, my love, what's the matter? Are you okay?" Petterman inquired with concern.

"She's fine, Petterman. We've just been having a woman-to-woman chat, that's all," Selika replied.

"I'm not sure I'm up to this task, my love. It's much bigger and more involved than I ever thought. It would take a thousand people like me to do half the job Rosella did," Eve said in a sad tone.

"Eve, my love, just a few minutes ago, I was sitting in a tree, its branches hugging me, keeping me safe from falling. The tree spoke to me, revealing what I needed to do to help save our world. At first, I thought it was a hopeless task. I pondered my options: stay here and help you, or go north as the tree advised; though there's more to that, which I'll explain later, or return to the garrison and live a predictable, stress-free life. As I wavered between the first and last choices, I heard noises from the bracken. Two of those creatures appeared, but I had the advantage of being hidden up in the tree, and with the aid of the old oak, I defeated them easily. That's when I realized that I had made up my mind and my choice became crystal clear. This world is worth fighting for, regardless of the cost. We cannot let Zeraphos win; we must unite and fight. It's what I was trained to do. You can do this, and you will do this. I'll provide all the help I can, and I'm sure M'Lady here will do the same," Petterman declared.

"Something has changed in you, Petterman," Selika remarked. "It's like you walked out of that door as a boy and came back as a man. What happened out there? I know you're accustomed to battle, so it wasn't just the creatures. What did the old oak do to you?"

"It seems I've been bestowed with a gift or a task; I'm not entirely sure which yet. Selika, M'Lady, I'll have to leave you for a while once we reach your destination up north. I need to accompany Tomoe to her village. The Nah-Vot have communicated to the old oak that I must go with her to find a secret cave, locate a hidden door, drink from an ancient chalice, and then find the man you're seeking. Beyond that, I have no idea what's expected of me," Petterman explained."

"I'm familiar with the cave you mentioned," Tomoe interjected. "It's where we hold ceremonies for the oath. I know of the hidden door, but it's never been opened. Legend says it was sealed from the inside tens of thousands of years ago by the highest of the Nah-Vot. According to the one we encountered earlier, they are all gone except for that one. So, how do we open the door?"

"If it's my destiny, then I'll find a way. If the Nah-Vot said I must do it, then there must be a way," Petterman affirmed.

"I think you'll need all the help you can get, Petterman. It might be wise for all of us to find the stranger, settle matters there, and then head over the mountains to Tomoe's village. We can shorten our stay with the stranger; the people he's staying with aren't that keen on me at the moment. Hopefully, that will change when we get there, as it did with Tomoe and me," Selika suggested.

"I'll accompany you to the northern borders," said Eve. "It'll give me a chance to test out some of this newly acquired knowledge. Rosella knew this forest like the back of her hand, and so should I. I'll put that to the test on my way back here. I'm sure I'll feel up to it in the morning."

"What about Rosella's horse? Will it stay with you now that she's gone?" Petterman inquired.

Tomoe responded to Petterman,

"From my experience, once the chosen rider has died, the Jumental goes out to pasture and lives the rest of its life as it wishes. I have never known one to have two chosen riders. So, Eve, I am very sorry to say that you might have a very long walk home if this is the case."

"Well, I am in no rush to go anywhere, and the walk back might do me good. Hopefully, there will be plenty of those mushysnacks to keep me fed till I get back here."

After they had finished another light meal, Selika suggested that they all try to get an early night so they could be up and ready at first light. She too was eager to make a move as soon as possible.

By the time the sun was even thinking of rising, Selika was already up and trying to get her things together. She woke all the others up by throwing things about in frustration. Tomoe shouted at her for being so impatient, saying,

"We'll get things done a lot sooner if you just go and sit down somewhere out of the way and let the ones that can see sort it all out"

"Oh… I hate this blindness. It is so frustrating. I thought that it might have gone by now, and I'd have my sight back," Selika sneered back at her.

In next to no time, after Selika had moved out of the way, they had everything ready to be put on the horses. Eve said that she would ride with Petterman again, as it would be the last time they could be together for the foreseeable future.

As they came to the entrance of the cave, two huge trees had moved and blocked their way, they completely covered the entrance. Eve walked up to them and asked them to move so that they could carry on their journey. Both trees shuddered and shook their leaves, and they all could hear one of them talk, they all looked at each other in disbelief, it had been the first time that they could all hear the trees talking. The tree said to Eve,

"Young Sylvan, we feel your loss, as you feel ours. We have all lost a very special person, one who has been with us in this forest for longer than most of us can remember. She will never be forgotten by us, and by the grace of the Nah-Vot, she is now one of us. Her mount, as you are probably aware, has now gone to pasture but will reside within the bounds of the forest. You may well see him from time to time. We thought that because you are only a human sapling and don't yet know what you are doing, we would ask for the assistance of another Jumental for you. During the night, five turned up, and one chose to stay and serve you. His name, in your tongue, is Leo because he growls and roars like a lion, and hopefully, he will be just as brave."

Both trees moved to the side of the entrance, and there in front of them, stood Leo, a jet-black Jumental. Perhaps a little smaller than the other three they had known, but just as beautiful, his silky coat glistened in the early morning light. Eve was so taken aback that she was speechless. She raised her hands to her face and started sobbing. She walked over to him, and he lowered his head to hers. She stroked and patted his neck, and he lowered himself to the floor so that she could climb aboard. He then stood up and gave a loud, humorous-sounding roar, then shook his head and whinnied. As he did that, Secronim and Decronim came trotting up the path toward them. They went, one on either side of Leo, and both nuzzled in with him for a second or two, then all three shook their heads and whinnied together. The remaining three came out of the cave and climbed aboard their mounts; Tomoe, once again, sat with Selika.

They set off down the path just as the sun broke through the trees, covering them all in a beautiful dappled early morning light. Their hearts now lightened, they intended to make haste and reach the northern borders before sundown. Fortunately, the forest was on their side today and gave them a straight, wide path north. All three Jumentals trotted side by side, and all three increased in size to the biggest any of them had seen before. They were more the size of elephants than horses, even Leo was huge. Their speed increased as their size increased, and very soon, they were travelling so fast that it was hard to keep their eyes open because of the wind. They could not talk to each other because they could not hear each other; the wind in their ears was too loud. So they just pressed onward in silence, stopping only once to stretch their legs. By early evening, they could see the edge of the forest. Shortly after, the horses started to slow the pace down a little, and their size decreased a little too.

They could see the mountains rising in the distance above the tree line. As they slowed down, they could now hear each other's voices while trotting along. The remarkable Jumentals showed no signs of exhaustion, having run all day long and still appearing as fresh as daisies.

They reached the edge of the forest just before darkness fell and decided to make camp for the night at the inner edge of the mighty forest. Eve dismounted from Leo and volunteered to find some food for them. Tomoe and Petterman got the bed rolls down from their mounts, leaving everything else in place to ensure an early start the next morning. As usual, Selika did nothing useful and grew increasingly frustrated by it.

Eve returned with some mushysnacks and some other strange-looking plants that she claimed were perfectly edible. They all sat down and ate them, finding the mushysnacks to be delicious but the other plants to be quite unpleasant, despite their nutritional value. Nonetheless, they acknowledged that Eve's knowledge was definitely expanding. Shortly after eating, the sun had already set, and the night quickly turned pitch black without the presence of the moon. They quietly went to bed.

They woke up early to a bright and crisp morning. Tomoe pointed to the mountains, now clearly visible in the distance.

"You see that narrow valley straight in front of us? That's where my home lies."

"But," said Selika, "We will be going to the right of that valley, somewhere over there. You should be able to see the pointed mountain, which is our destination for today. These three mountains are called the Triohex Mountains because each mountain supposedly holds a spell. We've recently learned about one spell, but the others remain unknown to us."

Eldoron

18 - Eve's Departure

By the time the small group was ready to travel, all three horses stood waiting. Petterman and Tomoe gathered their baggage and loaded it onto the horses. Eve went in search of more mushysnacks since they wouldn't find any outside the forest. Selika, once again, patiently waited, wishing she had asked the Nah-Vot how long her blindness would last.

Eve returned with a handful of good-sized mushrooms, enough for a couple each and one each for their mounts. She wrapped them in broad leaves that had fallen to the forest floor and handed them to Selika to distribute later in the morning.

"How far do you think you can go without being stopped? Will it be just before or just after the edge of this magnificent forest?" Tomoe asked Eve.

"I guess we're about to find out. I can't even imagine what could stop us," Eve replied.

As usual, Petterman helped Selika onto Secronim after Tomoe had mounted, and then he went to Eve and hugged her tightly.

"If this is the last time we meet, it's a very sad world. I have cherished every moment with you." Petterman whispered in her ear.

"We will meet again, I can feel it, see it even. Do you think some of Rosella's seer abilities have been passed on to me? I hope so." Eve replied.

"I'm not sure about the seer part, but it would have been nice to be able to communicate with each other over distances. Instead, I'll be stuck with these two. One is the epitome of self-righteousness, and the other is so stoic and stuck in the past. Yes, I know, she's new to this time and doesn't know any different yet, but she sounds like she's from the olden days." Petterman lamented.

"Enough complaining. Get on Decronim, and let's see how far I can get before I get turned back." Eve said playfully."

Petterman gave Eve a leg up onto Leo, then climbed aboard Decronim,

"Ok, let's go, forward and right. We head straight for the pointy one, is that correct M'lady?"

"They do have names, Petterman," Tomoe chuckled. "In my old tongue, 'Emrys', on the left, meant immortal. 'Ganna', the one in the middle meant paradise, and 'Balfor', the last one on the right meant pasture or grassland. You'll see why it's called that when we get there. My home is on the other side of Ganna, down the slopes. It used to be both beautiful and treacherous, with two waterfalls on either side of the village. When it rained and the wind blew, everyone got wet. The slippery stone roads made it perfect for sliding down the hill, but getting back up was quite challenging. As children, we used to have competitions to see who could slide the furthest without falling"

As they continued their journey, the density of trees gradually decreased. They followed the edge of the forest for a while, partly for Eve's enjoyment. Eventually, they veered more to the left, heading straight for the mountain. This meant leaving Sormoving Wood behind and saying farewell to Eve, a moment that was bound to be emotional for both her and Petterman. Over the past few weeks, they had grown quite close.

Petterman had found solace in Eve's company after the loss of his wife and child, and he was starting to develop feelings for her. But now, they had to part ways, each following their chosen paths. Only time and fate could reveal if they would ever meet again.

As they approached the forest's edge, Eve found it increasingly challenging to steer Leo outward. He kept trying to return to the depths of the forest, and eventually, she shouted for a stop, exclaiming,

"I cannot go any further; he refuses to go that way. My arms are aching from trying."

"That's your boundary line," said Tomoe. "Good, it's only a couple of hours' hard ride from the mountains."

Eve guided her mount over to Petterman and then leapt from Leo to Decronim, landing right at the back of Petterman. She wrapped her arms around his waist tightly, saying,

"Come back and see me as soon as you can. I'll be waiting for you, and the trees will be on the lookout for you. They trust you now, and you can come and go whenever you wish. Be careful, my soldier."

Petterman held her arms in front of him and returned the tight embrace.

"I'll be back before you realize I'm gone. You have a lot to do now, your knowledge of the forest is definitely increasing. You must get this forest to communicate with the other forests in far-off places and reunite them as one. Only then might we stand a chance of defeating Zeraphos once and for all. Go, my love. We will meet again soon, I promise."

She jumped back across to Leo, gently sat down, and patted him on his neck. Then she turned him around and rode off into the forest, tears streaming down her face.

They continued in silence for a while until Selika started humming a little tune to herself.

"I know that tune," Tomoe said quietly. "We used to

sing that song when we were children playing in the fields, but I can't for the life of me remember the words."

"The words I remember won't be the same as yours. My mother used to sing it after my father had knocked her senseless. She made up the words to hide her feelings; it was her way of coping and not showing him that she was hurt. As you know, he was not a nice man, and he's still not very nice. He's gaining strength again, which is very worrying. A few weeks ago, I had a little encounter with him, though I don't think he realized it was me. There was a young man there too, the one we're hoping to meet later today."

"M'lady, there's a village up ahead. Do you know it? Should we go through it or skirt around it?"

"There should be a small, narrow path quite a distance before the village. Take this path; it's the old way over the mountain, and it should be quieter. Do you know this way, Tomoe? It has been here for a very long time."

"I haven't been here in even longer than a very long time; I don't recall this road at all. The only road I remember was on the far side of Balfor, the one that goes around the base of the mountain, and this village wasn't there either. This village is too close to the forest. All it could take is one bad mood, and the forest could ensnare the whole village overnight, trapping the inhabitants and feeding on them. Petterman, you only saw the good side of the forest, but it can be terrifying! It has been known to move silently and raid animal farms, devouring all the livestock and the farm hands."

"Oh my!" Petterman exclaimed, "We do live in a nice world, don't we? Live in the South, and you might just get sacrificed; live in the North, and you might get eaten by trees! Go West, and you're in Zeraphos's world. Go East, and you're in the fabled giants' land, though I don't believe they ever really existed."

"Didn't you hear what Rosella said?" replied Selika. "She mentioned that Jorgon had recently passed through the forest. You'll meet him soon; he's a gentle giant most of the time, as you'll see."

"Yeah yeah yeah... probably just an overgrown man looking for a bit of adventure. I bet he's not much taller than I."

"This looks like it might be fun," Selika said. "A few surprises are coming up pretty soon. It's going to be an interesting few days. Just a shame I won't be able to see the looks on their faces.

Petterman, once we get a little further down the path, away from prying eyes, I think it's a good idea to stop and eat the mushysnacks that Eve found for us. They should sustain us for the rest of the journey."

After about ten minutes down the narrow path, Petterman called a halt. They were concealed from the village by a small outcrop of rocks, with an excellent view of the mountains ahead.

"This looks like an ideal spot for lunch, M'lady. I believe we're well hidden from anyone who might be watching. But may I ask why we need to keep our presence a secret?" Petterman inquired.

"We aren't exactly hiding, Petterman. I just prefer not to draw attention to ourselves until we reach the settlement, which lies just over the other side of this mountain. This path leads directly there. It won't take us long, especially considering how fast these Jumentals can run," Selika explained.

They all got down from their mounts and Selika put the folded leaves, that Eve had found for them on a ledge that they were all leaning on. Tomoe opened the package, and all that it contained was a sticky, horrible, decaying mess, it looked like the mushysnacks could not leave the forest without turning bad.

"Well," said Selika, "It appears we'll have to wait a

little while before we can eat. Thankfully, we don't have far to go. Let's take a few minutes to stretch our legs, and then we can set off again."

And so, they resumed the final leg of their journey. Selika estimated it would take only an hour or so, though the rough appearance of the road suggested it might take longer. The Jumentals increased in size to cope with the rugged stones on the path, ensuring they wouldn't attract much attention and could pass as unassuming travellers if they encountered anyone.

Eldoron

19 – Plans are Made

Jorgon, Eldoron, Volto, and Doron sat outside, near the fire they had used the other day for the Nah-Vot ceremony. As the air was getting a little cool, they decided to relight the fire. Jorgon spoke up,

"I don't know about you guys, but I'm feeling a bit peckish. We might have had breakfast a tad too early this morning. And if we start drinking that marvellous ale of yours on empty stomachs, we'll end up in trouble again with the ladies. You know how they dislike us drinking too much in the morning."

Valadora and Jarreen were approaching them with a nice hot brew just as Jorgon was speaking. They overheard everything. Jarreen chimed in,

"Well, we haven't been married very long, and you're already learning that married life doesn't come with the same freedoms as being single. But keep it up, my dear husband, and we'll have a long and happy marriage. Now, what do you desire for your evening meal? The rabbit population is abundant in the fields; you just need to catch some. I know your appetite, and you alone will need about five rabbits. So, if you bring back around ten, we can all have a decent meal tonight."

"Dora, Volto, and I will go catch some rabbits. It'll be good to be out for a few hours," said Doron.

"I don't think Volto has the energy for that just yet.

What do you say, Volto?" asked Valadora.

"I hate to admit it, but you're right. I think I'll sit this one out," replied Volto.

"Dora is in the kitchen; you can leave when she's finished making the potion, and not before. Understood, Doron? Not before!" Valadora emphasized.

"Alright, alright, I've got it. But tell her not to take forever, or we'll be having rabbits for breakfast tomorrow! Are you sure you don't want to come with us, Volto? We could have some fun," Doron suggested.

"No, I'm good here, thanks. Maybe another day. There's too much going on in my head right now, too many people messing with my brain," said Volto."

Dora quickly finished in the kitchen, impressing Doron for once.

"I'm going to try out this new bow that Jarreen made me the other day. It feels so light," she announced.

So they set off to hunt for meat for their evening meal, hoping to gather enough for the next few days, depending on Jorgon's appetite. They crossed the fields, heading toward Ganna, as rabbits from that direction always seemed to taste better.

Taking cover behind a small bush, they observed a fluffle of rabbits. Dora took out her bow and cocked an arrow, which made Doron giggle.

"You'll never reach them with that tiny bow. Even my bow isn't big enough for that distance. You'll just scare them all away," he teased."

"Let's see, shall we? Jarreen said it was a good one. Hold still while I fire it off," Dora replied. She positioned the bow horizontally just above the ground and pulled the arrow back as far as she could in that awkward position. Then, she released the arrow, and they both watched in astonishment as it flew in a perfectly straight line. It seemed to go on forever until suddenly, a big buck rabbit stood up on its back legs, and the arrow struck it right in the chest, killing it instantly. The arrow then lodged itself in another rabbit's neck, almost decapitating it. They were both amazed; there was no way that bow could send an arrow that far and accurately. Dora rolled over laughing, and Doron eagerly asked,

"Give me that bow; I want to try it!"

"Not a chance, you've got your own." They both sat up, still laughing.

"Come on, let's go and get them before some great big eagle beats us to it and steals them," Dora said, pulling him up. Just as they reached their quarry, Doron noticed movement on the road, right on the horizon.

"There is somebody on the road over there, can you see them?"

"No, but your eyes are better than mine; it's probably just some travellers. Look, this arrow is not even marked or damaged."

"Come on, get the rabbits. We need plenty more yet. Look, there are some more over there. It's my turn this time, but we will have to get a lot closer with this bow." This time there was no bush to hide behind, so Doron decided to use the same technique that Dora used, lying on the grass and putting the bow horizontally. His arrow fell short by a long way, not even scaring the rabbits.

"Give me one of your arrows quick, while they are still there." She handed one down to him and got one out for herself.

"If you miss this time, then it's mine," she said. He didn't miss, but as soon as she heard his arrow fly, she let hers loose too, aiming at one further away than his. Again, her arrow passed straight through the rabbit.

"Alright, show off. Come on, let's pick them up." They both looked to the horizon at the travellers, they could not believe how far they had come in just a few minutes.

As Dora collected these two rabbits, Doron was watching the travellers. He could see now that there were two horses, both running at an incredible speed. He said to her,

"Dora, look! Look how fast they are going. No horse can run that fast, and look how big they are; they must be three times as big as a normal horse."

"Maybe someone is bringing them for Jorgon and Jarreen, giant horses for giant people." They both crouched down in the grass as the travellers approached.

"I don't think they saw us," Doron said as the giant horses passed them.

"I think we need to go back and tell Mum and Dad about this. This is not normal; we will have to make do with just four rabbits for tonight," Dora said.

"Dora, they have turned off the road; they are going up the track to ours. We can still be there before them if we are quick and take the shortcut across the fields."

They ran as fast as they could to get back home before the strangers got there. They managed it with minutes to spare. They threw their catch down on the ground near the fire; neither of them could speak; they were so out of breath. They just pointed to the road.

Volto just said,

"Someone is approaching on horses. It sounds like two horses; they are very close." Dora and Doron just nodded their heads like idiots.

Jorgon stood up and looked down the road, but he could not see anybody. Volto said, "I can feel them. There are three people on two horses. They will be coming around the bend any second." They all stood up to see, and then they saw them, running like the wind, faster than any of them had ever seen a horse run.

"Look at the size of those horses," said Volto.

"They are not just horses; they are Jumentals. We have not seen these beasts for hundreds of years. Who is riding them? Can you see?" Valadora said.

Petterman signalled to the horses to start slowing down and go to normal size so that they did not cause too much of a stir. But it was too late; they had already been seen by the onlookers. As they got closer to where Eldoron and his gathering were, they were just about at walking speed.

Jorgon and Jarreen started walking down the path to meet them. Petterman and Tomoe could not see the others because of the size of the giants. Jarreen approached them first and said,

"Good afternoon and merry meet. We don't often encounter strangers in these parts. Can we be of any assistance to you? Have you lost your way?"

Selika leaned her head from the back of Tomoe and inquired,

"To whom am I speaking? I apologize, but I am currently blinded. My name is Selika, and I am searching for a stranger to this land who I believe is with you. Would you mind if we dismount and approach?" Volto responded in a loud voice, as he tried to pass the giants,

"That's her! She's the voice in my head. I would recognize that voice anywhere."

Valadora tried to stop him, snatching at his arm, but he pulled her along, and as soon as Tomoe saw her, she recognized her instantly and shouted,

"Oh my god! Valadora? Is it really you? I thought you had perished years ago." She slid down from Secronim and ran over to her

"Tomoe? Is it truly you?" they both embraced each other. "What in the world? I thought you died in the last battle. Where have you been all these years? Eldoron, look, it's Tomoe."

Petterman and Selika remained on their mounts. Petterman watched the two of them like a hawk, just in case of trouble. He also kept an eye on the giants, knowing that if things turned nasty, they would be in big trouble.

Volto had approached Selika to get a good look at her.

"You're the one who pulled me out of the water and saved me in the cave when that thing tried to kill me, aren't you? And you're the woman in my head too, aren't you? The one who made me set fire to the lake as well?"

"Yes, I am the same one, guilty as charged, young man. I'm thrilled to meet you again, and under better circumstances," Selika replied.

Jarreen stepped forward, looking rather menacing, and said,

"And you're the one who kicked me out of his head too, right?"

"Sorry, guilty of that too, but it was necessary at the time. I hope there are no hard feelings," Selika calmly responded.

Eldoron stood there with a big smile on his face, arms folded across his chest, observing everyone.

"Does this call for a celebration or not? Come down from your horses and join us up here. There are enough seats for all of us, and I think we can crack open a barrel. What say you, Jorgon? And you, sir, you've been quiet and watching all the time. Who might you be?"

"I am Petterman, Sir. I was a soldier of the garrison in Gehenna until I was commandeered by this lady. I am currently her guide as she is temporarily blinded."

"Then you too are welcome. Come and join us, and no need to call me Sir," Eldoron warmly said."

Petterman helped Selika down from her mount and guided her to the settlement. As Eldoron suggested, there was plenty of room for all of them to sit.

"Now, Petterman," Tomoe said with a smile on her face, "Do you still believe giants are a myth? And this is the lady I mentioned, the one who knows things about healing herbs and other matters. The same lady I was sworn to all those years ago, and she doesn't look a day older."

"I am so overwhelmed. I've heard countless tales throughout my life about these very people. I thought you were all myths. What am I doing in the company of such extraordinary individuals? I am just a nobody compared to all of you. What I've seen over the last few weeks is more than any ordinary person will see in their whole lifetime. Every day, I witness things that are talked about in legends, things people write songs about."

"Welcome to the peculiar company! I find myself in the same situation as you. Not long ago, I was a homeless man, wandering the streets of a city in a completely different world, so distinct from this one that explaining it to you would likely be futile. I, too, am uncertain about the true reason for my presence here, though I believe it will have significant, if not monumental, implications. I have experienced visions of thousands of lifeless bodies floating in the sea and a vast lake."

"I also had a vision of bodies in the lake. I was there when Selika set it on fire, a horrifying sight. However, miraculously, it caused no damage as she contained the flames within the lake. So, it was you who made her do it. I won't even inquire about how or why you managed that."

Doron approached with three flagons of ale, offering one to each of them,

"Do you mind if I join you?" he asked as he settled down. "Dora will be joining us shortly."

It wasn't long before she arrived and sat next to Volto.

"Did I hear correctly that you were a soldier in the

regiment? That must have been thrilling. Why did you leave?"

He proceeded to tell them about the loss of his wife and the birth of his child during the eruption of the volcano. He also spoke of Selika's cunning infiltration of the garrison and her single-handed overthrow of Jarroth, the head of state in Gehenna. He shared how she eventually became blind.

Meanwhile, Valadora and Tomoe reminisced about old times. Valadora expressed her delight at having a conversation with Tomoe, noting that during her time in the oath, Tomoe remained silent, ever vigilant, and dutiful without eating or sleeping.

"This is what perplexes me," said Tomoe. "Why have I been brought back, and why did I find myself in a desolate field with no knowledge of the time that has passed since my death? The Nah-Vot mentioned that my fellow sisters-in-arms have also returned, but I have no idea of their whereabouts. I must journey to my village over the mountains and attempt to find them. We might be required to take the oath again. I must admit, the thought of undergoing all those disciplines once more does not appeal to me. However, if it's necessary, so be it. I shall avoid her this time; she was the one who killed me in the great battle. Although we are friends now, it's still strange to be in the company of the one who took your life"

As Selika conversed with the two giants, a heated discussion ensued about Selika's expulsion of Jarreen from Volto's mind. Selika explained,

"I don't apologise because it was necessary at the time, he had just had a run-in with my father and I thought that he may be listening to him, he is very sly like that!"

"Wait, hold on a moment. Are you saying you are the daughter of Zeraphos?" asked one of the giants.

"Yes, that's true, and I'm not proud of it. For the past thousand years, I've been trying to keep him dormant, but I can no longer hold him back. He's awakening again, and his power is growing. He's becoming restless. I've had ample time to study his actions and deeds, and they are simply abhorrent. I believe in the potential for good in this world, not the harm he relishes so much. He killed my mother and subjected her to thousands of years of suffering. I can never forgive him for that. I also have a brother, Gorglothian, who despised our father passionately. However, I have no idea where he is, or if he's still alive. I want to render my father powerless; I know he can't truly die, but he can be made useless. He can be imprisoned in Quenilith, and as you know, she has awakened."

"So," retorted Jarreen, "you're merely switching allegiances and hoping your old enemy will believe what you say. That is a very tall order don't you think?"

"No, it's not a tall order, not from my perspective. In my own way, I've been fighting him ever since the battle in which I killed Tomoe. And what other choice do we have? He's waking and stealing souls, amassing a huge army. I've seen it, though it remains hidden from most people's eyes. The Nah-Vot know this and will be contacting you about Volto if they haven't already. They are in a dire predicament, fully aware of what he's doing, yet powerless to stop him. This task will be a collective effort; we all have a part to play in his downfall. But for now, it's Volto's actions that take precedence. He seeks to balance the living and the dead, a challenge far beyond my capabilities." Jarreen said to her.

"The Nah-Vot have already been and gone. They were here when Volto lost control, and you took the fire from him. They've given him 'the gift,' as they called it, something he must use to reclaim all the stolen souls. He also stopped time for a while and apparently went flying;

though we don't know how he managed that, you'll have to speak to Volto about it. But I don't even think he knows how or what he did. He says it just happened."

Selika was very interested in the notion of stopping time and flying, asking,

"How do you know that he actually stopped time? And for how long did he stop it? Surely we all would have known or felt something."

"How would we have known?" answered Jarreen. "If time stops, everything else would stop too, including clouds, wind, and the sun's movement across the sky. I don't think we would have had any idea, as long as it wasn't stopped for too long."

"This is getting a little too deep for me at this time of day," Jorgon said. "I think I'll go join Doron and that Petterman fellow. He might have an interesting story behind him."

Jarreen looked at him and said with a sly smile,

"You're just going over there because the ale is starting to flow, aren't you? You could fetch a tankard and bring it back here, getting one each for us while you're at it."

"Err... no thank you, my love. This conversation is a bit much for me this early in the day. But I'll gladly get you both some liquid refreshment."

Eldoron was sitting on his favourite chair, his throne, as he liked to call it, with his arms folded across his chest, as was his usual posture. He sat there, smiling slightly, and listened to all the different conversations going on simultaneously. He looked at Doron and Dora, feeling proud of how far they'd come in terms of their social skills over the last few years. They used to be shy and wouldn't talk to strangers, but now, they chatted away as if they'd known each other for years. Observing Valadora too, his lovely wife, engaged in a deep conversation with Tomoe, he found it odd to see her after all these years.

"Something is afoot here," he thought, "All of this isn't normal. I believe our peaceful little world is about to be turned upside down once again. It's a shame because I was starting to enjoy my life as it is now, with no stress or worries. Well, nothing lasts forever, I suppose."

Jorgon took a tankard each for Selika and Jarreen, placing them on the grass beside their bench, and then made his way over to Doron, Dora, Volto, and Petterman.

"Hey, old man!" he shouted to Eldoron, "Do you want me to bring your mighty throne over here so you can sit with us? You could tell us a story or two."

"It would take two of you to carry this thing over there," he replied.

"Nonsense, I could carry that thing with one hand and get you a drink with the other. Come on, my old friend, stand up and let me carry it."

"Okay, but I'll get my drink. I don't want you spilling it on the floor and wasting good ale, especially if Valadora has put some of my favourite herbs in it."

Soon after Eldoron joined them, Dora started to quiz Petterman about his adventures on the way there. When he got to the part about Eve wanting to be Rosella's apprentice and changing her name, Eldoron interrupted him, saying.

"Hang on a minute, soldier. I think this might be better heard by all of us. Matters concerning Rosella will be of great importance to Valadora; they were very good friends in the early days. Hey, Valadora my dear, I think you should come over here and listen to this. It concerns your old friend Rosella, and Jarreen, you too, please come and join us."

Once they had rearranged the seating to accommodate everyone in a small circle, Petterman continued to relate his story to the group. When he reached the part about Rosella's death, Valadora was devastated. She stood up and walked away from the group, not wanting to believe it. Tomoe got up and went to Valadora to console her.

"I have known her for thousands of years; she cannot be just snuffed out like that. And what about this Eve girl? Is she up for the task? Does she even know what it involves? Is she prepared to live the lonely life that Rosella did? I want to go and see her, tell her just what she has let herself in for. It is a major task that she has taken on, and she is just a child by the sound of it."

"Valadora, I was there too, and what Petterman has said is, in my opinion, very accurate. I think that the severed arm was aimed at me but was deflected in error; it was not meant to kill Rosella, it was meant to kill me. Eve had already agreed to be the new apprentice; she knew what she was doing. She might be just a child in your eyes, but trust me, she is very mature for her years. She could communicate with the trees long before we met Rosella but didn't realize it. She has been accepted by the Jumentals, and that says a lot. Come back to the circle; there is more to hear, I am sure."

Both Valadora and Tomoe went back and sat down, and Petterman stood up to apologize to Valadora, but she waved him on and told him to continue with the narrative.

"Yes, M'lady if that is what you wish."

Everyone else sat there in silence, stunned at the death of one of the oldest beings on the planet. Jorgon had his head cradled in his massive hands, tears streaming down his face. Jarreen had put her arm around his shoulder to help console him.

Petterman finished his account of the journey north on a lighter note, sharing his feelings for Eve and describing the rotten mushysnacks and the awful smell that emanated from the leaves they were wrapped in.

Eldoron suggested that they all take a few minutes to collect their thoughts and then formulate a plan to move forward.

Selika was the first to speak, addressing them all,

"I know that not all of you trust me as much as I would like, but I have thought out a basic plan. It needs a lot of work, but it is a starting point. I suggest that Tomoe goes with Petterman to her village over the mountain and see what has transpired there in terms of the others in the Protectorate. Then Petterman can go to the hidden cave and sort out what his part in all of this might be."

"What do you mean by the hidden cave?" asked Jarreen. "Is this something that you have not told us yet, Petterman?" Selika replied,

"It might not be much, but there again; it might be significant. The Nah-Vot told Petterman to go into the cave and find a secret door leading to a chamber. Then somehow open it and go inside. Then drink something from an old chalice on an altar; that most probably must have been sat there for a thousand years or more. The rest is not so clear; he must then come back over the mountain and find Volto again, for what purpose we are not yet sure. We have been led to believe that Petterman is a listener of the rock, as was I many thousands of years ago. Unfortunately, I lost that ability a long time ago."

"Wow! How exciting, I wonder what gossip the rock has to offer? Psst... the candlestick maker in the village is secretly seeing the baker..." Doron said sarcastically. Selika replied, rather angrily,

"I don't think the rock is interested in who is having an affair with whom, young man. But it might have an idea of where my father is hiding his army; an army like you have never heard of the likes of before. An army, where each being has at least three souls. Does that mean that we will have to kill it three times before it dies? Who knows? Now that sort of information would be very useful, don't you think Doron?"

"Well, yes, I didn't think of it like that. I'm not accustomed to considering wars and related matters; I've never experienced anything like this before. My life has been one of peace, and the only death I've witnessed is when animals are killed for food."

"Eldoron replied, 'Things are going to change, son. Not everything in this world is good. There are beings now that would love to kill you, consume you, and claim your soul. We've had wars like this before, several times, and the outcomes were never good for either side. There was death and suffering all around, and hardship lingered long after. Zeraphos, her father, is a formidable enemy; he can't be physically killed, only weakened and somehow imprisoned. The last war lasted many years and cost far too many lives on both sides. The rivers literally ran red with blood. We must avoid this at all costs.'"

Volto said,

"The Nah-Vot told me it won't be a physical war, but rather a battle of heart and mind or something like that. I'll need help to reclaim the stolen souls. How can I hold so many souls? Where will I put them all?"

Valadora replied,

"I believe that will become self-evident when the time comes, Volto."

Jorgon asked,

"Did the Nah-Vot say that it would not be a physical war for all of us, or just you, Volto? Perhaps you need protection while you carry out your part to avoid getting killed."

"I think we should take this one step at a time," suggested Jarreen. "Firstly, we should go over the mountain to find out what happened to the others in the Protectorate, assuming they've been brought back as you say, Tomoe. I also suggest we all go together to save time instead of waiting for Petterman to meet up with Volto again."

"I agree with Jarreen," said Selika. "Let's prepare tonight and set off at first light tomorrow. However, I don't think all of us need to go. Dora and Doron might be more useful staying here until we return."

Eldoron insisted,

"No, they are coming with us. They need to witness and understand what's unfolding. If anything happens, they should be in the know and able to react accordingly."

Jarreen also put in that,

"Dora is one of the finest with a bow and arrow that she has ever seen. She would be very useful if, as has been said, the magic is disabled in some way."

"Alright then," said Selika. "All ten of us shall go. I'm not sure how long it will take to reach Tomoe's village, but we'll probably be walking most of the way as the mountains appear too challenging for the Jumentals to climb. Plus, we'd need more Jumentals to accommodate all of us."

"Not at all, Selika," Tomoe reassured. "There used to be hidden paths we can take. I should remember most of them once we get closer. However, it's been quite a while since I've been there. The Jumentals should be fine for most of the journey."

Eldoron

20 – Hemmingstone

Valadora and Eldoron were the first to stand up and start preparing for their journey. Dora and Doron quickly followed suit, unsure of what to bring, so Valadora called out various items they should pack. The rest of the group had already packed up since they hadn't been there long enough to unpack, and Volto didn't have any belongings to worry about.

Jorgon and Jarreen took it upon themselves to cook a meal for the entire group. Somehow, they managed to turn the four rabbits, along with potatoes, vegetables, and some of Valadora's herbs, into a delicious stew that was enough for everyone.

Selika and Tomoe were discussing the best route to take. Selika suggested retracing their steps and then taking the road directly over the mountain, seeing it as the most logical and likely the shortest route. Tomoe, however, disagreed, proposing that they should go around the back of the mountain and approach Hemmingstone from the front to avoid any potential risks from the guardians. She also pointed out that approaching from the front would make them appear more friendly and less suspicious. Can you imagine the faces of any onlookers when they see two giants walking up the road?"

"Okay, yes, you do have a point there. Let's go your way then. What would your road be like at night? Would it be safe to travel in the dark?

Considering the safety of travelling at night, Tomoe admitted it was relatively safe based on her previous experiences but recommended travelling during daylight for added security. Everyone agreed to her plan, and they decided to enjoy the meal Jorgon and Jarreen had prepared before setting off at first light the following day. Unless you or anyone else has any other ideas or objections. Personally, I would like to get there as soon as possible. I think if I remember rightly that it should take us a good day and a half to get there if we are to go on foot."

"We have enough horses for all of us in the backfield," Eldoron said, "There was about fifteen there last week, we just need to catch them. That will create some fine entertainment for us in the morning."

The stew prepared by Jorgon and Jarreen was exceptionally tasty, comparable to a professionally cooked meal in a high-class restaurant. Everyone had their fill, and Dora and Doron kindly volunteered to handle the cleanup.

As the evening progressed, Tomoe answered questions about her life before taking the Protectorate Vow, and the atmosphere was filled with laughter and joy, thanks in part to Valadora's finest herb-infused ale.

"There will be some hangovers in the morning," Jorgon said in-between fits of laughter, "Dora, are you going to make some of that hangover cure that you are getting quite good at? I think we are all going to need it, especially if we are going to be up before the dawn chorus."

"Yes, I still have some left from the other day, Mother said I made much too much. I don't think it will get wasted now, will it?"

As the night grew colder, they all moved inside the cave and eventually fell asleep, enjoying a restful night despite the copious amount of drinks they had consumed.

Surprisingly, Jorgon and Jarreen were the first to rise the next morning, not feeling the effects of the previous night's indulgence. Dora, being next to wake, promptly brought out her hangover cure and offered it to the giants, who politely declined, saying they didn't need it. As the others woke up, she offered the cure to them, and they gladly accepted it.

As the sun started to rise, they were all ready to set off. Petterman led Selika to the cave entrance, and they stepped out into the dim pink light of dawn. The rest of the group followed, and to their surprise, the two Jumentals emerged from the back of the cave and stood in their path, blocking their way. Decronim nudged Petterman, urging him to go back the way they came. With little choice, they turned around, only to find four more jet-black Jumentals waiting for them, silhouetted against the morning light. They slowly, one by one came over to them and nuzzled up to each of them in turn, as if they were choosing their riders. One went to Valadora and stood next to her, one to Eldoron, and one each to the giants. The giants looked like they were far too big and heavy for their mounts, but as soon as they mounted them, they grew in size to match the giants. Volto rode with Petterman, Dora with Valadora, and Doron with Eldoron. Following a small track that Tomoe had suggested, leading to the other side of the mountains they crossed yesterday, they set off on their journey.

An hour later, they reached a crossroads and took the left-hand track, a wider and straighter road. The Jumentals increased their size and speed, allowing them to ride throughout the day without rest, making it to the bottom of Ganna by evening. The village was now just a short distance away. The Jumentals reduced their size and speed, and Jorgon and Jarreen dismounted, leading their horses on foot, easily keeping pace with the rest.

Tomoe felt a mix of excitement and nervousness as they approached her old home. They could see the familiar high wall surrounding the village, and the large black doors at the entrance appeared shut and well-maintained, quite different from Tomoe's memories of the past when the doors were often open and the road was narrower.

As they approached the doors, they could see that they were crafted from black granite, with very intricate carvings on them. There was a small door in one of them so that they did not need to open the larger doors. Just as they reached the smaller door, Tomoe jumped down from Secronim and did a strange little dance in front of the door, it opened silently, nobody was behind it, it just opened by itself. They were all taken aback, except Tomoe, she said to them,

"It has a secret switch on the floor, you have to step in a certain fashion to trigger it. I didn't think that it would still be working. There must be people inside looking after the old place, come on let's go in and see. Hang on there while I open the main doors, it will be easier for the horses and you two of course," signalling Jarreen and Jorgon, "I think you two would have to crawl on the floor to fit through that door." She stepped over the threshold and seconds later the massive stone doors started to slowly swing open. They opened to a large courtyard with some small official-looking stone buildings at the far end, these buildings were of the same black granite as the massive entrance doors. As they got closer to the buildings, the doors opened and a long line of men and older children came out, standing in a straight line in front of them, all holding large spears or bows. Jarreen push her way through the group, hand on her massive sword in readiness, Tomoe stopped her and said to her in a very loud voice,

"Jarreen, stay your sword this is not a threat, this is a traditional greeting for me, just stay still and watch, all is good and friendly at the moment."

The line of inhabitants began to surround the group of strangers, and more and more people came out of the buildings until they formed a full circle around them, standing two lines deep. Tomoe turned to the group and addressed them, saying,

"Just stay still and hold onto the horses. This is not a threat and will be over very shortly." With that, she started to walk around the circle, touching each and every weapon. As she touched them, the people laid their weapons down on the ground and sat down, their heads bowed low and hands together in front of their faces. When she touched the last weapon, a loud, deep-sounding gong thundered behind them, which none of them had noticed before. The gong signalled the arrival of the soldiers along the top of the wall, who had entered the courtyard unnoticed. These soldiers now marched along the wall, descended a set of stone stairs, and formed a circle around the seated inhabitants. The gong sounded again, and the soldiers all hammered their weapons once on the ground, removed their helmets, and stood at attention. Surprisingly, they were all women, while the seated inhabitants were all men of various ages, along with some older children. Tomoe spoke to the group again,

"Dismount and stand next to your horses, facing the buildings. I am hoping the others will come out."

The group followed her instructions, and soon four women dressed in red and gold silks emerged. Tomoe let out a loud gasp and said, "They are here, these are the others from the Protectorate. From left to right, they are Hangaku, Masako, Nakano, and Yaeko." Tomoe approached them, and as she passed the seated inhabitants, they quickly stood up and respectfully moved out of her way, bowing low. The sight of all five women embracing and hugging each other was heartwarming. The four newcomers then greeted Tomoe with "Merry meet sister and welcome back," before stepping back and giving her a respectful bow.

Tomoe signalled for the group to leave the horses and to come forward and meet the others. Eldoron bowed to them and said,

"Welcome back, I remember you well, all of you." Valadora did the same but said,

"Something big is about to happen, I am so glad you are here to help."

However, when the four ladies turned their attention to Selika, Hangaku accused her,

"We know you, what are you doing in this company? You should be imprisoned with your father. You are nothing but a cold-blooded murderer. If I had my weapon, I would take your head clean off right now." Tomoe quickly intervened, explaining that a lot of things had changed, and Selika deserved a chance to explain herself to everyone. The four reluctantly backed down but expressed their eagerness to hear her explanation and decide her fate.

Selika retorted,

"Well, thank you so much. That is so gracious of you not to kill a blind old woman."

"Blind? How are you blind?"

"Have you not noticed that this soldier has been guiding me all the way? I think it might be a good idea if we all sit down and talk about what has happened these last two thousand years, and what is going to happen very soon, don't you? And while we are at it, how do you think that you would kill me? You are not yet back in the Protectorate and is the Protectorate even going to be reinstated? If it is, then who is going to preside over the ceremony?"

Volto interjected, "This is getting us nowhere. Let's all settle down and hear each other out. We are all in this together for some reason, so let's share our stories and formulate a plan."

"Well said young man, I couldn't have put it better myself." Said Jorgon.

"Do you have any refreshments?" Dora said, quite nervously.

"We are so sorry, yes we do young lady, we have done you all a great disrespect. Please accept our sincere apologies. Will you please come with us to the new meeting house and we will arrange for some food and drinks to be served, and somewhere for you to rest if you wish." Hangaku said, with her head bowed down low.

"I don't need to rest or anything to eat really, I just wanted you all to stop arguing and be all nice and friendly again." They all burst out laughing at her and Jarreen said,

"You will make a very good diplomat one-day young lady, just keep doing what you do."

They all walked up to the meeting hall together, chatting in small groups about what could happen if things didn't go well. Jarreen advised Jorgon to keep a clear head and not drink too much. Valadora shared her nervousness about how things might turn out with Eldoron. Doron praised Dora for bravely interrupting that heated debate. Petterman guided Selika up the path, unsure about revealing the ability to hear the stone to Tomoe's friends. Tomoe, at the forefront of her old compatriots, engaged in another heated debate, while Volto trailed behind, thinking he should have stayed back at Eldoron's place as this matter didn't concern him.

As they reached the meeting house, a black granite building, they all paused outside, and Hangaku addressed them,

"This house is very sacred to us, built on the site of

our old meeting house, which unfortunately got destroyed by a fire a few years ago, as I am told. No weapons are allowed inside, and magic doesn't work here, though we know not how or why. Please enter with a peaceful mind, as it also serves as a place of worship for those who wish to pray to whoever they choose. Food and drink will arrive shortly."

They all entered through the large wooden doors, which had to be opened wide to accommodate the two giants. The original paved black granite floor contrasted nicely with the carved wood lining the rest of the hall, evoking thoughts of Eve for Petterman and the impact of cutting down trees for this construction.

They cooperated in arranging tables and chairs in a circle around a small fire pit at the room's centre. Logs burned on the fire, prompting Petterman to contemplate Eve and how the trees would not be happy to witness this. Two young men, probably around sixteen or seventeen years old, brought in a barrel of ale and some tankards, while two others carried trays with cheese, meat, and bread. Hangaku invited them all to partake, reassuring them that there was more if needed. As they ate, they chatted lightheartedly.

When everyone finished, Selika stood up and suggested,

"I think it's a good idea if I start this meeting by explaining my involvement in all this since the last battle. I apologize to those who have heard it several times before; it must be getting tedious." She then proceeded to tell the entire story as she saw it, from the end of the battle to the present day, answering questions along the way.

Valadora stood up next but was asked by Tomoe to wait a short while as she had something to attend to. The attendees refreshed their tankards, and Tomoe returned shortly after, dressed in the same red and gold silks as the other members of the Protectorate.

"Okay, now we can carry on," she said.

Valadora shared her version of the events from the battle until the present day, omitting anything about Volto. Eldoron added a few details and corrected some errors.

Next, Jorgon and Jarreen offered their side of the story, though it was brief.

Dora said that Doron and herself had nothing further to add, as her mother had said it all as usual.

Volto stood up next, and the four new Protectorates stood with him, bowing their heads low as Hangaku addressed him,

"Young man, we know not who you are, but we can feel a great power in you, a power that we have not sensed in many an age. Please share your tale in the greatest of detail, leaving nothing out." Volto proceeded to recount his version of events up until that day, and the Protectorates were enthralled by his experiences. They had many questions, but most of them he could not answer. In the end, Volto sat down, almost exhausted from the barrage of questions, but Jorgon comforted him by putting his massive hand on his shoulder and saying,

"Well done, lad. I think they understood all that"

Tomoe stood up, but Hangaku stopped her, claiming they didn't need her story. Tomoe objected and told it anyway, emphasizing the need for complete transparency from everyone. She insisted that she expected four different stories from four different members of the Protectorate in return. Each member then relayed their stories and the circumstances of how and where they had been brought back.

Petterman was the last to stand, Selika said,

"Tell us your tale, Goodman Petterman. Your story is a very interesting one too, miss nothing out, tell us everything." Petterman began recounting his story, starting from his first meeting with Selika, through the birth of his child, and the tragic loss of his lovely wife. He detailed every aspect, even his deepest feelings for Eve, with military precision. After he finished, Selika complimented him, saying,

"Last but not least, Petterman, well done. That is a full account of all events leading up to this day. Now that we know each other's stories, we must make a plan to move forward. But before that, we should find this secret chamber and see what is to happen with my guide."

Tomoe interjected,

"Selika, if we, the Protectorate, enter the cave, we will invoke the ceremony, and there will be no one to preside over it. We won't be able to leave until the ceremony is complete."

"I will preside over it, Tomoe. I have the power, knowledge, and authority. If you wish, we can conduct the ceremony before we enter the chamber. In fact, that would probably be the best approach, as we have no idea who or what awaits us there. Petterman, do you have any objections to this?" Selika inquired.

"Absolutely no objections from me, M'lady," Petterman replied.

Hangaku stood up once again and said,

"I think that concludes the business for today. The sun has set now, and it is dark outside. I suggest that we all bed down in here tonight; it is much warmer than the guest houses. I will ask for some blankets and more food and drink to be brought in. Let us have a friendly chat tonight and discuss the plan of action for tomorrow. The cave is only a few minutes walk from here"

That evening, they all relaxed more than they had in weeks. The atmosphere was warm and amiable, with no more heated debates; just friendly chatter. Even Masako, Nakano, and Yaeko were very talkative.

As the evening wore on, they slowly drifted off to sleep, one by one.

Eldoron

21 – Caves and Drinks in the Dark

They were all awakened by the sound of thunder outside as huge storm clouds had come over the mountain from the forest. Petterman was the first to get up, and he walked over to the wooden doors. It was only then that he noticed the beautiful carvings on the inside, covered with all manner of symbols and writing. Hangaku came over to him and said,

"The doors, when opened up and slid outside, reveal a fascinating sight. If the moon is full and in the right place in the sky, all the writing glows and forms a picture of a young woman sitting in a tree. We have only seen this phenomenon in the last few days, and tonight will be the last full moon, so you might get to see it if the sky clears up." Petterman expressed his keen interest in witnessing it.

Gradually, the others made their way to the doors to witness the lightning storm that was forking all over the sky, putting on a spectacular show. With such weather, heading to the cave was out of the question, so they settled down and finished the remaining food from last night. Once the lightning show subsided, they made plans to proceed to the cave, which was a short distance away and didn't require their mounts. As they stepped outside, the Jumentals were waiting for them. Petterman approached Decronim and told him that they didn't need their service for this journey. He instructed the horses to go outside the town walls and fill their bellies, and surprisingly, Decronim seemed to understand and whinnied to the other horses, leading them out through the massive stone gates.

Tomoe took the lead with Hangaku at her side, followed by Petterman and Selika, while the rest followed, chatting as they walked. The path they followed had a well-trodden feel to it, free of weeds and rocks. Tomoe pointed out a small path leading up to a cave on the side of the hill with a huge waterfall in front of it. She explained that they would have to go around the back of the waterfall to enter the cave, and she asked Petterman if he would be okay guiding Selika, considering it could get a little narrow in some places.

"I'll be fine, thank you. If necessary, I can carry her on my shoulders," Petterman replied with a chuckle.

"I think it might be better if Jorgon does that. He'd be more steady on his feet and capable of carrying her for a longer stretch," Tomoe suggested.

Selika interjected,

"I'm right here, you know! I can hear you! I do have a choice on how I get into the cave, and, Goodman Petterman, you won't be putting me over your shoulder at any time."

Approaching the waterfall, the loud, forceful sound of the water filled the air due to the earlier rainfall. However, the increased water flow created more space behind the waterfall, making it easier to enter the cave. The entrance was quite large, allowing even the giants to pass through without ducking their heads. Inside, they found a vast cavern with rough walls adorned with silver veins running across them.

It was quite dark inside, so they stood still for a moment, allowing their eyes to adjust. Curious, Volto went over to the wall and touched one of the silver threads, immediately illuminating the thread and sending waves of light throughout the cave. Unfortunately, this caused Petterman great pain, and he screamed while covering his ears and falling to his knees. Volto quickly withdrew his hand from the wall, leaving the threads of light behind.

"The invocation of the ceremony has begun," Selika said, "We cannot go any further until this is complete, the power of nature has initiated it with Volto's touch. I will have to do this now. Are you, The Protectorate ready for this? Everything I say from now on will be set in stone."

They all looked at one another, and in unison, they declared that they were once again ready to take their vows. Selika asked Doron to lead her to the centre of the cave while Petterman still knelt on the floor, covering his ears. Selika began to sing in a strange tongue, just as she had done by the lake in Sormoving Wood. Her song was so beautiful and enchanting that they all felt a warm and pleasant sensation inside. The five Protectorates involuntarily swayed from side to side, and the others, including Jarreen and Jorgon, sat on the floor, their heads slowly drooping until their chins rested on their chests, giving the impression that they were all asleep.

The five, still swaying, formed a circle around Selika while she turned slowly, singing and making hand gestures. The silvery light pulsated in rhythm with her song, and this continued for some time. Selika then reached out to touch each of them in turn, placing her hand on their foreheads and silently whispering something to them. As soon as they were touched, they sat cross-legged on the cave floor. When the last one was seated, Selika stopped singing and began speaking in a different tongue. They all raised their heads and looked around, puzzled by the lack of an experience they had anticipated.

Hangaku stood up and exclaimed,

"Well, that was a waste of time. I don't feel any different, and I can still talk. I don't think your little ceremony worked, Selika. Maybe you are the fraud we initially thought you were."

"It did work," Selika replied. "I have made some changes based on what you all shared in your stories last night. When you leave the cave, you will find that you can still talk, sleep, and eat. Everything else remains the same, and the vows I spoke on your behalf are just as binding as the last time you took them. To activate the changes, you must leave the cave and then re-enter it. When you come back in, we will attempt to open the chamber door."

The five stood up and exchanged glances, finding it hard to believe that it had worked. Tomoe said,

"Come on, ladies, let's see what happens. Selika has been right about everything so far. Let's take a little stroll outside and find out. Are you with me?"

The other four followed Tomoe out of the cave entrance. As they passed the entrance, the silvery light faltered slightly. They continued around the waterfall and onto the narrow pathway. There, an odd tingling sensation surged from their feet to their heads, leaving them feeling warm and euphoric. A bright flash in their eyes followed, confirming that they had all experienced the change. Hangaku couldn't contain her joy and laughed, swinging her arms around in circles.

"Oh, I love this! I feel so fit and strong. I feel incredible again. It's been a long time since I felt like this, the way I did the last time we took the vows, but I couldn't tell anyone. I was wrong about Selika. Let's go back in so I can apologize."

The five returned inside, flexing their hands and arms as if preparing for a fight. Selika was still standing in the same spot, seemingly looking at them or through them.

"I owe you an apology, Selika," Hangaku said sincerely. "I doubted you, and I shouldn't have. I judged you too quickly. I have no idea how you managed to do that. It was nothing like what we went through last time, and yet, I can still communicate with all of you."

"You don't owe me an apology, Hangaku. Your doubt is part of your nature, and that's precisely why you five are the Protectorate. As for what happens next, please guide me to this so-called secret chamber. Then, perhaps, we might discover what the Nah-Vot and trees meant about Petterman."

The chamber door was unexpectedly large and located about fifty paces back in the cave, concealed behind some sizable rocks. Like the walls, it featured the same silvery thread, but it was distinct, consisting of a series of rings with symbols in between. As they gazed at it in awe, Volto suggested,

"Maybe if I touch it like I did with the walls, it will glow or something." Without waiting for a response, he reached out and placed his hand on the door. To everyone's surprise, the rings started to glow brightly. "There you go! It's working. What if I put both hands on it?" He placed both hands on the door, and suddenly, it flashed brightly, throwing Volto backwards into Jorgon.

"Stop!" shouted Selika. "You cannot open it that way. It's like the door in Gehenna. It needs to be opened in a special way; you have to talk to it, nicely. Petterman, take me to the door. Volto, come here and touch the door gently."

"Not a chance! It just tried to kill me."

"It won't hurt if you use only one hand. Place one hand down on the right-hand corner, then hold my hand. Everyone else, move back a bit, give me some room." Selika started muttering some incomprehensible words, then suddenly shouted, "En Sephi Farragho, Annall Na-Graffico." As she did in Gehenna, the rings started to glow brightly, and she repeated the phrase. This time, the symbols between the rings glowed red, and Volto felt a strong tingling through his hands.

"En Sephi Farragho, Annall Na-Graffico." Selika pulled him away from the door and held him close to her, saying, "Do not move, no matter what happens or what you see."

The symbols on the door began rotating counterclockwise with a loud grating sound. Sparks and smoke emerged, and suddenly the symbols stopped turning. White light appeared around the edges and down the middle of the door. It split into two doors and started to open slowly inwards. It was pitch-black inside, but they could see movement as if the darkness was swirling and shifting.

A soft female voice emanated from within the chamber entrance, saying,

"Selika, Merry meet. It's good to see that you're still alive. You won't remember me, but I am the one who brought you back to life after you were slain in the last great battle. I cannot come out because, sadly, I have now diminished. I am not strong enough to have any substance. I am Nogho-Tilabive, or 'The Creator of Life' in your common tongue. I am your father's sworn enemy. He is gaining strength and becoming more physical. If he gains enough power to leave the cave, he will destroy everything. He must be stopped at all costs. You have all been summoned here to help prevent that from happening. How you do that, I cannot tell. You must all work together to achieve the desired outcome, or else we all die; along with many other worlds. He will have complete dominion over all time and space."

Jorgon was the only one not dumbstruck by the voice from the cave. He retorted,

"Wow! No pressure there then, eh? The fate of every world is on our shoulders. What could possibly go wrong?"

"Giant, you and your soon-to-be pregnant wife will be no more, and your child will not get the chance to live. It's rare enough that any giant gets pregnant these days. Don't you want this to happen?"

"I didn't mean it like that. I was just being a little sarcastic and trying to lighten the mood. And how do you know about my soon-to-be pregnant wife? How do you know this?"

"I am Nogho-Tilabive, giant. I know. I sanction all life and determine when, how, and why life is or is not given. I answer no questions about it to anyone. Your wife will soon be pregnant."

"I apologize; I didn't mean to be rude. It's fabulous news about the pregnancy, but now my lovely wife will not be able to go into battle, for fear of losing the child."

"As I said, giant, I decide who and when life will be given. She will be able to go into battle. I also said she will soon be pregnant; I didn't say she already is.

Now, on to more pressing matters. The five Protectorate members should enter the chamber and collect their weapons. After that, the soldier should come forward and enter the chamber with Selika. Everyone else must stay out."

The Protectorate ladies went to the entrance of the chamber. It was still pitch black inside. They were instructed to go to the far wall where their swords were hanging and named. They were to take their swords and then leave the chamber. Tomoe was the first to enter, and as soon as she stepped inside, she could feel the atmosphere change. It became very cold, and suddenly she could see; the walls emitted an eerie glow from the rocks. She walked straight to the back of the chamber, found her old sword hanging there, and removed it from the wall. She swung it around a few times and then exited the chamber as instructed. The other members of the Protectorate followed suit. They were all drenched in sweat but freezing at the same time. They gathered near the chamber entrance.

Petterman guided Selika to the chamber door and asked her,

"What do you think it wants you for? I thought it was only me who was going to go in there, drink some gooey stuff, and come out again."

"I do not know, Goodman Petterman. I have never been in such a privileged position before. I am uncertain about what will happen to either of us. Let us go in and find out," replied Selika."

"Petterman, merry meet young soldier. To ease your nerves, rest assured that nothing bad will happen in here. You simply need to go to the altar by the far wall, drink from the chalice there, and then leave the chamber immediately. Selika will be fine with me in here."

Petterman entered the darkness, and once again, the walls began to glow with the eerie light. He could clearly see a small altar near the far wall, and he noticed that the floor was almost transparent. He drank a few mouthfuls of the thick gooey liquid from the chalice, but nothing seemed to happen. On his way out, he looked down at the floor and saw people moving around in a room beneath. There were about ten or twelve of them, moving like maggots. Horror-stricken, he stared at them, and they all stopped moving, looking up at him. They spoke in unison,

"You have to succeed, or we all die. You cannot fail. We can help if you need us. You know who we are. Tell the stranger we are with him in this"

As he reached the chamber entrance, Nogho-Tilabive said to him,

"One more thing, soldier. Your daughter is growing fast and is very healthy and well looked after. Do not worry about her."

This nearly broke him, and he sat down at the side of the entrance, putting his head in his hands with tears rolling down his face.

The gentle voice then addressed Selika,

"Selika, you have done so much since the battle, and I appreciate it greatly. I will restore your sight for you, as it seems to be a hindrance. Go and drink from the chalice on the altar, just as the soldier did. When you leave the chamber, you will have your sight back."

Selika turned and began to walk towards where she thought the altar was. She missed it at first but eventually found it. She drank the remaining fluid from the chalice. At first, nothing happened, but as she turned to find the exit, she could see the floor and the people below, just as Petterman did. She recognized them instantly; they were the Zitons.

"So that's where they are! For all these years, they have been hidden from my eyes. No wonder I could not find them. They must still have some purpose in all of this."

She looked up, and suddenly everything was clear. She stumbled a couple of times before finding the exit. She came out of the chamber with her arms outstretched, and all of a sudden, the greyness disappeared, and everything became crystal clear. She could see each and every one of them. She was almost overwhelmed with emotion.

"I can see, I can see again. You all look so different from how I imagined. Oh, how good it feels to see everything again."

"What use am I to you now, M'lady? My task is done; I have done what you required of me. Do I now go back to my old life? Or do I go and see the lovely Eve?"

Selika looked at him. He was still sitting at the side of the chamber door. She said to him,

"Petterman, Goodman Petterman, your task is not

finished yet. What did Nogho-Tilabive say to you in there? The Nah-Vot said that you had to find Volto after you had been in the chamber. Have you been to him? I know he is standing over there, but have you been to him?"

"No, M'lady, I have not been to him. Nogho-Tilabive told me that my daughter is fit and healthy, nothing about hearing the stone."

"Then go to Volto now and see if anything happens. He does have some power within him. You saw the rings on the chamber door glow when he touched them."

Petterman stood up and walked over to Volto. Volto was still with Jorgon after leaving Selika to go into the chamber. Petterman said to him,

"Well, I am here. What are we supposed to do now? Do you touch me as you did with the chamber door?"

"I have no idea, Petterman. I am as new to all this as you are. We have no plans or customs. We have to play it by ear and see what happens. If nothing happens, then try something else. Give me your hands and let's see." Petterman stretched out both hands to him, and Volto took hold of them, but nothing seemed to happen. Jarreen said,

"It is your ears that are in question, is it not? You are supposed to be able to hear things that others cannot. Why don't you try holding his ears?" Petterman started to giggle and said,

"All this is getting a little ridiculous. How will holding my ears make any difference?"

"Well, it won't if we don't try, will it?" Volto said as he let go of Petterman's hands. "You are taller than me. Bend your head down a little so that I can get a good hold on them." Petterman did as instructed. Volto grabbed both ears firmly, but nothing happened. However, Petterman thought that he could hear a strange, very deep rumbling, a bit like far-off thunder.

"Did you hear that, Volto?"

"No, I didn't hear a thing. What did you hear?"

"Well, nothing really. It must have been my imagination. I thought that I heard thunder, but it was very far away."

"We didn't hear any thunder," Jarreen said. "Are you sure it was thunder?"

"Well, no, not really, seeing as none of you guys heard it. It was probably just in my mind."

Volto released his hands from Petterman's ears, and a few large sparks shot from his hands back to Petterman's ears. Petterman winced in pain as the sparks hit him.

"Thank you. What was that for?"

Volto laughed and said,

"I didn't do anything. It just happened. Stop moaning, you big softy. Well, it looks like this thing that was supposed to happen hasn't worked. What do we try now? Does anyone have any ideas?"

"I have an idea," Petterman answered. "Let's do nothing. I am not in favour of getting hurt again. Let's just leave it be. I said that I am not like all of you. I am just an ordinary soldier."

"Then why did the Jumental choose you to ride him? And why did the trees allow you into the forest and tell you, on behalf of the Nah-Vot, that you will be able to hear the stone? Have a little patience, soldier. All will come to pass in the fullness of time," replied Selika. "I suggest that we go back to Hemmingstone and talk about what has happened. Then we can formulate a plan, that is if nobody has any other plans or ideas."

Surprisingly, nobody had any other plans, so Selika asked Tomoe to lead them out of the cave and back to their village. Just as Petterman got to the entrance of the cave, he thought he heard Jorgon say something to him,

"Sorry, Jorgon, I did not hear that."

"I did not say anything; I was thinking things, but not

aloud. Perhaps the mountain is talking to you. Try listening in a different way, a bit like Volto has to do when Selika is talking to him in his head. Why don't you ask him how he does it? It won't do any harm to ask."

"Maybe I will later when we are back in Tomoe's village. It all feels a bit silly at the moment, and I feel like I have lost my purpose here now that Selika can see again."

"Don't dwell on it too much, soldier. Something will happen to change your mind," Jorgon replied

Apart from Petterman tripping over some stones at the edge of the road, the journey back to Hemmingstone was uneventful. They went straight to the meeting house, which had been prepared with a small meal for everyone. After they had eaten, Valadora suggested going back to their homes to discuss a plan, but Tomoe said,

"Why don't we just stay here? We have food, drink, and a comfortable place for all of us to stay, or we could go to the domestic quarters where we can each have our own rooms and get a good night's sleep."

Eldoron asked,

"Do you have any good ale here? I think we'll be needing some before this day ends."

"No, we don't have ale here, Eldoron, but we do have a couple of drinks I think you will enjoy just as much. One is a brew made from fermented fruit. It's much stronger and sweeter than your ale. The other is brewed from the honey we collect, but that's just for very special occasions. Would you like a sample of either of them?" replied Hangako.

"Yes, that would be very good of you. I think my rather large friend here would appreciate a taste too, right Jorgon?"

"Well, yes I would. I've had this fruity brew a few times in the past, and it's very nice. But mind how fast you drink it, Eldy. It has a habit of creeping up on you unawares. One minute you're chatting nicely, the next you're totally incomprehensible."

"Well, we can't have that at the moment, can we? We all need a clear head with all this new stuff happening. Better make that just a little taste, please Hangako."

"Does anyone else prefer to stay here?" Valadora asked. They all, except Volto, raised their hands in agreement to stay. "So be it then. Hangako, may we have the pleasure of your hospitality for the rest of this day and night? By then, I hope we will have formulated a plan to at least find out where all these stolen souls are hidden."

The debate about what they should do and where they should go continued for the rest of the day and into the evening. There were various suggestions made, ranging from the ridiculous to the plausible given their limited time. Volto asked,

"Would it not be possible for me to fly over different areas to see if I can spot anything?"

"What do you think you will see?" Selika asked.

"Well, I don't know. I was hoping one of you could tell me. I have no experience with this sort of thing. Maybe I might spot a large horde of creatures on the ground, similar to what you described in the forest. They must be hiding somewhere."

"Do you think that you could fly again without the Nah-Vot being here?" Selika said.

"I don't know that either. The Nah-Vot just said that when the time comes, I will know."

Petterman said,

"Something is not quite right. Volto, you have a power that you do not know how to use or even what it is. I, supposedly, have a power that I don't know how to use or how it could be of use. Selika, you have more powers than we could possibly imagine, and Eldoron and Valadora, your roles in all of this are yet to be discovered, and that includes Dora and Doron. Jarreen and Jorgon, well, I can only imagine that, with your sheer size and terrifying looks, you would be well-suited to a military role in this. The five Protectorate ladies, I can only imagine, are the guardians of the whole group, keeping everyone safe while they are going about their respective tasks."

Eldoron suggested that they all take some time out and reconvene in the morning, hopefully with clear minds.

Eldoron

22 – Back to Eve.

Petterman turned to Volto and said,

"There's something we need to do. I'm not sure what exactly, but the tree told me earlier to go back over the mountain and find the stranger; meaning you. Perhaps we should take a trip over there and see for ourselves. How long do you think it would take to walk there?"

"Walk over that mountain? Have you seen how steep it is? And the waterfall? It would be treacherous and take days, time we don't have," Volto replied.

"I still believe we have to do something, something to trigger a change. A catalyst, if you will," Petterman persisted.

"You're right about needing to take action, but climbing over this mountain isn't the answer. What if we go back around the base, the same way we came? Maybe if we call the horses, they can carry us, and it would be much faster."

As they all dispersed from the meeting, Volto turned to Selika and said,

"Petterman and I are going outside for a while to try and figure out what the Nah-Vot meant about finding the stranger. We know it refers to me, but we might have to call upon the horses for help. We'll probably be gone for a while, but we'll return before it gets too dark."

"Going alone might not be wise. Things are

happening that we don't fully understand yet. Take one of the Protectorate with you; they know this region like the back of their hands." Just as Selika finished speaking, Masako approached them and offered a respectful bow. She said,

"She said,

"It is my duty to accompany you to wherever you choose to go. I willingly serve both of you. We have retaken the vow, but this time, I have the freedom to choose whom I serve, and today it's both of you. Please follow me outside, and I'll guide you to your mounts."

They reached the large stone doors just as three Jumentals came trotting up to them. The horses stopped in front of them, lowered their heads, and nuzzled one person each, indicating who would ride each one. They all climbed onto their respective mounts, and Petterman asked,

"Where should we head first?" His mount reared up on its back legs, and the other two horses seemed to agree, whinnying back. Then, they galloped off down the road at an incredible speed. Petterman had never ridden so fast, and the wind made his eyes water, hindering his vision. Volto looked like he was holding on for dear life, while Masako seemed relaxed as if it were a regular occurrence to travel at such a pace. They knew not where they were being taken, but the Jumentals knew and they were not hanging around.

After an hour or so the Jumentals started to slow down, and Petterman recognised the road that they were on, it was the same road that they had travelled on when he, Selika and Tomoe had used to exit the forest. They slowed down some more and reduced their size to match. They were now walking three abreast. The thick forest was looming up on their left. Volto was the first to comment on it,

"This is Sormoving Wood, isn't it? I can feel its

dread, it feels so sad and heavy."

"Be cautious of what you say, young man. The forest has ears and eyes everywhere. We've known this place all our lives; it's both beautiful and treacherous. It may welcome you, but it can also hinder your entry or exit depending on its mood. A word of advice: approach with a kind heart and a joyful spirit."

Petterman just said, "It is a wondrous place, I love it here."

The Jumentals slowly made their way into the forest and headed for a small clearing not far ahead. In the centre of the clearing stood a circle of large stones, big enough for them to sit on; there were five stones. The horses stopped and lowered themselves to allow easy dismounting. Volto and Petterman sat down on the stones, with Masako standing behind them, while the horses remained in place. None of them knew what was meant to happen.

The forest was warm and humid, almost oppressive. A whisper emanated from the trees, saying,

"Welcome, friends, welcome to the ancient forest. Petterman, welcome back. Masako, you have not been around for many, many years; welcome back, please sit with your friends. And you, stranger. You are an enigma. We do not know you, but we know of you. Dangerous to the world, but not. A friend to us all, but not. A man to heal the world, but also a man to destroy it. Where do we stand with you? We can prohibit all natural magic within this forest, but we cannot stop yours. Your magic is not natural to this world. Will you do us harm?"

"I will do you no harm. I know nothing about you except what has been said recently. I am a man of peace and carry no weapon to hurt you."

"Your weapon is inside of you. You do not simply carry it like a sword, yet it is far more dangerous than any blade. Will you keep your weapon silent while in here?"

"Yes, of course, I will. As I said, I am a man of peace."

"Then you are welcome, stranger."

The voice fell silent, and then they heard a faint singing as a slight mist began to appear on the ground. The trees seemed to move closer to them. Volto tried to stand but found himself stuck to the rock. Petterman also struggled, and Masako giggled before explaining,

"Petterman, you are about to get your skill. I can stand, but you cannot, not until you learn how to listen to the stone. Only then will you be able to move away, and Volto too. You must both now think of a way to harness your new skill. And try not to take too long; it will be dark soon, and you don't want to spend the night here, do you?"

They both pondered how to solve this predicament when suddenly, Petterman had an idea. He asked,

"Masako, can the trees hear me?"

"Yes"

"Good. Beautiful and knowledgeable trees, will you please inform Eve of my presence in this fine forest? I am sure she will want to know. As you are aware, we are very good friends."

The roots of the nearby trees began to emit an eerie blue light, just like he had seen the other day while with Eve. The Jumentals seemed to nod their heads in amusement, and then another horse with Eve on top came trotting along the path. She dismounted and ran up to them, throwing her arms around Petterman in a big hug.

"What brings you here so soon, my love? I didn't think I would see you for months if not years. And who are these lovely people you bring with you?"

"Eve, my love, we are stuck to these rocks and

cannot move! This young man is Volto, and this lady is Masako, one of the ancient Protectorate. The Jumentals brought us here to try and open my skill or gift or whatever it is. We cannot move away from here until I learn how to use this skill, gift, thing. I need some help. I thought that if I eat a large amount of those lovely mushysnacks, I might be able to learn how to hear the rocks"

"Well, they will certainly open your senses, but you know you should not eat too many of them. You may see things that you really don't want to see, but I will get you some and see what happens."

"What are these mushysnacks?" asked Volto.

"They are special mushrooms that can do all sorts of things depending on how you use them. For this purpose, Petterman will just eat freshly picked ones. There will be some over there," she said, pointing toward the Jumentals. "Give me a moment, and I will bring some; I'll make sure there's enough for all of us."

Eve returned a few minutes later with a handful of mushrooms. She handed one to Volto, instructing him not to eat it yet. Then one to Masako, giving her the same advice. To Petterman, she gave four mushrooms, believing it would be enough. She kept one for herself and then stepped into the circle, sitting on the floor facing them. Masako asked,

"I haven't seen this ritual in many thousands of years. How do you know it? Rosella was the only person who knew it. Where is she?"

"She is dead," Petterman said, "I told you when I was relating my tale the other night."

"Then if she is dead, how does the girl know this ritual?"

"I am, or was supposed to be Rosella's apprentice, it was very unfortunate that she was killed by some strange beast, but the Nah-Vot have kindly given me a large portion of her knowledge, a lot more I have to learn but it is a good start. I know this little ritual, it is an easy one to learn."

Eve then turned to Petterman and said,

"Eat one now." He complied with her request. She began muttering words that nobody else could hear. "Now eat another one," she continued with her muttering and then turned to Volto, "Volto, eat yours and chew it well." Volto followed her instructions. "Masako, please eat yours now. Petterman, my love, eat a third one and chew it well. Don't swallow it, just keep chewing until I say. I'll eat mine now. I'll have to join you on the stones. If something goes wrong, we'll all be stuck here."

Eve stood up, went to one of the spare stones, and sat down on it, opening her arms wide as she spoke to the trees.

"Leaf and twig and branch and trunk, send the word to the rock and let him hear," she repeated the incantation three more times. The spare stone began to glow blue, the same blue as the light in the trees earlier. The ground started vibrating, emitting a deep resonant noise.

"Petterman, can you hear the stone? It's trying to talk to you. The trees are telling me what they say, but you must also tell me," Eve said.

Petterman stopped chewing the mushroom and said,

"I can only hear a deep droning noise."

Volto reached out his hand and said.

"Reach out and take hold of my hand. I can feel a strange power rising within me. It might help you hear better."

As Petterman took hold of Volto's hand, the spare stone turned black before flashing a brilliant white. Volto, Masako, and Eve were thrown off their stones onto the ground in front of Petterman. The spare stone then rose from the ground and began emitting a humming sound, audible to all of them. Petterman said,

"The rock is saying 'Welcome, rock friend.' I can hear it clearly."

Eve confirmed,

"Yes, that's what they said. You can hear them. Now, eat the last mushroom to seal the ritual." Petterman complied, and as soon as he swallowed the last mushroom, he was thrown off his rock just like the others. The spare stone slowly sank back to where it started, looking like any other ordinary rock. Petterman got up, walked over to the spare stone, and put his hand on it, feeling its warmth.

"Is it talking to you?" Volto asked.

"No, but I can feel the warmth in it. It's no longer cold."

"Put your ear to it and see if you can hear anything," Volto suggested. Petterman gently placed his ear on the rock, and this time, he heard something very faintly.

"I can hear something, but it sounds too far away to make out."

"Focus your mind, soldier," Masako said sternly. "It's like when you aim your arrow or sword at a target. Concentrate your mind on hearing, and channel your thoughts to your ears. Try again."

Petterman tried again, this time the sound was closer, he could hear a voice, a very deep gruff male-type voice, talking very slowly.

"I can hear a voice," he said. "I cannot make out the words because it is talking much too slowly; it is saying something to someone or something."

As he lifted his head from the rock, he could see the Jumentals walking toward them.

"It looks like it is time to go; the horses are coming back. Eve, I cannot thank you enough. It has been lovely to see you again. Next time, you can tell me what all the writing and pictures are on your skin." He took hold of her, and they embraced for a short while.

"Come back soon, my soldier. Go about your business and take care."

They all mounted their respective Jumentals and turned back to the road. They didn't need to steer the horses as they knew the way back. They were chatting about what had just happened in the forest, and Volto asked if he could still hear the rocks.

"No, but I can hear something; a deep rumbling noise coming from the ground, a sound a bit like a massive beast with an upset stomach, a grumbling noise. Maybe that is just how they talk, you know, how the mountains communicate with each other. I cannot believe that I am saying this. A few months ago, I would have thought anyone saying that they can hear stone talking was completely insane, but look at me now."

"Go easy on yourself, Petterman," Masako said. "I could tell you a tale or two that would make your little tale sound totally insignificant. You are just at the start of your journey through life. I have been here for a couple of thousand years and have seen things that you could not even imagine. Enjoy what is happening now, learn from your past, and let it shape your future. I can see that you have not finished your business with the young woman in the forest; you will see her again."

"I would like to hear her story," Volto said. "How do you become the apprentice of a forestall? How do you hear the trees?"

"I know most of her story. She was just a poor woman living in Gehenna with her grandmother when I met her, and her grandmother hated me, and rightly so. I used to send gathering parties to her village so that Jarroth could sacrifice them. I have seen the errors in my past ways. Sometimes, I think that I would give anything to reverse what I have done while in the military service. I did so much wrong to so many innocent people, and it was all at the behest of the wonderful General Jarroth. Everyone was scared to death of him."

"As I said, soldier, go easy on yourself. Your past shapes your future. When the time is right, and decisions need to be made, just think of your past and imagine your vision for the future. That may help you make any difficult decisions. You cannot look to the future to resolve the past; the past is gone. Only now, the present, can you affect the future."

"My thoughts exactly," Volto said with a sarcastic smile. "You've got your past, and I have mine. You wouldn't understand mine if I told you. You would only understand from the time I came to this world. My world, well, from the bits that I can remember, is a very different place altogether. The people are not as kind as here. They will leave you homeless and not give a thought; they will let you starve and not give a second thought. The rich and powerful rule and the poorer folk are just nothing. It is not a nice place to be."

Masako said,

"You will have to tell us all, the whole story of how and why you came to be here. Do you know much of the history of your world? I am very interested in the history of different places. There are places here that are very different from this land, like the lands in the far north, which are frozen for most of the year, or far to the south, where it is so hot that next to nothing can survive. And the seas, some are stormy all the time, and some are beautiful calm places. Some people make big boats that can go from one land to another, like the giants. They came on huge seafaring vessels that you would not believe could float, let alone sail across many miles of open water.

The Jumentals suddenly increased in size and started

to gallop. They knew the sun was setting soon, so they decided to take a different route home, one that shaved off a good few minutes from their journey.

They skirted much closer to the mountain and then took what appeared to be a disused path, just wide enough for one horse at a time, but they maintained their speed, not setting a foot wrong. With a turn to the left, they headed up the mountain for quite a distance, before making a right turn again and finding themselves suddenly at the top of the waterfall, beside the village. The view was stunning, so they stopped for a few minutes to take in the scenery. Masako said,

"This is one reason I love this village. Over there," she pointed to the left, "is another track similar to this one, with our other waterfall cascading down just like this one. As children, we used to race each other from one waterfall to the other. It would take nearly all day to run from one side to the other. It was a nice, simple life back then."

The Jumentals, still at full size, started to descend the hill. They were as sure-footed as ever, even on the wet, slippery ground. In no time, they were down at the back of the village, where they reduced their size back to that of normal-sized horses and trotted along the path back to the courtyard. It was just starting to get dark when they dismounted.

Eldoron

23 – Petterman Hears the Rock

Eldoron and Jorgon were sitting on the steps of the meeting house, each puffing on a pipe filled with some sweet-smelling leaf. As the riders approached, Eldoron called out to them,

"Well? Where did you get to? Did you sort out your hearing problem, Petterman?"

"They'll tell everything to all of you once we're back inside the meeting room, but until then, we need a drink," Masako replied.

"Well, I think that is you told, Old Eldy. We've been out here long enough, anyway. Come on, let's go see what has transpired. Don't you just love it when the Protectorate are in charge?"

"It's going to get even worse now that they can speak. Before, we just got the look, the kind that could kill at a thousand paces. Come on, Big Fella, let's head back in. It might even be interesting."

Volto and Petterman were seated at the big table. Petterman appeared to have had too much to drink. He was bleary-eyed and swaying a little. Volto insisted that they hadn't drunk anything, and Masako confirmed this, adding that they were all very thirsty, likely due to the mushysnacks they had eaten. Tomoe brought them a tankard full of water, and they gulped it down as if they hadn't had a drink for days.

Valadora came over to Volto and started to inquire about his well-being,

"I'm fine, just a little thirsty. We were given a mushroom to eat, and it was very salty."

"What kind of mushroom? Don't you know they can be poisonous?"

"Valadora, M'lady, they were not poisonous. They were what are known as mushysnacks. You may remember them from the old days when Rosella was the forestall. They are mostly used for nutrition, but they do have other uses. Would you like me to recount what has transpired since we left earlier?"

"Yes, Masako, I would like to hear your account of what happened. I don't think Petterman is in any fit state to tell his story at the moment. He might be better off going to bed and sleeping it off. And you, Volto, why did you partake in eating those mushrooms? Don't you know they can be fatal if you don't know which ones to eat?"

"Stop worrying; we were in good hands. Little Eve knew what she was doing. I believe she will be a valuable ally to have. Despite her youth, she possesses extensive knowledge of natural things, and she can even communicate with trees, believe it or not," Volto replied.

"Yes, Petterman told us the other day. She does seem a bit young to take on such a role, but never mind, it is what it is. I suppose Rosella was young once too. Let's just hope this one is as good."

"I think Petterman and the girl are very fond of each other. They make a good couple," Volto said.

"Yes, it will be quite interesting, joining the trees and the rocks together. Imagine what their offspring would be capable of," Valadora said.

"No forestall has ever been able to bear children, M'lady, so that is very unlikely to happen," Masako explained. Then she proceeded to give her account of the proceedings in the forest, and in the usual Protectorate style, she was very thorough and didn't miss a thing.

"Thank you, Masako, that is very enlightening. Conducting a ceremony like that at such a young age, I am very impressed. I would very much like to meet her. Now, our soldier can listen to the rocks; we will wait and see if it will be of any use to us."

Selika said to Valadora,

"Valadora, you know that I used to be able to listen to the stones, as Petterman can now do. Believe me, it will be a huge asset; he will, with practice, be able to pinpoint things like large gatherings and land movement. He may also be able to manipulate the rocks to cause a landslide. Think about that for a minute; that would be very useful."

"Yes, I suppose it would, if you look at it like that. Do you think that you could help him develop this skill? After all, you used to be able to do it."

"Yes, of course, I will help him. He will need to practice for many hours a day. It is a slow process because they speak so slowly. One small sentence may take many hours for them to say. The mountains have been here since the beginning of time, so they do not feel the need to rush for anything or anyone; patience is the key here."

"We need him to be able to find gatherings now; we have no time for long-winded practice. I feel like they, whoever they are, are two steps ahead of us. We need to know where they are now so that Volto can do his thing."

"Well, that might not be possible right away. As I said, it takes a lot of practice. It took me years to achieve what you want him to do tomorrow."

"Can we not use accelerated learning? Enter his mind and implant the knowledge? Surely, you can still remember how to hear them, even if you have not done it for such a long time."

"That might work, but we will have to ask him first. I am not going to enter anybody's mind without their consent; that is a very unethical thing to do."

"I think Eldoron and Jorgon have taken him to his bed for the night, to let him sleep off the effects of too many mushrooms. We will have to speak to him in the morning."

The rest of the evening was spent with most of them chatting amongst themselves. Eldoron and Jorgon were once again out on the steps having a smoke. Eldoron said to Jorgon,

"What are the chances of all this happening as it has done? Volto coming over to this world, Quenilith erupting, Petterman's baby being born, Rosella getting killed just after the apprentice arrives, you and Jarreen turning up, and that Selika woman, the Protectorate reforming, and all the other stuff that has happened recently. I think things are moving along way too fast. We are going to end up in one big muddle, not knowing what the others are doing. It is going to get very confusing if we are not careful, and I can sense a battle looming very soon, though with whom I have yet to figure out."

"I feel the same, Old Man. Something is looming, but I know not what it is. It is like a feeling of dread or the fear you get before a battle, the silence before the storm, but I cannot see any clouds. It is becoming a very uneasy calm. But I am sure that between these good ladies, all will end up calm and collected again soon. They do appear to be in control of the situation."

"Yes, they do at the moment. I hope it stays that way for a good while yet."

They both suddenly looked up toward the main gate as a commotion startled them. Two of the female soldiers were shouting for the gates to be closed immediately. They then armed their bows and loosed an arrow each at something out of sight. Instantly, more soldiers filed out of the living quarters and joined them on the high wall. The five Protectorate members came running out from the meeting room and, in no uncertain terms, told Eldoron and Jorgon to get back inside. Selika and Valadora burst out of the doors; Selika shouted to the soldiers,

"What the hell is going on? What is out there?"

"Two wild beasts. They have just killed one of the workers coming back from the fields. They have ripped him apart. We have never seen these beasts before." One of the soldiers replied.

"What sort of beasts?"

"See for yourself. They will be bringing them in shortly. I believe they have both been shot dead by the archers."

As the commotion quietened down a little, two soldiers galloped out of the gates and went straight to the corpses of the beasts. They quickly dismounted and tied ropes around the legs of the beasts before jumping back on their mounts and dragging the two carcasses back in through the large black gates. Tomoe and Masako were the first to see the beasts. Tomoe shouted to Selika that they were the same creatures that had killed Rosella.

Doron and Dora came out of the meeting house, supporting Volto between them. Dora shouted,

"Mother! Something is happening to Volto; he's not well, and he seems delirious. He's saying some really weird stuff." They dragged him over to Valadora and Selika and gently laid him on the ground. Valadora knelt beside him and placed her hand on his forehead.

"He's burning up. What happened in there? We've only just walked out," she said.

"As soon as you left, he started squirming around on the floor and speaking in another tongue. I couldn't understand any of it. We brought him out to you immediately," Dora explained.

Selika came to his side and whispered something to him. Volto suddenly opened his eyes wide and said,

"It has started. I feel a very strange thing in my body like I am hollow." He tried to stand, but Valadora stopped him. "Leave me be. I'm okay. I have to go over to those things over there," he said, pointing at the corpses, "I have to find a way to release their souls."

He went and stood next to the corpses and put a foot on one of them. Small, transparent bubbles started to emerge from both beasts. The bubbles rose above Volto's head and then suddenly dropped onto him, sinking into his skull. There must have been about twenty bubbles, and Volto started to laugh loudly, saying,

"The bubbles are the souls. I can feel them inside me. I didn't have to do anything; they just came to me. They are like the Nah-Vot but smaller. I can feel their pain, but they are happy, happy to be out of that beast. I don't know how to get them back to the Nah-Vot, though. I don't know how many I can carry inside me. I still feel like I am hollow."

Eldoron said to him,

"You will know when the time comes. Maybe they will come to you and find a way to return to the Nah-Vot. Remember, the Nah-Vot said that there were millions and millions of souls missing, so I would imagine you can carry quite a few at once."

"It's a strange feeling to have so many souls. It makes me feel elated, happy in some way," Volto replied.

A young woman returned through the small gate carrying the remains of the field worker. She mentioned that there were no other creatures out there and that these two might have been scouting for something. Jarreen suggested,

"Even so, I think it might be prudent if we all went back inside, just in case. After all, we do not yet know what these creatures are capable of."

They all, except Volto, slowly calmed down and went back inside. Volto was still in high spirits, laughing and giggling at the slightest thing. He kept apologizing to everyone and chattering all the time. He went over to the young woman and touched the body of the worker. It, too, released a single transparent orb, rising just like the others, then dropping into his head. He could feel it inside him, making its way down to his abdomen. He then went back inside with the others and sat next to Eldoron. Eldoron said to him,

"Things are starting to happen, that, hopefully, will change the fate of our lives for the better. The power that has been given to you is now active. The outcome of the world now rests on your shoulders, but fear not, young man. We are all with you in this. If we win in the end, that will be a good thing; but if we do not, we won't know anything about it. We will all be dead." Jorgon laughed and said to Eldoron,

"Hey, come on now, Old Man. You don't need to put so much pressure on him. I think he already knows. You don't need to say it. We will all have our part to play in this."

"I know how it is," Volto said. "If I mess up, we are all doomed, so I had better get it right the first time. We might not have a second shot at this. But what happens if there are too many of those creatures to deal with? What if they overwhelm us?"

"Now, don't worry about things like that. You don't know what we are capable of. My wife is one of the most formidable fighters you will ever see. Team her up with the likes of the Protectorate, and you have a small army. And don't forget Petterman; he is a trained soldier too."

"I can still feel them; their emotions. Some are happy they have been rescued, but others are very sad. I can also sense their memories from their past lives. What will it be like when I have a belly full? I think I'll be an emotional wreck after all this." Volto stood up and began pacing around the meeting house. As he passed the hearth, he felt a pull, similar to the one that drew him into the tomb at the start of all this. He looked at Eldoron and asked, "Was that you? Did you just send a push my way?"

"Young lad, I have no clue what you mean. I did not do anything. Was it you, Valadora?"

"No, it was not me. I was just talking to Selika, so it wasn't her either. Walk around again and see if it happens this time. Selika might be able to detect where it is coming from if it happens again." He circled the room once more, and sure enough, when he stood in front of the hearth, he could feel it again.

"It's coming from the fireplace," Selika said. "It is the Nah-Vot. Volto, sit down right where you are."

Volto sat on the floor in front of the hearth, and the others gathered around. The coals started to swirl, just as they did at Eldoron's home. Two small blue flames rose from the fire, taking on a solid form, and the red flame once again emerged. All three of them moved forward out of the fire. The red flame began to spin and increase in size. It moved toward Volto and, in a very gentle voice, said,

"Young man, you have done well. We set in motion the gift we have given to you, and you have reacted exactly how we wanted. You have recovered some of the stolen souls. I will shortly take them from you and return them to their rightful place. Do not concern yourself with how many you can carry; you have the capacity to hold millions of them inside you. It will feel the same with one soul as it will with a million. The souls are weightless and have no substance, so they won't take up any room at all."

"But what about their emotions and memories? Handling those will be near impossible."

"You will find a way. You could try to tell the souls to leave all their memories behind or try not to listen to them. Some of them may have been corrupted by Zeraphos to make you falter; he will try to trick you. Your mother, Valadora, should be able to help you cast a simple shield so that the memories and emotions cannot get through. We will be visiting often to reclaim the souls. As for the rest of you, rest well. You are going to need all the strength you can muster; this will not be an easy fight for any of us. We will try to help if things start to go wrong, but we cannot do much in your physical world. Rest now, all of you, for tomorrow the battle will begin. Volto, open your mind, let the souls free, they will come to me quite readily." The orb then made its way back to the fire.

Volto sat there and tried to open his mind, but there was too much going on. He was thinking of everything all at once. Valadora came over to him and put her hands on his shoulders, massaging them gently as she spoke in a calming voice,

"Relax, Volto. Empty your mind and let the souls free. You can do this; this is the easy part. Just breathe slowly and relax."

She could feel him starting to relax; the orbs, still as transparent as before, started to emerge from the top of his head, almost touching Valadora. Then, one by one, they floated to the fire and disappeared.

Petterman had risen from his bed and was standing behind them, looking on in amazement.

"What the hell is going on here? What have I missed?" he asked.

Jorgon turned to him and said,

"Nice to see you awake again, soldier. You haven't missed much, really, just a couple of unearthly beasts killing one of the locals and getting killed themselves by the archers on the wall. Volto sprang into action and collected the stolen souls, and the Nav-Vot visited us to reclaim them. Did you have a nice sleep?"

"I saw the orbs going to the fire, were they the souls?" Petterman inquired.

The red orb rose again from the fire and said to Petterman,

"Soldier, I can see that you have accepted our gift. Learn to use it wisely. I am sure Selika will help you with that, and remember, not all rocks will tell you the truth."

The red orb bid a fond farewell to them all and floated back into the flames, then disappeared. They spent the remainder of the evening in a sort of numb silence, slowly drifting off into a dreamless sleep.

Petterman was the first to awaken; it was still dark outside. He went out and sat on the meeting-house steps, listening to a faint rumbling noise in the distance. It sounded like a herd of cows stampeding. After trying to discern its location, he thought it might be coming from over the mountain they called Emrys. Selika had also awakened and was getting a brew ready for them all. Petterman went back inside and shared the news about the rumbling noise with her. She couldn't hear anything unusual and asked him if he thought it could be the mountain that he could hear.

"I honestly wouldn't know what they sound like, but I suppose it could be."

"You need to go somewhere quiet, where the rock is in direct contact with the ground. Put your ear to the rock and concentrate. It will take time to discern the words; it's like a very slow song, where a single word can take minutes to be said instead of seconds."

"We can go to the path at the back of the village, which is at the base of the mountain. I might be able to hear it clearer there."

"Let's wait till the others are awake, then we can go and see. Can you still hear the noise now?" inquired Selika.

"Yes, yes, I can still hear it. It's like a constant rumbling, and its tone does not waver."

They both went back inside and prepared the brews. A young man from the village brought some breakfast for them all, including toasted bread with honey and some oaty-looking cereal. As the lovely smell of toast reached the others, they woke up. Selika explained her plan to Petterman and Tomoe, stating that from now on, nobody should be travelling alone. Petterman laughed and said,

"We are quite capable of looking after ourselves. You know all too well about Selika's abilities, and I was a soldier for many years, so I can easily look after myself."

Hangako interjected firmly,

"Petterman, in these circumstances, when we, The Protectorate, are watching out for you, you will kindly not refuse the service. We are here for one reason: to protect. If we deem it necessary, we will accompany you wherever you may go, no arguments."

Selika added,

"It's pointless to argue. They will accompany us whether we like it or not."

"Okay, we will be setting off in 10 minutes or so."

When Petterman and Selika finished their breakfast, they both stood up and signalled Tomoe that they were ready to leave. Selika turned back and told the others to pack their belongings, as they would likely be leaving when they returned. The three of them started to walk around to the far side of the village, passing the village square where the younger children were playing, before turning up the narrow path toward the mountain.

After about ten minutes, Petterman stopped and remarked that the noise seemed to be getting louder. Selika explained that it was because they were now walking on rock instead of soil, causing the sound to reverberate and appear louder. She reassured him that this was actually a positive sign. They decided to halt at the top of a small rise to see if Petterman could better hear what was going on.

Once they had stopped, Petterman knelt down and pressed his ear against the rock. After listening intently, he lifted his head and exclaimed to Selika,

"Wow, that's so loud it could wake the dead."

Tomoe quickly responded,

"Please don't say things like that. You never know what might happen."

Curious about the situation, Selika asked,

"Has the tone changed? Is it wavering now?"

"It is wavering, very much so."

"That's a good sign," Selika said. "It means you have a strong connection. Now, stay silent, keep your ear on the rock, and listen for a few more minutes. You should be able to tune in to the different tones and make some sense of it."

"I don't even need to put my ear on the rock. I can hear it perfectly well while sitting up. It's that loud," Petterman replied.

They all fell silent for a few minutes, allowing Petterman to concentrate on the sounds. He then looked up at Tomoe and Selika with an amazed expression, saying,

"The rock is revealing the location of a horde of unnatural beings. Can you believe it? The rock is talking to me. There's a large horde near the bottom of the mountain, on the far side of Emrys."

"That's what I was afraid of," Selika said gravely. "We'll have to go over there and deal with it. I hope Volto is prepared for this."

Eldoron

24 – The Hidden Hordes

"M'lady, there are many caves and hidden gorges on the far side of Emrys. It can be a treacherous place, and we, the Protectorate, are well acquainted with its dangers. Several thousand years ago, we used it as a training ground for the military, as it once was. There are numerous locations that can be used to ambush small armies, but they can also be used to ambush us."

"Then we must survey the area and make plans, perhaps tackling one gorge or cave at a time. Let's return to the village and strategize with the others," Petterman said, his voice steady and resolute. Selika nodded in agreement, and Tomoe added,

"If we can secure the upper caves, we will gain a significant advantage. In every simulated battle we participated in, the side that claimed the upper caves always emerged victorious. We should focus on capturing those first. If I recall correctly, there are four caves, two on each side of the valley, nearly opposite each other."

"Very well, let's go back to the village and discuss this with the others," Selika said.

Once they were back in the meeting house, Tomoe informed the others of what had transpired and proposed that they formulate plans and prepare to depart by the next morning. She believed it would be best for them to launch the initial attack against the horde of beasts. The rest of the Protectorate agreed, showing visible satisfaction at the prospect of finally experiencing some action after years of relative silence.

Jarreen wondered how large an army could be assembled so quickly. Hangako replied,

"We should have around one hundred trained soldiers here, and perhaps more in the outlying villages. It may not be a significant number, but it should suffice if we manage to secure the caves, as Tomoe suggested. Before taking my oath, I served as a general in the army here, and it was my responsibility to coordinate simulated battles. I am familiar with Emrys. Once we gather information about the scale of the threat, I will plan an attack. Jarreen, I believe you would like to assist me with this."

"Yes, very much so. I too have experience in the planning and execution of such things. What of Eldoron and Valadora? What part will they have to play?"

Selika stood up and said,

"I have a proposition regarding that matter, but some of you may not be pleased with it. It involves dividing ourselves into different areas, if possible."

"Selika," Hangako responded, "Knowing the area as well as I do, that was my intention. I will describe the area to you, as I remember it. There is a small lake at one end of the valley, which is quite small but very deep. There is no way out beyond the lake; the sides are far too steep to climb without ropes. At the other end, there is a wide opening leading to the plains. This creates a gauntlet effect, and I intend to exploit it fully. I want the horde to be driven into the gauntlet somehow, where we can trap them and reclaim the souls. Can you handle that many souls at once, Volto?"

"Err... I'm not entirely sure. I don't know how many I can handle simultaneously. I'll have to trust what the Nah-Vot said. And what about the corrupted ones? How should I deal with them? How will I know which ones they are?"

"I believe everything will become clear when the time comes to pass. Everything you are currently concerned about will become evident," Valadora assured him.

Hangako began organizing the gathering of provisions they would need for the next few days. She instructed Tomoe to ready the soldiers for an early departure the next morning and asked Nakano to visit the surrounding villages and request additional soldiers. By late afternoon, most of the preparations were completed.

Hangako summoned everyone, including the soldiers, back to the meeting house one final time to explain her plan of action. She did so in a disciplined military manner, which greatly impressed Petterman. They were instructed to rest and engage in leisure activities for the remainder of the day, as the following day would be strenuous for all of them.

As dawn broke, they rose and enjoyed a light breakfast. The men of the village scurried around, gathering as many horses as possible and loading them with supplies. The Jumentals stood ready by the massive stone doors. When everyone was prepared, Hangako gave the signal to proceed. Petterman once again rode with Volto, Eldoron with Doron, and Valadora with Dora. Selika, now fully recovered, ventured on her own without a guide. The ladies of the Protectorate walked beside each of the Jumentals, with Hangako at the front.

The journey to the far side of Emrys was long and arduous, but the group pressed on with unwavering determination. The valley they traversed was lush and green, surrounded by imposing cliffs and dense forests. As they approached the hidden gorges and caves, the atmosphere grew tense, and the Protectorate remained vigilant, scanning for any signs of danger.

Hangako halted the army and went to address them. As she observed the soldiers, she sensed that their spirits were not as high as she would have liked. Gathering her courage, she rallied them around her and spoke with passion and conviction.

"Soldiers, warriors, and champions of the battlefield!

Today, as we stand united on the threshold of victory, I want to take a moment to recognize the extraordinary strength, courage, and resilience that each and every one of you brave ladies brings to this army. You are not merely the backbone; you are the heart and soul of this fighting force, and your valour knows no bounds.

From this moment on, we will face numerous challenges, fighting not just for victory on the battlefield but also to free the souls of the people of this world. Today, we stand shoulder to shoulder, unyielding in the face of adversity, ready to overcome whatever obstacles lie in our path.

I see the fire burning in your eyes, a fire that blazes brighter and fiercer with every hardship you endure. Your determination and commitment to this cause will inspire everyone around you, reminding us all why we fight and what we fight for.

At this moment, we must rise above every fear, every doubt, and every prejudice. Together, we will show this horde that courage, honour, and sacrifice know no bounds. On this battlefield, there is no distinction between young and old, only soldiers bound by duty and united in purpose.

Today, we must fight for all life, past, present, and future. Our legacy will be etched in the hearts of future generations, inspiring all to believe that they, too, can achieve greatness in mind and body.

As we march forward into battle, let the sound of our battle cry be heard far and wide. Let it echo through the ages, reminding all who hear it that in this army, there is no limit to what we can achieve when we stand as one.

No matter the odds, no matter the challenges, we will face them together. With unity, courage, and unyielding determination, we shall claim victory. For we are more than just soldiers; we are an unstoppable force, breaking barriers and paving the way for a better future.

So, my fellow soldiers, hold your heads high, grip your weapons tightly, and step into the fray with a resounding spirit. Today, we fight not just for ourselves but for the countless souls that Zeraphos has stolen. Today, we prove that there is no limit to what we can achieve.

Now, when I give you the signal that we have taken the caves, let us march into battle and show Zeraphos and his grotesque horde the strength of our unity, the power of our resolve, and the indomitable spirit that resides within each and every one of us! Forward, my brave warriors, forward to victory!"

She then left the small but now eager army and rejoined the others.

Upon reaching the first of the four caves, Hangako called for a brief halt. She gathered everyone around and laid out the plan. They would split into four groups, each guarded by a member of the Protectorate. Their objective was to simultaneously attack the caves and secure the upper grounds. Eldoron and Doron would attack the first cave, with Hangako as the Protectorate. Valadora and Dora would handle cave two, with Tomoe as the Protectorate. Jorgon and Jarreen, accompanied by Masako, would target cave number three, and Petterman and Yaeko, with Nakano as Protectorate, would attack the fourth cave.

"Remember, speed and coordination are key. We must gain control of the high ground before the enemy has a chance to react," Hangako emphasized

They proceeded with caution, each group moving swiftly towards their designated cave. The Protectorate's years of training and experience paid off, and they were able to reach their positions without alerting the enemy, a horde of ferocious creatures they, for some reason, named the Rokshar.

Selika and Volto rode on towards the deep lake. She told Volto that they were going to go into the middle of the lake where they would be safe from the battling horde.

"If all goes to plan, you should be able to collect the souls from here," Selika explained.

Volto was a bit apprehensive because he could remember all too well what had transpired when Selika told him to send the fire to her when she was in the lake. He didn't want to be so close to that sort of fire; he thought surely it would kill him.

The moment Hangako's group descended into the first cave, chaos erupted in a furious symphony of bloodshed and mayhem. The small horde of Rokshar caught off guard, fought back with a viciousness born of desperation, defending their precious territory ferociously. Both Petterman's group and Eldoron's group executed their parts of the plan with deadly precision. Petterman, Yaeko and Nakano struck like shadows, their blades glinting in the dim light of the cave as they engaged the enemy from different angles, hacking through flesh and bone.

Eldoron, the master of elements, along with Doron called upon the very forces of nature, conjuring raging winds and torrents of water to impede the Rokshar's advances, drowning them in a deluge of elemental wrath. While Hangako of the Protectorate sliced up any creature that escaped the watery grave.

Valadora, Dora and Tomoe's group, with steely determination, climbed and scrambled to secure the high ground, raining down a hail of arrows and spells upon their hapless foes. The cavern echoed with the screams of the dying creatures, the hum of flying arrows, the clash of metal, and the crackling of arcane power.

The two giants, along with Masako took the last cave with relative ease.

As the groups completed their assault on the caves, Hangako signalled for the army to push the horde further into the gauntlet, driving them deeper into the heart of darkness. The true slaughter had yet to begin.

As the battle started, Selika had already laid out her blanket and had started the invocations to get them safely to the middle of the lake. Volto sat on the blanket looking terrified; he never did like being on the water or swimming. Once in the middle, Selika changed her silent song to something more akin to a funeral dirge. Volto could see in the distance that the battle had started; he could also hear the screams and screeches of otherworldly creatures being killed, but he could not see any of the little, almost transparent orbs; the souls.

Back in the caves, Eldoron continued his manipulation of the elements, creating deadly obstacles for the enemy. He conjured swirling cyclones that tossed the Rokshar like ragdolls and summoned bolts of lightning that struck them down in electrifying agony.

Valadora stood with both arms in the air, shouting incantations and hurling balls of fire at the enemy below. Dora was firing arrows like a woman possessed at the horde closest to her, with an accuracy that defied belief.

Jorgon and Jarreen, two relentless giant warriors, leapt into the midst of the horde with unyielding determination. Their swords became a blur of death, severing limbs and heads with brutal efficiency. Masako, her sword split into twin blades, danced with deadly grace, moving like a demon amidst the enemy ranks, leaving nothing but devastation in her wake.

Petterman and Yaeko had also jumped into the fray. Yaeko, just like Masako, had split her weapon and was wielding it like a maniac, spinning and dancing around with an unworldly enthusiasm.

As the battle raged on, Hangako's little army successfully funnelled the majority of the Rokshar into the narrow gauntlet leading to the lake. The creatures were trapped, and Hangako seized the opportunity to strike a decisive blow. She shouted for the army and her newfound friends to retreat, then instructed Eldoron, Doron, Valadora, and Dora to weave a spell to send a firestorm at the trapped horde. But Petterman, in a moment of clarity, realized a different plan and shouted stop! He communicated with the very stone beneath his feet, and the ground shook with fury. The earth erupted in violent geysers, sending thousands of Rokshar flying into the air, only to be crushed as they fell back to the ground, their bodies broken and lifeless.

With unparalleled unity and determination, Hangako's army searched relentlessly, hunting down every last one of the Rokshar. The battleground became a gruesome display of death and destruction, as rivers of blood flowed among the shattered bodies of the fallen.

Finally, after what felt like an eternity of struggle, the last of the Rokshar breathed their final breath, and the valley fell silent once more. The air was heavy with the stench of death, and the Protectorate and its victorious army stood as a testament to the price of victory in this nightmarish battle.

Eldoron

25 – The Soul Collector

Selika and Volto were still in the middle of the lake when the battle ended. Volto trembled with fear, as he had never seen such a sight before. Even though there weren't many soldiers injured, there were thousands and thousands of horrible creatures lying dead all over the place. He turned to Selika and asked with concern,

"It will take forever to collect all these poor souls. Will I have to go and touch each one of them?"

Selika replied,

"I think you will have to do just that unless you see a way to collect several souls at once."

Volto then suggested,

"Will you get rid of that dome above us? I have an idea."

Selika hesitated before answering,

"That dome, as you call it, has been protecting you from my father's eyes and ears. If he knew you were here, he would have made this battle a million times worse. Before you go any further with your bright idea, I think you should run it by me. Also, you need to go to Valadora; she will weave a little spell to stop the corrupted souls from entering you."

"My idea," he said, "is to fly over all the bodies and ask the souls to come to me. If I fly over a few times, I should be able to collect them all. That would work, wouldn't it?"

Selika muttered some strange words, and the transparent dome above them disappeared. They floated slowly back to the shore. Once there, they both got off the blanket, folded it up, and started walking over to where the battle had been. Valadora, Dora, and the Protectorate ladies were all tending to the wounded soldiers; none of them was seriously injured except for one who had been gored through the stomach. She was not expected to survive her injuries, and preparations were being made to transport her body back to Hemmingstone.

As Volto and Selika approached the fallen soldier, Valadora covered her lifeless form. Selika, with her innate wisdom, said to them all,

"Life is but a fleeting moment and death comes for us all. Let us cherish these moments of pain and camaraderie, for they are what make life worth living."

When Valadora had finished tending to the wounded, Volto asked her to weave a spell to keep the corrupted souls from entering him. Glad of the distraction, she led him into one of the caves. She then began to chant, and the air around them started to crackle and sizzle.

"All done," she informed him after a few minutes. "What's the plan now? How are you going to release all those souls?"

"Well, I have a plan of sorts, but I don't know if it will work. I just need to try, but I don't want to stop time like I did the last time I flew," he replied.

"You intend to fly again? Where would you go to this time?" Valadora inquired.

"Oh, just over the bodies. I don't intend to go anywhere else. I just think it will be quicker to fly over them instead of having to touch them all individually. My idea is to call them out somehow. If I fly close enough to them, they might hear my call and rise up to me. That is the plan. Do you think it could work?"

"I think it could work if you did not need to touch each of the bodies. Are you sure you know how to fly again? The Nah-Vot are not here to help you this time, and what about stopping time? That could be disastrous for us all," she said with trepidation.

"I do not intend to stop time again, just fly over the bodies till I collect all the souls," he replied.

Both Valadora and Volto went back outside. Valadora said that she was going to continue tending to the wounded, and Volto went straight back to Selika. He said to her, "Now I have to find a way to fly again. I don't want to just jump from a cliff and hope for the best; that would be silly. I need to know if it is going to work first."

"I do not think that you will actually fly. I think it will be like last time, where your body will still be on the ground. But we won't know that until you try it. Let's go back over there, nearer to the lake. It is flatter over there, and you will be able to see the battlefield easier."

So, they went to the flat ground near the lake, and Selika said,

"You will probably have to be on solid rock for this to work, as you will need to be in contact with the earth power, with the Nah-Vot not being here. That piece of flat rock over there should be a good starting point." Once there, she told him to lie down and concentrate.

As he lay there, he could feel the warm fuzzy feeling again. He thought that he was drifting off to sleep. Even with all the clattering and shouting that was going on, he felt himself going into a dream. He was floating over his body, looking around, and seeing everyone still doing what they had been doing a few seconds ago. They were still moving around, so he knew that he had not stopped time.

He floated over to a creature that had been killed in battle and simply said,

"You are free, free from all the pain. Come to me, and I will take you home." Three small transparent orbs emerged from the corpse and floated towards him. They rose above him, then he could feel them drop onto his head; it felt like leaves or feathers had fallen onto him. He could feel them sink into his head and down the inside of his body, making him feel a little bit giddy. Then he remembered what the Nah-Vot had said about the memories; he must tell them to leave all their memories behind.

He flew to the next body, and this time there was no giddiness. Three more souls entered him, and he thought, "This is going to take all day at this rate." He rose a little higher and repeated what he had said. This time there must have been thirty or forty souls emerging, all rising above him and then dropping like light rain on his head. Higher still, he went, and more souls emerged. He went even higher and then flew faster over the battleground, shouting as he went,

"You are free, free from all the pain. Come to me, and I will take you home."

There were now hundreds, maybe thousands of small orbs rising from the ground and following him through the air. When they caught up with him, they all rose up and dropped into him. He kept circling over and over, for what felt like hours until no more orbs rose. He went back to where he started, and his body was still on the rocks as he had left it. Selika was still sitting next to him; she looked up and saw that he was approaching, she said to him,

"Welcome back, young man. That was very impressive, and it only took you half an hour or so. I wasn't expecting you back for a while yet. You know what we have to do now, don't you?"

"Yes, we have to get all these souls back to the Nah-Vot as soon as we can. We need to light a fire so that we can call them," Volto replied.

"I think it would be a good thing if we waited for everyone to finish what they are doing so that we can all celebrate our victory together. Maybe we can light a fire over there somewhere," she said, pointing to a flat piece of ground nearer to the lake that was large enough to accommodate the whole army. "Let's go back to the others and spread the word."

Valadora was still tending to the needs of the wounded with Dora and some of the Protectorate. Volto went to them and told them all of their plans to release the souls in a sort of celebration. Valadora said that they would only be a few minutes more as they had now seen all of the wounded.

Volto then went to Eldoron and Doron, who were collecting the arrows that had been fired. They said they would make their way over in a few minutes. He then went to the two giants and informed them. Jarreen said that she would tell Hangako so that she could relay it to the army.

When everybody was gathered in the flat area by the lake, and a small fire had been lit, Selika silently addressed them all, saying,

"I am going to call the Nah-Vot, and they will appear in the flames. Only Volto may approach them, nobody else may come near them. Volto will be releasing the souls back to their rightful place in the care of the Nah-Vot." Volto went nearer to the fire and sat down in front of it. Selika started to mumble a quiet chant again, and very soon the fire started swirling again. Just as before, the blue orbs rose from the fire to check the surroundings, and then the big red one made her appearance and told Selika to move back with the others. Volto was instructed to lie down and relax. Big Red then told everyone to sit down as there might be some turbulence.

Volto closed his eyes and relaxed a little. He could feel the souls making their way back up his body and out of the top of his head. All the onlookers could see the transparent orbs leaving him and making their way to the fire. It was a remarkable sight, one that had never been witnessed in public before. Everyone was smiling and clapping at the scene. Most had tears of joy or sadness in some cases rolling down their faces.

Suddenly, the ground on which they were all sitting started to vibrate, and then a very deep thudding sound started, a bit like enormous footsteps. It then slowly faded away into the distance. Selika stood up suddenly and said to the whole gathering,

"He has awakened, my Father is awake. Nobody move a muscle; he might overlook us." Big Red said to everyone,

"Be still and silent till this is complete; it will not take long."

The souls continued to flow out of Volto's head for a few minutes more, then stopped. Big Red addressed them all again and said,

"This is the end of this part of the war. We have successfully retrieved enough souls to tip the balance back into our favour, but it is not over yet. We have won this battle but not the war. There will be repercussions; I know not when or how, so all of you be on your guard. Volto, this is the end of this task that we required from you. We cannot thank you enough; you have been instrumental in saving all life on this and all the other worlds. Go in peace; we shall probably never meet again. I have to go now. I wish you all a peaceful life from here on." With that, the orb made its way back into the fire and disappeared.

Selika stood up and said to everyone,

"Before we depart this battlefield, I will have to clean it of all the evil bodies that lie on it. Please stay seated for a while longer and try not to watch what I do as there will be some very bright flashes of light." Just like when she was at the Coves, she stood on a piece of flat rock and started to mutter incomprehensible words again. The white orb appeared, spiralled up and around Selika, and then soared high over her, increasing its size massively as it went, then floated to the battlefield. No powder bags were needed this time; the massive orb sent tendrils to the four corners of the field and then started to pulse from the centre of the orb to the end of each tendril. All of a sudden, bright white flames sprouted from the tendrils, covering the whole field in flames. All of the creatures burned brightly for a few minutes, and then the soil started to bubble. White lightning struck all over the field, and then the bright white orb started to spin, then decreased in size and withdrew its tendrils; it then floated back to Selika, spiralled a few times around her then back into the ground.

Eldoron

26 – Selika's Fall

Just as Selika was walking back to the army, the ground underneath her heaved, and she fell into a deep pit that had opened up. Petterman, being the closest one to her, was the first to reach into the pit to try and grab her arm before she fell further down. He could hear the rock silently shouting at him,

"Run, all of you, he is coming. Leave the woman and save yourselves."

Jorgon and Jarreen were the next to arrive. Jorgon, with his long reach, could just about get a hold of Selika's hand. He tried to pull her back up, but something held her tight. She looked up at Jorgon and said,

"Let me go and guide everyone to safety. My Father has a hold of me; he will not let go. He wants me dead. This is beyond you all; go back to Hemmingstone. Go! Go now while you still can."

Reluctantly, Jorgon let go of her hand, and she fell beyond reach. They could all hear the struggle as she went further down; down into the abyss, screams, roars, and flashes of bright white and orange light filtered out from the pit, and then all went silent. The ground heaved again, and the hole shrank and then disappeared, taking Selika with it.

Everyone was stunned into silence, but Volto broke the quiet, saying,

"She is not dead; I can still feel her. I think she is fighting her Father, though it feels like He is winning."

Jorgon shouted to Hangako to get the army mobilized before He returns. Tomoe swung around and urged Valadora and her daughter to get moving. The rest of the Protectorate was rallying the troops into motion, but it didn't take much as they all looked horrified and just wanted to get out of the way and back home.

Eldoron was pushing Doron, making him go faster, back past the caves, past where all the dead bodies were just a few minutes ago. There was still the stench of death in the air even after the cleaning of the ground.

When everybody had exited the battlefield, the trauma of what had just happened kicked in, especially for Volto and Petterman. Petterman asked Volto,

"Can you still feel her? Is she still alive? After all that we have been through in the last few months, this is how it ends. What a waste of time it has been. I should have gone back to the garrison when I had the chance. Or stayed in the forest with Eve."

Eldoron walked up and joined them. He could see the anguish in Petterman's eyes and quietly said,

"Worry not, soldier, for she has been here before and returned even stronger. She will not die yet; she has more good to achieve before her time is up."

Volto turned to Eldoron and said,

"I can still feel her; she is like a presence in my head, but she is not speaking to me. I don't think she is dead yet. She is... just not here with us."

"Just leave her be for the time being. You might try to talk to her later tonight or tomorrow; she will be back, I can assure you. She thinks that I cannot remember her from times gone by, but I do; I remember her brother Gorglothian too, though I have not heard anything about him for a good few thousand years; he may be in hiding."

Valadora came up alongside and said to Eldoron,

"Can you not move us all to Hemmingstone? I don't feel safe here."

"No, I cannot risk that much noise, not when He is awake. He could open up the very ground we are walking on and swallow all of us as he has just done with Selika. It would take massive amounts of magic to pull that one off," Eldoron replied.

Every now and then, they could feel the ground shake, like a small tremor. They knew that a secret battle was going on somewhere.

Hangako moved from one soldier to another, inquiring about their condition and morale. As far as she could see, the whole army just wanted to get back to their respective villages, so they pressed on without a break.

Finally, they approached Hemmingstone after stopping at several small villages to drop off some of the soldiers. The younger men of the village came running out to meet them, two of them carrying poles and a canvas sheet for the body of the deceased.

The mood as they passed through the massive stone doors was a strange mixture of somberness and relief. Everyone wanted to know what had happened. Hangako told them that they would have a village meeting in due course, but before that, they needed to rest and have sustenance.

The injured went straight to the meeting room to have their wounds tended and redressed. Those who were not injured went either to their houses or to the meeting room for food.

Eldoron and his family sat at the table, discussing when they thought they should return home. They all agreed that the sooner, the better. Doron asked if Volto would be joining them, as apparently, he is family. Valadora told him not to be silly; yes, he is staying with us. He is family.

Jorgon and Jarreen said that they will join them too if that is okay. Eldoron asked Petterman to join them. He said that he would like that, but not for long because he would be going to the forest again to be with Eve.

Tomoe and Hangako came over to them, and Hangako said,

"We do not think this is over yet; we are still under oath to you. More is to happen before this is all done. At least one of us will have to accompany you. You too, Petterman, are under permanent protection now that you are a listener of stone, even when you go to the forest. Tomoe has requested that she stays with you, Valadora. Do you have any objections to this?"

"No, I d not have any objections, I would very much like to welcome her again into my household," Valadora replied.

"Petterman," Hangako continued, "I have assigned Yaeko to you. She will fill you in on the finer details of her duties. I think you will enjoy her company as she likes to train in our art of fighting every day, which you showed so much interest in before the battle. If she has time, she can, if you wish, find a weapon more similar to ours so that you may train with her."

Petterman thanked her and said that it would be very beneficial to train with her.

The ground under their feet lurched again. They all looked at each other but said nothing. They didn't need to speak; they all knew what was happening.

Volto stood up and asked,

"And what of me? What happens to me now? I have done what was asked of me. Do I just hang around and see if I am needed again? I can still feel her. She is still alive, but what happens if this feeling stops?"

Eldoron joined in, saying to Volto,

"Seek the silver stag amidst the thickest mist, for its

antlers hold the key to unlocking hidden truths and revealing the path ahead. Your true task has not yet come to fruition; you have more to do before the end of all days. I know not what this means; it is our ancestors saying things to me again."

He then turned to Petterman and said,

"The song of the stars whispers of a celestial dance, foretelling the rise of a mighty leader who shall unite the fractured kingdoms. I think this could relate to your daughter, Petterman. I know not why; I just get these strange messages."

He then turned to Jorgon and Jarreen,

"Jarreen, 'Within the tapestry of seashells lie the tales of distant shores, just as within you rests the collective wisdom of all the lives you've lived.'

Jorgon, my dearest old friend, the sea's embrace holds both serenity and tempest, just as life holds moments of calm and trial. Navigate with wisdom, for the currents of fate are as unpredictable as the waves."

Valadora said to Jorgon and Jarreen,

"Your little prophecies both say something about the sea. Do you think that you will be going back to your homeland? I would very much like to come with you and witness the marvels that you have both spoken of. Do you think that would be possible in the not-too-distant future? Both Eldoron and I have spoken about this many times in the past."

"The vessel that I came on, all those many years ago, may well have been destroyed, but the vessel that Jarreen arrived on should still be seaworthy. Petterman, I think you would find our ships very interesting as they are made of stone. Maybe you could talk to them and ask them if they are ready to sail again," Jorgon said.

"All this chatter is well and good, but it is not getting us ready to travel, is it? Maybe we should hit the road and continue this conversation while on the move," interrupted Hangako.

They all agreed with this, and then they all started their preparations to leave Hemmingstone.

Eldoron

27 – The Journey Home

Yaeko and Petterman made their way to the huge black gates, where five black Jumentals were waiting. One of them came forward to greet them, lowering its head in recognition and then lowering itself to allow easier mounting. Petterman mounted up and waited to see who would be the next to emerge from the meeting room. Eldoron and Doron were next, followed shortly by Volto and Hangako. Next came Valadora and Tomoe, with Dora at her side, and last but not least were the two giants.

The remaining four Jumentals approached to greet their respective riders and then bowed low to them. After they had mounted, Petterman asked,

"What are you ladies going to ride? I thought there would have been more horses."

"So did we. It looks like we are going to get fit again and run alongside you," Tomoe answered.

"Not so," said Jarreen, "Look over there towards Balfor. Three more horses are coming."

"As these horses converge, destinies align, a path to forge, a tapestry divine. Embrace their guidance, woven like a thread. For in their presence, the future's words spread," Eldoron said quietly. Valadora looked at him quizzically and asked,

"Are you feeling okay today, my husband? You seem to be saying some out-of-character things. Are the ancestors talking again?"

"Yes, yes, that is what I said to Volto earlier. Whenever they say something, I cannot help but repeat it. I think it might mean something, but I know not what. They seem to be talking a lot today," he answered.

They turned their mounts to face Balfor. The three other horses trotted up and nuzzled each mounted horse in turn, and then each went to the Protectorate and bowed to their chosen rider.

"That's it then, all mounted up? Let's move out! Decronim, take the fastest route to Valadora and Eldoron's home. We want to be there before nightfall."

Tomoe was looking at Petterman, she asked,

"What do you think became of Secronim now that Selika is not here?"

"Who do you think you are riding? Look at him, that is Secronim. It is plain to see. Can you not tell by the markings?" Petterman answered with a wide grin on his face.

"Markings? What markings? They all look exactly the same; they are all jet-black from mane to hoof."

"Then how do you know it is not him? Try speaking his name to him and see what he does. He might just surprise you," Petterman said.

The Beautiful Jumentals all raised their heads, gave a loud roar, then shook their heads and whinnied. Everyone was surprised and burst out laughing. They then set off down the rough road back to Balfor.

As they got around the bend, they could see the road was nice and straight for miles, and the Jumentals increased in size and speed. In what seemed like no time at all, they were approaching the ancient forest of Sormoving Wood. Valadora shouted to Petterman,

"Do you want to stop here and see your friend in the woods?"

"I think that would be a great idea. Maybe you would

like to meet her too? We could all have lunch with her, and then you can carry on to your house, cave."

They all shouted to each other that it was a good idea, so the Jumentals decreased their size and speed. Slowly they made their way off the road and onto the track that would lead them into the forest.

Valadora was feeling both excited and apprehensive about meeting the new Forestall. She had known Rosella for thousands of years and thought her shoes would be very hard to fill, especially with somebody as young as Eve.

The track got very narrow, and they had to travel in a single file. The ground was nice and soft for the horses to walk on, and Petterman could see what he thought was a patch of Mushysnacks. He held up his hand to stop the horses. He then jumped down from Decronim and went to pick up a couple of them.

"These are for Eve." He put them in the bag that was slung over his mount, then got eight more and gave one to each of the horses, and they accepted them gladly. Just as he was getting back onto Decronim, Volto said,

"She is coming. I can feel her presence getting stronger. She will come from down there," he said, pointing far down the lane they were travelling on. The horses started to rake the ground with their hooves and nod their heads.

Shortly after, they could see a big black shape in the distance. It looked as though she was running as fast as the wind on a stormy night. They could just make out the shape of her sitting on top of the Jumental; there was a cloud of dust following them like a tornado. As she got closer to the group, her Jumental reduced its size, slowed down, and the tornado faded and then disappeared. She strode up to them with a big grin on her face, her mount headed right for Decronim. As it pulled alongside, Eve stood up and jumped onto Petterman's mount, flinging her arms around him. She said,

"Well, this is a lovely surprise, my lovely. And such a big party with you too. What have I done to deserve this?"

"You don't need to do anything to deserve this, and you, my lovely, are worth much more than this," Petterman replied.

"Well, are you going to introduce me to your friends?" She asked.

After all the introductions were complete, Eve asked where Selika was. There was a small silence, and then Valadora spoke up and said,

"We think she has fallen into darkness. She was taken by her Father Zeraphos shortly after the battle."

"Oh no…" she replied, "I liked her. She was a good person. She has done a lot for my village, and no doubt many other villages too. I didn't expect her to die so soon."

"She is not dead," Volto replied, "I can still feel her now and then, especially when the ground lurches. Have you felt that? It was mainly this morning, but it did happen a few minutes ago. I think she is still fighting with her Father."

Petterman dismounted and helped Eve down to the ground. The rest of them then dismounted too. Petterman got the mushrooms out of his bag and gave them to Eve. She was very happy to receive them and gave him another hug, then said,

"How long are you staying, my love? You are all welcome to stay. I am sure I can put a meal together for us all."

Valadora answered,

"We won't be staying long, Eve. Thank you for asking, but we have a way to go yet, and we want to get there before it gets too dark. We live on the other side of Balfor, that is the mountain on the right over there. You would be most welcome to visit any time, that is if the forest will let you leave."

"I don't think it will. I tried when Petterman was here last time, but I got stopped. But thank you, and you will have to come back here to see me. Rosella told me about you; she was very fond of you and your husband. She also mentioned the giant too, but sorry, I cannot remember his name. Selika told me about you too, Valadora; she said that you and your husband were like salt and pepper, meaning that you were made for each other. She made me laugh with her little sayings. I will miss her."

Valadora said they could stay for a short while, just until they and the horses were refreshed. So they all sat and chatted for a while. Eve and Petterman scouted around for more Mushysnacks and refilled their water flasks with fresh spring water. Valadora promised to come back in the very near future for a longer visit, as she wanted to help Eve tend to the forest.

When they were ready to depart, Petterman addressed them all, "I think my journey in this ever-lasting battle has ended for the time being. I think I would like to stay here with Eve. That is if the trees will allow it. Do any of you have any objections?" Eldoron replied,

"Petterman, my dear friend, as the winds whisper through the ancient trees and the gentle streams murmur their secrets, I sense the harmonious bond that you and Eve share. The forest, with its sprawling embrace and nurturing spirit, reflects the sanctuary of your love. Just as the roots intertwine with the soil, so do your hearts entwine in a dance of devotion. Trust the guidance of the natural world, for it often mirrors the desires of our hearts. May the forest's tranquil wisdom guide you both towards a future of shared serenity and enduring love."

Valadora gave him that quizzical look again, and Jorgon said,

"My old friend, are you getting romantic in your old age? You are coming out with some really strange words today. This is just not like you," he said with a sly smile. Eve looked at Petterman and said,

"Oh my love, I would like that. How long will you stay? I can already hear the trees agreeing. I will show you all that I have learned, just as I promised."

"I will stay as long as I can. I have nowhere else to be at the moment, so I could stay indefinitely. Yaeko, will you have to stay as well? Or will you go back to your village?"

"I will discuss this with Hangako and Tomoe, but I think I will have to stay with you for a while. After all, I am still under the oath," Yaeko replied.

Hangako announced,

"Yaeko will stay here in the forest until further notice. That is what the oath says."

So the remaining few mounted up and said their goodbyes. The rest of the journey back to Eldoron and Valadora's home was rather uneventful. When they arrived, everything was just as it was a few days earlier. They all dismounted, and Jorgon suggested the inevitable,

"Shall we crack open a barrel? I think we all deserve a good drink tonight. What do you lot say?" Eldoron obviously agreed and went to fetch a barrel.

Doron said he would get the fire going, just to keep the evening chills at bay, and Volto said he would help gather the wood. Dora went with Valadora and Tomoe into the kitchen to sort out some food for them all.

Jorgon and Jarreen were sorting out the seating arrangement, as there weren't as many of them now. Just as they lowered one of the benches to the ground, the whole area lurched, and everyone staggered. Jorgon lost his balance and ended up sitting on the floor. The ground shifted again right underneath him. He began to sink into a hole that had appeared, and Jarreen was over to him in a flash. She grabbed his arms and pulled him back up.

"Something down there grabbed my foot. I could feel its claws. It must be fully awake!" Eldoron dropped the barrel, spilling its contents all over the floor, and came running over. Volto and Doron came running too. Volto was shouting,

"She is alive! She is screaming at me to run. She is saying that he is looking for me. Where the hell can I run and hide here?" Valadora was running from the cave towards them and shouted to Volto,

"Volto! This way, come with me. All of you, come with me. I know a place where we can hide." They all ran towards the cave, but just before they reached the entrance, the ground lurched again. This time, Volto and Jorgon sank into the resulting hole. Jarreen screamed for them to stop, and Hangako, who was immediately behind Volto, started to slide into the hole. She reached for Volto's arm and just caught hold of it. She pulled him up and saw a huge clawed hand holding his leg. Jarreen caught Jorgon's arm again and pulled him up. She too saw the claw and instantly drew her sword from its scabbard. She raised it high and shouted, "Hold on to him!" She then sliced the sword through the air with incredible force and severed the clawed hand from its owner.

Hangako started to pull Volto back from the brink, but another claw sprang out from the ground and smashed into Hangako's head, rendering her unconscious. It then grabbed Volto again and dragged him underground before anyone else could react. Just as his head was going under, he looked up at them all and in Selika's voice shouted,

"Run and hide, run now!" They all stood still, stunned into motionlessness. Nobody moved a muscle. Then, into their heads, she shouted again, "Run now or you will all die!" That got them moving. They all ran into the cave, and Valadora opened the secret door to her sanctuary. Everyone ran in. The sanctuary was hewn out of solid rock, so nobody could get in any other way. Valadora shut the door when they were all in. It was only small, but it offered them the protection they needed for the time being. There was nothing they could do to help either Volto or Selika. They just had to leave them to their own devices and hope for the best.

Eldoron

28 – Is This The End?

Volto tried to reach out for Jorgon's hand when the ground lurched. He felt himself being dragged underground. The soil and dirt were choking and suffocating him. He felt and heard Selika shout through his mouth as he was going under,

"Run and hide, run now!" Then he seemed to pass out.

Selika was still fighting her Father as all this was happening. She saw him grab Volto's leg, and she fired a huge fireball through the rocks at him. It hit him square in the back just as Jarreen's sword severed his hand. With his other hand, he pulled Volto down and through the rock to where Selika was. He then dropped Volto onto the rock and grabbed Selika, picked Volto up again with the same hand, and literally dragged them both through the rock all the way to his throne room.

He sat on his throne and threw Volto on the ground beside him. He put one of his feet on Volto's chest so that he could not move. He said some unutterable words, and Selika started to float away from him. She then hung motionless in the air. He reached down to grab Volto, who had regained consciousness again. Volto could see Selika floating helplessly in the air. He could feel the anger and the fire building up inside himself. He turned and saw Zeraphos's injured arm and immediately loosed his anger at the stump. A ball of fire hit Zeraphos right where it hurt. He dropped to the ground again and hurt his leg, thus increasing his anger. He looked at Selika again, and she said to him silently,

"Throw the fire at me!" This time he did not hesitate. A huge surge filled his whole body, and he just let fly at Selika. He could see the fireball hit her and send her across the cave, releasing Zeraphos's spell on her. She caught the fire and directed it at Zeraphos, sending him sprawling on the floor.

Just at the side of Selika, a huge orange glow erupted from the wall. Then Eldoron stood there with a million tendrils of orange fire dripping from him. She just simply said,

"Oh, I am so glad to see you." They both together sent a huge fireball at Zeraphos. Seeing this, Volto sent one of his own, hitting Zeraphos right in his chest, sending him sprawling on the floor. Before he could recover, Eldoron wove a spell that held him fast to the floor. He was being held by the million burning orange tendrils. He was trapped and beaten, and he knew it. He stopped struggling and said to them all,

"This is not over. You may have won this battle, but the war is far from done."

Volto went over to him to let him know his feeling, but Zeraphos grabbed him from beneath the tendrils and drew him close. Zeraphos said,

"Get out of my world, you puny child. Come back when we can fight this out by ourselves." He then threw Volto at the wall. Instead of hitting it, he went straight through it as if it wasn't there.

Selika and Eldoron were horrified and both increased their holding spell on Zeraphos. He laughed at them and said,

"Well done, you treacherous little worms. May you rot in my hell for all eternity. I will be back, I promise you that. Now be gone with you." He waved his arm at them and muttered something, and then he was alone again in his cave.

Feeling himself being thrown through the wall, Volto knew what was happening. But before he could react, he felt the cold damp air of the crypt and was ejected onto the hard ground by the crypt doors. It was raining and cold, which didn't bother him as it was quite refreshing. He rolled over to see who or what was around. There was one man, an old man standing by a headstone. He looked far too old for this world. He turned around and looked at Volto, saying,

"Just making sure you made it through the walls without too much pain. Well done in there. You did a fantastic job. But as you know, it is not over yet. We will meet again soon. Look after yourself, my son. We shouldn't be seen out here during the day. Go and make yourself scarce. We will talk again soon." With that, Eldoron turned and went into the crypt and was gone.

Volto stood up and looked around. The cemetery was now deserted. He made his way to the iron gates at the entrance and noticed that they had the same pattern as the massive stone gates at Hemmingstone. Chuckling and smiling to himself, he made his way to the car park where he last slept in this world. There was one of his homeless associates sleeping against the wall. He woke up as Volto sat down beside him and said,

"Hey Volto, where have you been? We all thought that you were dead." Volto just answered,

"I think I was."

This is the end of book one.

Volto's Rise

Eldoron Glossary

Eldoron (M): - Wizard.

Valadora (F): - Witch, Eldoron's wife.

Doron (M): - Son of Eldoron and Valadora, apprentice wizard. Twin to Dora.

Dora (F): - Daughter of Eldoron and Valadora, Apprentice witch, twin to Doron.

Volto (M): - Part human, unknown abilities.

Zeraphos (M): - God status. The Dark Lord.

Rosella (F): - Seer, eyeless, blind at birth, excellent foresight.

Selika (F): - Daughter to Zeraphos, beautiful, godlike powers. Renegade.

Jorgon (M): - Gentle giant, thought to be the last of his kind.

Jarreen (F): - Giant, warrior, sword master, last of her kind.

Jarroth (M): - Leader of Gehenna, clan chief.

Cadderman (M): - Captain of the Eastern regiment.

Petterman (M): - Captain of the Eastern regiment. Rock listener

Elita (F): - Petterman's wife.

Norak (M): - Soldier of the Eastern regiment.

Selenika (F): - Deceased wife to Zeraphos.

Gorglothian (M) Son to Zeraphos and Selenika, brother to Selika.

Vadoma (F): - Surrogate mother to Petterman's child.

Sormoving Wood: - Sacred forest of unknown size, the trees appear to move, so changing the dimensions of the forest. The trees capture animals and drag them underground to be devoured by the roots.

Quenilith: - Ancient volcano.

Na-Vot: - Place or beings? Keepers of souls.

Nogho-Tilabive: - God status, The Creator.

Nevet-Mudgh: - The stone of life.

Gehenna Coves: - City, Garrison, and coves on the southeast. An untold number of sacrifices to Zeraphos.

Triohex Range: - Mountain range in the north, Emrys – immortal, Ganna – paradise, Balfor – Pastureland

The Orbs: - Blue, protective orbs

The Orbs: - Red, Na-Vot only one left, pure spirit.

The Orbs: - Green, Information and learning, the wise ones.

The Orbs: - White, Cleansing.

The Orbs: - Orange, Gifts. (mythical)

The Orbs: - Transparent, the soul.

Secronim: - (Stallion) (Jumental) Large jet black Shire-type horse that Selika rides.

Decronim: - (Stallion) (Jumental) Large jet black Shire-type horse that Petterman rides.

Leo: - (Stallion) (Jumental) Large jet black Shire-type horse that Eve rides.

Rechina: - (F) The old hag in Gehenna Coves.

Sol or Eve or Sylvan-Eve: - (F) Rechina's granddaughter. Keeper of the forests.

Protectorate: - (F) Group of 5 women from Hemmingstone, a village over the Triohex Mountains. Almost immortal, sleepless warriors.

Tomoe: - (F) Protectorate Warrior.

Hangako: - (F) Protectorate Warrior.

Masako: - (F) Protectorate Warrior.

Nakano: - (F) Protectorate Warrior.

Yaeko: - (F) Protectorate Warrior.

The Zitons:- The ones the failed to rid Zeraphos of his power (The past ones)

Elohs: -   Ancient race of Gods.

Rokshar: - Ferocious enemy creatures with at least three stolen souls.

Volto's Rise

Volto's Rise

Printed in Great Britain
by Amazon